KB149569

주홍글자

I

강독 MP3 파일 다운로드 방법 안내

1. 방송대출판문화원 홈페이지에 접속한다.
   http://press.knou.ac.kr
2. 첫 화면 오른쪽 상단의 "고객만족센터"를 클릭한 뒤 "자료실"로 이동한다.
3. 자료실에서 "주홍글자 Ⅰ, Ⅱ 강독 MP3 파일"을 다운로드하고, 압축 비밀번호를 입력해서 압축을 푼다.

※ 압축 비밀번호 찾아내는 방법
   첫째 자리: 〈주홍글자 Ⅰ〉 26쪽 첫째 줄의 첫 알파벳
   둘째 자리: 〈주홍글자 Ⅰ〉 98쪽 첫째 줄의 마지막 알파벳
   셋째 자리: 〈주홍글자 Ⅰ〉 157쪽 첫째 줄의 첫 알파벳
   넷째 자리: p

신현욱 교수의 명작 강독 시리즈-1

주홍글자

I

너새니얼 호손 지음
신현욱 주해

THE
SCARLET
LETTER

에피스테메
EPISTEME

신현욱 교수의 명작 강독 시리즈-1

주홍글자 I

초판 1쇄 펴낸날 | 2015년 9월 15일

지은이 | 너새니얼 호손
주 해 | 신현욱
펴낸이 | 이동국
펴낸곳 | 한국방송통신대학교출판문화원
　　　　110-500 서울시 종로구 이화장길 54
　　　　전화 02-3668-4764
　　　　팩스 02-741-4570
　　　　홈페이지 http://press.knou.ac.kr
　　　　출판등록 1982년 6월 7일 제1-491호

출판문화원장 | 권수열
편집 | 신경진·양영희
마케팅 | 이상혁
편집 디자인 | (주)성지이디피
표지 디자인 | BOOKDESIGN SM

ISBN 978-89-20-01667-7　94840
　　　 978-89-20-01673-8　(세트)

값은 뒤표지에 있습니다.

이 도서의 국립중앙도서관 출판예정도서목록(CIP)은 서지정보유통지원시스템 홈페이지
(http://seoji.nl.go.kr)와 국가자료공동목록시스템(http://www.nl.go.kr/kolisnet)에서 이
용하실 수 있습니다.(CIP제어번호: CIP2015022933)

책을 펴내며

이상한 책을 내게 되었습니다. 원문에 주를 달아 단어 뜻을 적고 다소 복잡한 문장에 대한 해석과 해설을 덧붙였으니 주해서이기는 합니다. 그러나 작품 원문에 주를 단 곳을 표시하는 숫자 외에 밑줄이나 { }, [ ] 등의 기호가 들어가는 바람에 기존의 주해서들과는 달리 꽤나 '지저분한' 모양새가 되었습니다. 하지만 이 기호들은 만일 글로 표현했다면 몇 개의 문장을 사용하면서도 효과는 미약했을 설명을 대신합니다. 실제로 기호 없이 꼼꼼한 설명을 각주로 처리하는 작업을 꽤 진행했다가 차지하는 지면에 비해 효과가 덜하다고 판단하여 이렇게 방향을 돌렸습니다. { }와 [ ]는 같은 문장 내에서 서로 다른 부분들을 구별하여 묶기 위해 썼을 뿐 차이는 없고 특정 문형에 꼭 같은 기호를, 또 모든 경우에 사용한 것도 아닙니다. 복잡한 구문에서 한 묶음임을 보여 주기 위해, 그리고 같은 문장에서 같은 기호를 쓰는 데 따른 혼잡함을 피하기 위해서만 가려 쓰고 작품의 흐름을 따라가면서 필요에 따라 그때그때 썼을 뿐입니다.

작품 원문이 19세기 미국의 호손이 그린 밑그림이라면, 이 기호들은 21세기 한국의 독자가 독해의 필요에 따라 그 밑그림 위에 입힌 또 하나의 층(layer)이라고 할 수 있습니다. 이 기호들에 크게 의존할 필요가 없는 독자는 과연 주해자가 문맥을 제대로 끊고 있는지 따져 보면서 함께 읽어 가는, 조금은 색다른 느낌을 맛보지 않을까 생각됩니다.

그냥 주해서만 내면 일이 대폭 줄어 편하고 보기에도 좋을 것에 일일이 여러 가지 기호를 넣으며 사서 고생을 하게 된 데에는 나름의 이유가 있습니다. 이는 이 작품 전체를 읽고 해석한 것을 녹음해서 제공하게 된 과정과 연관되는데 이 사연은 잠시 뒤에 소개할까 합니다. 그냥 혼자 읽을 때와는 달리 녹음할 경우에는, 녹음 작업 이전에 작품을 꼼꼼히 읽어 가며 모든 문장까지는 아니라도 주요 문장구조들을 미리 표시해 두어야 합니다. 그렇지 않으면 복잡한 구문 앞에서 머뭇거리기 일쑤거나, 구문만큼 복잡한 작중의 상황과 인물의 내면 앞에서 당황하게 됩니다. 이렇게 편의에 따라 표시한 자료를 만들게 되었는데 학생들 입장에서도 녹음에만 의지해 읽어 가기가 쉽지 않았던지 방송대 교재와 같은 방식의 주해서가 없는지 물어 오는 학생들이 있었습니다. 이렇게 해서 기호와 각주 설명이 어울린 주해서를 내게 되었습니다.

사실 이 모든 과정의 시작은 방송대 영문학과의 『미국문학의 이해』과목에서 비롯되었습니다. 여기에 『주홍글자』의 11, 13장 두 장을 살펴보는 시간이 있습니다. 수업과는 별도로 그 사이의 12장을 강독해 주면 좋겠다는 자칭 '팬' 학생들의 은근한 요청에 '흠, 12장 하나 정도야 뭐……' 했다가 무지막지하게 작품 전체를 강독하게 된 것은, 한마디로 욕심꾸러기 학생들의 터무니없는 요청과 그 요청을 즐겁게 받아들인 선생의 턱없이 개념 없는 수락으로 인한 것입니다. 이에 대한 사연은, '달궁'이라는 이름이 붙은 마지막 파일, 즉 작품의 서문인 「세관」의 마지막 대목을 끝내며 언급했습니다. 강독녹음 준비를 위해 집중하여 기울인 시간은 말할 것도 없고 강독과 녹음 작업 자체에 들어간 시간만도 상당합니다. 이 작업이 가능하게 된 데에는, '달궁'이라는 이름이 붙은 마지막 파일에서 밝힌 대로 한글의 소리와 글자에 대한 주해자 나름의 작은 깨달음, 그리고 거기에 수반된 '힘,' 그리고 공부에 대한 학생들의 욕심과 열정이 있었기 때문입니다. 이런 것들이 버무려져 좀 엉뚱하게 외국문학 작품의 강독으로 행복하게 이어진 셈입니다.

우연치 않게 한글의 자음자모와 모음자모가 모두 24자인데 『주홍글자』 본 이야기가 전체 24장이어서 각 장마다 한글 자모를 순서대로 넣고 강독할 때에도 이를 염두에 두었는데, 이 전체가 참 재미있는 과정이 되었습니다. 작가가 이 작품의 서문으로 쓴 「세관」(The Custom-House)은 작가의 세일럼 세관에서의 경험과 이 작품이 나오기까지의 과정을 피력하는 부분입니다. 「세관」은 날카로운 풍자의 맛이 일품이지만 문장들이 꽤 길고 유난히 어렵습니다. 그런 한편, 「세관」 자체는 『주홍글자』의 본 이야기와 직접 연관된 것이 아니므로 「세관」에서 진을 빼다가 본 이야기가 나오기도 전에 지칠 기미가 보이는 경우에는 먼저 본 이야기를 읽고 나중에 「세관」을 읽어도 그 나름의 묘미가 있겠습니다.

이 주해서와 녹음파일들은 하나의 세트입니다. 이것들을 이용하여 독자 여러분 나름대로 멋진 세트플레이를 펼치시면 되겠습니다. 다만, 녹음파일들과 관련하여 일반 독자들에게는 양해를 구할 필요가 있겠습니다. 위와 같은 사연에서 비롯된 까닭에, 녹음파일에는 방송대 영문학과 학생과 방송대 학생 전체를 염두에 둔 발언이 간간이 있습니다. 그리고 아주 간혹 문장 일부분의 해석이 누락된 대목이 있습니다. 검토하면서 다시 녹음해서 끼워 넣었다가 이제는 목소리와 톤이 도무지 어울리지 않아 그냥 원래대로 두기로 했습니다. 다만 주해서에 해당부분의 해석을 좀 더 자세히 보충하는 것으로 독자들의 양해를 구합니다.

또 대개는 연구실에서 녹음을 했지만 (이때에도 잡음이 있는 경우가 있고, 연구실이 인접한 대학로의 상황이 생생하게 현장 중계되기도 합니다) 녹음한 시공간상의 '다양성'으로 인해 녹음상태가 들쭉날쭉합니다. 이를테면, 방송대 특성상 학기 중에 전국의 지역캠퍼스로 '출석수업'이라는 것을 가게 되는데, 시간여유가 될 때면 기차 역사 근처의 야외에서 새소리를 들으며 녹음한 경우도 있습니다. 그리고 지방의 숙소나 집에서 녹음한 경우도 있습니다. '여기는 어디고 지금은 무슨 시각이고' 등의 멘트를 넣은 파일에는 나름의 현장감이 살아 있어서 어쩌면 이런 '들쭉날쭉함'이 작품을 읽어 갈 때의 고단함을 잠깐씩 덜어 줄지도 모르지만 반대로 방해가 될 수도 있겠습니다.

다만, 직업, 신분, 나이, 지역, 기타 모든 점에서 우리 국민의 축도라고 할 방송대 학생들이 1인 2, 3, 4……역을 너끈히 수행하면서 공부에 시간과 장소를 따지지 않는 양상이 이 녹음의 상황에도 투영되어 있다는 점을 좋게 봐 주길 바랄 뿐입니다. 더불어 책을 펴고 녹음파일을 틀면 바로 공부자리가 펼쳐지는 방송대 학생들의 '마법'을 모든 독자가 자유자재로 쓸 수 있기를 희망합니다.

끝으로, 『주홍글자』 텍스트의 표준판은 오하이오 주립대학에서 1962년에 펴낸 센테너리(Centenary) 판본입니다. 하지만 판본에 따른 차이가 거의 없어서 어지간한 인터넷 사이트에서 제공하는 원문도 비교적 신뢰할 만합니다. 따라서 이 주해서는 특정 판본을 따르지는 않았고 필요한 경우에 위의 표준 판본을 참조하여 각주 설명을 붙였습니다. 주해서의 문단들 사이에 한 줄 넣은 여백은 원문에는 없지만, 지나치게 빡빡한 문장들, 더러 한 문단이 한 문장일 만큼 텍스트가 촘촘해서 독자들이 숨고를 공간이 필요하겠다는 판단에 따른 것입니다. 호손의 작품, 특히 『주홍글자』는 영어문장이 어렵기로 소문나 있고 호손 전공자들도 헤매는 일이 다반사이므로 문장이 너무 어렵다고 좌절할 필요는 없습니다.

한편, 문장이 어려운 만큼 그 어려운 문장들을 하나씩 딛고 나갈 때 이뤄지는 영어실력 향상은 비할 바 없이 큰 만족과 즐거움을 줍니다. 이 주해서와 녹음파일을 거친 독자들이 주해자보다 더 나은 실력을 갖추고 그 실력을 우리 사회 전체에 더 빛나게 펼쳐 내길 기원합니다.

기호가 많이 들어간 텍스트 작업과 훨씬 더 들쭉날쭉했던 녹음파일들을 가능한 선에서 다듬는 작업에 방송대 출판문화원의 신경진 선생님과 디지털미디어센터의 권기훈 피디께서 고생을 많이 해 주셨는데, 이 자리를 빌려 감사의 말씀을 전합니다. 길고 고되었을 강독작업을 신나는 일로 만들어 준

우리 학생들의 열정, 그리고 안수진 동학과 스승님의 보살핌에 감사드립니다.

주해서상의 모든 실수나 오류, 그리고 부족하고 부끄럽기 짝이 없는 강독에 대해서는 따뜻한 질책을!

독자 여러분들의 앞길에는 즐겁고, 기쁘고, 행복한 공부길이 열리길!

신현욱 씀

책을 펴내며(영문)

Introducing the annotated edition of *The Scarlet Letter* in Korean along with nearly 70 hours of audio recordings including translation notes on the text

The genesis of this project—a marathon recording of 70 hours of voice files along with the publication of the annotated edition of *The Scarlet Letter* in Korean—began simply enough. My students in the English Department of Korea National Open University wanted to read through the rest of *The Scarlet Letter* after taking my American literature survey class, in which I had read only two chapters (11 & 13) for them. I wanted to help them, of course, and to lead them into and out of the labyrinth of some of Hawthorne's most famous (or notorious!) sentences.

Everything starts with a wish, as the Fairy Godmother says. So I started to read and translate *The Scarlet Letter* in Korean while analyzing complicated sentences and adding brief explanations where needed. I started recording the entire book, uploading each finished voice file onto my homepage for students to use. When the recordings for the entire text were completed at last, students hesitantly asked me whether

I had any written material for them to use in order to follow my voice reading. Again, I prepared a Korean-annotated text in order for the students to better understand the sentence structures, inserting various symbols such as ( ), { }, [ ], etc., to help students understand the text more clearly and effectively.

I ask readers/listeners to kindly understand the somewhat rough condition of the voice files, though I am sure, there won't be major difficulties in listening to them. The files are somewhat uneven (containing surrounding noises in or near my office and from the street, including, at times, the sounds of birds chirping) because the files were not always recorded at our university recording studio according to any set schedule. Rather, I recorded them spontaneously and at whim—anytime and anywhere—utilizing my spare time whether it was at my office, at home, or on a park bench near a remote countryside railroad station during my lecture tours to regional campuses around the country. The whole process was similar to a written translation on the one hand, but totally different in that this became a long series of lectures or a kind of storytelling. It also became an intimate conversation with an invisible and as of yet imaginary audience, each completed within a limited time.

The Scarlet Letter consists of 24 chapters aside from the introductory "Custom House" and (not) altogether incidentally, corresponds to the 24 characters of the Korean alphabet, *Hangeul*. Thus, I have attached one Korean letter to each chapter of the novel, starting a little talk about the sound and meaning of the attached letter of our featural alphabet before reading and translating the chapter.

I found myself happy during the entire process, preparing the Korean-annotated chapters one by one, pondering over the complicated sentences and meandering along/between ambiguous meanings to the shining exit of each chapter, only to find myself standing before the door leading to the next chapter, where I once again embarked with an open-minded readiness and full of more expectation.

I hope that this annotated text with these voice files will be a pleasant help to my students, and that it will make even a small contribution to Nathaniel Hawthorne's cultural heritage. And I wish that someday readers/listeners around the world will enjoy *The Scarlet Letter*, one of the greatest classics in American and world literature, in their own language and voice while learning English.

Shin, Hyunwook
Written from Jongno, the main street of Seoul, South Korea

차례

Preface To the Second Edition

[Much to the author's surprise, and (if he may say so without additional offence)[1] considerably to his amusement], he finds that his sketch[2] of official life, [introductory[3] to *The Scarlet Letter*], has created an unprecedented excitement in the respectable community [immediately around him]. It could hardly have been more violent, indeed, {had he[4] burned down

---

1 이 대목의 ( )는 호손의 원텍스트상의 괄호이다.

2 sketch: 그림에서 '스케치'는 완성된 작품으로 의도한 것이 아니라 이후의 작업을 위한 예비적인 탐색의 성격을 지닌 그림을 의미한다. 이야기를 '스케치'라고 부를 때는 대개는 단편소설(short story)보다 더 짧으면서 단편소설이 담고 있는 플롯적인 요소가 거의 없는 이야기를 가리킨다. 16세기 영국에 기원을 둔 스케치 형식의 글은 이국적인 지역을 비교적 사실적으로 묘사하는 글에 대해 대중적인 관심이 커지면서 등장했는데 19세기에 이르러 대중적으로 널리 애용되는 읽을거리가 되었다. 여러 고장에 대한 여행 스케치, 사람들에 대한 인물 스케치 등 스케치는 특정 플롯 없이 묘사만으로 흥미를 끌어 간다. 스케치는 사람들이나 장소에 대한 인상을 묘사하지만 이런 묘사들을 플롯에 따라 긴밀히 연결하기보다는 개별적인 순간들에 집중함으로써 독자들에게 추가적인 궁금증과 상상력을 불러일으키는 데 주력한다. 스케치 형식을 애호한 작가의 예로는 미국의 워싱턴 어빙(Washington Irving)을 들 수 있고 그의 『스케치북』(*The Sketch Book*, 1819~1820)이 미국과 영국에서 큰 호응을 불러일으켰다. 디테일들의 시간순 배열보다는 어떤 인물에게 발생하는 강렬한 경험에 집중한 러시아의 안톤 체홉(Anton Chekhov, 1860~1904)의 경우도 이 범주에 해당하는 작품을 많이 썼다.

3 introductory: 서두(서론, 서문)의

4 had he(=if he had): 주어 동사의 도치를 활용한 가정법 문장

the Custom-House, and quenched[5] its last smoking ember[6] in the blood of a certain venerable[7] personage, [against whom he is supposed to cherish a peculiar malevolence[8]]}. {As the public disapprobation[9] would weigh[10] very heavily on him}, {were he conscious[11] of deserving it}, the author begs leave[12] to say, that he has carefully read over[13] the introductory pages, [with a purpose to alter or expunge {whatever might be found amiss}, and to make the best reparation[14] in his power for the atrocities[15] {of which he has been adjudged[16] guilty}]. But it appears to him, that the only remarkable features of the

---

5 quench: (타는 불을) 끄다, 목마름을 해소하다

6 ember: (장작·숯이 타다 남은) 잉걸불

7 venerable: 존경할 만한

8 휘그당(Whig Party)의 재커리 테일러(Zachary Taylor)가 대통령 선거에서 승리하자 1849년에 호손은 세관직을 잃었다. 세관에 대한 묘사에서 호손이 휘그파의 인사를 풍자한 뒤로 그의 휘그파 동료들이 지역 신문에서 호손을 맹비판하였다. 문제의 중심에 있던 인물은 매사추세츠 휘그당원의 실세였던 찰스 웬트워스 업햄(Charles Wentworth Upham) 목사로 호손이 세관직을 잃게 하는 데 책임이 있는 인물이었고 호손은 그를 '더할 나위 없는 악당'이라고 여겼다.

9 disapprobation: (도덕적으로 틀렸다고 생각하는 것에 대한) 반감

10 weigh: 압박하다, 영향을 주다

11 were he conscious(=if he were conscious): 주어 동사의 도치를 활용한 가정법 문장

12 leave: 허가

13 read over: (틀린 부분·내용들을 확인하기 위해) 꼼꼼히 읽다

14 reparation: 배상

15 atrocity: (특히 전시의) 잔혹 행위

16 adjudge: 판단을 내리다

sketch are its frank and genuine good-humor, and the general accuracy {with which he has conveyed his sincere impressions of the characters [therein described]}. [As to enmity[17], or ill-feeling[18] of any kind, personal or political], he utterly disclaims[19] such motives. The sketch might, perhaps, have been wholly omitted, [without loss to the public, or detriment[20] to the book]; but, having undertaken to write it, he conceives {that it could not have been done in a better or a kindlier spirit, nor, [so far as his abilities availed[21]], with a livelier effect of truth}.

The author is constrained[22], therefore, to republish his introductory sketch without the change of a word.

---

17 enmity: 원한, 증오, 적대감
18 ill-feeling: 반감, 악감정
19 disclaim: (무엇에 대해 모르거나 책임이 없다고) 말하다, (책임 등을) 부인하다
20 detriment: 손상(을 초래하는 것)
21 avail: 도움이 되다, 소용에 닿다
22 constrain: ~하게 만들다[강요하다]

The Scarlet Letter

THE CUSTOM-HOUSE

INTRODUCTORY TO "THE SCARLET LETTER"

It is a little remarkable, {that—[though disinclined[1] to talk overmuch of myself and my affairs at the fireside, and to my personal friends[2]]—an autobiographical impulse[3] should twice in my life have taken possession of[4] me, in addressing the public[5]}. The first time was three or four years since, {when I favoured[6] the reader—[inexcusably[7], and for no earthly reason that either the indulgent reader or the intrusive author[8] could imagine]—with a description of my way of life in the deep quietude of an Old Manse[9]}. And now—{because, beyond my deserts[10], I was happy enough to find a listener or two on the former occasion}—I again seize the public

---

1 disincline: 싫증나게 하다(여기에서는 수동태로 쓰여 '싫증난')

2 though disinclined ... to my personal friends: 나 자신과 내 개인적 관심사에 대해 난롯가에서 사적인 친구들에게도 지나치게 많이 말하는 것을 내켜하지 않는 편이면서도

3 autobiographical impulse: 자서전적인 충동, 자신의 이야기를 하고픈 충동

4 take possession of: 사로잡다

5 address the public: 대중들에게 말을 걸다

6 favour: 호의를 베풀다. *favour A with B(이 문장에서는 favoured the reader ... with a description ...으로 쓰임)

7 inexcusably: 특별한 구실도 없이

8 either the indulgent reader or the intrusive author: 너그럽게 받아준 독자나 주제넘게 억지로 들이민 꼴이 된 저자 어느 쪽도

9 Old Manse: 오래된 목사관. 호손은 에머슨(R. W. Emerson) 가문의 오래된 목사관에서 결혼 이후 신혼살림을 시작하였고 여기에서 『옛 목사관의 이끼』(*Mosses from an Old Manse*, 1846)를 완성했다. 이때의 '자전적인 충동'은 「옛 목사관」("The Old Manse")이라는 제목의 스케치를 통해 자신의 이야기를 한 것을 가리킨다.

10 beyond my deserts: 분에 넘치게도

by the button[11], and talk of my three years' experience in a Custom-House. The example of the famous "P. P., Clerk of this Parish,"[12] was never more faithfully followed. The truth seems to be, however, that {when he casts his leaves[13] forth upon the wind[14]}, the author addresses, not the many {who will fling aside his volume, or never take it up}, but the few {who will understand him better than most of his schoolmates or lifemates[15]}. Some authors, indeed, do far more than this, and indulge themselves in such confidential depths of revelation {as could fittingly be addressed only and exclusively to the one

---

11 seize the public by the button(=hold[take] a person by the buttons): ~을 붙잡아 놓고 긴 이야기를 늘어놓다

12 P. P., Clerk of this Parish: 이 인물은 스크리블러러스 클럽(Scriblerus Club)의 일원인 존 아버스닛(John Arbuthnot), 알렉산더 포프(Alexander Pope), 조너선 스위프트(Jonathan Swift), 존 게이(John Gay), 토머스 파넬(Thomas Parnell), 로버트 할리(Robert Harley)가 공동으로 썼다고 알려진 익명의 작품 『마티너스 스크리블러러스의 예외적인 삶, 저작, 발견들에 대한 회상』(*Memoirs of the Extraordinary Life, Works and Discoveries of Martinus Scriblerus*)의 일부분을 이루는 패러디, 「이 교구의 목사 P. P.의 회상」("Memoirs of P. P., Clerk of this Parish")에 등장하는 수다스러운 주인공이다. 이 작품은 지루하고 샛길로 빠지기 일쑤인 길버트 버넷(Gilbert Burnet) 주교(bishop)의 『자기 자신의 시대에 대한 역사』(*A History of His Own Times*, 1723)를 패러디하고 있다. 스크리블러러스 클럽의 멤버들 중에서 이 "P. P., Clerk of this Parish"의 실제 저자를 정확히 짚어 내기는 쉽지 않다고 여겨진다.

13 leaves: 잎이 아니라 책의 낱장을 의미한다.

14 when he ... the wind: 자기 책장들을 바람에 실어 보내면서

15 schoolmates or lifemates: 학교 때 친구나 평생의 반려

heart and mind of perfect sympathy[16]}; as if the printed book, [thrown at large on the wide world[17]], were certain to find out the divided segment of the writer's own nature[18], and complete his circle of existence by bringing him into communion with it.[19] It is scarcely decorous[20], however, to speak all, {even where we speak impersonally}. But, {as thoughts are frozen and utterance benumbed[21], [unless the speaker stand in some true relation with his audience]}, it may be pardonable[22] to imagine {that a friend, a kind and apprehensive, [though not the closest friend], is listening to our talk}; and then, [a native reserve being thawed by this genial consciousness[23]], we may prate[24] of the circumstances {that lie around us}, and even of ourself, but still keep the inmost Me[25] behind its veil. [To this

---

16 indulge ... sympathy: 오로지 완전히 공감하는 마음과 정신에게만 건네는 게 알맞을 그런 뜻밖의 사실들을 밝히는 그런 내밀한 깊이에 빠져 있다

17 thrown at large on the wide world: 넓은 세상에 되는 대로 던져 놓으면

18 the divided segment of the writer's own nature: 작가 자신의 본성에서 분리되어 나간 조각

19 by bringing him into communion with it: 그를 그것[작가 자신의 본성에서 분리되어 나간 조각]과 교감하게 함으로써

20 scarcely decorous: 격(식)에 거의 맞지 않다

21 utterance (is) benumbed: 말이 혀에서 굳어 버리다

22 pardonable: 용서할 수 있는, 어쩔 수 없는

23 a native reserve ... consciousness: 타고난 수줍음이 이런 다정한 자각에 의해 누그러들면서

24 prate: 지절거리다

25 the inmost Me: 가장 깊은 곳의 나

extent, and within these limits], an author, methinks, may be autobiographical, without violating either the reader's rights or his own.[26]

It will be seen, likewise, that this Custom-House sketch has a certain propriety[27], of a kind [always recognised in literature, as explaining {how a large portion of the following pages came into my possession[28]}, and as offering proofs of the authenticity of a narrative [therein contained[29]]]. This, in fact — [a desire to put myself in my true position as editor, or very little more, of the most prolix[30] among the tales {that make up my volume[31]}] — this, and no other[32], is my true reason for assuming a personal relation with the public. In accomplishing the main purpose, it has appeared allowable, [by a few extra touches[33]], to give a faint representation of a mode of life [not heretofore described[34]], together with some of the characters

---

26 either A or B: A거나 B거나

27 propriety: 타당, 적당

28 came into my possession: 내 수중에 들어왔다

29 the authenticity of a narrative therein contained: 그 속에 담긴 이 야기의 진실성

30 prolix: 지루한, 장황한

31 as editor, or very little more, of the most prolix among the tales that make up my volume: 사실 이것, 즉 내 책을 구성할 이야기들 가운데 가장 장황한 것을 편집하는 이, 혹은 그에서 거의 벗어나지 않는 자로서의

32 this, and no other: 다른 게 아니라 바로 이것이

33 by a few extra touches: 몇몇 별도의 손질을 통해서

34 give a faint representation of a mode of life not heretofore

{that move in it}, {among whom the author happened to[35] make one}.

In my native town of Salem, {at the head of what, half a century ago, in the days of old King Derby[36], was a bustling wharf—[but which is now burdened with decayed wooden warehouses[37], and exhibits few[38] or no symptoms of commercial life; except, perhaps, a bark or brig, half-way down its melancholy length, discharging hides[39]; or, nearer at

---

described: 지금까지 묘사된 바 없는 삶의 양식을 희미하게나마 재현하다

35 happen to: 우연히 ~하게 되다

36 old King Derby: 에일리어스 해스켓 더비(Elias Hasket Derby, 1739~1799)는 동양과의 무역을 개척한 이로 독립혁명기에는 정부에 고용되어 자기 소유의 배로 적선과 교전을 벌이기도 했으며 '올드 킹 더비'라는 별명을 얻었다. 예루살렘을 가리키는 이름(창세기 14:18)으로 신세계에서 청교도들의 새로운 예루살렘을 이룩하겠다는 의도를 담아 건설된 세일럼은 독립전쟁 당시 민간 무장선들의 중심지였고, 1790년대에는 미국에서 여섯 번째로 큰 도시이자 특히 중국과의 무역 때문에 세계적으로 유명한 항구이기도 했다. 서인도제도에서 사탕수수와 당밀을, 중국에서 차를, 수마트라에서는 후추를 들여와 유럽, 아프리카, 러시아, 일본, 오스트레일리아 등지까지 선박이 출항했다. 해운업이 쇠퇴하면서 침니(沈泥)항인 세일럼이 보스턴과 뉴욕에 밀리게 되었다. 호손이 1846~1849년 사이에 검사관으로 근무한 세관이 있던 세일럼의 피커링 부두(Pickering Wharf)는 『주홍글자』 앞 대목의 배경이 되었다.

37 is now burdened with decayed wooden warehouses: 이제는 서서히 쇠락한 목조창고들이 성가신 짐으로 남아 있다

38 few: 거의 없는. *a few: 몇몇의

39 half-way down its melancholy length, discharging hides: 길게 뻗은 우울한 선창가 저 아래 중간쯤에서 피혁을 부려 놓고 있는

---

hand, a Nova Scotia[40] schooner[41], pitching out her[42] cargo of firewood]} — at the head, I say, of this dilapidated[43] wharf, {which the tide often overflows, and along which, [at the base and in the rear of the row of buildings], the track of many languid years is seen in a border of unthrifty grass[44]} — here, [with a view from its front windows adown this not very enlivening prospect, and thence across the harbour], stands a spacious edifice of brick[45]. From the loftiest point of its roof, [during precisely three and a half hours of each forenoon], floats or droops, [in breeze or calm], the banner of the republic; but [with the thirteen stripes turned vertically, instead of horizontally[46], and thus

---

40 Nova Scotia: 뉴스코틀랜드(New Scotland)를 의미하는 라틴어. 캐나다 동남부 해안반도나 그 주(州)를 가리키는 말로 대서양에 인접한 캐나다 지역에서는 가장 인구가 많다.

41 schooner: 바크, 브릭, 스쿠너 등의 형태와 설명은 http://www.pem.org/sites/archives/guides/rigs.htm(2014.4.5.) 참조.

42 her: 배는 여성형 대명사인 'she', 'her' 등으로 받는다.

43 dilapidated: 황폐한

44 which the tide ... unthrifty grass: 파도가 종종 흘러넘쳐 들어오고 줄을 지어 늘어선 건물들의 밑단과 뒤쪽에는 시르죽은 풀밭의 가장자리로 수많은 세월이 나른하게 지나간 자국이 보이는. *여기에서 두 번의 'which'의 선행사는 앞의 'this dilapidated wharf'(이 황폐한 부두)이다.

45 긴 부사구문들이 께느른하게 앞부분을 잔뜩 메우고 있는 이 문장에서 주어는 문장 맨 끝의 'a spacious edifice of brick'이며, 동사는 'stands'이다. 황폐하고 나른한 부두의 풍경 묘사를 앞으로 끌어내고 주어를 맨 끝에 배치함으로써 주어인 그 건물에 외지고 낙후된 부두의 느낌들이 잔뜩 고여 드는 듯하다.

46 with the thirteen stripes turned vertically, instead of horizontally: 13개의 줄이 수평이 아니라 수직으로 돌려져 있어서

indicating {that a civil, and not a military, post of Uncle Sam[47]'s government is here established[48]}]. Its front is ornamented with a portico of half-a-dozen wooden pillars, supporting a balcony, {beneath which a flight of wide granite steps descends towards the street[49]}. [Over the entrance] hovers an enormous specimen[50] of the American eagle, [with outspread wings, a

---

47 Uncle Sam: 미국 정부를 의인화한 것으로 독립 이후 해외 무역이 나 신대륙의 서북 지역으로의 변경개척 등을 영국이 간섭하고 방 해한 데 맞서 일으킨 1812년 전쟁 무렵부터 이 표현이 쓰인 것으로 알려져 있다. 엉클 샘은 은발의 백인으로 모자를 비롯한 차림새가 미국 국기를 연상시키는 복장을 하고 있다.

48 미국에서 민간용 국기가 처음 나온 것은 영국의 인지세에 반대하여 '자유의 아들들'(Sons of Liberty)을 중심으로 들고 일어난 1767년 경으로 영국 동인도회사의 깃발을 옆으로 돌려 수평선이 수직으로 서게 함으로써 영국 왕보다 우위에 있는 개인의 독립적 존엄성을 표현하려 했다고 한다. 이후 독립혁명기인 1776년에 조지 워싱턴 이 '대연방기'(Grand Union Flag)를 도입하여 미국 국기로 승인된 이후로 수평 줄은 군사용으로 사용되었고, 군사용보다는 드물게 사 용되었던 수직 줄의 민간용 깃발은 한때 세관에서 항구에 대한 세 금 강화와 감찰을 강화하면서 채택되기도 했다. 남북전쟁 이후 각 주를 연방에서 관리하며 통제하는 과정에서 군사용 깃발이 강제되 면서 민간기가 단종된 것으로 여겨진다. [참조: http://www.civil-liberties.com/pages/mystery_of_the_flag.htm(2009.12.5.)]

49 beneath which a flight of wide granite steps descends towards the street: 그[발코니] 아래로는 일련의 화강암 계단이 내리받이가 되면서 길로 이어진다. *flight: 층계참까지의[층에서 층까지의] 일 련의 계단

50 an enormous specimen: 거대한 표본. *현관 위에 위치하여 이 건 물이 관청임을 나타내는 이 '미국 독수리의 거대한 표본'은 몸통 길 이가 1m에 육박하고 펼친 날개 폭이 2.5m에 이르는 거대한 독수 리종인 흰머리수리를 가리킨다. 미국 대통령 인장과 국새를 비롯하 여 대부분의 공식인장에 등장한다. 독립 시에 13개 주였음을 의미

shield before her breast, and, {if I recollect aright}, a bunch of
intermingled thunderbolts and barbed arrows in each claw[51]].
With the customary infirmity of temper[52] {that characterizes
this unhappy fowl}, she appears [by the fierceness of her
beak and eye, and the general truculency of her attitude[53]],
to threaten mischief to the inoffensive community[54]; and
especially to warn all citizens, [careful of their safety], against[55]
intruding on the premises[56] {which she overshadows with her
wings[57]}. Nevertheless, {vixenly as she looks[58]}, many people

---

하는 숫자 13을 따서 한쪽에는 13개 잎이 달린 올리브 가지를, 다
른 쪽에는 13개의 (갈고리진) 미늘화살을 쥐고 있다. 작가는 평화
를 상징하는 올리브 나뭇가지는 '혹시 제대로 기억을 못 했을 수도
있다'는 암시와 함께 은근슬쩍 빼놓고 있다. 이후의 묘사에서도 계
속 이어지지만 작가의 비판적이고 풍자적인 시각이 여기에서도 드
러난다. 작가는 이 독수리를 여성형으로 지칭하고 있다.

51 with ... a bunch of intermingled thunderbolts and barbed arrows
   in each claw: 갈고리진 각 발톱에는 번개와 미늘화살을 혼합한 것
   과 같은 것을 한 묶음씩 움켜쥔 채

52 the customary infirmity of temper: 고질적인 결함이 있는 성깔

53 the general truculency of her attitude: 몸 전체에서 드러나는 호전
   적인 태도. *truculent: 흉포한, 잔혹한, 사나운; truculency: 호전성

54 the inoffensive community: (새의 성미를) 거스를 생각이 없는 공
   동체

55 warn against ...: ~하지 못하게 하다

56 premises: 관내

57 주절이 she appears ... to threaten ... and especially to warn ...인
   구조이다.

58 vixenly as she looks: 그녀[독수리]가 잔소리 심한 여자같이 보임
   에도 불구하고. *vixenly: 잔소리 심한 여자다운. 'though' 구문이
   도치되면서 'as'가 쓰였다.

are seeking at this very moment to shelter themselves under the wing of the federal eagle; imagining, {I presume}, that her bosom has all the softness and snugness of an eider-down pillow[59]. But she has no great tenderness even in her best of moods, and, sooner or later — [oftener soon than late[60]] — is apt to fling off her nestlings with a scratch of her claw, a dab of her beak, or a rankling[61] wound from her barbed arrows[62].

MP3 ★ [2] 시작 The pavement round about the above-described edifice — {which we may as well name at once as the Custom-House of the port} — has grass enough growing in its chinks[63] to show {that[64] it has not, of late days, been worn[65] by any multitudinous resort[66] of business}. In some months of the

---

59 imagining, I presume, that her bosom has all the softness and snugness of an eider-down pillow: 추정컨대 그녀의 품이 솜털오리의 부드러운 가슴 털로 만든 베개같이 보드라움과 아늑함을 잔뜩 지니고 있다고 상상하는. * 'imaging'의 의미상의 주어는 'many people'이다.

60 sooner or later—oftener soon than late—: 조금 이르든 아니면 조금 늦든 간에—늦기보다는 이를 때가 더 잦지만. * 새의 성미가 급함을 풍자하고 있다.

61 rankle: 곪다, 쑤시다

62 fling off ... her barbed arrows: 발톱으로 할퀴거나 부리로 쪼거나 미늘화살로 쑤시는 상처를 입혀 둥지에 자리를 잡은 젖먹이들을 내동댕이치다

63 chink: 갈라진 틈새

64 grass enough ... to show that ...: 'that ...'을 보여 주기에 충분한 풀

65 wear: 사용하여 낡게 하다

66 resort: 자주 드나들기, 여러 사람이 드나들기

28

year, however, there often chances[67] a forenoon {when affairs move onward with a livelier tread[68]}. Such occasions might remind the elderly citizen of that period, before the last war with England[69], {when Salem was a port by itself[70]; not scorned, [as she is now], by her[71] own merchants and ship-owners, [who permit her wharves to crumble to ruin while their ventures go to swell, needlessly and imperceptibly, the mighty flood of commerce[72] at New York or Boston]}. On some such morning, {when three or four vessels happen to have arrived at once usually from Africa or South America— or to be on the verge of[73] their departure thitherward[74]}, there is a sound of frequent feet[75] [passing briskly up and down the granite steps]. Here, {before his own wife has greeted him}, you

---

67 chance: 어쩌다(우연히) ~하다

68 there ... tread: 좀 더 경쾌한 발걸음으로 업무가 진행되는 아침나 절이 어쩌다 종종 있을 때가 있다. *chance: 우연히 ~하다, 우연 히 ~이다

69 the last war with England: 1812년의 전쟁을 가리킨다.

70 that period, ... itself: [지금처럼 바로 이곳의 상인들과 선주들에게 조차 웃음거리가 되지 않고] 혼자서도 너끈히 항구의 역할을 하던 시절. *중간에 'before ...' 구가 삽입되었고 'that period, when ...' 으로 'that period'가 'when' 관계부사절의 수식을 받고 있다.

71 she, her는 도시인 Salem을 받는 대명사이다.

72 swell, ... the mighty flood of commerce: 거대한 상업의 물결을 더 커지게 하다

73 on the verge of ...: 막 ~하려고 하다

74 thitherward: 그쪽[아프리카나 남아메리카]으로

75 there is a sound of frequent feet ...: ~하는 발자국 소리가 종종 들린다

may greet the sea-flushed[76] ship-master, just in port, with his vessel's papers under his arm in a tarnished tin box[77]. Here, too, comes his owner, cheerful, sombre, gracious or in the sulks, accordingly {as[78] his scheme of the now accomplished voyage has been realized in merchandise [that will readily[79] be turned to gold], or has buried him under a bulk of incommodities [such as nobody will care to rid him of[80]]}. Here, likewise — [the germ of the wrinkle-browed, grizzly-bearded, careworn[81] merchant] — we have the smart young clerk, {who gets the taste of traffic[82] [as a wolf-cub does of blood[83]], and already sends adventures[84] in his master's ships, [when he had better be sailing mimic boats upon a mill-pond]}. Another figure in the scene is the outward-bound sailor[85], [in quest of a protection[86]]; or the recently arrived one, pale and feeble,

---

76 sea-flushed: 바다생활로 얼굴이 홍조가 된, 그을린

77 with his vessel's papers under his arm in a tarnished tin box: (with+목적어+전치사구의 구조) 배의 서류를 녹슨 양철상자에 넣어 옆구리에 낀 채

78 cheerful ... accordingly as ...: ~에 따라 기운차 있기도 하고 침울하기도 하고 찌무룩해 있기도 하다

79 readily: 즉시, 쉽사리

80 a bulk of incommodities ... rid him of: 아무도 처분해 주고 싶어 하지 않는 그런 마땅치 않은 화물 더미

81 careworn: 근심걱정에 찌든

82 traffic: 장사, 상업

83 as a wolf-cub does of blood(=as a wolf-cub gets the taste of blood): 늑대 새끼가 피 맛을 보듯

84 sends adventures: 투기(모험)에 나서다

85 the outward-bound sailor: 외항선원

[seeking a passport[87] to the hospital]. Nor must we forget the captains of the rusty little schooners {that bring firewood from the British provinces[88]}; a rough-looking set[89] of tarpaulins[90], [without the alertness of the Yankee aspect[91]], but contributing an item of no slight importance[92] to our decaying trade.

[Cluster all these individuals together, {as they sometimes were}, with other miscellaneous ones to diversify the group], and[93], for the time being[94], it made the Custom-House a stirring scene[95]. More frequently, however, on ascending the steps, you would discern — in the entry {if it were[96] summer time}, or in their appropriate rooms {if wintry or inclement weather[97]} —

---

86 protection: 통행증, 외항선원에 대한 국적증명서
87 passport: 여권, 통행허가증, 통행권, 입장권
88 British provinces: 영국령 식민지
89 a rough-looking set: 거칠어 보이는 일단의 무리들
90 tarpaulin: 방수외투
91 the alertness of the Yankee aspect: 빈틈없는 뉴잉글랜드의 양키 같은 풍모
92 an item of no slight importance: 얕잡아 볼 수 없는 중요성을 지닌 품목. *글의 맥락상 '장작'(firewood)을 가리키는 것으로 보인다.
93 cluster ..., and: 동사원형(명령문)+and의 구조로서 '~해라. 그러면~'의 뜻이다. 실제로 이 사람들을 모아 놓는다는 의미가 아니라 앞에 열거한 그런 개개인들이 무리 지어 모이고 거기에 다른 잡다한 인물들까지 더해지면 세관이 떠들썩한 장소가 되었다는 내용이다.
94 for the time being: 잠시 동안이나마
95 a stirring scene: 떠들썩한 장면[장소]
96 가정법 문장에서는 주어가 삼인칭 단수(이 문장에서는 it)여도 was 대신 were를 사용한다.

a row of venerable figures[98], sitting in old-fashioned chairs, {which were tipped on their hind legs back against the wall}. Oftentimes they were asleep, but occasionally might be heard talking together, in voices between a speech and a snore[99], and with that lack of energy {that distinguishes the occupants of alms-houses[100], and all other human beings [who depend for subsistence on charity, on monopolized labour, or anything else but their own independent exertions[101]]}. These old gentlemen — [seated, like Matthew at the receipt of custom[102], but not very liable to be summoned thence, like him, for

---

97 in the entry ... inclement weather: 여름이면 문간에서, 그게 아닌 겨울철 혹은 궂은 날씨에는 다들 제각기의 방에 있겠지만. *'or in their appropriate rooms if wintry or inclement weather' 부분은 'discern'의 목적어 부분, 즉 '줄지어 벽에 기댄 채 앉아 있는 모습들'과는 호응을 이루고 있지 않으므로 '겨울철 혹은 궂은 날씨에는 다들 제각기의 방에 있겠지만'이라고 해석하는 것이 자연스럽다.

98 a row of venerable figures: 줄지어 있는 위엄 있는 모습

99 in voices between a speech and a snore: 말소리인지 코고는 소리인지 모를 목소리로

100 alms-house: 구빈원

101 depend ... exertions: 구빈원 신세를 지는 이들, 아니면 자선이나 독점된 노동, 여하튼 자기 자신의 독립적인 노력이 아닌 그 밖의 다른 것에 자신의 생존을 의탁하는. *예컨대, 거지의 경우는 자신의 생존을 '자선'에, 주인의 경우는 노예의 '독점된 노동'에 자신의 생존을 의존하게 되는데, 두 경우 모두 '자신의 독립적인 노력'과는 거리가 있다고 볼 수 있다.

102 Matthew at the receipt of custom: 세금수령(징수)대의 마태. *예수의 부름을 받을 당시 마태는 로마의 세금을 징수해 주는 일을 통해 꽤 돈을 벌던 세리였다.

apostolic errands] — were Custom-House officers[103].

Furthermore, on the left hand {as you enter the front door}, is a certain room or office[104], about fifteen feet square, and of a lofty height; with two of its arched windows [commanding a view of[105] the aforesaid dilapidated wharf[106]], and the third [looking across a narrow lane, and along a portion of Derby Street]. All three[107] give glimpses of the shops of grocers, block-makers, slop-sellers, and ship-chandlers[108], {around the doors of which[109] are generally to be seen, [laughing and gossiping], clusters of old salts, and such other wharf-rats [as haunt the Wapping[110] of a seaport]}. The room itself is cobwebbed, and

---

103 중간에 삽입된 부분을 풀지 않고 문장구조 그대로 직역하면, "세금 받는 자리에 있던 마태와 마찬가지의 위치에 있었으나 그와는 달리 사도의 부름을 받아 그 자리로부터 소환되어 나올 가능성은 매우 희박한 이 노신사들은 세관의 관리들이었다"가 된다. 그런데 문장 끝의 '세관의 관리들이었다'는 서술은 삽입된 앞 대목의 마태 이야기에 이미 포함된 내용이라 반복적이다. 따라서 "이 노신사들은 세금 받는 자리에 있던 마태와 마찬가지로 세관의 관리들이었지만 그와는 달리 사도의 부름을 받아 그 자리로부터 소환되어 나올 가능성은 매우 희박했다"로 풀어서 해석하는 것이 자연스럽다.

104 도치문장으로 문장 전체의 주어는 'a certain room or office'

105 commanding a view of ...: ~의 전경이 보이다

106 the aforesaid dilapidated wharf: 앞서 말한 황폐한 부두

107 'all three (windows)'가 주어, 'glimpse of ...'(~이 얼핏 보임)가 목적어이다.

108 grocers, block-makers, slop-sellers, and ship-chandlers: 식료품 점들, 건축용 각재(角材)상들, 싸구려 기성복 판매상들, 선박 용 구상들

109 around the doors of which: 그 문들 주변에. ＊관계절 계속적 용법으로 'which'가 가리키는 것은 앞에 열거한 상점들

dingy[111] with old paint; its floor is strewn with grey sand, in a fashion {that has elsewhere fallen into long disuse[112]}; and it is easy to conclude[113], [from the general slovenliness[114] of the place], that this is a sanctuary {into which womankind, with her tools of magic, the broom and mop, has very infrequent access[115]}. In the way of[116] furniture, there is a stove[117] with a voluminous funnel[118]; an old desk with a three-legged stool beside it; two or three wooden-bottom chairs, exceedingly decrepit[119] and infirm[120]; and — not to forget the library —

---

110 Wapping: 런던 시 동쪽에 붙어 있는 부둣가 지역의 옛 장소를 가리키며 템스 강이 인접해 있어서 부두의 특성이 두드러졌다. 19세기 들어 런던 독스(London Docks)가 건설됨에 따라 이 지역에서는 일반주택이 대거 헐리고 인구가 줄면서 대규모 창고들의 벽으로 가로막혀 런던과 격리된 외지고 황폐한 곳이라는 인상을 주기도 했다.

111 dingy: 음침한

112 fall into disuse: 사용되지 않게 되다

113 it ... to conclude ...: 가주어, 진주어 구문으로 'conclude'의 목적어는 'that ...' 부분. 이 'that ...' 목적절 안에는 보어 '성소'(sanctuary)를 꾸며 주는 'which' 관계절이 들어 있다.

114 slovenliness: 단정치 못함, 꾀죄죄함, 초라함

115 have access into ...: (into which의 into와 함께) ~ 안으로 접근해 들어가다

116 in the way of ...: ~ 점에서는, ~으로서는, ~에 관하여, ~라고 할 만한 것

117 'a stove'를 포함하여 이후 세미콜론(;)으로 연결된 것들은 모두 'there is'의 주어 부분에 해당된다.

118 a voluminous funnel: 덩치 큰 굴뚝

119 decrepit: 늙어빠진, 덜컥거리는, 노후한

120 infirm: (몸이) 약한, 허약한, (의지, 성격이) 우유부단한

on some shelves, a score or two of volumes[121] of the Acts of Congress[122], and a bulky Digest of the Revenue laws[123]. A tin pipe ascends through the ceiling, and forms a medium of vocal communication with other parts of the edifice[124]. And here, some six months ago, ─[pacing from corner to corner, or lounging on the long-legged tool, with his elbow on the desk, and his eyes wandering up and down the columns of the morning newspaper[125]], ─you might have recognised, honoured reader, the same individual {who welcomed you into his cheery little study, where the sunshine glimmered so pleasantly through the willow branches on the western side of the Old Manse[126]}. But now, {should you go[127] thither to seek him}, you would inquire in vain[128] for the Locofoco[129]

---

121 a score or two of volumes: 20~30권

122 the Acts of Congress: 의회제정 법률

123 a bulky Digest of the Revenue laws: 한 권의 두툼한 세법 요약집

124 a medium of vocal communication with other parts of the edifice: 건물의 다른 부분들과 음성을 통해 의사소통하기 위한 수단

125 삽입된 'pacing ... newspaper'는 주절의 목적어인 'the same individual'을 꾸며 주는 목적보어의 역할을 한다. 'the same individual'을 꾸며 주는 관계절─이 안에 또 'where' 관계부사절이 포함되어 있는─이 뒤에 길게 이어지기 때문에 'pacing ... newspaper'를 앞으로 위치시키면서 삽입으로 처리했다.

126 the same individual ... the Old Manse: 옛 목사관 서편에 자라는 버드나무 가지들 사이로 햇살이 즐겁게 반짝이며 비쳐드는 유쾌한 작은 서재로 그대를 반갑게 맞아들였던 바로 그이

127 should you go: 가 보아야

128 in vain: 헛되이

129 Locofoco: 성냥을 가리키는 스페인어에서 나온 말로 1835년에 뉴

Surveyor. The besom[130] of reform hath swept him out of office, and a worthier successor wears his dignity and pockets[131] his emoluments[132].

この This old town of Salem — my native place, {though I have dwelt much away from[133] it both in boyhood and maturer years} — possesses, or did possess, a hold on[134] my affection, {the force of which[135] I have never realized during my seasons of actual residence here}. Indeed, {so far as its physical aspect is concerned[136], with its flat, unvaried surface, [covered chiefly

MP3 ★ 표시 (3) 시작

욕의 급진파 민주당원들이 보수파가 회의를 해산시키려고 가스등을 꺼 버리자 성냥을 그어 초에 불을 붙인 뒤 정치집회를 계속하였는데 이때부터 민주당 급진파를 비난하는 용어가 되었다. 로코포코 검사관(Locofoco Surveyor)은 호손 자신을 가리킨다. 호손이 민주당 친구들의 도움으로 세관직에 올랐다가 정권교체에 따라 물러나게 된 상황을 여기에서도 내비치고 있다.

130 besom: 커다란 마당비

131 pocket: ~을 포켓에 넣다(감추다), ~을 착복하다, 횡령하다

132 emolument: (직무 따위에서 생기는) 이득, 수입, 보수. * a worthier ... emoluments: 더 훌륭하신 후임자가 위엄을 두르고 수당을 챙기고 계시다

133 dwell away from ...: ~로부터 떨어져 지내다

134 possess a hold on ...: ~을 잡다, 손에 넣다, 사로잡다

135 the force of which: 관계대명사 계속적 용법으로 쓰였고 'which'가 가리키는 것은 'my affection'

136 so far as ... is concerned: ~에 관한 한. * 이 대목에서 시작되는 긴 문장의 주요 구조는 so far as ... is concerned, it would be ...로 세일럼의 물리적인 외관만으로 보자면 차라리 헝클어진 장기판에 애착을 갖는 것이 더 납득할 만하다는 내용으로 중간의 'with its flat … surface, (with) its irregularity, (with) its long and lazy

36

with wooden houses[137], few or none of which[138] pretend to[139] architectural beauty] — its irregularity, [which is neither picturesque[140] nor quaint[141], but only tame] — its long and lazy street, [lounging wearisomely through the whole extent of the peninsula, with Gallows Hill[142] and New Guinea[143] at one end, and a view of the alms-house at the other]}[144] — [such being the features of my native town], it would be quite as reasonable[145] to form a sentimental attachment to a

---

street' 부분은 부사절의 주어 'its physical aspect'의 보잘것없는 측면들을 보충해 주는 대목이다. 이 부분들의 'its'는 모두 세일럼 을 가리킨다.

137 with its flat, unvaried surface, covered chiefly with wooden houses: 평평하고 변화가 없는 지표면이 주로 목조 가옥들도 덮 여 있는. *with 목적어 과거분사의 꼴로 'its physical aspect'를 설명해 주고 있다.

138 few or none of which ...: [그 목조 가옥들 중에] ~인 것은 거의 혹은 전혀 없다

139 pretend to ...: ~을 자부하다, ~을 지녔다고 주장하다

140 picturesque: 그림 같은, 생생한

141 quaint: 기묘한

142 Gallows Hill: 1692년 세일럼 마녀재판 때 교수형을 행하던 장소

143 New Guinea: 호손 당시 세일럼에는 꽤 커다란 흑인 집단거주지 가 있었다. 이들은 하이스트리트(High Street) 뒤쪽에 위치한 버 펌 모퉁이(Buffum's Corner) 근처의 통행료 징수소 근방에서 100 여 채의 움막을 짓고 살았다. 호손은 이 하이스트리트 지역을 '뉴 기니'로 부르고 있다.

144 so far as ... at the other: 여기까지가 so far ...로 이끌리는 부분 으로 밑줄 친 its flat, unvaried surface, its irregularity, its long and lazy street를 with로 묶으면서 세일럼의 외관상 특징들을 설 명하고 있다.

145 as reasonable: as reasonable (as my affection for the old town

disarranged checker-board[146]. And yet, [though invariably happiest elsewhere[147]], there is within me a feeling for Old Salem, {which, in lack of a better phrase[148], I must be content to call affection}. The sentiment is probably assignable to[149] the deep and aged roots {which my family has stuck into the soil}. It is now nearly two centuries and a quarter {since the original Briton, the earliest emigrant of my name, made his appearance in[150] the wild and forest-bordered settlement [which has since become a city]}. And here his descendants have been born and died, and have mingled their earthly substance[151] with the soil, {until no small portion of it must necessarily be akin

---

of Salem)은 앞에서 말한 세일럼에 대한 애착과 비교하고 있는 것을 생략한 것이다.

146 to form … checker-board: 진주어 부분으로 '헝클어진 장기판에 애착을 갖는 것'의 의미

147 though invariably happiest elsewhere: 가장 행복했던 곳은 늘 다른 데였기는 하나

148 in lack of a better phrase: 더 나은 표현이 없어서, 달리 더 잘 표현할 말이 없어서

149 assignable to …: ~에 돌릴 수 있는

150 since the original Briton, the earliest emigrant of my name, made his appearance in …: 원래 잉글랜드인으로 내 성을 지닌 맨 처음의 이주민이 (~에) 모습을 드러낸 이래. *made his appearance: 모습을 드러냈다. 호손의 미국의 첫 조상은 윌리엄 호손(William Hathorne)으로 1630년에 존 윈스롭(John Winthrop)이 이끄는 이주민들과 함께 잉글랜드에서 매사추세츠로 왔다. 식민지를 대표하는 (그러나 의결권은 없던) 하원의 일원으로 세일럼 민병대의 소령이었다.

151 earthly substance: 직역하면 '이 세상의 물질'로 '육신'을 가리킨다.

to the mortal[152] frame[153] [wherewith[154], for a little while, I walk the streets [155]]}. In part, therefore, the attachment {which I speak of} is the mere sensuous sympathy of dust for dust[156]. Few of my countrymen can know {what it is}; nor, {as frequent transplantation is perhaps better for the stock}, need they[157] consider it desirable to know [158].

But the sentiment has likewise its moral quality. The figure of that first ancestor, [invested by family tradition with a dim and dusky grandeur[159]], was present to my boyish imagination {as far back as I can remember}. It still haunts me, and induces a sort of home-feeling with the past, {which[160] I scarcely claim

---

152 mortal: 죽을 운명의, 인간의, 이 세상의

153 frame: 신체, 체격, 육체

154 wherewith: 그것으로 ~하는, 그것에 의해 ~하는(=with which)

155 no small portion … the streets: 필시 그 적잖은 부분이 내가 잠시 의탁해 이 거리를 걷고 있는 이승의 내 육체와 유사할 터이다

156 the mere sensuous sympathy of dust for dust: 흙먼지가 흙먼지에게 갖는 감각적인 공명일 뿐

157 need they(=if they need): 주어 동사의 도치를 활용한 가정법 문장

158 nor … to know: 자주 옮겨 심으면 아마 뿌리줄기에는 더 나을 터이니 사실 [한 군데 오래 있게 되어] 그것이 무엇인지 안다는 것을 바람직하다고 여길 필요도 없다

159 invested by family tradition with a dim and dusky grandeur: 가문의 전통에 의해 어두침침한 위풍을 띠고

160 which … the town: 이 읍의 현재 모습과 관련해서 그런 느낌[고향의 느낌]이 든다고 할 수 있는 경우는 거의 없다. 고향의 느낌이 현재의 장소와 관련해서보다는 조상과의 관계에서 느껴진다는 의미이다. *which: home-feeling

in reference to[161] the present phase of the town}. I seem to have a stronger claim to a residence here[162] on account of this grave, bearded, sable[163]-cloaked, and steeple-crowned[164] progenitor[165], —{who came so early, with his Bible and his sword, and trode the unworn street with such a stately port, and made so large a figure[166], as a man of war and peace}, —a stronger claim than for myself, {whose name is seldom heard and my face hardly known[167]}. He was a soldier, legislator, judge; he was a ruler in the Church; he had all the Puritanic traits, both good and evil. He was likewise a bitter persecutor; {as witness the Quakers, [who have remembered him in their histories[168], and

---

161 in reference to …: ~에 관하여

162 have a stronger claim to a residence here: 이곳에 거주할 자격이 있다고 더 그럴 듯하게 주장하다

163 sable: 검은, 어두운, 음침한, 음울한

164 steeple-crowned: (모자의) 꼭대기가 뾰족한, 원추 모양의

165 progenitor: 선조

166 make a large figure: 우람한 풍채를 드러내다

167 a stronger claim than for myself, whose name is seldom heard and my face hardly known: 내 이름을 말해 봐야 아는 이가 거의 없고 얼굴도 알려졌을 리가 없으니 내 자신을 이유로 드는 것보다는 [위와 같은 이유가] [내가 이곳에 거주할 자격이 있음에 대한] 더 그럴 듯한 주장

168 their histories: 그들의 역사(서). *여기에서 언급한 퀘이커교도의 역사(서)는 윌리엄 시웰(William Sewel)의 『퀘이커라고 불리는 기독교도의 발흥, 증가, 발전의 역사』(History of the Rise, Increase, and Progress of the Christian People called Quakers, 1722)로 호손이 주요하게 참조한 사료로 여겨진다. 이 책은 윌리엄 호손(William Hathorne)을 그 종파에 대한 '맹렬한 박해자'(fierce persecutor)라며 그의 잔인함을 기록하고 있다고 한다. 퀘

relate[169] an incident of his hard severity towards a woman of their sect, {which will last longer, it is to be feared, than any record of his better deeds, although these were many[170]}]}.
His son[171], too, inherited the persecuting spirit, and made

---

이커교도인 앤 콜먼(Ann Coleman)을 잔인하게 매질하여 거의 죽을 지경이 되게 한 것은 그가 발부한 영장 때문이었다고 한다.

169 as witness the Quakers and relate …: 이 대목은 'as the Quakers witness and relate'의 구조로 보아 'an incident'를 '목격하고 상술하다'의 목적어로 볼 수 있는 한편, witness를 자동사로 본 뒤 who 이하를 통째로 묶어서 볼 수도 있다. 후자의 경우 '그를 기억하고 그 사건을 상술한다'의 의미가 된다. 어느 쪽으로 보든 전체적인 의미는 서로 통한다.

170 which … many: which는 an incident를 가리킨다. 그것[자신들(퀘이커들)의 종파에 속한 한 여인에 대해 그(작가의 선조)가 매우 가혹했던 한 사건]이 염려스럽게도 그[작가의 선조]의 많은 더 나은 행적에 대한 어떤 기록보다도 더 오래 남을 것이다. *호손은 「유순한 소년」("The Gentleboy")에서 퀘이커 여인과 그녀의 어린 사내아이가 가혹한 청교도들에게 박해받는 이야기를 한 바 있다. 작가는 종교적·인종적 타자에 대해 전반적으로 매우 엄혹한 태도를 취했던 청교도사회의 모습을 묘사함과 동시에 이 퀘이커 여인과 아이를 대하는 청교도들 내의 차이에도 주목하고 있다. 호손은 더 나아가 청교도 내부의 이런 차이가 단지 개인의 심성 차이에만 기인하는 것이 아니라 이들 각각이 어떤 계기로 어느 때에 신대륙으로 건너왔으며 그 이전에 영국에서는 어떤 종류의 삶을 살았는가 하는 점과도 매우 밀접한 것임을 치밀하게 보여 주고 있다.

171 his son: 치안판사 존 호손(John Hathorne)을 가리킨다. 그는 윌리엄의 아들로 1692년 세일럼 마녀재판의 판사 중 하나였다. 청교도사회 내부의 문제를 징후적으로 드러낸 그 사건이 지나간 이후 대다수의 판사가 참회한 것과는 달리 존 호손은 자신이 한 역할에 대해 참회하지 않았다. 윌리엄과 존의 내력에 대한 것은 「젊은 굿맨 브라운」("Young Goodman Brown")에서 주인공 브라운의 선조에 대한 이야기로도 활용되고 있다.

himself so conspicuous[172] in the martyrdom of the witches, that their blood may fairly be said to[173] have left a stain upon him. So deep a stain, indeed, that his old dry bones, in the Charter Street[174] burial-ground, must still retain it, {if they have not crumbled utterly to dust}![175] I know not {whether these ancestors of mine bethought[176] themselves to repent, and ask pardon of Heaven for their cruelties}; or {whether they are now groaning under the heavy consequences of them in another state of being}. At all events, I, the present writer, as their representative, hereby take shame upon myself for their sakes, and pray {that any curse [incurred by them] — [as I have heard, and as the dreary and unprosperous condition of the race, for many a long year back, would argue to exist[177]] — may

---

172 conspicuous: 눈에 잘 띄는, 이목을 끄는

173 may fairly be said to ...: ~라고 말해도 괜찮을 것이다

174 the Charter Street: 특허장거리. *매사추세츠 세일럼에 있는 '자유'(Liberty), '더비'(Derby), '중앙'(Central), '특허장'(Charter) 등의 이름을 가진 거리들이 경계가 되어 '특허장거리 역사지구'를 이루고 있다.

175 So deep a stain ... to dust!: so ... that ... 구문을 활용한 감탄문이다. "그 핏자국이 너무나 깊이 스며들어 특허장거리의 묘지에 묻혀 있는 오래되고 메마른 그의 유골이 부스러져 완전히 가루가 되지 않았다면 아직도 그 자국이 남아 있을 것이다!"

176 bethink: ~을 숙고하다, 생각이 미치다, 결심하다

177 as ... exist: 삽입된 유사관계절로서 heard의 목적어, 그리고 argue의 목적어 자리에 'any curse'를 놓고 문맥을 파악해야 한다. 'any curse'의 술어 부분은 'may be ... removed' 부분이다. 삽입절은 "내가 들은 것도 있고 또 이전 그 많은 세월 동안 자손이 황량하고 불운한 상태였던 것으로 보아 존재한다고 주장할 수 있을

be now and henceforth removed}.

Doubtless, however, either of these stern and black-browed[178] Puritans would have thought it quite a sufficient retribution[179] for his sins {that[180], [after so long a lapse of years], the old trunk of the family tree, [with so much venerable moss upon it], should have borne, [as its topmost[181] bough], an idler like myself}. No aim {that I have ever cherished[182]} would they recognise[183] as laudable[184]; no success of mine — {if my life, beyond its domestic scope, had ever been brightened by success[185]} — would they deem[186] otherwise than worthless[187],

---

[그들로 인해 초래된 저주]"의 의미이다.

178 brow: 이마, 안색, 표정

179 quite a sufficient retribution: 꽤 충분한 응보

180 that ...: 앞의 가목적어 it에 해당하는 진목적어절로서 "고색창연한 이끼가 핀 오래 묵은 가문의 나무기둥이 그렇게 오랜 세월이 지난 뒤에 맨 꼭대기 가지에서 나같이 빈둥거리는 이를 맺고 말았다는 것"의 뜻

181 topmost: (위치, 지위 등이) 맨 꼭대기의, 최고의

182 No aim that I have ever cherished: recognise의 목적어

183 would they recognise(= if they would recognise): 주어 동사의 도치를 활용한 가정법 문장

184 laudable: 기특한

185 if ... by success: 성공을 통해 내 삶이 가정의 영역 너머로까지[바깥세상에서] 밝게 빛난 적이 있다고 하더라도

186 deem: 여기다, 생각하다. *deem의 목적어는 앞의 "no success of mine"

187 otherwise than worthless: no success of mine을 설명해 주는 목적보어로 '하찮은 것과는 다른', '하찮지 않은'의 뜻. '내가 이룬 성

if not positively disgraceful[188]. "What is he?" murmurs one grey shadow of my forefathers to the other. "A writer of story books! What kind of business[189] in life—what mode of glorifying God, or being serviceable to mankind in his day and generation—may that be? Why, the degenerate fellow[190] might as well[191] have been a fiddler[192]!" Such are the compliments [bandied[193] between my great grandsires[194] and myself, across the gulf of time]! And yet, let them scorn me as they will, strong traits of their nature have intertwined themselves with mine.

[Planted deep, in the town's earliest infancy and childhood, by these two earnest and energetic men], the race[195] has ever

---

공 중에 어떤 것도 하찮지 않다고 여기지는 않을 것이다'라는 의미로 결국 '내가 이룬 어떤 성공도 하찮다고 생각할 것이다'라는 의미

188 if not positively disgraceful: 명확하게[단호히][확신을 가지고] 부끄럽다고 여기지는 않더라도, 누가 봐도 분명 남부끄러운 일은 아닐지언정

189 business: 본분, 직업, 일

190 degenerate fellow: 타락한 녀석

191 might as well ...: ~하는 편이 낫다

192 fiddler: 바이올리니스트, 사기꾼, 게으름뱅이. *이 용어는 엔터테이너들에 대한 청교도의 경멸을 담고 있는데, 이것은 예술가들에게도 마찬가지로 확대적용될 수 있다.

193 bandy: [주먹이나 말 따위를] 주고받다

194 grandsire: 조부, 조상, 노인

195 race: 혈통, 가계, 자손

since[196] subsisted[197] here; always, too, in respectability; never, {so far as I have known}, disgraced by a single unworthy member; but seldom or never, on the other hand, after the first two generations, performing any memorable deed, or so much as[198] putting forward[199] a claim to public notice[200]. Gradually, they have sunk almost out of sight; {as old houses, here and there about the streets, get covered half-way to the eaves by the accumulation of new soil[201]}. From father to son, for above a hundred years, they followed the sea[202]; a grey-headed shipmaster, in each generation, retiring from the quarter-deck[203] to the homestead[204], {while a boy of fourteen

---

196 ever since: 그 후로 쭉
197 subsist: 살아가다, 존재하다, 존속하다
198 not so much as: ~조차 없다[않다]. *not so much as putting forward a claim to public notice: 그저 세상 일반의 이목을 끄는 일조차 [좀처럼 없었거나 전혀 없었다]
199 put forward: ~을 내놓다, ~을 두드러지게[남의 눈에 띄게] 하다
200 이 긴 문장의 주어는 'the race'이며 앞에는 이를 꾸며 주는 과거분사 구문이 위치하고, 뒤에는 전치사구(in respectability), 과거분사 구문(disgraced ...), 현재분사 구문(performing ... or ... putting ...)이 위치해 있다.
201 as ... new soil: 마치 오래된 집이 거리의 이곳저곳에서 새 흙이 쌓여 처마까지 반쯤 덮인 것처럼
202 follow the sea: 뱃사람이 되다
203 quarter-deck: 후갑판(보통 고급 선원이나 1등 선객이 전용하는 갑판)
204 homestead: 집과 대지, 선조 대대로의 집, (부속 건물, 부근의 밭을 포함한) 농장

took the hereditary[205] place before the mast[206], confronting the salt spray and the gale [which had blustered against his sire and grandsire]}. The boy, also in due time, passed from the forecastle to the cabin, spent a tempestuous[207] manhood, and returned from his world-wanderings[208], [to grow old, and die, and mingle his dust[209] with the natal earth[210]]. This long connexion of a family with one spot, [as its place of birth and burial], creates a kindred[211] between the human being and the locality, quite independent of[212] any charm in the scenery or moral circumstances {that surround him[213]}. It is not love but instinct. The new inhabitant — {who came himself from a foreign land}, or {whose father or grandfather came} — has little claim to be called a Salemite[214]; he has no conception of[215] the

---

205 hereditary: 유전하는, 선조 대대의 대물림의

206 before the mast: 앞돛대 앞에서, 평선원으로서

207 tempestuous: 비바람 치는, 폭풍우의, 사나운

208 world-wanderings: 세상을 떠도는 일

209 his dust: 자신의 유해

210 natal earth: 태어난 고향의 대지

211 kindred: 친족, 일족, 혈연, 혈연관계, 동질

212 quite independent of ...: ~와는 전혀 관계없이, ~와는 전혀 별도로

213 quite ... him: 그[인간]를 둘러싼 풍경이나 도덕적 환경의 매력과는 전혀 관계없이

214 Salemite: 세일럼 사람. *-ite는 '~의 주민, ~의 신봉자, ~에 소속된 사람'이라는 의미를 띤다. 그 밖에 광물, 화석의 이름, 혹은 폭발물이나 합성물의 이름으로 쓰이기도 한다.

215 have no conception of: ~을 전혀 알지 못하다, ~을 전혀 생각해 내지 못하다

oyster-like tenacity[216] {with which an old settler, [over whom his third century is creeping[217]], clings to the spot [where his successive[218] generations have been embedded[219]]}. It is no matter that the place is joyless for him; that he is weary of[220] the old wooden houses, the mud and dust, the dead level[221] of site[222] and sentiment, the chill east wind, and the chillest of social atmospheres;—all these, and {whatever faults besides[223] he may see or imagine}, are nothing to the purpose[224]. The spell survives, and just as powerfully {as if the natal[225] spot were an earthly paradise}. So has it been in my case[226]. I felt it[227] almost as a destiny to make Salem my home; so that the mould of features[228] and cast[229] of character {which had all along been familiar here—ever, as one representative of the

---

216 tenacity: 고집, 완고, 끈덕짐, 끈기
217 creep: 느릿느릿 기어가다, 퍼지다
218 successive: 연속적인, 연이은
219 embed(=imbed): 묻다, 심다
220 be weary of: 싫증나다, 넌더리나다
221 the dead level: 평평한 고장에 적용되는 용어. *dead: 평평한, 단조로운; level: 평평한, 높낮이가 없는, 수평, 평면
222 site: 장소, 용지, 부지
223 besides: 그 밖에, 그 외에
224 nothing to the purpose: [이 고장에 대한 집착을 버리게 하는 데] 아무 소용이 없다. *to the purpose: 적절한, 요령 있는, 유익한
225 natal: 출생의, 탄생의
226 So has it been in my case: 내 경우에도 마찬가지였다
227 it: =to make Salem my home
228 the mould of features: 이목구비의 생김새[틀, 뼈대]
229 cast: 외형, 외관, 성질

race lay down in the grave, another assuming, as it were, his sentry-march[230] along the main street}—might still in my little day[231] be seen and recognised in the old town.[232] Nevertheless, this very sentiment is an evidence {that the connexion, [which has become an unhealthy one], should at least be severed[233]}. Human nature will not flourish, any more than a potato, {if it be planted and re-planted, for too long a series of generations, in the same worn-out soil[234]}. My children have had other birth-places, and, {so far as their fortunes may be within my control}, shall strike their roots[235] into unaccustomed earth.

On emerging from the Old Manse, it[236] was chiefly this strange, indolent, unjoyous attachment for my native town {that brought me to fill a place in Uncle Sam's brick edifice, [when I might as well, or better, have gone somewhere else]}. My doom was on me. It was not the first time, nor the second, {that I had gone away—[as it seemed, permanently]—but yet

---

230 sentry-march: 보초를 서며 도는 순찰. *sentry: 감시, 파수꾼
231 in my little day: 보잘것없으나 한창 때의 내 모습에서
232 the mould of features ... in the old town: 이 부분의 내용을 요약하면 세일럼이 작가의 조상들이 살고 죽은 고장이어서 가문사람들 특유의 이목구비와 성격을 익히 보아 왔을 것이고 또 조상들의 모습이 내게도 유전되었을 것이기 때문에 내 모습을 통해서도 조상들의 모습을 알아차릴 것이라는 뜻이다.
233 sever: 절단하다
234 in the same worn-out soil: 지력(地力)이 떨어진 똑같은 토양에
235 strike root: 뿌리를 내리다, 정착하다
236 it ... that ...: 강조용법

returned, like the bad halfpenny[237], or [as if Salem were for me the inevitable centre of the universe]}. So, one fine morning I ascended the flight of granite steps, with the President's commission[238] in my pocket, and was introduced to the corps of gentlemen {who were to aid me in my weighty responsibility as chief executive officer[239] of the Custom-House[240]}.

I doubt greatly — or, rather, I do not doubt at all — {whether any public functionary[241] of the United States, [either in the civil or military line], has ever had such a patriarchal[242] body of veterans under his orders as myself}. The whereabouts[243] of the Oldest Inhabitant was at once settled[244] when I looked

---

237 like the bad halfpenny: 아무짝에도 소용없는 반 페니 동전처럼 원하지 않는데도 빠지지 않고 꼬박꼬박

238 commission: 위임, 임명

239 chief executive officer: 최고 경영 책임자, 최고 행정관, 조직의 장(長)

240 호손은 1846년에서 1849년까지 세일럼 세관에서 검사관(surveyor)으로 근무했다.

241 public functionary: 공무원

242 patriarchal: 존경할 만한, 원로의

243 whereabouts: 행방, 소재

244 settle: 해결하다, 결정하다, 매듭짓다. *이 마을에서 가장 나이 든 주민이 누구이며 어디 있을까 하는 것이 문제라고 한다면 다른 곳에서 찾을 것도 없이 여기에 속해 있을 것이라는 것을 금세 알겠다는 내용으로, 바로 앞에서 같이 일하게 될 사람들이 '원로 노병집단'이라고 말한 것과 상통하는 호손의 우스꽝스러운 어조가 여기서도 느껴진다.

at them. For upwards of twenty years before this epoch[245], the
independent position of the Collector[246] had kept the Salem
Custom-House out of the whirlpool of political vicissitude[247],
{which makes the tenure[248] of office generally so fragile[249]}.
A soldier — New England's most distinguished soldier,[250] —
he stood firmly on the pedestal[251] of his gallant services[252];
and, [himself secure in the wise liberality of the successive
administrations {through which he had held office}], he had
been the safety[253] of his subordinates[254] in many an hour

---

245 this epoch: 호손 당대를 가리키는 말로 바로 뒤의 정치적인 소용
     돌이에 따라 관직이 영향을 받는다는 이야기와 연관되어 있다고
     볼 수 있다. 뒤에서도 언급되지만, 1848년 대통령 선거에서 휘그
     당의 재커리 테일러(Zachary Taylor)가 대통령이 되면서 그 반대
     파인 민주당의 영향으로 세관직을 얻었던 호손이 자리에서 밀려
     났다. 일종의 전리품 챙기기의 측면이 큰 엽관제(spoils system,
     patronage system)로 인해 호손의 공직임용은 애초부터 안정성
     이 보장되기 어려운 취약한 것이었다.

246 collector: 징세관

247 vicissitude: 변천

248 tenure: 보유, 재직기간, 재임자격, 임기

249 fragile: 부서지기 쉬운, 오래 못 가는

250 New England's most distinguished soldier: 이 인물은 제임스 F.
     밀러(James F. Miller)로 24년 동안 징세관(collector) 또는 주임
     관리(chief officer)였다. 이 인물은 영국과 싸운 1812년 전쟁에서
     두각을 드러낸 바 있고 정식 주가 되기 이전 준주 아칸소의 첫 주
     지사였다.

251 pedestal: 받침대, 기초, 중요한 지위

252 gallant services: 용감한 군복무

253 safety: 안전판, 안전장치

254 subordinates: 부하, 하급자

of danger and heart-quake. General Miller was radically conservative; a man {over whose kindly nature habit had no slight influence[255]}; attaching himself strongly to familiar faces, and [with difficulty] moved to change, {even when change might have brought unquestionable improvement}. Thus, on taking charge of[256] my department, I found few but[257] aged men. They were ancient sea-captains, for the most part, {who, [after being tossed[258] on every sea, and standing up sturdily against life's tempestuous blast[259]], had finally drifted into this quiet nook[260], [where, with little to disturb them, except the periodical terrors of a Presidential election[261], they one and all acquired a new lease of existence[262]]}. [Though by no means less liable[263] than their fellow-men to age and infirmity], they

---

255 habit had no slight influence (over): 습관이 적잖은 영향을 미 쳤다

256 take charge of: 떠맡다

257 but: = except

258 toss: 던져 올리다, 심하게 흔들리다, 시달리다

259 tempestuous blast: 폭풍우를 동반한 돌풍, 사나운 돌풍, 폭풍우 몰아치는 세찬 바람

260 nook: 구석진 곳, 은신처

261 with little to disturb them, except the periodical terrors of a Presidential election: 정기적으로 불어닥치는 대통령선거의 공포 를 제외하면 그들을 괴롭힐 것이 거의 없는

262 new lease of existence: 존재의 새로운 임차기간(임차권, 임대차 계약서). 새롭게 주어진 존재의 기간. *바다에서의 삶과 달리 육 지에서의 새로운 삶을 살 기회를 얻었음을 이렇게 표현하고 있다. lease: 임차기간, 생명 등의 주어진 기간

263 liable: 책임을 져야 할, 면할 수 없는, (병 따위에) 걸리기 쉬운

had evidently some talisman or other {that kept death at bay[264]}. Two or three of their number[265], {as I was assured}, [being gouty and rheumatic, or perhaps bed-ridden[266]], never dreamed of making their appearance[267] at the Custom-House during a large part of the year; but, [after a torpid[268] winter], would creep out into the warm sunshine of May or June, go lazily about[269] {what they termed duty}, and, [at their own leisure and convenience[270]], betake themselves to[271] bed again. I must plead guilty to[272] the charge of abbreviating the official breath[273] of more than one of these venerable servants of the republic. They were allowed, on my representation[274], to rest from their arduous[275] labours, and soon afterwards—{as if their sole principle of life had been zeal for their country's

---

264 keep ... at bay: ~을 가까이 오지 못하게 하다, 저지하다. *bay: (사냥개의) 으르렁거리는 소리, 쫓겨서 몰린 상태

265 number: 사람의 모임, 집단, 무리

266 bed-ridden: 누워만 있는, 지쳐빠져 있는

267 make appearance: 출두하다, 모습을 드러내다

268 torpid: (신체기관 등이) 둔한, 움직이지 않는, (동물이) 휴면(동면)하고 있는

269 go about: 돌아다니다, ~와 사귀다, 열심히 ~하다, ~하려고 애쓰다

270 at their own leisure and convenience: 자기들이 틈이 나고 편할 때

271 betake oneself to ...: ~로 가다

272 plead guilty to ...: ~의 죄를 인정하다

273 abbreviate the official breath: 관직의 생명을 단축시키다

274 on my representation: 나의 주장에 의거하여, 내 제안에 따라

275 arduous: 힘든, 정력적인

service—as I verily believe it was}—withdrew to a better world. It is a pious consolation to me {that, [through my interference[276]], a sufficient space was allowed them for repentance of the evil and corrupt practices [into which, as a matter of course, every Custom-House officer must be supposed to[277] fall]}. Neither the front nor the back entrance of the Custom-House opens on the road to Paradise.

The greater part of my officers were Whigs[278]. It was well for their venerable brotherhood[279] {that the new Surveyor was not a politician, and [though a faithful Democrat in principle], neither received nor held his office with any

---

276 through my interference: 나의 간섭으로 인해. ＊고령의 사람들 몇을 권고 사직시켜 내보낸 일을 두고 그냥 두면 세관에서 하릴없이 시간만 보내거나 세관에 있으면서 빠져들 수밖에 없었을 악덕들로부터 이들을 벗어나게 해서 죽기 전에 회개할 시간을 준 셈이라고 하고 있다. 호손의 풍자적인 필치가 여기에서도 드러난다.

277 be supposed to …: ～하기로 되어 있다, ～하리라 생각되다

278 Whig: 미국 독립혁명기에는 영국을 지지한 왕당파(Tory)에 맞선 독립당원을 가리키는 말이었으나 여기에서는 잭슨 민주주의 시기에 잭슨과 민주당에 반대하여 결성되었던 휘그정당(Whig Party, 1833～1856)의 당원들을 가리킨다. 앤드류 잭슨(Andrew Jackson)이 대통령이 된 1828년부터 그 기조를 유지한 1850년대까지 걸쳐 있는 잭슨 민주주의는 참정권 확대, '명백한 운명'(Manifest Destiny)을 내세운 서부로의 팽창정책, 자유방임 경제, 엄격한 입헌주의의 원리에 의거한 연방정부의 권한 제한 등을 특징으로 한다.

279 their venerable brotherhood: 휘그 성향 세관의 나이 많은 사람들을 이렇게 지칭하고 있다.

reference to political services}. {Had it been otherwise}—
{had an active politician been put into this influential post,[280]
to assume the easy task of making head against[281] a Whig
Collector, [whose infirmities withheld him from the personal
administration of his office[282]]}—hardly a man of the old
corps[283] would have drawn the breath of official life within
a month {after the exterminating angel had come up the
Custom-House steps[284]}. [According to the received code[285]

---

280 had it ... post: 주어 동사의 도치를 활용한 가정법 문장. ＊if
it had been otherwise → had it been otherwise, if an active
politician had → had an active politician

281 make head against ...: ～에 맞서다, 대항하다

282 Had it been otherwise ... of his office: 그렇지 않았다면, 즉 활
동적인 정치가가 이 영향력 있는 지위에 임명되어, 이제는 쇠약해
져서 자기 임무를 몸소 관리하지 못하는 휘그파 징세관에 만만하
게 맞서는 일을 떠맡았다면

283 the old corps: 노쇠한 군단

284 징세관(collector)과 검사관(surveyor) 모두 대통령이 임명하
는 직위이다. 징세관은 검사관을 제외한 직급들을 재정부 장관
의 승인을 얻어 임명하는 권한을 가지며, 검사관은 징세관의 지시
에 따라 그렇게 임명된 하위에 있는 조사관(inspectors), 계량사
(weighers), 측량사(measurers), 검량관(gaugers) 등의 모든 직
책을 관리 감독하는 권한이 있다. 따라서 징세관이 제 임무를 수
행하지 못하는 경우 검사관이 행사할 수 있는 권한은 막강하다고
할 수 있다. '전멸시키는 천사'라는 표현에는 노쇠한 징세관을 대
신해서 권한을 행사했을 경우 노령의 직원들 거의 대부분이 '공직
생활의 숨통'이 끊겼을 것이라는 독설이 실려 있다. ＊해당 직책들
이 한 일이나 그 직책에 대해 정확한 우리말 명칭을 대입시키기
는 쉽지 않으나 각기 무게, 길이, 숫자, 액체의 양 등과 같이 다양
한 품목의 점검에 따른 세분화된 직책들이라고 볼 수 있다.

285 the received code: 받아들여진(일반에 인정된) 불문율(관례)

54

in such matters], it would have been nothing short of[286] duty, in a politician, [to bring every one of those white heads under the axe of the guillotine[287]]. It was plain enough to discern[288] that the old fellows dreaded some such discourtesy[289] at my hands. It[290] pained, and at the same time amused me, [to behold the terrors {that attended my advent[291]}]; [to see a furrowed cheek, weather-beaten[292] by half a century of storm, turn[293] ashy pale at the glance of so harmless an individual as myself]; [to detect, as one or another addressed me, the tremor of a voice {which, in long-past days, had been wont[294] to bellow[295] through a speaking-trumpet[296], hoarsely enough to frighten Boreas[297] himself to silence}]. They knew, these excellent old persons, {that, [by all established rule—and, {as regarded some of them}, weighed by their own lack of

---

286 nothing short of ...: 아주 ~한, ~로 보아 부족한 게 전혀 없는
287 to bring every one of those white heads under the axe of the guillotine: 머리카락이 하얗게 센 그들의 머리를 모두 단두대의 도끼 아래로 옮겨 놓는 것
288 plain enough to discern: 알아차릴 정도로 빤하다
289 discourtesy: 무례, 무례한 언행
290 it: 가주어. 진주어는 이후에 나오는 to behold, to see, to detect
291 the terrors that attended my advent: 나의 출현에 따른 공포
292 weather-beaten: 비바람에 시달린, 풍상을 다 겪은
293 see ... turn: see+목적어+동사원형 목적보어 turn
294 wont: ~에 익숙한, ~하는 것이 예사인
295 bellow: 큰소리로 울다
296 had been wont to bellow through a speaking-trumpet: 확성기를 통해 고함치는 것이 예사였던
297 Boreas: 보리어스(북풍의 신)

efficiency for business[298]] — they ought to have given place to younger men, more orthodox[299] in politics, and altogether fitter than themselves to serve our common Uncle[300]}. I knew it, too, but could never quite find in my heart to act upon the knowledge[301]. [Much and deservedly to my own discredit, therefore, and considerably to the detriment of my official conscience], they continued, [during my incumbency[302]], to creep about the wharves, and loiter up and down the Custom-House steps. They spent a good deal of time, also, asleep in their accustomed corners, [with their chairs tilted back against the walls]; awaking, however, once or twice in the forenoon, to bore one another with the several thousandth repetition of old sea-stories and mouldy jokes, {that had grown to be passwords and countersigns among them}.

The discovery was soon made[303], I imagine, {that the new Surveyor had no great harm in him}. So, [with lightsome

---

298 as regarded ... business: 그들 중 어떤 이들과 관련해서는 그들 자신의 업무 능력 결여에 의해 평가되어

299 orthodox: (일반적으로) 정통의, 옳다고 인정된, 공인된

300 our common Uncle: 앞에서 나온, 미국을 의미하는 엉클 샘 (Uncle Sam)을 가리킨다.

301 could never quite find in my heart to act upon the knowledge: 알고 있는 것에 따라 행동할 마음을 전혀 먹을 수가 없었다

302 incumbency: 재직 기간

303 make a discovery: 발견하다. *뒤의 'that ...' 부분은 주어 'the discovery'와 동격인 명사절이다.

hearts and the happy consciousness of being usefully employed—in their own behalf at least, if not for our beloved country[304]]—these good old gentlemen went through the various formalities of office. Sagaciously[305] under their spectacles, did they peep[306] into the holds[307] of vessels! Mighty was their fuss[308] about little matters, and marvellous, sometimes, the obtuseness[309] {that allowed greater ones to slip between their fingers}. Whenever such a mischance[310] occurred—when a waggon-load of valuable merchandise had been smuggled ashore, at noonday, perhaps, and directly beneath their unsuspicious noses—nothing could exceed the vigilance[311] and alacrity[312] {with which they proceeded[313] to lock, and double-lock, and secure with tape and sealing-wax[314], all the avenues[315] of the delinquent[316] vessel}. [Instead of a

---

304 in their own behalf at least, if not for our beloved country: 우리의 사랑하는 국가를 위해서는 아닐지라도 적어도 자기들 자신의 이익을 위해

305 sagacious: 현명한

306 peep: 훔쳐보다, 살짝 보다

307 hold: (배, 비행기의) 짐 선반, 잡는 것, 지탱하는 것(곳)

308 fuss: 호들갑, 법석, 야단

309 obtuse: 둔감한, 무딘. *〈명사〉 obtuseness

310 mischance: 불운

311 vigilance: 경계, 조심, 불침번

312 alacrity: 민첩성

313 proceed: 진행하다, 계속해서 ~을 하다, 나아가다

314 sealing-wax: 납봉

315 avenue: 거리, 길, 진입로, 도달(접근) 수단

316 delinquent: 비행의 범죄성향을 보이는, 채무를 이행하지 않는,

reprimand[317] for their previous negligence], the case seemed rather to require an eulogium[318] on their praiseworthy caution {after the mischief[319] had happened}; a grateful recognition of the promptitude of their zeal {the moment that there was no longer any remedy[320]}.

Unless people are more than commonly disagreeable[321], it is my foolish habit to contract[322] a kindness for them. The better part of my companion's character, {if it have a better part}, is that {which usually comes uppermost[323] in my regard[324], and forms the type [whereby I recognise the man]}. {As most of these old Custom-House officers had good traits}, and {as my position in reference to them, being paternal and protective, was favourable to the growth of friendly sentiments}, I soon grew to[325] like them all. It was pleasant in the summer

---

연체된. *a delinquent borrower: 채무 불이행 채무자

317 reprimand: 질책

318 eulogium: 칭찬

319 mischief: (특히 아이들이 하는 크게 심각하지 않은) 나쁜 짓(장난), (사람, 평판에 대한) 피해

320 a grateful ... any remedy: 더 이상 어떤 대책도 없는 순간에 그들이 보인 열정의 신속함에 대해 감사해하는 인정. *promptitude: 민첩, 신속; remedy: 처리 방안, 해결책, 치료, 구제방법

321 disagreeable: 유쾌하지 못한, 무례한

322 contract: 일을 계약하다, ~의 습관이 붙다, 병에 걸리다

323 uppermost: 가장 위의, 가장 중요한, 가장 높은 위치의

324 regard: 관계, 관련, 주의, 관심, 고려, 평가

325 grow to: 점점 ~하게 되다

forenoons—when the fervent heat, {that almost liquefied the rest of the human family}, merely communicated a genial[326] warmth to their half torpid[327] systems—it was pleasant to hear them chatting in the back entry, [a row of them all tipped against the wall, as usual]; while the frozen witticisms of past generations were thawed out, and came bubbling with laughter from their lips. Externally, the jollity[328] of aged men has much in common with the mirth[329] of children; the intellect, any more than a deep sense of humour, has little to do with the matter; it is, with both, a gleam[330] {that plays upon the surface, and imparts a sunny and cheery aspect alike to the green branch and grey, mouldering[331] trunk[332]}. In one case, however, it is real sunshine; in the other, it more resembles the phosphorescent[333] glow[334] of decaying wood. It would be sad injustice, the reader must understand, to represent all my excellent old friends as in their dotage[335]. In the first place, my coadjutors[336] were not invariably old; there were men among

---

326 genial: 온화한, 쾌적한, 상냥한
327 torpid: 무감각한, 마비된
328 jollity: 유쾌함, 명랑
329 mirth: 명랑, 유쾌한 법석, 떠들썩한 소동, 즐거운 웃음소리
330 gleam: 어슴푸레한 빛, 반짝거림
331 moulder: (서서히) 썩다
332 trunk: 나무 몸통
333 phosphorescent: 인광을 내는
334 glow: (특히 불꽃이 일지 않는 은은한) 불빛
335 dotage: 노망, 망령
336 coadjutor: 조수, 보좌관

them in their strength and prime, of marked ability and energy, and altogether superior to the sluggish and dependent mode of life {on which their evil stars had cast them}. Then, moreover, the white locks of age were sometimes found to be the thatch[337] of an intellectual tenement[338] in good repair. But, {as respects the majority of my corps of veterans}, there will be no wrong done if I characterize them generally as a set of wearisome old souls[339], {who had gathered nothing worth preservation from their varied experience of life}. They seemed to have flung away all the golden grain of practical wisdom, {which they had enjoyed so many opportunities of harvesting, and most carefully to have stored their memory with the husks[340]}. They spoke with far more interest and unction[341] of their morning's breakfast, or yesterday's, to-day's, or tomorrow's dinner, than of the shipwreck of forty or fifty years ago, and all the world's wonders {which they had witnessed with their youthful eyes}.

The father of the Custom-House — {the patriarch[342], not only of this little squad[343] of officials, but, I am bold to say, of

---

337 thatch: 초가지붕. *thatch of hair: 숱 많은 머리

338 tenement: 주택

339 soul: 영혼, 마음, 정신, ~의 전형, (특정 유형의) 사람

340 husk: (특히 곡식의) 겉껍질

341 unction: 도유(종교의식에서 머리나 몸에 기름을 바르는 일), 번
지르르한 말

342 patriarch: (가정의) 가장, (공동체의) 족장, 원로

343 squad: 반, 단, 분대, 소집단

the respectable body[344] of tide-waiters[345] all over the United States} — was a certain permanent Inspector[346]. He might truly be termed a legitimate son of the revenue[347] system, dyed in the wool[348], or rather born in the purple[349]; since his sire, a Revolutionary colonel, and formerly collector of the port, had created an office for him, and appointed him to fill it, at a period of the early ages {which few living men can now remember}. This Inspector, when I first knew him, was a man of fourscore[350] years, or thereabouts, and certainly one of the most wonderful specimens of winter-green[351] {that you would be likely to discover in a lifetime's search}. {With his florid cheek, his compact[352] figure smartly[353] arrayed in a bright-buttoned blue coat, his brisk and vigorous step, and his hale[354] and hearty[355] aspect}, altogether he seemed — not

---

344 body: 몸통, 본체, 조직, 많은 양

345 tide-waiter: 승선세관 감시인

346 inspector: 조사관, 감독관

347 revenue: (정부 · 기관의) 수익(수입/세입)

348 dyed in the wool: dyed-in-the-wool로 붙여서 명사 앞에 쓰면, '골수~'라는 뜻이다. * 원재료일 때 염색을 한 양모가 색상이 더 고르고 오래간다는 맥락에서 나온 표현

349 born in the purple: 왕후의 집안에 태어난

350 fourscore: 80. * score = 20; fourscore = 4 × 20 = 80

351 winter-green: (식물) 바위앵도류의 관목, 북미산의 상록수

352 compact: 소형의, 작은, 촘촘한

353 smartly: 거세게, 엄하게, 현명하게, 말쑥하게

354 hale: (특히 노인이) 건강한, 노익장의

355 hearty: (마음이) 따뜻한, 원기왕성한, 쾌활한

young, indeed—but a kind of new contrivance[356] of Mother
Nature in the shape of man, {whom age and infirmity had no
business to touch}. His voice and laugh, {which perpetually
re-echoed through the Custom-House}, had nothing of the
tremulous[357] quaver[358] and cackle[359] of an old man's utterance;
they came strutting[360] out of his lungs, like the crow[361] of a
cock, or the blast[362] of a clarion[363]. Looking at him merely as
an animal—and there was very little else to look at—he was
a most satisfactory object, from the thorough healthfulness
and wholesomeness of his system, and his capacity, at that
extreme age, to enjoy all, or nearly all, the delights {which
he had ever aimed at or conceived of}. The careless security
of his life in the Custom-House, [on a regular income], and
[with but slight and infrequent apprehensions of removal],
had no doubt contributed to make time pass lightly over him.
The original and more potent causes, however, lay in [the rare
perfection of his animal nature], [the moderate[364] proportion

---

356　contrivance: (글이나 행을) 억지로 짜맞춘 것, 부자연스러움,
　　　(교묘한) 장치, 수완
357　tremulous: 약간 떠는, 떨리는
358　quaver: (목소리의) 떨림, 떨리는 목소리
359　cackle: 꽥꽥하고 날카롭게 울다, 꽥꽥 우는 소리, 새된 목소리
360　strut: 뽐내며 걷다, 활보하다
361　crow: 수탉의 울음소리
362　blast: 한바탕의 바람, 돌풍, (나팔, 피리의) 취주, 경적
363　clarion: 클라리온(명쾌한 음색을 지닌 옛 나팔)
364　moderate: 적당한, 보통의, 중도의

of intellect], and [the very trifling admixture[365] of moral and spiritual ingredients[366]]; these latter qualities, indeed, being in barely enough measure to keep the old gentleman from walking on all-fours. He possessed no power of thought, no ★ MP3 [6] 시작 depth of feeling, no troublesome[367] sensibilities: nothing, in short, but a few commonplace instincts, {which, [aided by the cheerful temper which grew inevitably out of his physical well-being], did duty very respectably, and to general acceptance, in lieu[368] of a heart}. He had been the husband of three wives, all long since dead; the father of twenty children, {most of whom, at every age of childhood or maturity, had likewise returned to dust}. Here, one would suppose, might have been sorrow enough [to imbue the sunniest disposition through and through with a sable[369] tinge[370]]. Not so with our old Inspector! One brief sigh sufficed[371] to carry off[372] the entire burden of these dismal reminiscences. The next moment he was as ready for sport as any unbreeched[373] infant: far readier than the

---

365 admixture: 혼합(물), 약간 섞인 것
366 ingredient: 재료, 성분, 구성요소
367 troublesome: 골칫거리인, 고질적인
368 in lieu of: ~의 대신으로
369 sable: 검은담비, 아메리카 족제비, 검은, 어두운, 음울한
370 tinge: 엷은 색조
371 suffice: 충분하다
372 carry off: 강력하게 제거하다, 이기다, 성공적으로 처리하다, 죽게 하다
373 unbreeched: 바지를 입고 있지 않은

Collector's junior clerk, who at nineteen years was much the elder and graver man of the two. I used to watch and study this patriarchal personage [with, I think, livelier curiosity than any other form of humanity {there presented to my notice}]. He was, in truth, a rare phenomenon[374]; so perfect, in one point of view; so shallow, so delusive[375], so impalpable[376], such an absolute nonentity[377], in every other. My conclusion was that he had no soul, no heart, no mind; nothing, as I have already said, but instincts; and yet, withal[378], so cunningly had [the few materials of his character] been put together {that there was no painful perception of deficiency, but[379], on my part, an entire contentment with [what I found in him]}. It might be difficult—and it was so—to conceive {how he should exist hereafter, so earthly[380] and sensuous did he seem}; but surely his existence here, [admitting that[381] it was to terminate with his last breath], had been not unkindly[382] given; [with no higher moral responsibilities than the beasts of the field], but

---

374 phenomenon: 현상, 경이로운 사람(것)
375 delusive: 현혹시키는, 미혹케 하는, 기만적인, 알쏭달쏭한
376 impalpable: 손으로 만져서 알 수 없는, 쉽게 이해할 수 없는
377 nonentity: 보잘것없는 사람(것), 존재하지 않는 것, 비실재
378 withal: 게다가, 한편, 그럼에도 불구하고
379 no ... but: 의미상 not A but B의 꼴로 보고 해석하는 게 자연스럽다.
380 earthly: 세속적인, 현세적인, 이 세상의
381 admitting that(=while admitting that): ~이기는 하나
382 unkindly: 불친절하게, 몰인정하게

[with a larger scope of enjoyment than theirs], and [with all their blessed immunity[383] from the dreariness and duskiness of age].

One point {in which he had vastly the advantage over his four-footed brethren} was his ability to recollect the good dinners {which it had made no small portion of the happiness of his life to eat}. His gourmandism[384] was a highly agreeable trait; and [to hear him talk of roast meat] was as appetizing as a pickle or an oyster. {As he possessed no higher attribute, and neither sacrificed nor vitiated[385] any spiritual endowment[386] [by devoting all his energies and ingenuities[387] to subserve[388] the delight and profit of his maw[389]]}, it always pleased and satisfied me [to hear him expatiate[390] on fish, poultry, and butcher's meat[391], and the most eligible[392] methods of preparing them for the table]. His reminiscences of good cheer[393],

---

383 immunity: 면역력, 면제
384 gourmandism: 미식주의, 식도락
385 vitiate: (무엇의 효과를) 해치다, 떨어뜨리다
386 endowment: (학교 등의 기관에 주는) 기부(금), (타고난) 자질 (재능)
387 ingenuity: 기발한 재주, 재간
388 subserve: 거들다, 촉진하다, 모시다, 섬기다
389 maw: (뭐든지 집어삼킬 듯 쩍 벌어진) 구멍, (동물의) 위(목구멍)
390 expatiate: 상세히 설명하다
391 butcher's meat: 정육점에서 팔고 있는 고기, 가축의 고기
392 eligible: 적격인, 신랑(신부)감으로 좋은
393 cheer: 환호, 격려(words of cheer), 기분, 음식, 성찬. *a cheer

{however ancient the date of the actual banquet}, seemed to bring the savour of pig or turkey under one's very nostrils. There were flavours[394] on his palate[395] {that had lingered there not less than sixty or seventy years, and were still apparently as fresh as that of the mutton chop[396] [which he had just devoured[397] for his breakfast]}. I have heard him smack[398] his lips over[399] dinners, {every guest at which, except himself, had long been food for worms}. It was marvellous to observe {how the ghosts of bygone meals were continually rising up before him — [not in anger or retribution, but as if grateful for his former appreciation, and seeking to reduplicate[400] an endless series of enjoyment. at once shadowy[401] and sensual]. A tender

---

section: 웅원단; birthday cheer: 생일잔치; The fewer the better cheer. 맛있는 음식은 사람이 적을수록 좋다

394 flavour: 풍미, 맛

395 palate: 구개(입천장), 미각, 감식력

396 chop: (특히 돼지나 양의 뼈가 붙은) 토막(갈비) 살

397 devour: 걸신들린 듯 먹다

398 smack: 입맛을 다시다

399 smack one's lips over: ~가 먹고 싶어 입맛을 다시다

400 reduplicate: 복제하다. *이 작품의 원고는 표제지(title-page) 외에는 호손이 파기하여 남아 있지 않다. 이 주해본은 reduplicate로 되어 있는 초판본의 예를 따랐다. 이 단어 reduplicate는 같은 해에 2판을 내면서 작품에 대한 세간의 반향에 대한 작가의 반응을 담은 새로운 서문을 추가하면서 '한 글자도 바꾸지 않고 낸다'고 했으나 repudiate로 바뀌었다. 이후 판본들에서는 초판본을 따라 reduplicate로 다시 바뀌거나 더러 resuscitate로 되어 있는 경우가 있다.

401 shadowy: 그림자가 있는, 그늘진, 그림자 같은, 몽롱한, 실체[실

loin[402] of beef, a hind-quarter[403] of veal[404], a spare-rib[405] of pork, particular[406] chicken, or a remarkably praiseworthy turkey, {which had perhaps adorned his board in the days of the elder Adams[407]}, would be remembered; while all the subsequent experience of our race, and all the events {that brightened or darkened his individual career}, had gone over him with as little permanent effect as the passing breeze. The chief tragic event of the old man's life, {so far as I could judge}, was his mishap[408] with a certain goose, {which lived and died some twenty or forty years ago}: a goose of most promising[409] figure, but which, at table, proved so inveterately[410] tough, that the carving-knife[411] would make no impression on

---

질]가 없는 *a shadowy tree: 그늘지게 하는 나무; a shadowy garden: 그늘진 정원; ashadowy outline[form]: 희미한 윤곽[형상]; the shadowy past: 어렴풋한 과거

402 tender loin: 안심

403 hind-quarter: (짐승고기의) 뒤쪽 4분의 1. *〈복수〉 hind-quarters: 뒷다리와 궁둥이

404 veal: 송아지 고기

405 squrar-rib: 평방 늑골

406 particular: 하나하나의, 개개의, 독특한, 각별한, 보통 이상의

407 John Adams(1735~1826). 본인이 미국의 2대 대통령이었고 그의 아들은 여섯 번째 대통령이 되었기 때문에 'the elder Adams'라고 했다. *elder: (혈연관계에서) 나이가 위인, 연장의, (인명 앞이나 뒤에 붙여, 같은 이름 또는 성을 지닌 사람·부자·형제 중에서) 연상의

408 mishap: 작은 사고, 불행

409 promising: 전도유망한, 장래성이 있는, 전망이 좋은

410 inveterately: 뿌리 깊이, 만성적으로

its carcass[412], and it could only be divided with an axe and handsaw[413].

But it is time to quit this sketch; on which, however, I should be glad to dwell[414] at considerably more length, because of all men {whom I have ever known}, this individual was fittest to be a Custom-House officer. Most persons, {owing to causes which I may not have space to hint at}, suffer moral detriment from this peculiar mode of life. The old Inspector was incapable of it; and, {were he to continue in office to the end of time}, would be just as good as he was then, and sit down to dinner with just as good an appetite.

There is one likeness[415], {without which my gallery of Custom-House portraits would be strangely incomplete}, but {which my comparatively few opportunities for observation enable me to sketch only in the merest outline}. It is that of the Collector, our gallant old General, {who, after his brilliant military service, [subsequently to which he had ruled over a wild Western territory], had come hither, twenty years before,

---

411 carving-knife: (식탁에서) 요리된 큰 고기 덩어리를 저미는 칼
412 carcass: (큰 동물의) 시체, (식용으로 쓸) 죽은 동물
413 handsaw: (한 손으로 쓸 수 있는) 가는 톱, 손톱
414 dwell on ...: ~을 깊이 생각하다, ~을 자세히 설명하다[이야기하다]
415 likeness: (어떤 사람과 아주 닮은) 화상(畫像)

[to spend the decline[416] of his varied and honourable life]. The brave soldier had already numbered[417], nearly or quite, his three-score years and ten[418], and was pursuing the remainder of his earthly march, burdened with infirmities {which even the martial music of his own spirit-stirring recollections could do little towards lightening}. The step was palsied[419] now, that had been foremost in the charge[420]. It was only [with the assistance of a servant, and by leaning his hand heavily on the iron balustrade[421]], that he could slowly and painfully ascend the Custom-House steps, and, [with a toilsome progress across the floor], attain[422] his customary chair beside the fireplace. There he used to sit, gazing [with a somewhat dim serenity[423] of aspect] at the figures {that came and went, amid the rustle of papers, the administering of oaths, the discussion of business, and the casual talk[424] of the office}; all which sounds and circumstances seemed but indistinctly to impress his

---

416 decline: 경사, 내리막, 만년(in the decline of one's life)

417 number: ~의 수에 이르다

418 three-score years and ten: [3×20]+10=70세. 그런데 성서의 「시편」(Psalms) 제90편에 따라 인간의 수명을 70세로 보면, 이 대목은 장군이 이미 수명을 다했다는 말로 풀이할 수 있다.

419 palsy: 마비, 저림, ~을 마비시키다, 저리게 하다

420 charge: 여러 뜻이 있는데 여기에서는 '돌격', '진격'의 의미

421 balustrade: 난간, 난간이 달린

422 attain: (대개 많은 노력을 기울여) 이루다(획득하다), 이르다, 달하다

423 serenity: 고요함, 맑음, 평온,

424 casual talk: 평상시의 가벼운 이야기(=small talk)

senses, and hardly to make their way into his inner sphere of contemplation. His countenance, in this repose, was mild and kindly. If his notice was sought, an expression of courtesy[425] and interest gleamed out upon his features, proving {that there was light within him}, and {that it was only the outward medium of the intellectual lamp that obstructed the rays in their passage}. The closer you penetrated to the substance of his mind, the sounder it appeared. {When no longer called upon to speak or listen — either of which operations cost[426] him an evident effort} — his face would briefly subside into its former not uncheerful quietude. It was not painful to behold this look; for, though dim, it had not the imbecility[427] of decaying age. The framework of his nature, originally strong and massive, was not yet crumpled[428] into ruin.

MP3 ★
[7] 시작 To observe and define his character, however, under such disadvantages[429], was as difficult a task as to trace out[430] and build up anew, in imagination, an old fortress, like

---

425 courtesy: 공손함, 정중함, 예의상 하는 말(행동)

426 cost: (값·비용이) 들다, 희생시키다, 겪게 만들다

427 imbecility: 저능, 우둔

428 crumple: 구겨지다, 일그러지다, 쓰러지다, 허물어지다

429 세월이 가면서 세월에 따른 정신적·육체적 쇠약이라는 불리한 점들이 그의 정신과 본래의 성격 위로 덮여 쌓이게 된다는 의미를 담고 있다.

430 trace out: [윤곽]을 그리다, [흔적]을 찾아내다

Ticonderoga[431], [from a view of its grey[432] and broken ruins]. Here and there, perchance, the walls may remain almost complete; but elsewhere may be only a shapeless mound, cumbrous[433] with its very strength[434], and overgrown, through long years of peace and neglect, with grass and alien weeds.

Nevertheless, looking at the old warrior with affection— for, slight as was the communication between us, my feeling towards him, like that of all bipeds and quadrupeds who knew him, might not improperly be termed so,—I could discern the main points of his portrait. It was marked with the noble and heroic qualities {which showed it to be not a mere accident, but of good right, that he had won a distinguished name}. His spirit could never, I conceive, have been characterized by an uneasy activity; it must, at any period of his life, have required an impulse to set him in motion; but [once stirred up], [with obstacles to overcome, and an adequate object to be attained], it was not in the man to give out or fail. The

---

431 Ticonderoga: 타이컨데로가는 미국 뉴욕 주 동북부 챔플레인 (Champlain) 호수에 인접한 마을로 1759년에 영국군이 점령했던 곳인데, 1775년에는 이산 앨런(Ethan Allen)과 베네딕트 아널드 (Benedict Arnold)가 이끄는 미국 정규군이 영국으로부터 빼앗 았다.

432 grey(=gray): 태고의, 고대의. *the gray past: 먼 과거, 태고

433 cumbrous(=cumbersome): 방해가 되는, 번거로운, 성가신

434 strength: 내구력, 견고성. *이 대목은 성채의 견고함 때문에 오 히려 빨리 흙으로 돌아가지 못한 상황을 말한다.

heat {that had formerly pervaded his nature}, and {which was not yet extinct}, was never of the kind {that flashes and flickers in a blaze}; but rather a deep red glow, as of iron in a furnace. Weight, solidity, firmness — this was the expression of his repose[435], even in such decay as had crept untimely over him[436] at the period of which I speak. But I could imagine, even then, that, [under some excitement which should go deeply into his consciousness] — roused by a trumpet-peal, loud enough to awaken all of his energies that were not dead, but only slumbering — he was yet capable of flinging off his infirmities like a sick man's gown, dropping the staff of age to seize a battle-sword, and starting up once more a warrior. And, [in so intense a moment], his demeanour[437] would have still been calm. Such an exhibition[438], however, was but to be pictured in fancy; not to be anticipated, nor desired. What I saw in him — [as evidently as the indestructible ramparts[439] of Old Ticonderoga, already cited as the most appropriate simile] — was the features of stubborn and ponderous[440]

---

435 repose: 휴식

436 in such decay as crept untimely over him: 그의 위에 때 이르게 천천히 덮인, 심지어 그런 쇠락 속에서도. *앞에서 타이컨데로가 옛 성채의 묘사에 이어 장군에게도 세월의 흔적이 쌓이는 것으로 묘사하고 있으며, 그런 외관에도 불구하고 아직은 그의 정신이 쇠락한 것이 아님을 말하고 있다.

437 demeanour: 태도, 품행, 행실

438 exhibition: 전시, 발휘, 표현

439 rampart: 성곽, 성벽

endurance[441], {which might well have amounted to[442] obstinacy[443] in his earlier days}; of integrity, {that, like most of his other endowments[444], lay in a somewhat heavy mass, and was just as unmalleable[445] or unmanageable as a ton of iron ore[446]}; and of benevolence {which, fiercely as he led the bayonets[447] on at Chippewa or Fort Erie[448], I take to be of quite

---

440　ponderous: 대단히 무거운, 크고 무거운, 육중한

441　endurance: 인내, 지구력, 내구력, 지속

442　amount to: 총계가 ~에 이르다, 결과적으로 ~이 되다, ~에 해당하다

443　obstinacy: 완고함, 고집, 집요한 끈기, 강퍅함

444　endowment: 기증, 기부, 유증

445　unmalleable: (금속 등이) 단조할 수 없는, 두드려서 늘이기 힘든

446　iron ore: 철광석

447　bayonet: 대검, 총검

448　Chippewa or Fort Erie: 치페와 혹은 이리 요새. *1812년 전쟁의 와중이었던 1814년 여름에 나이아가라 전선에서 벌어진 전투를 가리키며 전쟁의 흐름을 바꾸었다. 이리 요새 지역은 부싯돌(flint) 산지로 창, 화살촉 기타 도구를 만드는 데 중요한 지역이자 전투적인 인디언 부족인 휴론(Huron)과 이라쿠아(Iroquois) 사이에서 중립을 유지했다는 뜻에서 중립부족(Neutral Nation)이라고 불린 인디언의 거주지역이었다. 프렌치-인디언 전쟁 이후 캐나다 지역이 프랑스에서 영국으로 넘어가면서 영국은 이 지역에 이리 요새를 비롯하여 여러 요새를 건설하였고 미국독립혁명 기간에는 영국 군대의 보급기지 역할을 했다. 여기에서 치페와 [혹은 치파와(Chippawa)]는 위의 전투가 벌어진 해당 지역의 지명이다. 오지브웨(Ojibwe)로도 불린 치페와는 나바호, 체로키, 라코타 부족에 이어 북미 최대의 원주민 부족으로 주로 오대호의 슈피리어(Superior) 호 인근을 근거지로 했다. 대개의 북미 인디언 부족들이 프랑스와 영국의 식민지 쟁탈 분쟁의 틈바구니에서 어려움을 겪었듯이, 치페와 역시 프렌치-인디언 전쟁 때에는 영국에 맞서 프랑스편을 들었다가 프랑스가 패한 뒤로는 영국과 동

as genuine a stamp[449] as [what actuates any or all the polemical philanthropists of the age]}. He had slain men with his own hand, for aught I know — certainly, they had fallen like blades of grass at the sweep of the scythe before the charge {to which his spirit imparted its triumphant energy} — but, be that as it might, there was never in his heart so much cruelty {as would have brushed the down off[450] a butterfly's wing}. I have not known the man {to whose innate kindliness I would more confidently make an appeal}.

Many characteristics — and those, too, {which contribute not the least forcibly[451] to impart resemblance in a sketch} — must have vanished, or been obscured, before I met the General. All merely graceful attributes are usually the most evanescent[452]; nor does nature adorn the human ruin with blossoms of new beauty, {that have their roots and proper nutriment only in the chinks and crevices of decay}, as she sows wall-flowers[453] over the ruined fortress of Ticonderoga. Still, even in respect of grace and beauty, there were points

---

맹을 맺고 있었다. 1812년 전쟁 때에는 영국이 승리하면 미국 개척자들의 영토 잠식을 막을 수 있으리라 생각하고 영국편을 들어 미국에 맞서 싸웠다.

449 stamp: 우표, 도장, 특징, 유형
450 brush off: (솔이나 손으로) 털어내다
451 forcibly: 〈법률〉 강제적으로, 우격다짐으로, 강력하게, 유효하게
452 evanescent: 덧없는, 순간의
453 wall-flower: 꽃무(십자화과의 여러해살이풀)

well worth noting. A ray of humour, now and then, would make its way through the veil of dim obstruction, and glimmer pleasantly upon our faces. A trait of native elegance, [seldom seen in the masculine character after childhood or early youth], was shown in the General's fondness for the sight and fragrance of flowers. An old soldier might be supposed to prize only the bloody laurel[454] on his brow; but here was one {who seemed to have a young girl's appreciation of the floral tribe}.

There, beside the fireplace, the brave old General used to sit; while the Surveyor — though seldom, when it could be avoided, taking upon himself the difficult task of engaging him in conversation — was fond of standing at a distance, and watching his quiet and almost slumberous countenance. He seemed <u>away from us</u>, {although we saw him but a few yards[455] off}; <u>remote</u>, {though we passed close beside his chair}; <u>unattainable</u>[456], {though we might have stretched forth our hands and touched his own}. It might be that he lived a more real life within his thoughts than amid the unappropriate environment of the Collector's office. The evolutions[457] of the parade; the tumult of the battle; the flourish[458] of old heroic music, heard thirty years before — such scenes and sounds,

---

454 laurel: 월계수
455 yard: 3피트, 36인치, 0.914미터
456 unattainable: 도달 불가능한
457 evolution: 진화, 발전의 산물, (행진 시의) 전개, 기동연습
458 flourish: 번창하다, 과장된 동작, (말, 글의) 수식, 팡파르

perhaps, were all alive before his intellectual sense. Meanwhile, the merchants and ship-masters, the spruce[459] clerks and uncouth[460] sailors, entered and departed; the bustle of his commercial and Custom-House life kept up its little murmur round about him; and [neither with the men nor their affairs] did the General appear to sustain the most distant relation. He was as much out of place[461] {as an old sword— [now rusty, but which had flashed once in the battle's front, and showed still a bright gleam along its blade] — would have been among the inkstands[462], paper-folders, and mahogany rulers on the Deputy Collector's desk}.

There was one thing {that much aided me in renewing and re-creating the stalwart[463] soldier of the Niagara frontier — the man of true and simple energy}. It was the recollection of those memorable words of his — "I'll try, Sir!"[464] — [spoken

---

459 spruce: 가문비나무, 말쑥한, 맵시 있는

460 uncouth: 무례한, 상스러운, 투박한

461 out of place: 제자리에 있지 않는, (특정한 상황에) 맞지 않는(부적절한)

462 inkstand: 책상 위에 놓아 두고 잉크를 담아 찍어 쓸 수 있게 만든 문방구

463 stalwart: 튼튼한, 용감한, 건장한

464 "I'll try, Sir!": 해보겠습니다, 장군! *밀러 장군은 런디즈 레인 (Lundy's Lane: 캐나다 온타리오 주 나이아가라 부근의 도로로 1814년 영미전쟁의 싸움터)에 있는 영국 포병대를 탈취하라는 스콧(Scott) 장군의 명령에 이렇게 답변했다고 한다.

on the very verge of a desperate and heroic enterprise[465], and breathing[466] the soul and spirit of New England hardihood[467], comprehending all perils, and encountering all]. {If, in our country, valour[468] were rewarded by heraldic[469] honour[470]}, this phrase—{which it seems so easy to speak, but which only he, with such a task of danger and glory before him, has ever spoken}—would be the best and fittest of all mottoes for the General's shield of arms.

It contributes greatly towards a man's moral and intellectual ★ MP3 [B] 시작 health [to be brought into habits of companionship[471] with individuals unlike himself, {who care little for his pursuits, and whose sphere and abilities he must go out of himself to appreciate}. The accidents of my life have often afforded me this advantage, but never with more fulness and variety than during my continuance in office. There was one man, especially, {the observation of whose character gave me a new idea of talent}. His gifts were emphatically[472] those of a man of

465 enterprise: 기획, 기도, 회사, 진취적 정신. ＊a spirit of enterprise: 진취적 기상
466 breathe: (어떤 느낌이나 특성이) 가득하다
467 hardihood: 대담, 배짱, 불굴의 정신
468 valour: (특히 전쟁터에서의) 용기
469 heraldic: 전령의, 문장(紋章)의
470 honour: 영예를 나타내는 것, 훈장, 서훈
471 companionship: 친구 사이, 우의, 교우, 동료
472 emphatically: 강조하여, 단호히, 단연코

business; prompt[473], acute, clear-minded; with an eye {that saw through all perplexities[474]}, and a faculty of arrangement {that made them vanish as by the waving of an enchanter's wand}. Bred up from boyhood in the Custom-House, it was his proper field of activity; and the many intricacies[475] of business, [so harassing[476] to the interloper[477]], presented themselves before him with the regularity of a perfectly comprehended system. In my contemplation, he stood as the ideal of his class[478]. He was, indeed, the Custom-House in himself[479]; or, at all events, the mainspring {that kept its variously revolving wheels in motion}; for, in an institution like this, {where its officers are appointed to subserve[480] their own profit and convenience, and seldom with a leading[481] reference[482] to their fitness for the duty to be performed}, they must perforce[483] seek elsewhere the dexterity[484] {which is not in them}. Thus, by an inevitable

---

473 prompt: 즉각적인, 지체 없는, 시간을 엄수하는
474 perplexity: 당혹감, 당혹스러운 것
475 intricacy: 복잡한 사항(내용)
476 harassing: 괴롭히는, 귀찮게 구는
477 interlope: 무허가 영업을 하다, 남의 일에 간섭하다
478 class: 계층, 부류
479 in oneself: ~자신, ~자체
480 subserve: 돕다, 보조하다
481 leading: 가장 중요한, 선두적인
482 reference: 추천, 참고, 추천서, 추천인(신원보증인)
483 perforce: 부득이
484 dexterity: (손이나 머리를 쓰는) 재주

necessity, {as a magnet attracts steel-filings[485]}, so did our man of business[486] draw to himself the difficulties {which everybody met with}. With an easy[487] condescension[488], and kind forbearance towards our stupidity — {which, to his order of mind, must have seemed little short of crime} — would he forth-with[489], by the merest touch of his finger, make the incomprehensible as clear as daylight. The merchants valued him not less than we, his esoteric[490] friends. His integrity was perfect; it was a law of nature with him, rather than a choice or a principle; nor can it be otherwise than the main condition of an intellect [so remarkably clear and accurate as his] to be honest and regular in the administration of affairs. A stain on his conscience, {as to anything that came within the range of his vocation}, would trouble such a man very much in the same way, though to a far greater degree, than [an error in the balance of an account[491]], or [an ink-blot on the fair page of a book of record]. Here, in a word — and it is a rare instance in

---

485 file: (쇠붙이, 손톱 가는) 줄, 줄질하다. *filing: 줄밥

486 a man of business: 사업가였던 재커리아 버치모어(Zachariah Burchmore, 1809~1894)를 가리킨다. 호손과 죽을 때까지 친구 관계를 유지했던 인물로 민주당과 연관이 있던 그 역시 휘그 정부에 의해 직위에서 물러났다.

487 easy: (성격이) 수월한, 너그러운

488 condescension: 낮추보는 태도, 생색내는 태도

489 forth-with: 곧, 당장

490 esoteric: 심원한, 난해한, 선택된, 소수만 이해하는, 비전(秘傳)의

491 balance of account: 계정잔액

my life — I had met with a person thoroughly adapted to the situation {which he held}.

Such were some of the people {with whom I now found myself connected}. I took it in good part, at the hands of Providence, {that I was thrown into a position [so little akin to my past habits]}; and set myself seriously to gather from it {whatever profit was to be had}. [After my fellowship[492] of toil and impracticable schemes with the dreamy brethren of Brook Farm[493]]; [after living for three years within the subtle influence of an intellect like Emerson's]; [after those wild, free days on the Assabeth[494], indulging[495] fantastic speculations, beside our fire of fallen boughs, with Ellery Channing[496]]; [after

---

492 fellowship: 유대감, 동료애, (이해관계, 목표, 사상을 공유하는) 단체, (대학원생에게 주는) 연구비, 장학금

493 Brook Farm: 조지 리플리(George Ripley)의 지도 아래 보스턴 에서 9마일 떨어진 곳에 설립된 이상주의 공동체 실험을 가리킨 다. 호손은 1841년 4월에서 11월 동안 브룩팜에 거주했으나 환멸 을 느끼고 떠났다. 이곳에서의 경험은 나중에 『블라이드데일 로맨 스』(The Blithedale Romance)의 소재가 된다.

494 Assabeth: 아사벳(Assabet)으로도 표기한다. 이 강은 서드베리 (Sudbury) 강과 합쳐져서 매사추세츠 콩코드 타운을 지나는 콩 코드 강을 이룬다. 호손은 신혼 시절 1842~1845년 동안 콩코드 에서 살면서 윌리엄 엘러리 채닝(William Ellery Channing) 등과 종종 보트를 타러 가곤 했다.

495 indulge: (특히 좋지 않다고 여겨지는 것을) 마음껏 하다, (특정 한 욕구, 관심 등을) 채우다, 충족시키다

496 William Ellery Channing(1818~1901). 시인. 호손과 소로의 친구

talking with Thoreau[497] about pine-trees and Indian relics in his hermitage at Walden]; [after growing fastidious[498] by sympathy with the classic refinement[499] of Hillard's[500] culture]; [after becoming imbued[501] with poetic sentiment at Longfellow's[503] hearthstone[503]] — it was time, at length, that I should exercise other faculties of my nature, and nourish[504] myself with food {for which I had hitherto had little appetite}. Even the old Inspector was desirable, [as a change of diet], to a man who had known Alcott[505]. I looked upon it as an evidence, in some measure, of a system [naturally well balanced, and lacking no

---

497 Henry David Thoreau(1818~1862). 소로는 거의 평생 콩코드에서 살았으며 에머슨(Emerson)의 『자연』(*Nature*)을 읽고 큰 영향을 받았다. 콩코드 주변의 지역에서 원주민의 유적을 조사하는 등 그 문화와 사회에 큰 관심을 두고 있었다.

498 fastidious: 세심한, 꼼꼼한, 까다로운

499 refinement: 개선, 개량, 정제, 교양, 품위, 세련

500 George Stillman Hillard(1808~1879). 힐러드는 보스턴의 변호사이자 박애주의자로 문학계에서도 이름이 잘 알려진 인물인데, 호손에게 친구이자 실제적인 조언자로서 도움을 주었다. 비록 휘그당파였으나 호손이 세관직에 계속 있을 수 있도록 애를 썼는데 호손이 면직되자 재정적인 도움을 주고자 모금운동을 벌이기도 했다.

501 imbue: 감염시키다, 스며들게 하다

502 Henry Wadsworth Longfellow(1807~1882). 호손과 보든대학(Bowdoin College) 동기. 이후 계속 친분을 유지했는데 여기에 언급된 시기는 1843년 무렵으로 롱펠로(Longfellow)가 하버드(Harvard)대학에서 교수로 재직 중일 때이다. 보든대학은 1794년에 인가받은 학부 중심의 인문대학으로 메인 주에 소재한다.

503 hearthstone: 벽난로의 바닥돌, 노변, 가정

504 nourish: 영양분을 공급하다, (감정, 생각 등을) 키우다

505 Bronson Alcott(1799~1888). 브론슨 올컷은 미국 초절주의자들

essential part of a thorough[506] organization, {that, with such associates to remember, I could mingle at once with men of altogether different qualities, and never murmur at the change}.

Literature, its exertions[507] and objects, were now of little moment[508] in my regard[509]. I cared not at this period for books; they were apart from me. Nature — except it were human nature — the nature {that is developed in earth and sky}, was, in one sense, hidden from me; and all the imaginative delight {wherewith[510] it had been spiritualized} passed away out of my mind. A gift, a faculty, {if it had not been departed[511]}, was suspended and inanimate[512] within me. There would have been something [sad, unutterably dreary], in all this, {had I not been

---

중에서 가장 이상주의적인 인물로 보스턴에 실험학교를 세우기도 했다. 『작은 아씨들』(*Little Women*, 1868~1869)의 저자인 루이자 메이 올컷(Louisa May Alcott, 1832~1888)의 아버지이다.

506 thorough: 빈틈없는, 철두철미한

507 exertion: 노력, 행사, 발휘, 활동

508 of moment: 아주 중요한. *여기에서 호손은 문학이 '거의 중요하지 않게 되었다'(of little moment)고 하고 있으나 1846~1847년 사이에도 창작이 잠시 뜸했던 시기를 빼면 세관에 있는 동안 내내 단편소설을 계속 쓰고 있었다.

509 in my regard: 나와 관련하여, 나의 관심에 있어서. * in this regard: 이것과 관련하여

510 wherewith: 그것을 가지고, 그것으로 .

511 depart: 출발하다, 벗어나다, ~을 떠나다, 죽다. *depart this life: 이 세상을 뜨다

512 inanimate: 무생물의, 죽은, 죽은 것 같은

conscious that it lay at my own option to recall [whatever was valuable in the past]}. It might be true, indeed, that this was a life {which could not, with impunity[513], be lived too long}; else, it might make me permanently other than I had been, without transforming me into any shape {which it would be worth my while to take}. But I never considered it as other than a transitory life. There was always a prophetic instinct, a low whisper in my ear, {that [within no long period], and [whenever a new change of custom should be essential to my good], change would come}.

Meanwhile, there I was, a Surveyor of the Revenue and, so far as I have been able to understand, as good a Surveyor as need be[514]. A man of thought, fancy, and sensibility (had he ten times the Surveyor's proportion of those qualities[515]), may, at any time, be a man of affairs[516], {if he will only choose to give himself the trouble}[517]. My fellow-officers, and the merchants and sea-captains {with whom my official duties brought me into any manner of connection}, viewed me in no other

★ MP3
[9] 시작

---

513 impunity: 처벌받지 않음. ＊with impunity: 무사히

514 as ... as need be: 필요한 만큼, 필요한 범위 내에서

515 had he(＝if he had): 주어 동사의 도치를 활용한 가정법 문장

516 a man of affairs: 업무가, 실무가

517 이 문장 전체의 내용을 간략히 간추리면 사고, 상상, 감수성 등은 검사관의 업무와 전혀 관계가 없고 방해가 된다고 보는데, 자기보다 사고력, 상상력, 감수성 등이 열 배나 더 풍부해도 좀 고생하며 적응하기로 마음만 먹는다면 불가능한 것은 아니라는 의미이다.

light[518], and probably knew me in no other character[519].

None of them, I presume, had ever read a page of my inditing[520], or would have cared a fig the more for me {if they had read them all}; nor would it have mended the matter, in the least, {had those same unprofitable pages been written with a pen like that of Burns or of Chaucer[521], each of whom was a Custom-House officer in his day, as well as I}. It is a good lesson—though it may often be a hard one—for a man {who has dreamed of literary fame, and of making [for himself] a rank among the world's dignitaries[522] by such means}, to step aside out of the narrow circle {in which his claims are recognized} and to find {how utterly devoid of significance, beyond that circle, is all [that he achieves], and all [he aims at]}[523]. I know not {that I especially needed the lesson, either

---

518 light: 관점
519 검사관이라는 실무가 외에 '어떤 다른 성격을 띤 나' 혹은 '(검사관 외에) 어떤 다른 것에 더 잘 맞을 것 같은 나'의 의미로도 볼 수 있다. '검사관 양반에 더 잘 맞는 다른 일이 있지 않을까' 식으로 생각하는 것을 상상해 볼 수 있다. *in character: ~다운, ~어울리는, [배역에] 꼭 맞는
520 indite: (시, 글 등을) 짓다, 쓰다
521 로버트 번즈(Robert Burns, 1759~1796)는 1789~1791년 동안 덤프리즈(Dumfries)의 소비세 징수관이었고, 제프리 초서(Geoffrey Chaucer, 1343~1400)는 1374~1386년 동안 런던 세관의 관리자(controller)였다.
522 dignitary: 고위 관리
523 it ... for a man ... to step ... and to find ...: 가주어+진주어+의미상의 주어(to 부정사) 구문이다. 마지막의 to find의 목적어절

in the way of warning or rebuke[524]}; but at any rate, I learned it thoroughly: nor, {it gives me pleasure to reflect}, did the truth, {as it came home to[525] my perception}, ever cost me a pang, or require to be thrown off[526] in a sigh. In the way of[527] literary talk, {it is true}, the Naval Officer — an excellent fellow, who came into the office with me, and went out only a little later — would often engage[528] me in a discussion about one or the other of his favourite topics, Napoleon or Shakespeare. The Collector's junior clerk, too, — a young gentleman who, it was whispered occasionally, covered a sheet of Uncle Sam's letter paper with {what (at the distance of a few yards) looked very much like poetry} — used now and then to speak to me of books, as matters {with which I might possibly be conversant[529]}. This was my all of lettered[530] intercourse; and it was quite sufficient for my necessities.

No longer seeking or caring that my name should be blazoned[531] abroad[532] on title-pages[533], I smiled to think that

---

how ... 부분에서는 all ... all 부분이 주어로서 도치되어 있다.

524 rebuke: 힐책(질책)하다

525 come home to: ~에 뼈저리게 와 닿다

526 throw off: (고통스럽거나 짜증스러운 것 등을) 떨쳐 버리다

527 in the way of: ~라고 할 만한 것이

528 engage: ~을 끌어들이다

529 conversant: 정통한

530 lettered: 글자를 넣은, 학문(교양, 문학적 소양)이 있는

531 blazon(=emblazon): (주로 수동태로) 새겨져 있다. *make a blazon of: ~을 과시하다

532 abroad: 해외에, 널리, 유포되어, 퍼져서

it had now another kind of vogue[534]. The Custom-House marker[535] imprinted it, with a stencil and black paint, on pepper-bags, and baskets of anatto[536], and cigar-boxes, and bales[537] of all kinds of dutiable merchandise, {in testimony that these commodities had paid the impost[538], and gone regularly[539] through the office}. Borne on such queer[540] vehicle[541] of fame, a knowledge of <u>my existence</u>, {so far as a name conveys it}, was carried {where it had never been before, and, I hope, will never go again}.

But the past was not dead. Once in a great while[542], the thoughts {that had seemed so vital[543] and so active, yet had been put to rest so quietly}, revived again. One of the most

---

533 title-page: (책의) 속표지, 표제지

534 vogue: 인기. *have a vogue: 인기가 있다

535 marker: 표지(부호)를 붙이는 사람(것), 표지(가 되는 것), 득점 기록자, 채점자, 마커펜

536 anatto(=annatto): 잇꽃나무. 아나토(색소의 일종). 작은 북미산 열대 식물로 붉은색이나 핑크색 꽃과 펄프질의 씨를 맺는데 이것이 색소의 원료가 된다. 향신료로 이용하는 것은 잇꽃나무의 씨 부분이다. 씨 껍질을 기름에 녹여서 나온 빨간색은 주로 유제품에 착색료로 이용한다.

537 bale: (배에 싣는 상품의) 곤포(梱包), 짐짝, 화물

538 impost: 세금, 수입세

539 regularly: 규칙 바르게, 어김없이, 정식으로

540 queer: 기묘한, 괴상한

541 vehicle: 차량, 탈것, 운송수단, 매개체

542 once in a great while: 아주 드물게, 어쩌면

543 vital: 필수적인, 활력이 넘치는

remarkable occasions, {when the habit of bygone days awoke in me}, was that[544] {which brings it within the law of literary propriety[545] to offer the public the sketch [which I am now writing]}.

[In the second story of the Custom-House], there is a large room, {in which the brick-work[546] and naked[547] rafters[548] have never been covered with panelling[549] and plaster}. The edifice — originally projected on a scale [adapted to the old commercial enterprise of the port], and with an idea of subsequent prosperity [destined never to be realized] — contains far more space {than its occupants[550] know what to do with}. This airy[551] hall, therefore, over the Collector's apartments, remains unfinished to this day, and, [in spite of the aged cobwebs {that festoon[552] its dusky[553] beams[554]}],

---

544 that: = the occasion
545 propriety: (행동의 도덕적 · 사회적) 적절성, 예의범절, 예절. *작가는 자신의 스케치가 문학적인 관례와 예의에 부응한다는 판단을 피력하고 있다.
546 brick-work: (벽에 쌓아 놓은) 벽돌
547 naked: 벌거벗은, 적나라한, 드러난
548 rafter: 서까래
549 panelling: (벽 · 천장 등에 붙이는 나무) 판자
550 occupant: (주택, 방, 건물 등의) 사용자, 입주자, 타고(앉아) 있는 사람
551 airy: 바람이 잘 통하는, 대수롭지 않은, 비현실적인
552 festoon: (흔히 축제를 위해 꽃, 색종이 등으로) 장식하다
553 dusky: 어스름한, (색깔이) 탁한

appears still to await the labour of the carpenter and mason[555]. At one end of the room, in a recess[556], were a number of barrels[557] [piled one upon another], containing bundles[558] of official documents. Large quantities of similar rubbish[559] lay lumbering[560] the floor. It was sorrowful to think {how many days, and weeks, and months, and years of toil had been wasted on these musty[561] papers, [which were now only an encumbrance[562] on earth, and were hidden away in this forgotten corner, never more to be glanced at by human eyes]}. But then, what reams[563] of other manuscripts — [filled, not with the dulness of official formalities, but with the thought of inventive brains and the rich effusion[564] of deep hearts] — had gone equally to oblivion; and that, moreover, without serving a purpose in their day, {as these heaped-up papers had},

---

554 beam: 빛줄기, 기둥, 들보

555 mason: 석공, 석수

556 recess: 휴회기간, (방의 벽에서) 우묵 들어간 부분, 구석진(후미진) 곳

557 barrel: (목재, 금속으로 된 대형) 통, 한 통의 양

558 bundle: 꾸러미, 묶음, 보따리, 거액, 거금

559 rubbish: 쓰레기, 형편없는 것

560 lumber: 재목, 목재, 잡동사니, (물건이) 쓸모없게 되다, ~을 난잡하게 쌓아 올리다, (장소)를 잡동사니로 메우다, 어지르다

561 musty: 퀴퀴한 냄새가 나는

562 encumbrance: 지장, 짐, 폐

563 ream: 연(連). *전에는 480매(short ...), 지금은 500매(long ...); 〈줄임말〉 rm.; 〈보통 복수〉 다량(특히 종이나 문서)

564 effusion: (특히 액체의) 유출, (감정의) 토로

and — saddest of all — without purchasing for their writers the comfortable livelihood {which the clerks of the Custom-House had gained by these worthless scratchings of the pen}. Yet not altogether worthless, perhaps, as materials of local history. Here, no doubt, statistics of the former commerce of Salem might be discovered, and memorials[565] of her princely[566] merchants — old King Derby — old Billy Gray[567] — old Simon Forrester[568] — and many another magnate[569] in his day, {whose powdered[570] head, however, was scarcely in the tomb [before[571] his mountain pile of wealth began to dwindle]}. The founders

---

565 memorial: 기념비, 기념비(적인 것), 청원서, 비공식문서, 기록, 연대기

566 princely: 엄청난, 웅장한, 왕자(대공/군주)의

567 Billy Gray(= William Gray, 1750~1825). 빌리 그레이는 선단을 소유한 세일럼의 거부로 인도, 중국, 러시아 등과 처음으로 무역을 한 초기 뉴잉글랜드 상인들 중 하나였고 말년에 매사추세츠 부지사가 되었다.

568 Captain Simon Forrester(1748~1823). 아일랜드 태생의 거부. 사이먼은 농부였으나 교육열이 컸던 아버지 덕택에 클로인 컬리지(Cloyne College)에서 공부를 다 마치고도 가족의 농장으로 돌아와 일을 했다. 그러나 농사일이 맞지 않아 1767년에 "이번이 아일랜드 땅에서의 마지막 추수다"라고 선언하고는 짐을 꾸려 영국으로 갔다가 다시 신대륙으로 건너왔다. 이때 대니얼 호손(Daniel Hathorne)의 배를 탔고 이 선장의 마음에 들어 세일럼에 정착하게 되었는데 이 선장이 호손의 조부이다. 사이먼은 해상 무역을 통해 세일럼의 최대거부로 알려졌던 인물이다.

569 magnate: (특히 재계의) 거물(큰손)

570 powdered: 가루(분말)로 만든, 파우더(분)를 바른

571 scarcely ... before ...: ~하자마자 ~ 하다

of the greater part of[572] the families {which now compose the aristocracy of Salem} might here be traced, from [the petty and obscure[573] beginnings of their traffic, at periods generally much posterior to the Revolution], upward to [what their children look upon as long-established rank].

MP3 ★
(10) 시작 Prior to the Revolution there is a dearth[574] of records; the earlier documents and archives[575] of the Custom-House having, probably, been carried off to Halifax, {when all the king's officials accompanied the British army in its flight from Boston[576]}. It has often been a matter of regret[577] with me; for, [going back, perhaps, to the days of the Protectorate][578], those papers must have contained many references[579] to forgotten or remembered men, and to antique customs, {which would have

---

572 greater part of: ~의 대부분

573 obscure: 잘 알려져 있지 않은, 무명의, 모호한

574 dearth: 부족(결핍)

575 archive: 공적 기록, 공문서 보관소, 기록

576 독립혁명이 발발하자 영국군이 보스턴 항을 폐쇄하고 점령하였는데, 1776년 조지 워싱턴(George Washington)의 군대에 의해 포위되자 보스턴에서 노바스코샤(Nova Scotia)의 핼리팩스(Halifax)로 철수했다.

577 a matter of regret: 유감스러운 일

578 protectorate: (약소국에 대한 강대국의) 보호제도(정책), 보호령. *the Protectorate: 호민관시대(1653~1658). 올리버 크롬웰(Oliver Cromwell)이 호민관(Lord Protector)으로 국가원수였던 기간

579 reference: 언급, 참조

affected me with the same pleasure [as when I used to pick up Indian arrow-heads in the field near the Old Manse]}.

But, one idle and rainy day, it was my fortune to make a discovery of some little interest. [Poking[580] and burrowing[581] into the heaped-up rubbish in the corner], [unfolding one and another document], and [reading the names of vessels {that had long ago foundered[582] at sea or rotted at the wharves}, and those of merchants [never heard of now on 'Change[583], nor very readily decipherable on their mossy tombstones]]; [glancing at such matters with the saddened, weary, half-reluctant interest {which we bestow on the corpse of dead activity}] — and [exerting my fancy, sluggish[584] with little use, to raise up [from these dry bones] an image of the old town's brighter aspect, {when India was a new region, and only Salem knew the way thither}] — I chanced to lay my hand on a small package, [carefully done up[585] in a piece of ancient yellow parchment]. This envelope had the air of an official record of

---

580 poke: (손가락으로) 쿡 찌르다, 뒤적이다
581 burrow: 굴을 파다, 들추다, 파고들다, 뒤적이다
582 founder: (배가) 침수하여 침몰하다, 내려앉다
583 'Change(=Merchant's Exchange): 보스턴 상공거래소를 가리키며 이 거래소 건물은 1841년에 지어져서 1842~1890년까지 시의 업무활동의 주축으로 기능했다.
584 sluggish: 느릿느릿 움직이는, 부진한
585 do up: 싸다, 치장하다

some period long past, {when clerks engrossed[586] their stiff and formal chirography[587] on more substantial[588] materials than at present}. There was something about it {that quickened an instinctive curiosity, and made me undo[589] the faded red tape [that tied up the package], with the sense [that a treasure would here be brought to light]}. [Unbending the rigid folds of the parchment[590] cover], I found it to be a commission, [under the hand and seal[591] of Governor Shirley], [in favour of[592] one Jonathan Pine, as Surveyor of His Majesty's Customs for the Port of Salem, in the Province[593] of Massachusetts Bay]. I remembered to have read (probably in Felt's "Annals") a notice of the decease of Mr. Surveyor Pue, about fourscore years ago[594]; and likewise, in a newspaper of recent times, an account of the digging up of his remains in the little graveyard of St. Peter's Church, during the renewal of that edifice. Nothing, {if I rightly call to mind}, was left of my respected[595] predecessor,

---

586 engross: ~에 몰두하다, ~을 크고 똑똑하게 쓰다(베끼다)

587 chirography: 필법, 서체

588 substantial: (양, 가치, 중요성이) 상당한, 크고 튼튼한, 단단히
지은. *a substantial house: 크고 튼튼한 집

589 undo: (잠기거나 묶인 것을) 풀다(열다, 끄르다)

590 parchment: 양피지, 두꺼운 담황색 종이, 양피지 문서

591 under the hand and seal: 서명 날인되어. *hand: 필체; seal: 직인

592 in favour of: ~에 찬성하여, ~ 앞으로 발행된

593 province: 북미의 영국령 식민지

594 실제로 『연보』(Annals)의 1760년 3월 24일 항목에 세일럼의 검
사관인 조너선 퓨(Jonathan Pue)라는 사람의 부고가 실려 있다.

595 respected: 훌륭한, 높이 평가되는

save an imperfect skeleton, and some fragments of apparel, and a wig of majestic[596] frizzle[597], {which, unlike the head [that it once adorned], was in very satisfactory preservation}. But, on examining the papers {which the parchment commission served to envelop}, I found more traces of Mr. Pue's mental part, and the internal operations of his head, {than the frizzled wig had contained of the venerable skull itself}[598].

They were documents, in short, not official, but of a private nature, or, at least, written in his private capacity[599], and apparently with his own hand. I could account for their being included in the heap of Custom-House lumber[600] only by the fact {that Mr. Pue's death had happened suddenly}, and {that these papers, [which he probably kept in his official desk], had never come to the knowledge of his heirs, or were supposed to relate to the business of the revenue}. [On the transfer of the archives to Halifax], this package, [proving to be of no public concern[601]], was left behind, and had remained ever since unopened.

---

596 majestic: 위풍당당한, 장엄한

597 frizzle: 고수머리

598 양피지 커버와 그 안의 내용, 퓨(Pue)의 가발과 그 안의 두개골을 병치하여 비교하고 있다.

599 private capacity: 사적인 자격. *in her capacity as teacher: 선생으로서의 역할, 지위

600 lumber: 잡동사니

601 public concern: 공적인 관심사

The ancient Surveyor — {being little molested[602], suppose, at that early day with business pertaining to[603] his office} — seems to have devoted [some of his many leisure hours] to researches as a local antiquarian[604], and other inquisitions of a similar nature. These supplied [material for petty[605] activity] to a mind {that would otherwise have been eaten up with rust}. A portion of his facts, by-the-by[606], did me good service in the preparation of the article entitled "MAIN STREET," included in the present volume.[607] The remainder may perhaps be applied to purposes [equally valuable] hereafter, or not impossibly may be worked up, {so far as they go[608]}, into a regular[609] history of Salem, {should my veneration[610] for the natal soil ever impel[611] me to so pious a task}. Meanwhile, they shall be at the command[612]

---

602 molest: 괴롭히다

603 pertain to: ~와 관계가 있다

604 antiquarian: 골동품 전문가

605 petty: 사소한, 하찮은

606 by-the-by(e): 그건 그렇고

607 「중심가」("Main Street")라는 스케치는 1849년에 엘리자베스 파머 피바디(Elizabeth Palmer Peabody)가 편집하던 『미학지』(*Aesthetic Papers*)에 발표되었는데, 원래는 『주홍글자』(*The Scarlet Letter*)에 포함시키려고 했다가 그만두었다. 이 스케치는 나중에 『눈의 이미지와 다른 케케묵은 이야기들』(*The Snow-Image and Other Twice-Told Tales*, 1852)에 실렸다.

608 so far as … go: ~로 판단할 때, 보아하니

609 regular: 평상시의, 평범한, 일상사의

610 veneration: 존경, 숭앙

611 impel: (생각, 기분이) ~해야만 하게 하다

612 at the command: 장악하고 있는, 자유로이 쓸 수 있는

of any gentleman, [inclined and competent, to take the unprofitable labour off my hands]. As a final disposition[613], I contemplate depositing them with the Essex Historical Society.[614]

But the object {that most drew my attention to the mysterious package} was a certain affair[615] of fine red cloth, [much worn and faded], There were traces about it of gold embroidery, {which, however, was greatly frayed[616] and defaced[617], [so that none, or very little, of the glitter was left]}. It had been wrought, {as was easy to perceive}, with wonderful skill of needlework; and the stitch (as I am assured by ladies conversant with such mysteries) gives evidence of a now forgotten art, [not to be discovered even by the process of picking out[618] the threads[619]]. This rag[620] of scarlet cloth —{for time, and wear[621], and a sacrilegious[622] moth[623] had reduced it to little other than a

---

613 disposition: 타고난 기질, 성향, 배치, (재산의) 양도
614 퓨의 서류와 주홍글자 A는 허구적인 창조물이므로 이 학회에 맡겨진 것은 당연히 아무것도 없었다.
615 affair: 일, 업무, (특이한) 물건(것)
616 fray: 해어지게 하다
617 deface: 외관을 훼손하다
618 pick out: 뽑아내다, 가려내다
619 thread: 가닥
620 rag: 해진 천, 자선행사. *rag week: 자선행사 주간
621 wear: 착용, (오랜 기간의) 사용, (많이 사용되어) 닳음
622 sacrilegious: 신성을 더럽히는, 죄받을, 무엄한
623 moth: 좀

rag} — on careful examination, assumed the shape of a letter. It was the capital letter A. By an accurate measurement, each limb proved to be precisely three inches and a quarter in length. It had been intended, {there could be no doubt}, as an ornamental article of dress; but {how it was to be worn}, or {what rank, honour, and dignity, in by-past[624] times, were signified by it}, was a riddle {which (so evanescent[625] are the fashions of the world in these particulars) I saw little hope of solving}. And yet it strangely interested me. My eyes fastened[626] themselves upon the old scarlet letter, and would not be turned aside. Certainly there was some deep meaning in it [most worthy of interpretation], and {which, as it were, streamed forth from the mystic symbol, [subtly communicating itself to my sensibilities, but evading the analysis of my mind]}.

MP3 ★
(11) 시작 {When thus perplexed — and cogitating[627], among other hypotheses, [whether the letter might not have been one of those decorations ⟨which the white men used to contrive in order to take the eyes of Indians⟩]} — I happened to place it on my breast. It seemed to me — {the reader may smile, but must not doubt my word} — it seemed to me, then, that I

---

624 by-past: 과거의, 옛날의

625 evanescent: 쉬이 사라지는, 덧없는, 무상한

626 fasten: 매다, 잠그다, 꽉 잡다, (눈, 시선 등을 오랫동안) 고정시키다

627 cogitate: 숙고하다

experienced a sensation[628] [not altogether physical, yet almost so], [as of burning heat], and [as if the letter were not of red cloth, but red-hot iron]. I shuddered, and involuntarily[629] let it fall upon the floor.

In the absorbing[630] contemplation of the scarlet letter, I had hitherto neglected to examine a small roll of dingy[631] paper, {around which it had been twisted[632]}. This I now opened, and had the satisfaction to find [recorded by the old Surveyor's pen], a reasonably[633] complete explanation of the whole affair. There were several foolscap[634] sheets, containing many particulars respecting the life and conversation of one Hester Prynne, {who appeared to have been rather a noteworthy personage in the view of our ancestors}. She had flourished[635] during the period between the early days of Massachusetts and the close of the seventeenth century. Aged persons, [alive in the time of Mr. Surveyor Pue], and {from whose oral testimony he had made up his narrative}, remembered her, in their youth, [as

---

628 sensation: (자극을 받아서 느끼게 되는) 느낌
629 involuntarily: 모르는 사이에, 부지불식간에, 본의 아니게
630 absorbing: 몰입하게(빠져들게) 만드는
631 dingy: 우중충한, 거무칙칙한
632 twist: (어떤 것에 대고) 두르다, 휘감다
633 reasonably: 상당히, 꽤, 타당하게
634 foolscap: 풀스캡판(13×16[33cm×40.64cm]인치 대형 인쇄용지)
635 flourish: 번영하다, 전성기이다, 활약하다

a very old, but not decrepit[636] woman, of a stately and solemn aspect]. It had been her habit, [from an almost immemorial[637] date], {to go about the country as a kind of voluntary nurse, and [doing whatever miscellaneous[638] good she might]; [taking upon herself, likewise, to give advice in all matters, especially those of the heart]}; by which means — {as a person of such propensities[639] inevitably must} — she gained from many people the reverence due[640] to an angel, but, I should imagine, was looked upon by others as an intruder[641] and a nuisance[642]. Prying[643] further into the manuscript, I found the record of other doings and sufferings of this singular woman, {for most of which the reader is referred to[644] the story entitled "THE SCARLET LETTER"}; and it should be borne carefully in mind {that the main facts of that story are authorized[645] and authenticated[646] by the document of Mr. Surveyor Pue}. The original papers, together with the scarlet letter itself —

---

636 decrepit: 노후한, 노쇠한
637 immemorial: 태곳적부터의
638 miscellaneous: 여러 종류의, 이것저것, 다양한
639 propensity: 경향, 성질
640 due: 상응하는
641 intruder: 불법침입자, 불청객
642 nuisance: 성가신(귀찮은) 존재, 골칫거리
643 pry: 엿보다, 탐색하다, 파고들다, 꼬치꼬치 캐다
644 refer ... to ...: (~에게 ~을) 알아보도록 하다, 참조하게 하다
645 authorize: 재가(인가)하다, 권한을 부여하다
646 authenticate: 진짜임을 증명하다

a most curious[647] relic — are still in my possession, and shall be freely[648] exhibited[649] to {whomsoever, induced by the great interest of the narrative, may desire a sight of them}. I must not be understood affirming that, [in the dressing up of the tale, and imagining the motives and modes of passion {that influenced the characters who figure[650] in it}], I have invariably confined myself within the limits of the old Surveyor's half-a-dozen sheets of foolscap[651]. On the contrary, I have allowed myself, as to such points, nearly, or altogether, {as much license as if the facts had been entirely of my own invention}. {What I contend for}[652] is the authenticity[653] of the outline.

This incident recalled my mind, in some degree, to its old track[654]. There seemed to be here the groundwork[655] of a tale. It impressed me {as if the ancient Surveyor, in his garb of a hundred years gone by, and wearing his immortal wig — [which was buried with him, but did not perish in the grave] — had met me in the deserted[656] chamber of the Custom-House}. In

---

647 curious: 궁금한, 별난, 특이한, 기이한
648 freely: 자유롭게, 거리낌없이, 기꺼이
649 exhibit: 전시하다, (감정, 특질 등을) 보이다(드러내다)
650 figure: (어떤 과정, 상황 등에서) 중요하다, 중요한 부분이다
651 foolscap: 풀스캡판 용지
652 contend for: ~을 주장하다, ~을 얻으려고 다투다
653 authenticity: 진짜임, 진실성
654 track: (사람들이 걸어다녀서 생긴) 길, 자국, 자취
655 groundwork: 준비(기초) 작업

his port was the dignity of one {who had borne His Majesty's commission}, and {who was therefore illuminated by a ray of the splendour [that shone so dazzlingly about the throne]}. How unlike, alas! the hangdog[657] look of a republican official[658], {who, as the servant of the people, feels himself less than the least, and below the lowest of his masters[659]}. [With his own ghostly hand], the obscurely[660] seen, but majestic, figure[661] had imparted to me the scarlet symbol and the little roll of explanatory manuscript. [With his own ghostly voice] he had exhorted[662] me, [on the sacred consideration of[663] my filial[664] duty and reverence towards him — {who might reasonably regard himself as my official ancestor}] — to

---

656 deserted: (장소가) 사람이 없는, 버림받은

657 hangdog: (표정이) 처량한, 겸연쩍은

658 a republican official: 여기에서의 'republican'은 노예제 확산에 반대하여 1854년에 형성된 미국의 공화당(Republican Party) — 에이브러햄 링컨이 공화당 출신의 첫 대통령이 된다—과는 관계가 없고 퓨가 근무할 때의 영국령 식민지의 상황과 비교하여 독립한 후의 미국의 공화주의적 정치형태를 지칭하기 위해 쓰였다고 볼 수 있다. 따라서 '공화국의 관리'는 호손 자신을 가리킨다고 볼 수 있다.

659 masters: 앞에서 국민들의 '종복'이라고 했으므로 여기의 주인들은 곧 국민들을 가리킨다.

660 obscurely: 어둡게, 침침하게, 애매하게

661 figure: 인물, 사람[모습]

662 exhort: 열심히 권하다, 촉구하다

663 on the sacred consideration of: ~을 성스럽게 숙고하여

664 filial: (부모에 대한) 자식의

bring his mouldy[665] and moth-eaten lucubrations[666] before the public. "Do this," said the ghost of Mr. Surveyor Pue, emphatically nodding the head {that looked so imposing[667] within its memorable wig}; "do this, and the profit shall be all your own! You will shortly need it; for it is not in your days as it was in mine, {when a man's office was a life-lease[668], and oftentimes an heirloom[669]}. But I charge you, in this matter of old Mistress[670] Prynne, give to your predecessor's memory[671] [the credit[672] {which will be rightfully its due[673]!}]" And I said to the ghost of Mr. Surveyor Pue — "I will!"

On Hester Prynne's story, therefore, I bestowed much thought. It was the subject of my meditations for many an hour, while pacing to and fro across my room, or traversing, with a hundredfold repetition, the long extent[674] from the

---

665 mouldy: 곰팡내가 나는, 케케묵은
666 lucubration: 역작. *lucubrate: 열심히 공부하다, 깊이 연구하다, 고심하여 노작하다
667 imposing: 인상적인, 눈길을 끄는, 당당한
668 life-lease: 종신제
669 heirloom: (집안의) 가보
670 mistress: (보통 기혼 남자의) 정부, 〈영국 구식표현〉 여교사, (과거 하인을 부리던 집의) 여자 주인, 권한을 가진 여자, 여류 명인
671 to one's memory: ~을 기려 바치는
672 credit: 칭찬, 인정, (영화나 기타 제작 프로그램 등에서) 이름 언급
673 due: 마땅히 주어져야 하는 것, 마땅히 내야 할 돈(회비, 요금 등)
674 extent: 정도, 규모, 크기, 거리

front door of the Custom-House to the side entrance, and back again. Great were the weariness[675] and annoyance of the old Inspector and the Weighers and Gaugers, whose slumbers were disturbed by the unmercifully lengthened tramp of my passing and returning footsteps. Remembering their own former habits, they used to say that the Surveyor was walking the quarter-deck[676]. They probably fancied that my sole object — and, indeed, the sole object for which a sane man could ever put himself into voluntary motion — was to get an appetite for dinner. And, to say the truth, an appetite, sharpened[677] by the east wind that generally blew along the passage, was the only valuable result of so much indefatigable exercise. So little adapted[678] is the atmosphere of a Custom-house to the delicate harvest of fancy and sensibility, that, had I remained there through ten Presidencies yet to come[679], I doubt whether the tale of "The Scarlet Letter" would ever have been brought before the public eye. My imagination was a tarnished[680] mirror. It would not reflect, or only with miserable dimness, the figures with which I did my best to people it. The characters of the narrative would not be warmed and rendered

---

675 weariness: 권태, 피로
676 quarter-deck: 후갑판(보통 고급선원이나 1등 선객의 전용 갑판)
677 sharpen: 날카롭게 하다, 더 강렬하게(분명하게) 하다
678 adapt: 맞추다, 조정하다
679 yet to come: 아직 오지 않은, 앞으로 오게 될
680 tarnish: 흐려지다, 변색되다

malleable[681] by any heat that I could kindle at my intellectual forge. They would take neither the glow of passion nor the tenderness of sentiment, but retained all the rigidity of dead corpses, and stared me in the face with a fixed and ghastly grin of contemptuous defiance. "What have you to do with us?" that expression seemed to say. "The little power you might have once possessed over the tribe of unrealities is gone. You have bartered[682] it for a pittance[683] of the public gold. Go then, and earn your wages" In short, the almost torpid[684] creatures of my own fancy twitted[685] me with imbecility[686], and not without fair occasion[687].

It was not merely during the three hours and a half [which ★ MP3 [12] 시작 Uncle Sam claimed as his share of my daily life] {that this wretched numbness held possession of me}. It went with me on my sea-shore walks and rambles[688] into the country, {whenever — which was seldom and reluctantly[689] — I bestirred myself[690] to seek that invigorating[691] charm of Nature [which

---

681 malleable: 유순한, 두드려 펼 수 있는
682 barter: 교환하다, 바꾸다
683 pittance: 적은 급여
684 torpid: 둔한, 뻣뻣한
685 twit: 꾸짖다
686 imbecility: 저능, 허약, 무능
687 occasion: 근거, 이유
688 ramble: 걷기, 긴 산책, 소요, 횡설수설
689 reluctantly: 마지못해서
690 bestir oneself: 분발하다
691 invigorating: 기운 나게 하는, 상쾌한

used to give me such freshness and activity of thought, the moment that I stepped across the threshold of the Old Manse]}. The same torpor[692], [as regarded the capacity for intellectual effort], accompanied me home, and weighed upon[693] me in the chamber {which I most absurdly termed my study[694]}. Nor did it quit me when, late at night, I sat in the deserted[695] parlour, [lighted[696] only by the glimmering[697] coal-fire and the moon], [striving to picture forth imaginary scenes, which, the next day, might flow out on the brightening page in many-hued description].

If the imaginative faculty refused to act at such an hour, it might well be deemed a hopeless case. Moonlight, [in a familiar room, falling so white upon the carpet, and showing all its figures so distinctly] — [making every object so minutely[698] visible, yet so unlike a morning or noontide visibility] — is a medium [the most suitable for a romance-

---

692 torpor: 무기력

693 weigh upon: 짓누르다, 압박하다

694 which I most absurdly termed my study: 아주 터무니없이 내 서재라고 부른. * 서재라고 하기에는 보잘것없는 공간이었거나, 아니면 서재는 뭔가 지적인 작업을 하는 곳이어야 함에도 불구하고 전혀 그렇지 못한 상황을 의미하는 것으로 볼 수 있는데, 여기에서는 후자의 맥락으로 이해된다.

695 deserted: 사람이 없는, 빈

696 light: 비추다, 밝혀 주다

697 glimmering: 깜박이는, 희미하게 빛나는

698 minutely: 자세하게, 상세하게, 정밀하게

writer to get acquainted with[699] his illusive[700] guests]. There is the little domestic[701] scenery of the well-known apartment; the chairs, [with each its separate individuality[702]]; the centre-table, [sustaining a work-basket[703], a volume or two, and an extinguished lamp]; the sofa; the book-case; the picture on the wall — all these details, [so completely seen], are so spiritualized[704] by the unusual light, {that they seem to lose their actual substance, and become things of intellect}. Nothing is too small or too trifling to undergo this change, and acquire dignity thereby. A child's shoe; the doll, seated in her little wicker[705] carriage[706]; the hobby-horse — {whatever, in a word, has been used or played with during the day} is now invested[707] with a quality of strangeness and remoteness[708], {though still almost as vividly present as by daylight}. Thus, therefore, the floor of our familiar room has become a neutral territory, [somewhere between the real world and fairy-land], {where the Actual and the Imaginary may meet, and each

---

699 get acquainted with: 교제를 맺다
700 illusive(=illusory): 환상에 의한
701 domestic: 가정의, 집안의
702 individuality: 개성, 특성
703 work-basket: 반짇고리, 작업 용구 바구니
704 spiritualize: 정신적으로(영적으로) 하다, 영화하다, 정신적인 의미로 생각하다, ~에 영성을 부여하다
705 wicker: 고리버들
706 carriage: 객차, 마차,
707 invest: 투자하다, 부여하다
708 remoteness: 멀리 떨어져 있음

imbue[709] itself with the nature of the other}. Ghosts might enter here without affrighting[710] us. It would be too much in keeping with the scene to excite surprise, were we[711] to look about us and discover a form, [beloved, but gone hence[712], now sitting quietly in a streak[713] of this magic moonshine], with an aspect {that would make us doubt whether it had returned from afar, or had never once stirred from our fireside}.

The somewhat dim coal fire has an essential influence in producing the effect {which I would describe}. It throws its unobtrusive[714] tinge[715] throughout the room, [with a faint ruddiness[716] upon the walls and ceiling, and a reflected gleam upon the polish[717] of the furniture]. This warmer light mingles itself with the cold spirituality of the moon-beams, and communicates, as it were, a heart and sensibilities of human tenderness to the forms {which fancy summons up}. It converts them from snow-images into men and women. Glancing at the looking-glass, we behold — [deep within its haunted verge] —

---

709 imbue: 가득 채우다

710 affright: 공포, 위협, 두려워하게 하다

711 were we(＝if we were): 주어 동사의 도치를 활용한 가정법 문장

712 hence: 따라서, 지금으로부터, 이 장소에서, 여기서부터

713 streak: 바탕을 이루는 부분과 색깔이 다른 기다란 줄 모양의 것

714 unobtrusive: (보기 싫게) 눈에 띄지 않는, 두드러지지 않는

715 tinge: 엷은 색조, 기, 기미, 기운

716 ruddiness: 빨간 빛, 불그스레함

717 polish: 광택, 윤

the smouldering[718] glow of the half-extinguished anthracite[719], the white moon-beams on the floor, and a repetition[720] of all the gleam[721] and shadow of the picture, [with one remove further from the actual, and nearer to the imaginative]. Then, at such an hour, and with this scene before him, {if a man, sitting all alone, cannot dream strange things, and make them look like truth}, he need never try to write romances.

But, for myself, during the whole of my Custom-House experience, moonlight and sunshine, and the glow of firelight, were just alike in my regard; and neither of them was of one whit[722] more avail than the twinkle[723] of a tallow-candle. An entire class[724] of susceptibilities[725], and a gift connected with them — of no great richness or value, but the best I had — was gone from me.

It is my belief, however, that {had I attempted a different order of composition[726]}, my faculties would not have been

---

718 smoulder: (불이 불꽃은 없이 서서히) 타다
719 anthracite: 무연탄
720 repetition: 석탄불이 반복적으로 일렁이면서 내는 효과
721 gleam: (흔히 어디에 반사된) 어슴푸레한 빛
722 whit: 조금. ＊not a whit: 조금도 ~ 않다
723 twinkle: 반짝거림(빛남)
724 class: 부류, 종류
725 susceptibility: 감수성
726 composition: 구성, 작품, 작곡, 작문

found so pointless[727] and inefficacious[728]. I might, for instance, have contented myself with writing out[729] the narratives of a veteran shipmaster[730], one of the Inspectors, {whom I should be most ungrateful not to mention, since scarcely a day passed that he did not stir me to laughter and admiration by his marvelous gifts as a story-teller}. {Could I have preserved the picturesque[731] force of his style, and the humourous[732] colouring [which nature taught him how to throw over his descriptions]}, the result, I honestly[733] believe, would have been something new in literature. Or I might readily[734] have found a more serious task. It was a folly, [with the materiality of this daily life pressing so intrusively[735] upon me], {to attempt to fling[736] myself back into another age}, or {to insist on creating the semblance of a world out of airy[737] matter, [when, at every moment, the impalpable[738]

---

727 pointless: 무의미한, 할 가치가 없는
728 inefficacious: 효력[효능]이 없는
729 write out: 써내다
730 veteran shipmaster: 스티븐 버치모어 선장(Captain Stephen Burchmore)을 가리킨다. 이 인물의 동생이 앞에서 '사업계의 인물', '사업가'(a man of business)로 묘사된 재커리아 버치모어이다.
731 picturesque: 그림 같은, 생생한
732 humourous: 유머러스한, 익살스러운, 해학적인, 우스운
733 honestly: 솔직히
734 readily: 손쉽게, 순조롭게, 선뜻, 기꺼이
735 intrusively: 침입하여, 주제넘게 참견하여
736 fling: 던지다, 쏟아 붓다, 매달리다, 몰두하다
737 airy: 공허한, 비현실적인
738 impalpable: 손으로 만지거나 느낄 수 없는, 아주 미묘한

beauty of my soap-bubble was broken by the rude contact of some actual circumstance]}. The wiser effort would have been [to diffuse[739] thought and imagination through the opaque substance of to-day, and thus to make it a bright transparency]; [to spiritualise the burden that began to weigh so heavily]; [to seek, resolutely, the true and indestructible value {that lay hidden in the petty and wearisome incidents, and ordinary characters with which I was now conversant[740]}]. The fault was mine. The page of life {that was spread out before me} seemed dull and commonplace only because I had not fathomed[741] its deeper import[742]. A better book {than I shall ever write} was there; leaf after leaf presenting itself to me, {just as it was written out by the reality of the flitting hour}, and vanishing as fast as written, {only because my brain wanted the insight, and my hand the cunning[743], to transcribe[744] it}. At some future day, it may be, I shall remember a few scattered fragments and broken paragraphs, and write them down, and find the letters turn to gold upon the page.

These perceptions had come too late. At the Instant, I was ★MP3 [13] 시작 only conscious that {what would have been a pleasure once}

---

739 diffuse: 분산[확산]시키다, 퍼지다, 번지다
740 conversant: ～을 아는, ～에 친숙한
741 fathom: 헤아리다, 가늠하다, 깊이를 재다
742 import: (즉각 분명해 보이지 않는) 의미, 중요성
743 cunning: 교활, 간사, 솜씨, 기량
744 transcribe: (생각, 말을) 글로 기록하다, 바꾸다, 옮기다

was now a hopeless toil. There was no occasion to make much moan[745] about this state of affairs. I had ceased to be a writer of tolerably poor tales and essays, and had become a tolerably good Surveyor of the Customs. That was all. But, nevertheless, it is anything but agreeable[746] to be haunted by a suspicion {that one's intellect is dwindling[747] away, or exhaling[748], without your consciousness, like ether out of a phial[749]; so that, at every glance, you find a smaller and less volatile[750] residuum[751]. Of the fact, there could be no doubt; and, examining myself and others, I was led to conclusions, [in reference to the effect of public office on the character], not very favourable to the mode of life in question. In some other form, perhaps, I may hereafter develop these effects[752]. Suffice[753] it here to say that a Custom-House officer of long continuance can hardly be a very praiseworthy or respectable personage, for many reasons; one of them, the tenure[754] by which he holds his situation, and another, the very nature of his business, {which — though, I

---

745 moan: 신음, 넋두리, 불평. *make a moan: 탄식하다
746 agreeable: 기분 좋은, 쾌활한, 선뜻 동의하는, 받아들일 수 있는
747 dwindle: 줄어들다
748 exhale: 증발하다, 발산하다
749 phial: 작은 유리병
750 volatile: 휘발성의, 증발하기 쉬운
751 residuum: 잔재, 남아 있는 것
752 이 대목에서 호손은 공직이 미친 영향을 마치 병증처럼 묘사하고 있다.
753 suffice: 충분하다
754 tenure: 보유, 유지, 보유기간, 보유조건, 재임자격

trust, an honest one—is of such a sort that he does not share in the united effort of mankind}.

An effect—which I believe to be observable, more or less, in every individual {who has occupied the position}—is, that {while he leans on the mighty arm of the Republic}, his own proper strength departs from him. He loses, [in an extent proportioned to the weakness or force of his original nature], the capability of self-support[755]. {If he possesses an unusual share of native energy, or the enervating[756] magic of place do not operate too long upon him}, his forfeited[757] powers may be redeemable. The ejected[758] officer—fortunate in the unkindly[759] shove[760] {that sends him forth betimes[761], to struggle amid a struggling[762] world}—may return to himself, and become all {that he has ever been}. But this seldom happens. He usually keeps his ground[763] just long enough for his own ruin, and is then thrust out, [with sinews[764] all unstrung[765]], to totter along the difficult footpath

---

755 self-support: 자활, 자영, 독립경영

756 enervate: 기력을 떨어뜨리다

757 forfeit: 몰수(박탈)당하다

758 eject: 쫓아내다, 내쫓다

759 unkindly: 무정하게, 무정한

760 shove: (거칠게) 밀치다, 떠밀다, 힘껏 밀침

761 betimes: 때마침, 늦기 전에

762 struggling: 발버둥이 치는, 기를 쓰는

763 ground: (특정) 장소. *a holy ground: 성역; baseball grounds: 야구장; one's house and grounds: 집과 대지

764 sinews: 힘줄, 정력, 힘

of life as he best may. Conscious of his own infirmity—that his tempered[766] steel and elasticity[767] are lost—he for ever afterwards looks wistfully[768] about him in quest of support external to himself. His pervading[769] and continual hope—[a hallucination, {which, [in the face of all discouragement, and making light of impossibilities], haunts him {while he lives}, and, I fancy, [like the convulsive throes[770] of the cholera], torments him for a brief space[771] after death}]—is, {that finally, and in no long time, by some happy coincidence of circumstances, he shall be restored to office}. This faith, more than anything else, steals the pith[772] and availability[773] out of whatever enterprise {he may dream of undertaking}. Why should he toil[774] and moil[775], and be at so much trouble [to pick himself up[776] out of the mud], {when, in a little while hence[777],

---

765 unstrung: 산산조각이 나, 엉망이 되어

766 tempered: 조절된, 달구어 단련된

767 elasticity: 탄력성

768 wistfully: 탐내는 듯, 아쉬운 듯

769 pervade: 만연하다, 속속들이 배어들다

770 throe: 격통

771 space: 공간, 기간

772 pith: 골자, 핵심, 고갱이, 본질, 정수, 활력

773 availability: 유효성, 효용

774 toil: 힘들게 고생하다

775 toil and moil: 악착스럽게 일하다, 노역하다

776 pick oneself up: 일어서다, 회복하다

777 ... hence: 지금부터 ~ 후에. *when ... support him: 지금부터 조금만 있으면 그의 아저씨[국가]의 건장한 팔이 그를 일으켜 주고 부축해 줄 텐데

the strong arm of his Uncle will raise and support him}? Why should he work for his living here, or go to dig gold in California, {when he is so soon to be made happy, at monthly intervals, with a little pile of glittering coin out of his Uncle's pocket}? It is sadly curious to observe how slight a taste of office suffices to infect a poor fellow with this singular disease. Uncle Sam's gold — meaning no disrespect[778] to the worthy[779] old gentleman — has, in this respect, a quality of enchantment like that of the devil's wages. {Whoever touches it} should look well to himself, or he may find the bargain to go hard against him, [involving, if not his soul, yet many of its better attributes; its sturdy force, its courage and constancy[780], its truth, its self-reliance, and all {that gives the emphasis to manly character}].

Here was a fine prospect[781] in the distance[782]. Not that the

---

778 disrespect: 무례, 결례

779 worthy: 훌륭한, 괜찮은

780 constancy: 지속성, 지조, 절개

781 prospect: 전망, 가망, 예상. ＊이 대목은 '멋진 전망'이라는 게 무슨 의미인지 모호한데, 자기는 그런 꼴을 당하지 않을 자신이 있으니 '그래도 먼 곳에는 멋진 전망이 있다'는 자기긍정인지, 아니면 아이러니한 시선으로 풍자적인 언급을 하는 것인지 애매하다. 바로 다음 대목을 봐도 마찬가지이다. 교훈을 절절하게 새기면서 자기도 그 꼴이 될 수도 있다는 것을 인정한다면 그래도 멀리 있는 전망은 나쁘지 않을 터이나, 이런 인식이 없는 상태인데도 전망이 나쁘지 않다고 말하는 맥락은 정확히 와 닿지 않는다. 이 대목은 나중에 이런 걱정과는 무관하게 잘리게 되므로 걱정거리가 사라져 버렸으니 그게 멋진 전망이 아니고 무엇인가의 취지라면 이 얘기는 좀 나중에 나오는 게 자연스러웠을 것이다.

Surveyor brought the lesson home to himself, or admitted {that he could be so utterly undone[783], either by continuance in office or ejectment}. Yet my reflections[784] were not the most comfortable. I began to grow melancholy and restless; continually prying[785] into my mind, to discover {which of its poor properties were gone}, and {what degree of detriment had already accrued[786] to the remainder}. I endeavoured to calculate {how much longer I could stay in the Custom-House, and yet go forth a man}. To confess the truth, it was my greatest apprehension — {as it would never be a measure of policy to turn out so quiet an individual as myself; and it being hardly in the nature of a public officer to resign} — it was my chief trouble, therefore, {that I was likely to grow grey and decrepit[787] in the Surveyorship, and become much such another animal as the old Inspector}. Might it not, [in the tedious lapse of official life {that lay before me}], finally be with me {as it was with this venerable friend} — [to make the dinner-hour the nucleus[788] of the day, and to spend the rest of it, {as an old dog spends it}, asleep in the sunshine or in the shade]? A dreary look-forward, this, for a man {who

---

782 in the distance: 먼 곳에
783 undone: 파멸한, 몰락한
784 reflection: 심사숙고
785 pry: 꼬치꼬치 파고들다
786 accrue: 저절로 생기다
787 decrepit: 늙어빠진, 노쇠한
788 nucleus: 핵, 중심

felt it to be the best definition of happiness [to live throughout the whole range of his faculties and sensibilities]}! But, all this while, I was giving myself very unnecessary alarm. Providence had meditated better things for me than I could possibly imagine for myself.

A remarkable[789] event of the third year of my Surveyor-ship[790]—to adopt[791] the tone of "P. P."—was the election of General Taylor to the Presidency[792]. It is essential, in order to form a complete estimate of the advantages of official life, to view the incumbent[793] at the in-coming[794] of a hostile administration. His position is then one of the most singularly[795] irksome[796], and, in every contingency[797], disagreeable[798], {that a wretched mortal can possibly occupy}; with seldom an alternative of good on either hand, although {what presents itself to him as the worst event} may very probably be the best.[799] But it is a strange experience, to a man

★ MP3
(14) 시작

---

789 remarkable: 주목할 만한, 놀랄 만한
790 surveyor-ship: surveyor의 직, 지위, 신분
791 adopt: 쓰다, 취하다
792 presidency: 대통령직(임기)
793 incumbent: (공적인 직위의) 재임자, 재임 중인
794 in-coming: 새로 당선된, 선출된, 도착하는, 도래
795 singularly: 아주, 몹시, 특이하게
796 irksome: 짜증 나는, 귀찮은
797 contingency: 만일의 사태
798 disagreeable: 유쾌하지 못한
799 although ... the best: 비록 그에게 최악의 사건으로 나타나는 것

of pride and sensibility, to know that his interests are within the control of individuals {who neither love nor understand him}, and {by whom, since one or the other must needs happen, he would rather be injured than obliged[800]}. Strange, too, for one {who has kept his calmness throughout the contest}, to observe the bloodthirstiness[801] {that is developed in the hour of triumph}, and to be conscious that he is himself among its objects! There are few uglier traits of human nature than this tendency— {which I now witnessed in men no worse than their neighbours}—to grow cruel, merely because they possessed the power of inflicting harm. {If the guillotine, as applied to office-holders, were a literal fact, instead of one of the most apt of metaphors}, it is my sincere belief that the active members of the victorious party were sufficiently excited to have chopped off all our heads, and have thanked Heaven for the opportunity! It appears to me—{who have been a calm and curious observer, as well in victory as defeat}—that this fierce and bitter spirit of malice and revenge has never distinguished[802] the many triumphs of my own party {as it now did that of the Whigs}. The Democrats take the offices, as a general rule, {because they need them}, and {because the

---

이 최상이 될지 모른다고 하여도. *'최악이라고 해 봐야 잘리기밖에 더하겠어', '잘리면 차라리 잘된 거지' 식의 태도

800 oblige: 부득이 ~하게 되다, 돕다, 베풀다
801 bloodthirstiness: 피에 굶주림, 잔인함
802 distinguish: 특징짓다

practice of many years has made it the law of political warfare, [which {unless a different system be proclaimed}, it was weakness and cowardice to murmur at]}. But the long habit of victory has made them generous. They know {how to spare[803] when they see occasion}; and {when they strike}, the axe may be sharp indeed, but its edge is seldom poisoned with ill-will; nor is it their custom ignominiously[804] to kick the head {which they have just struck off}.

In short, {unpleasant as was my predicament[805], at best}, I saw much reason to congratulate myself {that I was on the losing side rather than the triumphant one}. {If, heretofore, l had been none of the warmest of partisans}, I began now, [at this season of peril and adversity], to be pretty acutely sensible {with which party my predilections[806] lay}; nor was it without something like regret and shame {that, [according to a reasonable calculation of chances], I saw my own prospect of retaining office to be better than those of my democratic brethren}. But who can see an inch[807] into futurity beyond his nose? My own head was the first {that fell}!

---

803 spare: 모면하게 하다, 피하게 해 주다
804 ignominiously: 비열하게, 불명예스럽게
805 predicament: 곤경
806 predilection: 매우 좋아함, 선호
807 inch: 2.54cm. *한 치의 치는 한 자의 10분의 1로 약 3.03cm

The moment {when a man's head drops off} is seldom or never, {I am inclined to think}, precisely the most agreeable of his life. Nevertheless, like the greater part of[808] our misfortunes, even so serious a contingency[809] brings its remedy and consolation with it, {if the sufferer will but make the best[810] [rather than the worst[811]], of the accident which has befallen him}. In my particular case, the consolatory topics were close at hand, and, indeed, had suggested[812] themselves to my meditations a considerable time {before it was requisite to use them}. [In view of[813] my previous weariness of office, and vague thoughts of resignation], my fortune somewhat resembled that of a person {who should entertain[814] an idea of committing suicide, and although beyond his hopes, meet with the good hap to be murdered}. In the Custom-House, as before in the Old Manse, I had spent three years—a term long enough to rest a weary brain: long enough to break off old intellectual habits, and make room for new ones: long enough, and too long, to have lived in an unnatural state, {doing what was really of no advantage nor delight to any human

---

808 greater part of: ～의 대부분
809 contingency: 만일의 사태
810 make the best of: ～을 최대한 이용하다, 어떻게든 극복하다
811 make the worst of: ～을 비관하다, ～의 나쁜 면만 보다
812 suggest: 제안(제의)하다, 추천하다, 시사하다, 비치다
813 in view of: ～을 고려하여
814 entertain: 즐겁게 해 주다, 접대하다, (생각, 감정, 희망 등을) 품다

being}, and {withholding[815] myself from toil[816] that would, at least, have stilled[817] an unquiet[818] impulse in me}. Then, moreover, as regarded his unceremonious[819] ejectment, the late Surveyor was not altogether ill-pleased to be recognised by the Whigs as an enemy; since his inactivity in political affairs—his tendency to roam, at will, in that broad and quiet field {where all mankind may meet}, rather than confine himself to those narrow paths {where brethren of the same household must diverge from one another}—had sometimes made it questionable with his brother Democrats whether he was a friend. Now, after he had won the crown of martyrdom (though with no longer a head to wear it on), the point might be looked upon as settled. Finally, little heroic as he was, it seemed more decorous[820] [to be overthrown in the downfall of the party with which he had been content to stand] than {to remain a forlorn survivor, [when so many worthier men were falling]: and at last, after subsisting[821] for four years on the mercy of a hostile administration, to be compelled then to define his position anew, and claim the yet more humiliating mercy of a friendly one}.

---

815 withhold: ~을 주지 않다
816 toil: 노역, 고역
817 still: 고요해(잠잠해)지다. 고요하게 하다
818 unquiet: 침착하지 못한, 불안해하는, 동요하는
819 unceremonious: 예의를 차리지 않는
820 decorous: 점잖은, 예의 바른
821 subsist: 근근히 살아가다, 먹고살다

Meanwhile, the press had taken up my affair, and kept me for a week or two careering[822] through the public prints, in my decapitated state, [like Irving's Headless Horseman], ghastly[823] and grim[824], and longing to be buried, {as a political dead man ought}. So much for my figurative self. The real human being all this time, [with his head safely on his shoulders], had brought himself to the comfortable conclusion {that everything was for the best}; and [making an investment in ink, paper, and steel pens], had opened his long-disused writing desk, and was again a literary man.

MP3 ★
'(15) 시작 Now it was that the lucubrations[825] of my ancient predecessor, Mr. Surveyor Pue, came into play[826]. Rusty through long idleness, some little space was requisite {before my intellectual machinery could be brought to work upon the tale with an effect in any degree satisfactory}. Even yet, {though my thoughts were ultimately much absorbed in the task}, it wears, to my eye, a stern and sombre[827] aspect: too much ungladdened[828] by genial[829] sunshine; too little relieved[830] by

---

822　career: 제멋대로 달리다
823　ghastly: 무시무시한
824　grim: 음산한
825　lucubration: 노작, 역작
826　come into play: 활동(작동)하기 시작하다
827　sombre: 어두침침한, 거무스름한
828　ungladden: gladden(기쁘게 하다)의 부정
829　genial: 다정한, 상냥한
830　relieve: (불쾌감, 고통 등을) 없애(덜어) 주다, 안도하게 하다

the tender and familiar influences {which soften almost every scene of nature and real life, and undoubtedly should soften every picture of them}. This uncaptivating[831] effect is perhaps due to the period of hardly accomplished revolution, and still seething[832] turmoil, {in which the story shaped itself}.

It is no indication, however, of a lack of cheerfulness in the writer's mind: for he was happier while straying through the gloom of these sunless fantasies than at any time {since he had quitted the Old Manse}. Some of the briefer articles, {which contribute to make up the volume}, have likewise been written {since my involuntary withdrawal from the toils and honours of public life}, and the remainder are gleaned[833] from annuals and magazines, of such antique[834] date {that they have gone round the circle[835], and come back to novelty again}. Keeping up the metaphor of the political guillotine, the whole may be considered as the POSTHUMOUS PAPERS OF A DECAPITATED SURVEYOR: and the sketch {which I am now bringing to a close}, {if too autobiographical for a modest person to publish in his lifetime}, will readily be excused in a

---

831 uncaptivate: captivate(마음을 사로잡다)의 부정
832 seething: 펄펄 끓는, 소용돌이치는, 들끓는
833 glean: (정도 지식 등을 어렵게 여기저기서) 얻다, 모으다. *glean grains: 이삭을 줍다
834 antique: 오래된, 고풍스러운
835 circle: 공전주기, 궤도, 순환, 주기

gentleman {who writes from beyond the grave}. Peace be with all the world! My blessing on my friends! My forgiveness to my enemies! For I am in the realm of quiet!

The life of the Custom-House lies like a dream behind me. The old Inspector — {who, by-the-bye[836], I regret to say, was overthrown and killed by a horse some time ago, else he would certainly have lived for ever} — he, and all those other venerable personages {who sat with him at the receipt of custom[837]}, are but shadows in my view: white-headed and wrinkled images, {which my fancy used to sport with, and has now flung aside for ever}. The merchants — Pingree, Phillips, Shepard, Upton, Kimball, Bertram, Hunt — these and many other names, {which had such classic[838] familiarity for my ear six months ago}, — these men of traffic, {who seemed to occupy so important a position in the world} — how little time has it required to disconnect me from them all, not merely in act, but recollection! It is with an effort that I recall the figures and appellations[839] of these few. Soon, likewise, my old native town will loom upon me through the haze[840] of memory, a mist [brooding over and around it]; {as if it were no portion of the

---

836 by-the-bye: 그런데, 말이 났으니 말이지
837 the receipt of custom: 세관(마태복음 9:9)
838 classic: 최고 수준의, 대표적인
839 appellation: 명칭, 호칭
840 haze: 아지랑이

real earth, but an overgrown village[841] in cloud-land[842], with only imaginary inhabitants to people its wooden houses and walk its homely lanes, and the unpicturesque[843] prolixity[844] of its main street}. Henceforth it ceases to be a reality of my life; I am a citizen of somewhere else. My good townspeople will not much regret me, for[845] — {though it has been as dear an object as any, in my literary efforts, to be of some importance in their eyes, and to win myself a pleasant memory in this abode and burial-place of so many of my forefathers} — there has never been, for me, the genial[846] atmosphere {which a literary man requires in order to ripen the best harvest of his mind}. I shall do better amongst other faces; and these familiar ones, {it need hardly be said}, will do just as well without me.

---

841 overgrown village: (못마땅하게) 너무 커진 마을. *overgrown children: 덩치(만) 큰 아이들

842 cloud-land: 구름나라, 공상의 세계

843 unpicturesque: 비회화적인(보아서 재미없는)

844 prolixity: 장황함

845 for: 앞 문장의 이유, 왜냐하면. *그런데 바로 뒤에 나오는 이야기가 고향 사람들이 호손을 아쉬워하지 않을 것이란 점에 대한 이유는 아니다. 더 뒤의 "나는 다른 얼굴들 사이에서 더 잘 해 나갈 것이고 이 낯익은 얼굴들 역시 나 없이 마찬가지로 잘 해 나갈 것이란 점은 언급할 필요도 거의 없다"(I shall do better amongst other faces; and these familiar ones, it need hardly be said, will do just as well without me) 부분이 for 다음의 이유로 되어야 자연스럽다.

846 genial: 쾌적한, 온화한

It may be, however — Oh, transporting[847] and triumphant thought! — that the great-grandchildren of the present race may sometimes think kindly of the scribbler[848] of bygone days, {when the antiquary[849] of days to come, among the sites memorable in the town's history, shall point out the locality of THE TOWN PUMP[850]}.

---

847 transport: 황홀하게 하다, 기뻐 어쩔 줄 모르게 하다
848 scribbler: (못마땅함, 유머) 기자, 작가, 저자, 잡기장
849 antiquary: 골동품 연구가
850 THE TOWN PUMP: 「마을의 펌프에서 흘러나오는 실개천」("A Rill from the Town Pump")이라는 제목의 단편소설은 세일럼에서의 삶을 묘사하는 독백체의 작품으로 단편모음집 『케케묵은 이야기들』(*Twice-Told Tales*, 1837)에 실렸다.

The Scarlet Letter **1장**

The Prison-Door

A throng of bearded men, in sad-colored garments and gray, steeple[1]-crowned[2] hats, [intermixed with women, some wearing hoods, and others bareheaded], was assembled[3] in front of a wooden edifice[4], {the door of which was heavily timbered[5] with oak, and studded[6] with iron spikes[7]}.

The founders of a new colony, {whatever Utopia of human virtue and happiness they might originally project}, have invariably[8] recognized it among their earliest practical necessities [to allot a portion of the virgin soil as a cemetery, and another portion as the site of a prison]. In accordance with this rule, it may safely be assumed that the forefathers of Boston had built the first prison-house, somewhere in the vicinity[9] of Corn-hill, almost as seasonably[10] as they marked out[11] the first burial-ground, on Isaac Johnson's lot[12], and round

---

1 steeple: 교회의 첨탑
2 crowned: 왕관을 씌우다, 꼭대기에 ~이 있다(덮여 있다), 치아에 인공 치관을 씌우다. *steeple-crowned: 꼭대기가 높고 뾰족한
3 assemble: 모이다, 모으다, 집합시키다
4 edifice: 크고 인상적인 건물
5 timber: 목재, ~을 재목으로 세우다[짓다]
6 stud: ~에 장식 단추를 달다, 장식 못(징)을 박다
7 spike: (굵은 목재를 고정시키는) 대못
8 invariably: 변함(예외)없이, 언제나
9 vicinity: 인근, 근처
10 seasonably: 시기적절하게
11 mark out: 표시하다, 그리다, 계획하다
12 Issac Johnson은 보스턴의 첫 정착민들과 함께 도착한 바로 그 해

about his grave, {which subsequently became the nucleus of all the congregated sepulchres in the old church-yard of King's Chapel}. Certain it is, that, some fifteen or twenty years[13] after the settlement of the town, the wooden jail was already marked with[14] weather-stains[15] and other indications of age, {which gave a yet darker aspect to its beetle-browed[16] and gloomy front}. The rust on the ponderous iron-work[17] of its oaken door looked more antique than any thing else in the new world. Like all {that pertains to crime}, it seemed never to have known a youthful era. Before this ugly edifice, and between it and the wheel-track of the street, was a grass-plot, much overgrown with burdock[18], pig-weed[19], apple-peru[20], and such unsightly[21] vegetation[22], {which evidently found something

---

인 1630년에 죽었다. 그 후 그의 땅이 감옥, 묘지, 교회 부지로 제공되었는데 각각 죄, 죽음, 구원이라는 청교도의 드라마를 상징했다.

13 정착이 1630년이고 그 후 약 15~20년 후면 1646~1650년 정도가 되는데 이를 좀 더 정확히 보면, 실제 작중의 사건은 1642~1649년에 벌어지는 것으로 설정되어 있다. 이 근거는 12장에 언급된 존 윈스롭(Winthrop) 총독의 죽음은 1642년의 일이며, 이때가 작품의 서두 이후 '7년의 긴 세월이 지난 후'라고 언급하고 있기 때문이다.

14 marked with: ~의 자국이 남은

15 weather-stain: 비바람으로 인한 변색(얼룩)

16 beetle-browed: 눈썹이 검고 짙은, 상을 찌푸린, 뚱한

17 iron-work: 철제 부품

18 burdock: 우엉

19 pig-weed: 명아주

20 apple-peru: 흰독말풀(=jimsonweed)

21 unsightly: 보기 흉한

22 vegetation: (특히 특정 지역, 환경의) 초목(식물)

congenial[23] in the soil [that had so early borne the black flower of civilized society, a prison]}. But, on one side of the portal, and rooted almost at the threshold[24], was a wild rose-bush[25], covered, in this month of June, with its delicate gems, {which might be imagined to offer their fragrance[26] and fragile beauty to the prisoner as he went in, and to the condemned criminal as he came forth to his doom, in token that the deep heart of Nature could pity and be kind to him}.

This rose-bush, by a strange chance, has been kept alive in history; but whether it had merely survived out of the stern old wilderness, so long after the fall of the gigantic pines and oaks {that originally overshadowed it}, — or whether, as there is fair authority for believing, it had sprung up under the footsteps of the sainted Ann Hutchinson[27], as she entered the prison-

---

23 congenial: 마음이 맞는(통하는), 알맞은

24 threshold: 문지방, 문턱

25 rose-bush: 장미 덤불

26 fragrance: 향기

27 Ann(=Anne) Hutchinson(1591~1643). 앤 허치슨은 영국 국교회 목사이자 교사인 아버지 덕분에 당시 여성들에 비해 더 나은 교육을 받았다. 영국에서 존 코튼(John Cotton)의 영향을 많이 받았는데, 존 코튼이 신대륙으로 이주할 수밖에 없게 되자 1년 뒤 허친슨 부부는 11명의 아이를 데리고 뒤따른다. 앤은 산파로 남들을 돕는 데 열성적인 성격으로 집에서 매주 여성들을 모아 놓고 최근의 설교에 대해 코멘트를 했는데, 모임이 인기가 있자 남성들에게도 모임을 제공했다. 그녀는 covenant of grace(은총성약)를 주장하는 한편, covenant of works(선행성약)를 주장하는 목사들을 비

door, — we shall not take upon us to determine. Finding it so directly on the threshold of our narrative, {which is now about to issue from that inauspicious portal}, we could hardly do otherwise than pluck one of its flowers and present it to the reader. It may serve, let us hope, to symbolize some sweet moral blossom, {that may be found along the track}, or relieve the darkening close of a tale of human frailty and sorrow.

판하고, 신심에 따른 구원, 개인에 내재하는 신의 은총의 직관적인 계시 등 Antinomianism(도덕률 폐기론)을 주장했다. 따라서 선행을 통해서 구원을 받는다는 입장과는 거리가 있었고 선행을 규정하는 사회와 제도에 대해서도 비판적인 입장이었다. 위에 'sainted'라고 했으나 청교도들이 그녀를 '성인'으로 간주한 것은 아니고 오히려 존 윈스롭(John Winthrop), 리처드 벨링햄 (Richard Bellingham), 존 윌슨(John Wilson) 등이 이끄는 제도화된 청교도 신정체제에 비판적이었기 때문에 추방되었다.

The Scarlet Letter **2장**

The Market-Place

ㄴ

The grass-plot[1] before the jail, in Prison Lane, on a certain summer morning, not less than[2] two centuries ago, was occupied[3] by a pretty large number of the inhabitants of Boston; all with their eyes intently[4] fastened[5] on the iron-clamped[6] oaken door. Amongst any other population, or at a later period in the history of New England, the grim[7] rigidity[8] {that petrified[9] the bearded physiognomies[10] of these good people} would have augured[11] some awful business in hand. It could have betokened[12] nothing short of the anticipated[13] execution of some noted[14] culprit[15], {on whom the sentence of a legal tribunal[16] had but confirmed the verdict of public sentiment}. But, in that early severity of the Puritan character, an inference[17] of this kind could not so indubitably[18] be

---

1 grass-plot: 잔디밭

2 not less than: (수사와 함께) 적어도(at least)

3 occupy: (공간, 지역, 시간을) 차지하다, 사용하다, 점령(점거)하다

4 intently: 골똘하게, 여념없이

5 fasten: 매다, 잠그다, 묶다, (눈, 시선 등을 오랫동안) 고정시키다

6 clamp: 죔쇠로 고정시키다, 꽉 물다

7 grim: 엄숙한, 단호한, 암울한

8 rigidity: 단단함, 강직, 엄격

9 petrify: 겁에 질리게 하다, 석화하다(시키다)

10 physiognomy: 얼굴 모습, 골상

11 augur: (상서로운 또는 상서롭지 못한) 전조(조짐)가 되다

12 betoken: 징조(전조)이다

13 anticipated: 기대하던, 대망의

14 noted: 유명한, 잘 알려져 있는

15 culprit: 범인, (문제를 일으킨) 장본인

16 tribunal: 재판소, 법원

drawn. It might be that a sluggish[19] bond-servant[20], or an undutiful[21] child, {whom his parents had given over to the civil authority[22]}, was to be corrected[23] at the whipping-post[24]. It might be, that an Antinomian[25], a Quaker, or other heterodox religionist, was to be scourged[26] out of the town, or an idle[27] or vagrant[28] Indian, {whom the white man's fire-water[29] had made riotous[30] about the streets}, was to be driven with stripes[31] into the shadow of the forest. It might be, too, that a witch, like old Mistress Hibbins[32], the bitter-tempered[33] widow

---

17 inference: 추론

18 indubitably: 의심할 여지없이, 틀림없이

19 sluggish: 느릿느릿 움직이는, 부진한, 느려터진

20 bond-servant: 종, 노예

21 undutiful: 의무를 다하지 않은, 불충한

22 civil authority: 행정당국

23 correct: 바로잡다

24 whipping-post: 태형기둥

25 Antinomian: 도덕률 폐기론자. 1장 126쪽 앤 허치슨(1591~1643)에 대한 설명 참조.

26 scourge: 재앙, 골칫거리, 채찍, 채찍으로 때리다

27 idle: 게으른, 놀고먹는

28 vagrant: (특히 구걸을 하며 다니는) 부랑자

29 fire-water: 화주(위스키 같은 독한 술)

30 riotous: 소란을 피우는

31 stripe: 줄, 줄무늬, 길쭉한 조각

32 앤 히빈스(Ann Hibbins)는 리처드 벨링햄(Richard Bellingham) 총독의 누이로 소설에 간간이 등장하는데 1656년에 마녀로 몰려 사형당했다. 두 번째 남편 윌리엄 히빈스(William Hibbins, 1600~1654)는 부유한 상인으로 뉴잉글랜드 식민지 지방의회의 부판사였고, 1648년 마거릿 존스(Margaret Jones)의 마녀재판 때 판결을 내

of the magistrate[34], was to die upon the gallows. In either case, there was very much the same solemnity of demeanour on the part of the spectators; as befitted a people {amongst whom religion and law were almost identical}, and {in whose character both were so thoroughly interfused, that the mildest and severest acts of public discipline were alike made venerable and awful}. Meagre, indeed, and cold, was the sympathy {that a transgressor might look for, from such bystanders at the scaffold}. On the other hand, a penalty {which, in our days, would infer a degree of mocking infamy[35] and ridicule}, might then be invested with almost as stern a dignity as the punishment of death itself.

It was a circumstance to be noted, on the summer morning when our story begins its course, that the women, {of whom there were several in the crowd}, appeared to take a peculiar interest in {whatever penal[36] infliction[37] might be expected

---

린 판사 중 하나였다. 1640년에 앤 히빈스는 자신이 집 공사를 위해 고용한 일단의 목수들을 과다비용청구로 고소해서 소송에 이겼으나 그녀의 행동은 거슬리는(abrasive) 것으로 여겨졌고 이 일로 종교재판을 받게 된다. 또한 목수들에게 자신의 행동에 대한 사과를 거부하자 훈계 파문되고, 남편의 권위를 남용했다는 비난도 추가되었다. 1654년에 그녀의 남편이 죽고 난 몇 달 뒤부터 마녀재판 절차가 시작되어 1656년에 교수형을 당했다.

33 bitter-tempered: 매서운, 혹독한 성미의
34 magistrate: 치안판사, 행정관
35 infamy: 오명
36 penal: (특히 법에 의한) 처벌의, 형벌의

to ensue}. The age had not so much refinement[38], that any sense of impropriety[39] restrained[40] the wearers of petticoat and farthingale[41] from stepping forth into the public ways, and wedging[42] their not unsubstantial[43] persons, if occasion were, into the throng[44] [nearest to the scaffold at an execution]. Morally, as well as materially, there was a coarser fibre[45] in those wives and maidens of old English birth and breeding, than in [their fair descendants, separated from them by a series of six or seven generations]; for, [throughout that chain[46] of ancestry[47]], every successive[48] mother has transmitted [to her child] a fainter bloom[49], a more delicate and briefer beauty, and a slighter physical frame, if not a character of less force and solidity[50], than her own. The women, who were now standing

---

37 infliction: (고통, 벌, 타격을) 가함, 형벌

38 refinement: 개선, 세련, 고상, 품위

39 impropriety: 부적절한(부도덕한) 행동

40 restrain: 제지(저지)하다

41 farthingale: 파딩게일(과거 여자들이 치마를 불룩하게 하려고 안에 입던 둥근 틀)

42 wedge: 쐐기 모양의 것. (좁은 틈 사이에) 끼워 넣다

43 unsubstantial: 실체(실질)가 없는, 견고하지 않은, 약한, (식사가) 내용이 빈약한, 비현실적인(unreal)

44 throng: 인파, 군중

45 fibre(=fiber): 섬유, 성격, 기질. *a man of fine[coarse] fiber: 섬세한[거친] 성격의 사람

46 chain: 사슬, 띠, 일련

47 ancestry: 가계, 혈통

48 successive: 연속적인, 잇따른

49 bloom: 꽃, (건강한) 혈색

about the prison-door, stood within less than half a century of the period {when the man-like Elizabeth had been the not altogether unsuitable representative of the sex}. They were her countrywomen; and the beef and ale of their native land, [with a moral diet not a whit[51] more refined], entered largely into their composition[52]. The bright morning sun, therefore, shone on broad shoulders and well-developed busts, and on round and ruddy cheeks, {that had ripened in the far-off island, and had hardly yet grown paler or thinner in the atmosphere of New England}. There was, moreover, a boldness and rotundity[53] of speech among these matrons[54], as most of them seemed to be, that would startle us at the present day, whether in respect to its purport or its volume of tone.

"Goodwives[55]," said a hard-featured[56] dame of fifty, "I'll tell ye a piece of my mind. It would be greatly for the public behoof, if we women, being of mature age and church-members in good repute, should have the handling of such malefactresses[57] as this Hester Prynne. What think ye, gossips[58]? If the hussy[59]

---

50 solidity: 견고함, 탄탄함
51 whit: 아주 조금
52 composition: 기질, 성질
53 rotundity: 둥근 것, 통통함, (목소리가) 우렁참
54 matron: 나이 지긋한 부인
55 Goodwife: ~여사, ~부인(Mrs.)(여자의 경칭)
56 hard-featured: 얼굴이 험상궂은, 인상이 나쁜
57 malefactress: (여자) 악한. *malefactor: 악인, 악한

stood up for judgment before us five, that are now here in a knot[60] together, would she come off[61] with such a sentence as the worshipful magistrates have awarded[62]? Marry[63], I trow[64] not!"

"People say," said another, "that the Reverend[65] Master[66] Dimmesdale, her godly[67] pastor, takes it very grievously[68] to heart[69] that such a scandal should have come upon his congregation[70]."

"The magistrates are God-fearing gentlemen, but merciful overmuch,—that is a truth," added a third autumnal[71] matron.

---

58 gossip: 뜬소문, 험담, 뒷공론, 쑥덕공론, 가벼운 이야기[읽을 거리], 남의 말하기 좋아하는 사람, 수다쟁이, 〈고어〉 (특히 여자끼리의) 친구(=friends, acquaintances)

59 hussy: 제멋대로인[마구 놀아나는] 여자

60 knot: 매듭, 올린 머리, 옹이, (함께 가까이 모여 서 있는 사람들) 무리

61 come off: 벗어나다

62 award: 수여하다, 판정을 내리다

63 marry: 저런, 어머나(놀람·분노 등)

64 trow: 〈고어〉 생각하다, 믿다

65 reverend: 목사

66 master: 주인, 대가, 스승

67 godly: 경건한

68 grievously: 슬프도록, 지독히, 격렬하게

69 take ... to heart: ~을 통감하다

70 congregation: (특정 교회의) 신자[신도]들

71 autumnal: 가을의, 나이 지긋한

"At the very least, they should have put the brand of a hot iron on Hester Prynne's forehead. Madame Hester would have winced at that, I warrant[72] me. But she,—the naughty[73] baggage[74],—little will she care what they put upon the bodice[75] of her gown! Why, look you, she may cover it with a brooch, or such like heathenish[76] adornment, and so walk the streets as brave as ever!"

"Ah, but," interposed, more softly, a young wife, holding a child by the hand, "let her cover the mark as she will, the pang of it will be always in her heart."

"What do we talk of marks and brands, whether on the bodice of her gown, or the flesh of her forehead?" cried another female, the ugliest as well as the most pitiless of these self-constituted[77] judges. "This woman has brought shame upon us all, and ought to die. Is there no law for it? Truly there is, both in the Scripture and the statute-book[78]. Then let the magistrates, {who have made it of no effect[79]}, thank

---

72 I warrant: 장담컨대, 분명히
73 naughty: 버릇없는, 무례한, 외설적인
74 baggage: (경멸적) 말괄량이 아가씨, 시끄러운 노파, 창녀
75 bodice: 보디스(드레스의 상체 부분)
76 heathenish: 이교(도)의, 이교도적인, 비그리스도교적인
77 self-constituted: 스스로 결정한, 자기 설정의
78 statute-book: 법령집
79 of no effect: (기대한) 효과를 거두지 못한 채(법령을 만들어 놓기

themselves if their own wives and daughters go astray!"

"Mercy on us, goodwife," exclaimed a man in the crowd, "is there no virtue in woman, save {what springs from a wholesome[80] fear of the gallows}? That is the hardest word yet[81]! Hush, now, gossips; for the lock is turning in the prison-door, and here comes Mistress[82] Prynne herself."

[The door of the jail being flung open from within], there appeared, in the first place, like a black shadow emerging into sunshine, the grim and grisly[83] presence of the town-beadle[84], with a sword by his side and his staff of office in his hand. This personage[85] prefigured[86] and represented in his aspect the whole dismal[87] severity of the Puritanic code[88] of law, {which it was his business to administer in its final and closest application to the offender}. Stretching forth the official staff

---

만 했으니)

80 wholesome: 건강에 좋은, 건전한, 몸보신
81 yet: (앞에 최상급과 같이 써서) 지금[그때]까지 있은 것 중 가장 ~한
82 mistress: 권한[지배력]을 가진 여자, 여류 명인[대가]
83 grim and grisly: 엄숙하고 소름끼치는
84 beadle: 교구(敎區) 직원
85 personage: 인물, 인사
86 prefigure: 예시하다
87 dismal: 음울한
88 code: 암호, 코드(프로그램의 데이터 처리 형식에 맞는 데이터), 관례, 법규. *code of law: 법계, 법체계

in his left hand, he laid his right upon the shoulder of a young woman, {whom he thus drew forward until, on the threshold of the prison-door, she repelled[89] him, by an action [marked[90] with natural dignity and force of character], and stepped into the open air, as if by her own free-will}. She bore in her arms a child, a baby of some three months old, {who winked and turned aside its little face from the too vivid light of day; because its existence, heretofore, had brought it acquainted only with the gray[91] twilight[92] of a dungeon, or other darksome apartment of the prison}.

{When the young woman — the mother of this child — stood fully revealed before the crowd}, it seemed to be her first impulse to clasp the infant closely to her bosom; not so much by an impulse of motherly affection, as that she might thereby conceal a certain token, which was wrought[93] or fastened into her dress. In a moment, however, wisely judging that one token of her shame would but poorly serve to hide another, she took the baby on her arm, and, [with a burning blush[94], and yet a haughty smile, and a glance that would not be abashed[95]],

---

89 repel: 뿌리치다, 밀어내다
90 mark: 특징(성격)짓다
91 gray: 어스레한
92 twilight: 황혼, 땅거미
93 wrought: 세공된, 장식된
94 blush: 얼굴이 붉어짐

looked around at her townspeople and neighbours. On the breast of her gown, in fine red cloth, surrounded with an elaborate embroidery and fantastic flourishes[96] of gold thread, appeared the letter A. It was so artistically done, and with so much fertility and gorgeous luxuriance of fancy, that it had all the effect of a last and fitting decoration to the apparel[97] {which she wore}; and which was of a splendor[98] in accordance with the taste of the age, but greatly beyond {what was allowed by the sumptuary[99] regulations of the colony}.

The young woman was tall, with a figure[100] of perfect elegance, on a large scale. She had dark and abundant hair, so glossy[101] that it threw off the sunshine with a gleam[102], and a face {which, besides being beautiful from regularity of feature and richness of complexion, had the impressiveness belonging to a marked brow and deep black eyes}. She was lady-like, too, after the manner of the feminine gentility[103] of those days; characterized by a certain state and dignity, rather than by the

---

95 abashed: 창피한, 겸연쩍은

96 flourish: 과장된 동작, (말, 글의) 수식, (글씨의) 장식체

97 apparel: 의류, 복장

98 splendor: 훌륭함, 장려(壯麗), 화려함

99 sumptuary: 비용 절감의, 출비를 규제하는, 사치 규제의.
　　＊sumptuary law: 〈법〉 윤리 규제 법령, (개인 소비를 제한하는)
　　사치 금지법[령]

100 figure: (특히 여성의 매력적인) 몸매

101 glossy: 윤이 나는

102 gleam: (흔히 어디에 반사된) 어슴푸레한 빛

103 gentility: 고상함, 품위

delicate, evanescent, and indescribable grace, {which is now recognized as its indication}. And never had Hester Prynne appeared more lady-like, [in the antique interpretation of the term], than as she issued from the prison. Those {who had before known her, and had expected to behold her dimmed and obscured by a disastrous cloud}, were astonished[104], and even startled[105], to perceive {how her beauty shone out, and made a halo of the misfortune and ignominy in which she was enveloped}. It may be true, that, to a sensitive observer, there was something exquisitely painful in it. Her attire, {which, indeed, she had wrought for the occasion, in prison, and had modelled[106] much after her own fancy}, seemed to express the attitude of her spirit, the desperate recklessness of her mood, by its wild[107] and picturesque[108] peculiarity[109]. But the point {which drew all eyes, and, as it were, transfigured the wearer,—so that both men and women, who had been familiarly acquainted with Hester Prynne, were now impressed as if they beheld her for the first time}, —was that SCARLET LETTER, so fantastically embroidered and illuminated upon her bosom. It had the effect of a spell, taking her out of the

---

104 astonish: 깜짝[크게] 놀라게 하다
105 startle: (약간 충격·공포의 감정을 동반하여) 몸이 움찔할 정도로 깜짝 놀라게 하다
106 model: 모형(견본)을 만들다
107 wild: 격렬한, 날뛰는, 무모한
108 picturesque: 그림 같은, 생생한
109 peculiarity: 기이한 특징, 특이함

ordinary relations with humanity, and inclosing her in a sphere by herself.

"She hath good skill at her needle, that's certain," remarked ★ MP3 2장 (2) 시작 one of the female spectators; "but did ever a woman, before this brazen[110] hussy, contrive[111] such a way of showing it! Why, gossips, <u>what is it but to laugh</u>[112] in the faces of our godly magistrates, and make a pride[113] out of what they, worthy gentlemen, meant for a punishment?"

"It were well," muttered the most iron-visaged[114] of the old dames, "if we stripped Madam Hester's rich[115] gown off her dainty[116] shoulders; and as for the red letter, which she hath stitched so curiously[117], I'll bestow a rag of mine own rheumatic[118] flannel[119], to make a fitter one!"

---

110 brazen: 뻔뻔한, 놋쇠로 만든, 황동색의

111 contrive: 용케(어떻게든) 하다, (어려운 가운데도) 성취하다, 고안하다

112 what is it but to ...: 'to ...'(to 이하)가 아니고 뭐겠어요? *but: =except

113 pride: 자랑, 긍지, 교만, 우쭐대기, 자랑거리. *make a pride out of ...: ~을 가지고 자랑거리를 만들다

114 visaged: (복합어를 이루어) ~얼굴의

115 rich: 호화로운, 사치스러운

116 dainty: 앙증맞은, 얌전한

117 curiously: 기묘하게, 정교하게

118 rheumatic: 류머티즘의, 류머티즘에 걸리기 쉬운, 류머티즘을 걸리게 하는

119 flannel: 플란넬(면이나 양모를 섞어 만든 가벼운 천), 목욕 수건, 때 (미는) 수건. *a face flannel: 얼굴 씻는 수건; rheumatic

"O, peace, neighbours[120], peace!" whispered their youngest companion. "Do not let her hear you! Not a stitch in that embroidered letter, but[121] she has felt it in her heart."

The grim beadle now made a gesture with his staff.

"Make way, good people, make way, in the King's name," cried he. "Open a passage; and, I promise ye, Mistress Prynne shall be set where man, woman, and child may have a fair sight of her brave[122] apparel, from this time till an hour past meridian. A blessing on the righteous Colony of the Massachusetts, {where iniquity is dragged out into the sunshine}! Come along, Madam Hester, and show your scarlet letter in the market-place!"

A lane was forthwith[123] opened through the crowd of spectators. Preceded[124] by the beadle, and attended by an irregular[125] procession of stern-browed men and unkindly-

---

flannel: 몸을 따뜻하게 유지시켜 류머티즘으로 인한 관절 통증을 완화시키려고 걸치는 천

120 neighbours: (이름을 모르는 사람을 친근하게 부르는 말) 여보세요, 저보세요

121 not A ... but B: B하지 않는 A는 없을 것이다

122 brave: 용감한, 〈반어적〉 멋진

123 forthwith: 곧, 당장

124 precede: 앞서다

125 irregular: 고르지 못한, 불규칙적인

visaged women, Hester Prynne set forth towards the place [appointed for her punishment]. A crowd of eager and curious schoolboys, [understanding little of the matter in hand, except that it gave them a half-holiday], ran before her progress, turning their heads continually to stare into her face, and at the winking baby in her arms, and at the ignominious letter on her breast. It was no great distance, in those days, from the prison-door to the market-place. Measured by the prisoner's experience, however, it might be reckoned a journey of some length; for, haughty[126] as her demeanour was, she perchance underwent an agony from every footstep of those that thronged to see her, {as if her heart had been flung into the street for them all to spurn[127] and trample upon}. In our nature, however, there is a provision[128], alike marvellous and merciful[129], that the sufferer should never know the intensity of {what he endures} by its present torture, but chiefly by the pang {that rankles[130] after it}. With almost a serene deportment, therefore, Hester Prynne passed through this portion[131] of her ordeal, and came to a sort of scaffold, at the western extremity of the market-place. It stood nearly beneath the eaves of

---

126 haughty: 오만한, 거만한

127 spurn: 쫓아내다, 추방하다, 걷어차다

128 provision: 조항, 규정, 대책

129 merciful: 자비로운, 다행스러운

130 rankle: (어떤 사건·누구의 말 등이 오랫동안) 마음을 괴롭히다 [마음에 맺히다]

131 portion: (더 큰 것의) 일부(부분)

Boston's earliest church, and appeared to be a fixture[132] there.

In fact, this scaffold constituted a portion of a penal machine[133], which now, for two or three generations past[134], has been merely historical and traditionary among us, but was held, in the old time, to be as effectual an agent in the promotion of good citizenship[135], as ever was the guillotine among the terrorists of France. It was, in short, the platform[136] of the pillory[137]; and above it rose the framework of that instrument of discipline, so fashioned as to confine the human head in its tight grasp, and thus hold it up to the public gaze. The very ideal of ignominy was embodied and made manifest in this contrivance of wood and iron. There can be no outrage[138], methinks, against our common nature,—whatever be the delinquencies of the individual,—no outrage [more flagrant[139] than to forbid the culprit to hide his face for shame]; as it was the essence of this punishment to do. In Hester Prynne's instance, however, as not unfrequently in other cases, her sentence bore, that she should stand a certain time upon

---

132 fixture: 고정, 붙박이
133 penal machine: 처벌 장치
134 past: 지난, 최근의
135 citizenship: 시민(공민)권, 시민의 신분(자질)
136 platform: 단, 대
137 pillory: (옛날 죄인에게 씌우던) 칼
138 outrage: 격분, 잔학행위, 잔인무도한 일
139 flagrant: 노골적인, 명백한

the platform, but without undergoing that gripe[140] about the neck and confinement[141] of the head, the proneness to which[142] was the most devilish characteristic of this ugly engine[143]. Knowing well her part, she ascended a flight of wooden steps, and was thus displayed[144] to the surrounding multitude, at about the height of a man's shoulders above the street.

Had there been a Papist[145] among the crowd of Puritans, he might have seen in this beautiful woman, [so picturesque in her attire and mien, and with the infant at her bosom], an object to remind him of the image of Divine Maternity[146], {which so many illustrious[147] painters have vied[148] with one another to represent}; something {which should remind him, indeed, [but only by contrast], of that sacred image of sinless motherhood, whose infant was to redeem the world}. Here, there was the taint of deepest sin in the most sacred quality of human life, {working such effect, that the world was only the

---

140 gripe: 꽉 쥐기, 제어

141 confinement: 갇힘, 얽매임

142 the proneness to which: 이렇게[목 주위를 꽉 죄고 머리를 움직이지 못하게 가둬 두는 일] 되기 쉬운 것. *prone: ~하기 쉬운

143 this ugly engine: 앞의 pillory를 가리킨다.

144 display: 전시(진열)하다, 보이다

145 Papist: 가톨릭신자

146 maternity: 어머니임, 모성, 어머니다움. *a maternity benefit: 출산수당

147 illustrious: 저명한, 걸출한

148 vie: 다투다, 경쟁하다

darker for this woman's beauty, and the more lost for the infant that she had borne}.

The scene was not without a mixture of awe, such[149] {as must always invest the spectacle of guilt and shame in a fellow-creature, before society shall have grown corrupt enough to smile, instead of shuddering, at it[150]}. The witnesses of Hester Prynne's disgrace had not yet passed beyond their simplicity[151]. They were stern enough to look upon her death, {had that been the sentence}, without a murmur at its severity, but had none of the heartlessness of another social state, {which would find only a theme for jest in an exhibition like the present}. {Even had there been a disposition to turn the matter into ridicule}, it must have been repressed and overpowered[152] by the solemn presence of men [no less dignified than[153] the Governor, and several of his counsellors[154], a judge, a general, and the ministers of the town]; all of whom sat or stood in a balcony of the meeting-house[155], looking down upon the platform. {When

---

149 such: = such awe
150 as must always ... at it: 동료 인간에게서 보는 죄와 수치의 광경에 사회가 몸서리를 치는 대신에 웃어넘길 만큼 충분히 타락하기 전이기에, 그 광경을 언제나 둘러싸고 있기 마련인 경외감. *invest: 덮다, 싸다, 둘러싸다
151 simplicity: 소박함, 순박함
152 overpower: 제압하다
153 no less ... than: ~ 못지않게 ~한
154 counsellor: 고문, 참사관

such personages could constitute a part of the spectacle, without risking the majesty or reverence of rank and office}, it was safely to be inferred that the infliction of a legal sentence would have an earnest and effectual meaning[156]. Accordingly, the crowd was sombre[157] and grave[158]. The unhappy culprit sustained herself as best a woman might, under the heavy weight of a thousand unrelenting[159] eyes, all fastened upon her, and concentrated at her bosom. It was almost intolerable to be borne. Of an impulsive and passionate nature[160], she had fortified herself to encounter the stings and venomous stabs of public contumely[161], wreaking[162] itself in every variety of insult; but there was a quality so much more terrible in the solemn mood of the popular mind, that she longed rather to behold all those rigid countenances contorted with scornful merriment[163], and herself the object. {Had a roar of laughter

---

155 meeting-house: 교회당, 예배당

156 이 대목을 보면 헤스터와 관련된 사건에 어떤 선고가 내려지든 말든 상관하지 않는 분위기가 아님을 알 수 있다. 지위고하를 막론하고 헤스터의 사건을 이 사회 전체에 중대한 의미를 띤 사안으로 여기고 있으며, 이를 사회성원 전체의 참여를 통해 치러야 할 중요한 행사로 집행하고 있다.

157 sombre(=somber): 어둠침침한, 침울한

158 grave: 심각한

159 unrelenting: 수그러들 줄 모르는, 가차 없는

160 impulsive and passionate nature: 충동적이고 열정적인 성격을 지닌

161 contumely: (언어·태도의) 오만불손, 모욕, 모욕받음, 굴욕

162 wreak: (큰 피해 등을) 입히다[가하다]

burst from the multitude,—each man, each woman, each little shrill-voiced child, contributing their individual parts},— Hester Prynne might have repaid them all with a bitter and disdainful smile. But, under the leaden infliction[164] {which it was her doom to endure}, she felt, at moments, {as if she must needs shriek out with the full power of her lungs, and cast herself from the scaffold down upon the ground, or else go mad at once}.

Yet there were intervals when the whole scene, {in which she was the most conspicuous object}, seemed to vanish from her eyes, or, at least, glimmered indistinctly before them, like a mass of imperfectly shaped and spectral images. Her mind, and especially her memory, was preternaturally active, and kept bringing up other scenes [than this roughly hewn street of a little town, on the edge of the Western wilderness]; other faces [than were lowering upon her from beneath the brims of those steeple-crowned hats]. [Reminiscences], [the most trifling and immaterial, passages[165] of infancy and school-days], [sports], [childish quarrels], and [the little domestic traits of her maiden years], came swarming back upon her, intermingled with recollections of {whatever was gravest in

---

163 merriment: 유쾌하게 떠들썩함
164 infliction: (고통 · 벌 · 타격을) 가함[줌], 형벌, 고통, 시련
165 passage: 시간의 경과

her subsequent life}; one picture precisely as vivid as another; as if all were of similar importance, or all alike a play. Possibly, it was an instinctive device of her spirit to relieve itself, by the exhibition of these phantasmagoric[166] forms, from the cruel weight and hardness of the reality.

{Be that as it might}, the scaffold of the pillory was a point of view {that revealed to Hester Prynne the entire track along which she had been treading, since her happy infancy}. Standing on that miserable eminence, she saw again her native village, in Old England, and her paternal home; a decayed house of gray stone, with a poverty-stricken aspect, but retaining a half-obliterated shield of arms over the portal, in token of antique gentility. She saw her father's face, with its bold brow, and reverend white beard, {that flowed over the old-fashioned Elizabethan ruff[167]}; her mother's, too, with the look of heedful[168] and anxious[169] love {which it always wore in her remembrance}, and {which, even since her death, had so often laid the impediment[170] of a gentle remonstrance in her daughter's pathway}. She saw her own face, glowing with girlish beauty, and illuminating all the interior of the dusky

---

166 phantasmagoric: 환영 같은, 주마등같이 변하는
167 ruff: (특히 16~17세기 의류의) 주름 칼라[옷깃]
168 heedful: 세심한 주의를 기울이는
169 anxious: 불안해하는, 염려하는
170 impediment: 장애(물)

mirror {in which she had been wont to gaze at it}. There she beheld another countenance, of a man well stricken in years[171], a pale, thin, scholar-like visage, with eyes [dim and bleared[172] by the lamp-light that had served them to pore over many ponderous books]. Yet those same bleared optics[173] had a strange, penetrating power, when it was their owner's purpose to read the human soul. This figure of the study and the cloister[174], {as Hester Prynne's womanly[175] fancy failed not to recall}, was slightly deformed, with the left shoulder a trifle higher than the right. Next rose before her, in memory's picture-gallery, the intricate and narrow thoroughfares, the tall, gray houses, the huge cathedrals, and the public edifices, ancient in date and quaint in architecture, of a Continental city; {where a new life had awaited her, still in connection with the misshapen[176] scholar; a new life, but feeding itself on time-worn materials, like a tuft of green moss on a crumbling wall}. Lastly, [in lieu of[177] these shifting scenes], came back the rude market-place of the Puritan settlement, [with all the townspeople assembled and levelling their stern regards[178] at

---

171 stricken in years: 〈고어〉 연로한, 노령의. *stricken: 상처를 받은, 병에 걸린, 괴로워하는

172 blear: (눈물이나 염증으로) 흐린, 침침한, 그렇게 하다

173 optic: 〈고어〉 눈, 안구

174 cloister: 수도원 생활

175 womanly: 여성스러운. *이 대목은 '여성으로서의' 의미

176 misshapen: 모양이 정상이 아닌, 기형의

177 in lieu of: 대신에

Hester Prynne, — yes, at herself, — {who stood on the scaffold of the pillory, an infant on her arm, and the letter A, in scarlet, fantastically embroidered with gold thread, upon her bosom}]!

Could it be true? She clutched the child so fiercely to her breast, that it sent forth a cry; she turned her eyes downward at the scarlet letter, and even touched it with her finger, to assure herself {that the infant and the shame were real}. Yes! — these were her realities, — all else had vanished!

---

178 regard: 응시, 주목, 주시

The Scarlet Letter 3장

The Recognition[1]

From this intense consciousness of being the object of severe and universal observation, the wearer of the scarlet letter was at length relieved[2] by discerning, on the outskirts of the crowd, a figure {which irresistibly[3] took possession of her thoughts}. An Indian, in his native garb, was standing there; but the red men were not so infrequent visitors of the English settlements, that one of them would have attracted any notice from Hester Prynne, at such a time; much less[4] would he have excluded all other objects and ideas from her mind. By the Indian's side, and evidently sustaining[5] a companionship with him, stood a white man, clad in a strange disarray[6] of civilized and savage costume.

He was small in stature, with a furrowed visage, which, as yet, could hardly be termed aged. There was a remarkable intelligence in his features, as of a person {who had so cultivated his mental part that it[7] could not fail to[8] mould

---

1 recognition: 알아봄(이전에 보거나 듣거나 냄새를 맡아 본 경험 등으로 인해 알아보는 것) 'I am sorry I didn't realize you—you've had your hair cut!(×) realize → recognize. *realize: 어떤 사실이나 그 진정한 의미를 갑자기 깨달을 때

2 relieve: 없애(덜어) 주다, 구출하다

3 irresistibly: 저항할 수 없이

4 much less: 하물며(더구나) ~은 아니다

5 sustain: 유지하다, 지속하다, 인정하다

6 disarray: 혼란. *in a disarray: 혼란해져, 어지럽게 뒤섞여; total disarray: 완전 엉망진창

7 it: =his mental part

the physical to itself[9], and become manifest by unmistakable tokens[10]}. {Although, by a seemingly careless arrangement of his heterogeneous[11] garb, he had endeavoured to conceal or abate the peculiarity}, it was sufficiently evident to Hester Prynne, that one of this man's shoulders rose higher than the other. Again[12], [at the first instant of perceiving that thin visage, and the slight deformity of the figure,] she pressed her infant to her bosom, with so convulsive a force that the poor babe uttered another cry of pain. But the mother did not seem to hear it.

At his arrival in the market-place, and some time before she saw him, the stranger had bent[13] his eyes on Hester Prynne. It was carelessly, at first, like a man [chiefly accustomed to look inward], and [to whom external matters are of little value

---

8 not fail to: ~하지 않을 수 없다

9 mould the physical to itself: 육체적인 면을 자신[정신적인 면]에 맞춰 만들다

10 become manifest by unmistakable tokens: [정신적인 면이] 오해의 여지가 없는 상징들을 통해 눈으로 보아 알아볼 수 있을 정도로까지 분명해지다. *정신적인 면은 외형적인 것이 아니기에 금방 눈에 두드러지지 않으나 정신적인 면이 너무 강하다 보니 육체적인 면도 크게 영향을 받았고 눈에 두드러지는 특징들을 통해 정신적인 면이 겉으로 두드러졌다는 의미

11 heterogeneous: 여러 다른 종류들로 이뤄진

12 again: 뒤의 she pressed her infant 부분으로 연결하여 '다시 한 번 그녀는 아이를 끌어안았다~'로 해석

13 bend: (방향을) 틀다

and import, unless they bear relation to something within his mind]. Very soon, however, his look became keen and penetrative. A writhing horror twisted itself across his features, [like a snake] gliding swiftly over them, and making one little pause, with all its wreathed[14] intervolutions[15] in open sight[16]. His face darkened with some powerful emotion, {which, nevertheless, he so instantaneously controlled by an effort of his will, that, [save at a single moment], its expression might have passed for calmness}. After a brief space, the convulsion grew almost imperceptible, and finally subsided into the depths of his nature. {When he found the eyes of Hester Prynne fastened on his own, and saw that she appeared to recognize him}, he slowly and calmly raised his finger, made a gesture with it in the air, and laid it on his lips.

Then, touching the shoulder of a townsman {who stood near to him}, he addressed him in a formal and courteous manner.

"I pray you, good Sir," said he, "who is this woman? — and wherefore is she here set up to public shame?"

---

14 wreathe: 휘감듯 움직이다

15 intervolve: 서로 얽히게 하다, 한데 감기게 하다

16 in sight: 시야에. *There was no one in sight. 아무도 눈에 띄지 않았다.; At last we came in sight of a few houses. 마침내 우리 눈에 집 몇 채가 들어왔다.; The end is in sight. 끝이 눈에 보인다.

"You must needs[17] be a stranger in this region, friend," answered the townsman, looking curiously at the questioner and his savage companion; "else you would surely have heard of Mistress Hester Prynne, and her evil doings. She hath raised a great scandal, I promise you, in godly Master Dimmesdale's church."

"You say truly," replied the other. "I am a stranger, and have been a wanderer, sorely against my will. I have met with grievous[18] mishaps by sea and land, and have been long held in bonds among the heathen-folk, to the southward; and am now brought hither by this Indian, to be redeemed out of my captivity. Will it please you, therefore, to tell me of Hester Prynne's,—have I her name rightly?—of this woman's offences, and what has brought her to yonder scaffold?"

"Truly, friend, and methinks it must gladden your heart, after your troubles and sojourn[19] in the wilderness," said the townsman, "to find yourself, at length, in a land {where iniquity is searched out, and punished in the sight of rulers and people, as here in our godly New England}. Yonder woman, Sir, you must know, was the wife of a certain learned man,

---

17 needs: 필시
18 grievous: 통탄할, 극심한
19 sojourn: 체류

English by birth, but who had long dwelt in Amsterdam[20], {whence[21], some good time agone[22], he was minded[23] to cross over and cast in[24] his lot with us of the Massachusetts}. To this purpose, he sent his wife before him, remaining himself to look after some necessary affairs. Marry, good Sir[25], in some two years, or less, {that the woman has been a dweller here in Boston}, no tidings have come of this learned gentleman, Master Prynne; and his young wife, look you, being left to her own misguidance[26]... ."

"Ah!—aha!—I conceive you," said the stranger with a bitter smile. "So learned a man {as you speak of} should have learned this too in his books. And who, by your favor, Sir, may be the father of yonder babe—it is some three or four months old, I should judge—which Mistress Prynne is holding in her arms?"

---

20 Amsterdam: 박해를 받은 영국의 분리주의자(separatist)—순례자 (Pilgrim)들—와 청교도들(puritan)은 1608년경 네덜란드의 암스 테르담으로 도피해 있다가 1620년에 신대륙으로 항해했다.

21 whence: 그곳으로부터

22 agone(=ago): 전에

23 minded: ~하고 싶어 하는, ~할 의향이 있는

24 cast in: 준비하다, 사전에 계획하다. *cast himself in의 의미로 보 아서 '자신을 ~ 운명에 맡기다'의 뜻으로 파악할 수 있다.

25 Marry, good Sir: '아 그런데 말이죠 선생님' 정도의 의미

26 misguidance: 그릇된 지도

"Of a truth, friend, that matter remaineth a riddle; and the Daniel {who shall expound[27] it} is yet a-wanting," answered the townsman. "Madam Hester absolutely refuseth to speak, and the magistrates have laid their heads together in vain. Peradventure[28] the guilty one stands looking on at this sad spectacle, unknown of man[29], and forgetting that God sees him."

"The learned man," observed the stranger, with another smile, "should come himself to look into the mystery."

"It behooves[30] him well, if he be still in life," responded the townsman. "Now, good Sir, our Massachusetts magistracy[31], {bethinking themselves that this woman is youthful and fair, and doubtless was strongly tempted to her fall;—and that, moreover, as is most likely, her husband may be at the bottom of the sea};—they have not been bold to put in force the extremity of our righteous law against her. The penalty thereof[32] is death. But, in their great mercy and tenderness of heart, they have doomed Mistress Prynne to stand only a space

---

27 expound: 자세히 설명하다
28 peradventure: 아마, 혹시나
29 unknown of man: 알려지지 않은 사람
30 behoove: (사람에게) (~하는 것이) 의무이다, 마땅하다
31 magistracy: 치안판사들
32 thereof: 〈격식 또는 법률〉 (앞에 언급된) 그것의

of three hours on the platform of the pillory, and then and thereafter, for the remainder of her natural life, to wear a mark of shame upon her bosom."

"A wise sentence!" remarked the stranger, gravely bowing his head. "Thus she will be a living sermon against sin, until the ignominious letter be engraved upon her tombstone. It irks[33] me, nevertheless, that the partner of her iniquity should not, at least, stand on the scaffold by her side. But he will be known! — he will be known! — he will be known!"

He bowed courteously to the communicative[34] townsman, and, whispering a few words to his Indian attendant[35], they both made their way through the crowd.

While this passed, Hester Prynne had been standing on her pedestal, still with a fixed gaze towards the stranger; so fixed a gaze, that, at moments of intense absorption, all other objects in the visible world seemed to vanish, leaving only him and her. Such an interview[36], perhaps, would have been more terrible than even to meet him {as she now did}, with the hot,

---

33 irk: 〈격식 또는 문예체〉 짜증스럽게[귀찮게] 하다

34 communicative: (다른 사람들에게) 말을 잘 하는, 속을 잘 털어 놓는

35 attendant: 종업원, 수행원

36 such an interview: 단 둘만 만나는 것

midday sun burning down upon her face, and lighting up its shame; with the scarlet token of infamy on her breast; with the sin-born infant in her arms; with a whole people, drawn forth as to a festival, staring at the features[37] {that should have been seen only in the quiet gleam of the fireside, in the happy shadow of a home, or beneath a matronly veil, at church}. {Dreadful as it was}, she was conscious of a shelter in the presence of these thousand witnesses. It was better to stand thus, with so many betwixt him and her, than to greet him, face to face, they two alone. She fled for refuge, as it were, to the public exposure[38], and dreaded the moment {when its protection should be withdrawn from her}. Involved in these thoughts, she scarcely heard a voice behind her until it[39] had repeated her name more than once, in a loud and solemn tone, audible to the whole multitude.

"Hearken unto me, Hester Prynne!" said the voice.

It has already been noticed, that [directly over the platform {on which Hester Prynne stood}] was a kind of balcony, or open gallery, appended to the meeting-house. It was the place whence proclamations were wont to be made, amidst an

---

37 the features: 헤스터의 이목구비
38 exposure: 노출, 폭로
39 it: =the voice

assemblage of the magistracy, with all the ceremonial[40] {that attended such public observances[41] in those days}. Here, to witness the scene {which we are describing}, sat Governor Bellingham[42] himself, with four sergeants[43] about his chair, bearing halberds[44], as a guard of honor[45]. He wore a dark feather in his hat, a border of embroidery on his cloak[46], and a black velvet tunic[47] beneath; a gentleman advanced in years, and with a hard experience written in his wrinkles. He was not ill fitted to be the head and representative of a community, {which owed its origin and progress, and its present state of development, not to the impulses of youth, but to the stern and tempered[48] energies of manhood, and the sombre[49] sagacity[50] of age; accomplishing so much, precisely because it imagined and hoped so little}. The other eminent

---

40 ceremonial: 의식절차

41 observance: 준수, (종교·전통) 의식

42 Richard Bellingham(1592~1672). 영국 링컨셔 출신의 변호사로 1634년에 식민지의 보스턴에 와서 매사추세츠 식민지 총독을 1641, 1654, 1665~1672 기간 동안 여러 차례 지냈다.

43 sergeant: 하사관

44 halberd: 미늘창(도끼와 창을 결합시킨 형태의 옛날 무기)

45 guard of honor: 의장병

46 cloak: 망토

47 tunic: 튜닉(고대 그리스나 로마인들이 입던, 소매가 없고 무릎까지 내려오는 헐렁한 웃옷). *tunic dress: 여성용의 짧고 심플한 드레스

48 tempered: 단련된

49 sombre: 칙칙한

50 sagacity: 총명, 기민

characters, {by whom the chief ruler[51] was surrounded}, were distinguished by a dignity of mien, belonging to a period {when the forms of authority were felt to possess the sacredness of divine institutions}. They were, doubtless, good men, just, and sage. But, out of the whole human family, it would not have been easy to select the same number of wise and virtuous persons[52], {who should be less capable of sitting in judgment on an erring woman's heart, and disentangling its mesh[53] of good and evil, than the sages of rigid aspect [towards whom Hester Prynne now turned her face]}. She seemed conscious, indeed, that {whatever sympathy she might expect} lay in the larger and warmer heart of the multitude; for, as she lifted her eyes towards the balcony, the unhappy woman grew pale and trembled.

The voice {which had called her attention} was that of the reverend and famous John Wilson[54], the eldest clergyman of ★ MP3
3장 (2)
시작

---

51 the chief ruler: = Bellingham

52 다음과 같은 면에서는 능력이 부족한 사람들을 이렇게 한자리에 모아 놓기도 쉽지 않을 것이라는 의미

53 mesh: 그물망(같이 복잡하고 어려운 상황)

54 John Wilson(1588~1667). 매사추세츠 베이 식민지의 첫 정착민들 중 하나로, 1638년에 앤 허치슨(Anne Hutchinson)이 추방되기 직전에 그녀를 이교도로 낙인찍어 파문한 인물. 리처드 벨링햄(Richard Bellingham)의 총독 임기가 1642년 5월에 끝나므로 이 작품의 스토리가 시작되는 6월은 벨링햄 이후의 존 윈스롭(John Winthrop)이 총독으로 설정되어 있어야 하지만 여전히 벨링햄이 총독으로 재임하면서 헤스터의 죄를 단죄하는 입장에 세운 상황

Boston, a great scholar, like most of his contemporaries in the profession, and withal a man of kind and genial spirit. This last attribute, however, had been less carefully developed than his intellectual gifts, and was, in truth, rather a matter of shame than self-congratulation with him. There he stood, with a border of grizzled locks beneath his skull-cap[55]; while his gray eyes, accustomed to the shaded[56] light of his study, were winking, like those of Hester's infant, in the unadulterated[57] sunshine. He looked like the darkly engraved portraits which we see prefixed[58] to old volumes of sermons; and had no more right than one of those portraits would have, to step forth, as he now did, and meddle with[59] a question of human guilt,

---

설정은 아이러니하다. 왜냐하면 역사적 기록으로 볼 때 바로 6월에 벨링햄 자신이 '부적절한 행동'—자기 집에 거주하는 친구와 이미 결혼 약속을 한 여성인 페닐플 펠햄(Penelple Pelham)을 '뺏어서' 결혼해 버린 행동—으로 고소된 상태였기 때문이다. 벨링햄이 내세운 정당화는 '자신의 애정이 강하고 그녀가 다른 신사에게 완전히 약속한 상태가 아니다'라는 것이었는데, 이런 이유를 내세우자면 헤스터도 못할 게 없다. 물론 호손은 작중의 몇몇 인물이 헤스터에게 판결을 내릴 자격이 있느냐 없느냐 자체에 큰 관심을 두고 있기보다는 청교도 사회 자체가 인간의 자연스러운 감정을 어떤 방식으로 왜곡하고 억누르는가, 이런 상황에서 헤스터의 사랑과 저항이 어떤 의미를 지니는가에 더 큰 관심을 두고 있다고 봐야 한다.

55 skull-cap: 스컬캡, 테두리 없는 베레모(특히 유대인 남성 · 가톨릭 주교가 쓰는 모자)

56 shaded: 그늘진

57 unadulterated: 완전한, 섞이지 않은

58 prefix: 앞에 붙이다

59 meddle with: 관여하다

passion, and anguish.

"Hester Prynne," said the clergyman, "I have striven with my young brother here, under whose preaching of the word[60] you have been privileged[61] to sit,"—here Mr. Wilson laid his hand on the shoulder of a pale young man beside him,—"I have sought, I say, to persuade this godly youth, that he should deal with you, here in the face of Heaven[62], and before these wise and upright[63] rulers, and in hearing of all the people, as touching the vileness[64] and blackness[65] of your sin. Knowing your natural temper better than I, he could the better judge what arguments to use, whether of tenderness or terror, such as might prevail over your hardness and obstinacy; insomuch that[66] you should no longer hide the name of him {who tempted you to this grievous[67] fall}. But he opposes to me, (with a young man's over-softness, albeit wise beyond his years,)

---

60 the word: 하느님 말씀의 설교, 성경의 가르침

61 privileged: 특권을 가진

62 in the face of Heaven: 하늘의 정면으로 마주해, 하늘이 바로 보는 앞에서

63 upright: 강직한

64 vileness: 몹시 나쁨, 비도덕, 비열함

65 blackness: 흉악, 음흉

66 insomuch that ...: ~라는 점에서. *윌슨을 비롯한 여타 지도층의 지배적인 태도는 헤스터로 하여금 그 상대의 이름을 밝히도록 한다는 것이며 이를 위해 딤즈데일이 적절한 언변을 구사할 것이라고 보았다.

67 grievous: 통탄할[극심한]

that it were wronging the very nature of woman to force her to lay open her heart's secrets in such broad daylight, and in presence of so great a multitude. Truly, as I sought to convince him, the shame lay in the commission[68] of the sin, and not in the showing of it forth. What say you to it, once again, brother Dimmesdale? Must it be thou or I that shall deal with this poor sinner's soul?"

There was a murmur among the dignified and reverend occupants of the balcony; and Governor Bellingham gave expression to its purport, speaking in an authoritative voice, although tempered[69] with respect towards the youthful clergyman whom he addressed.

"Good Master Dimmesdale," said he, "the responsibility of this woman's soul lies greatly with you. It behooves you, therefore, to exhort her to repentance, and to confession, as a proof and consequence thereof[70]."

The directness of this appeal drew the eyes of the whole crowd upon the Reverend Mr. Dimmesdale; a young clergyman, who had come from one of the great English universities, bringing all the learning of the age into our wild

---

68 commission: 위원회, 수수료, 의뢰, 범함, 저지름
69 temper: 완화하다, 조절하다
70 thereof: 그것의

forest-land[71]. His eloquence and religious fervor had already given the earnest[72] of high eminence[73] in his profession. He was a person of very striking[74] aspect, with a white, lofty, and impending[75] brow, large, brown, melancholy eyes, and a mouth which, unless when he forcibly compressed it, was apt to be tremulous, expressing both nervous sensibility and a vast power of self-restraint. Notwithstanding[76] his high native gifts and scholar-like attainments, there was an air about this young minister, — an apprehensive[77], a startled, a half-frightened look, — as of a being {who felt himself quite astray and at a loss in the pathway of human existence, and could only be at ease in some seclusion of his own}. Therefore, so far as his duties would permit, he trode in the shadowy by-paths[78], and thus kept himself simple and childlike; coming forth, when occasion was[79], with a freshness, and fragrance, and dewy purity of thought, which, as many people said, affected them like the speech of an angel.

---

71 forest-land: 삼림지

72 earnest: 성실한, 진심 어린

73 eminence: (특히 전문 분야에서의) 명성

74 striking: 눈에 띄는, 두드러진

75 impend: (위험 · 파멸 등이) 임박하다, 절박하다, 머리 위에 걸리다, 드리워지다

76 notwithstanding: ～에도 불구하고

77 apprehensive: 불안한

78 by-path: 옆길, 샛길

79 when occasion was: 때가 되면

Such was the young man whom the Reverend Mr. Wilson and the Governor had introduced so openly to the public notice[80], bidding him speak, in the hearing of all men, to that mystery of a woman's soul, so sacred even in its pollution. The trying[81] nature of his position drove the blood from his cheek, and made his lips tremulous.

"Speak to the woman, my brother," said Mr. Wilson. "It is of moment to her soul, and therefore, as the worshipful Governor says, momentous to thine own, in whose charge hers[82] is. Exhort her to confess the truth!"

The Reverend Mr. Dimmesdale bent his head, in silent prayer, {as it seemed}, and then came forward.

"Hester Prynne," said he, leaning over the balcony, and looking down steadfastly[83] into her eyes, "thou hearest {what this good man says}, and seest the accountability {under which I labor}. If thou feelest it[84] to be for thy soul's peace, and {that thy earthly punishment will thereby be made more effectual to salvation}, I charge thee to speak out the name of thy fellow-

---

80 public notice: 공고, 대중의 이목
81 trying: 괴로운, 난감한
82 hers: =her soul
83 steadfastly: 확고부동하게, 고정되게, 불변으로
84 it: 뒤의 to speak out ... 부분

sinner and fellow-sufferer! Be not silent from any mistaken[85] pity and tenderness for him; for, believe me, Hester, though he were to step down from a high place, and stand there beside thee, on thy pedestal of shame, yet better were it so, than to hide a guilty heart through life. What can thy silence do for him, except it tempt him — yea, compel him, as it were — to add hypocrisy to sin? Heaven hath granted thee an open ignominy, that thereby thou mayest work out an open triumph over [the evil within thee, and the sorrow without]. Take heed how thou deniest to him — {who, perchance, hath not the courage to grasp it for himself} — the bitter, but wholesome, cup {that is now presented to thy lips}!"

The young pastor's voice was tremulously sweet, rich, deep, and broken[86]. The feeling {that it[87] so evidently manifested}, rather than the direct purport of the words, caused it to vibrate within all hearts, and brought the listeners into one accord of sympathy. Even the poor baby, at Hester's bosom, was affected by the same influence; for it directed its hitherto vacant gaze towards Mr. Dimmesdale, and held up its little arms, with a half pleased, half plaintive[88] murmur. So powerful seemed the minister's appeal, that the people could not believe but

---

85 mistaken: 잘못 알고[판단하고] 있는
86 broken: 연속되지 못한, 계속적이지 못한, 끊어지는
87 it: = the voice
88 plaintive: 애처로운, 애달픈

that Hester Prynne would speak out the guilty name; or else that the guilty one himself, {in whatever high or lowly place he stood}, would be drawn forth by an inward and inevitable necessity, and compelled to ascend the scaffold.

Hester shook her head.

"Woman, transgress not beyond the limits of Heaven's mercy!" cried the Reverend Mr. Wilson, more harshly than before. "That little babe hath been gifted with a voice, to second and confirm the counsel[89] {which thou hast heard}. Speak out the name! That, and thy repentance, may avail[90] to take the scarlet letter off thy breast."

"Never!" replied Hester Prynne, looking, not at Mr. Wilson, but into the deep and troubled[91] eyes of the younger clergy-man. "It is too deeply branded. Ye cannot take it off. And would that[92] I might endure his agony, as well as mine!"

"Speak, woman!" said another voice, coldly and sternly, proceeding from the crowd about the scaffold. "Speak; and give your child a father[93]!"

---

89 counsel: 조언, 충고
90 avail: 도움이 되다, 소용에 닿다
91 troubled: 걱정하는, 불안해하는
92 would that: 원컨대

"I will not speak!" answered Hester, turning pale as death[94], but responding to this voice, which she too surely recognized. "And my child must seek a heavenly Father; she shall never know an earthly one!"

"She will not speak![95]" murmured Mr. Dimmesdale, who, leaning over the balcony, with his hand upon his heart, had awaited the result of his appeal. He now drew back, with a long respiration[96]. "Wondrous strength and generosity of a woman's heart! She will not speak!"

Discerning the impracticable[97] state of the poor culprit's mind, the elder clergyman, who had carefully prepared himself for the occasion, addressed to the multitude a discourse on sin, in all its branches, but with continual reference to the ignominious letter. So forcibly did he dwell upon[98] this symbol, for the hour or more during which his periods[99] were rolling[100]

---

93 give your child a father: 아이에게 아버지의 이름을 말해 주다. ＊Give me your name and address. 당신의 이름과 주소를 말해 주세요.; Give me a job. 나에게 일을 제공해 주세요.; Give them a drink. 그들에게 마실 것을 갖다 주세요.

94 pale as death: 죽은 사람처럼 창백한

95 She will not speak!: 그녀는 말하지 않을 거예요!

96 respiration: 호흡

97 impracticable: 실행[실현]이 불가능한

98 dwell upon(＝dwell on): 곱씹다

99 period: 기간, 주기, 순환. ＊periods: 문장, 명문, 미문

100 roll: 구르다, 밀어 펴다, 돌아가다, 작동하다

over the people's heads, that it assumed new terrors in their imagination, and seemed to derive its scarlet hue from the flames of the infernal pit. Hester Prynne, meanwhile, kept her place upon the pedestal of shame, with glazed[101] eyes, and an air of weary indifference. She had borne, that morning, all that nature could endure; and {as her temperament was not of the order[102] [that escapes from too intense suffering by a swoon], her spirit could only shelter itself beneath a stony crust of insensibility, {while the faculties of animal life remained entire}. In this state, the voice of the preacher thundered remorselessly[103], but unavailingly, upon her ears. The infant, during the latter portion of her ordeal, pierced the air with its wailings and screams; she strove to hush it, mechanically, but seemed scarcely to sympathize with its trouble. With the same hard demeanour, she was led back to prison, and vanished from the public gaze within its iron-clamped portal. It was whispered, [by those {who peered[104] after her}], {that the scarlet letter threw a lurid[105] gleam along the dark passage-way[106] of the interior}.

---

101 glazed: 멀건, 멍한

102 order: 종류

103 remorselessly: 끝날 줄을 모르는, 갈수록 심해지는 듯한, 무자비한, 가차 없는

104 peer: 자세히 들여다보다, 응시하다, 주의해서 보다(into, at)

105 lurid: 타는 듯이 밝게 빛나는, 무서운, 섬뜩한

106 passage-way: 복도, 통로

The Scarlet Letter **4장**

The Interview[1]

2

After her return to the prison, Hester Prynne was found to be in a state of nervous[2] excitement {that demanded constant watchfulness, [lest she should perpetrate violence on herself[3], or do some half-frenzied[4] mischief to the poor babe[5]]}. {As night approached}, [it proving impossible to quell her insubordination[6] by rebuke[7] or threats of punishment], Master Brackett, the jailer, thought fit to introduce a physician. He described him as a man of skill[8] in all Christian modes of physical science, and likewise familiar with whatever the savage people could teach, in respect to medicinal herbs and roots {that grew in the forest}. To say the truth, there was much need of professional assistance, not merely for Hester herself, but still more urgently for the child; {who, [drawing its sustenance from the maternal bosom[9]], seemed to have drank in with it all

---

1 interview: 면담, 면회

2 nervous: 신경과민의, 불안해하는

3 lest she should perpetrate violence on herself: 그녀 스스로를 자해하지 않도록. ＊perpetrate: (범행·과실·악행을) 저지르다, 자행하다

4 frenzied: 광분한, 광란한

5 or do some half-frenzied mischief to the poor babe: 혹은 반쯤 미친 상태로 그 가엾은 아이에게 해를 끼칠지. ＊do mischief: 해를 끼치다

6 it proving impossible to quell her insubordination: 그녀의 불복종을 가라앉히는 것이 불가능함이 드러나자. ＊quell: 평정하다, 가라앉다; insubordination: 불복종, 반항

7 rebuke: 힐책, 질책

8 a man of skill: 명인. 여기서는 의술가를 의미한다.

9 drawing its sustenance from the maternal bosom: 어머니의 가슴

the turmoil[10], the anguish, and despair, [which pervaded[11] the mother's system[12]]}. It now writhed in convulsions[13] of pain, and was a forcible[14] type, in its little frame, of the moral agony which Hester Prynne had borne throughout the day.

Closely following the jailer into the dismal apartment, appeared that individual, of singular aspect, {whose presence in the crowd had been of such deep interest to the wearer of the scarlet letter}. He was lodged[15] in the prison, not as suspected of any offence[16], but as the most convenient and suitable mode of disposing of him, {until the magistrates should have conferred with the Indian sagamores[17] respecting his ransom[18]}. His name was announced as Roger Chillingworth. The jailer, after ushering him into the room, remained a

---

에서 자양분을 먹는(젖을 빠는). *sustenance: 생명을 건강하게 유지시켜 주는 것, 자양물; maternal: 어머니의, 모성의

10 turmoil: 혼란, 소란

11 pervade: 만연하다, 스며들다

12 system: 몸

13 convulsion: 경련, 경기

14 forcible: 물리력에 의한, 강제적인, 강력한

15 lodge: 셋방을 얻다, ~를 재워 주다[머무르게 해 주다]

16 not as suspected of any offence: 어떤 범죄 혐의가 있어서가 아니라

17 sagamore: 추장(= sachem)

18 until the magistrates should have conferred with the Indian sagamores respecting his ransom: 그의 몸값에 대하여 관리들과 인디언 추장과 협의를 끝낼 때까지. *confer with: 협의하다; Indian sagamores: 인디언 추장; ransom: 몸값, 몸값을 지불하다

moment, marvelling at[19] the comparative quiet {that followed his entrance[20]}; for Hester Prynne had immediately become as still as death[21], {although the child continued to moan}.

"Prithee[22], friend, leave me alone with my patient," said the practitioner[23]. "Trust me, good jailer, you shall briefly have peace in your house; and, I promise you, Mistress Prynne shall hereafter[24] be more amenable to[25] just authority {than you may have found her heretofore[26]}."

"Nay, if your worship[27] can accomplish that," answered Master Brackett, "I shall own[28] you for a man of skill indeed! Verily, the woman hath been like a possessed one[29]; and there lacks little[30], {that I should take in hand[31] to drive Satan out of

---

19 marvel at ...: ~에 깜짝 놀라다

20 the comparative quiet that followed his entrance: 그의 입장으로 상대적으로 조용해진. *comparative: 상대적인, 비교적

21 as still as death: 죽은 듯 조용해진

22 prithee: 부디, 제발

23 practitioner: (전문직 종사자, 특히) 의사, 변호사

24 hereafter: 이후로, 장차

25 amenable to ...: 말을 잘 듣는, ~을 잘 받아들이는

26 heretofore: 예전에

27 your worship: 각하(시장, 고관을 호칭할 때의 경칭)

28 own: 소유하다, 인정하다

29 like a possessed one: 악령에 홀린 사람 같은. *possessed: (사람이나 마음이 악령에) 홀린

30 there lacks little: 부족한 게 거의 없다, 할 수 있는 게 많다, 모든 것이라도 할 수 있다

her with stripes[32]}."

The stranger had entered the room with the characteristic quietude of the profession {to which he announced himself as belonging}. Nor did his demeanour change, {when the withdrawal[33] of the prison-keeper left him face to face with the woman, [whose absorbed notice of him[34], in the crowd, had intimated[35] so close a relation between himself and her]}. His first care was given to the child; {whose cries, indeed, [as she lay writhing on the trundle-bed[36]], made it of peremptory[37] necessity to postpone all other business to the task of soothing her}. He examined the infant carefully, and then proceeded to unclasp[38] a leathern case, {which he took from beneath his dress}. It appeared to contain certain medical preparations[39],

---

31 take in hand: 떠맡다, 착수하다, 처리하다

32 to drive Satan out of her with stripes: 채찍으로 때려서 마귀를 몰아내는 것. *there … with stripes: 채찍으로 때려서라도 그녀로부터 악마를 몰아내기 위해서 일을 착수해야 한다면, 모든 것이라도 할 수 있다

33 withdrawal: 철수

34 whose absorbed notice of him: 그녀가 골똘히 쳐다보았던 그 사나이

35 intimate: 암시하다

36 trundle-bed(=truckle bed): 바퀴 달린 침대. *trundle: (천천히 시끄러운 소리를 내며) 굴러가다[굴리다, (굴려서) 나르다]

37 peremptory: 위압적인, 독단적인

38 unclasp: 걸쇠를 벗기다

39 preparation: (약·화장품 등으로 사용하기 위한) 조제용 물질. *medical preparations: 조합약제

{one of which he mingled with a cup of water}.

"My old studies in alchemy[40]," observed he, "and my sojourn, for above a year past, [among a people well versed[41] in the kindly[42] properties of simples[43]], have made a better physician of me {than many [that claim the medical degree]}. Here[44], woman! The child is yours, — she is none of mine, — neither will she recognize my voice or aspect as a father's. Administer[45] this draught[46], therefore, with thine own hand."

Hester repelled[47] the offered medicine, at the same time gazing with strongly marked apprehension[48] into his face.

"Wouldst thou avenge thyself on the innocent babe?" whispered she.

---

40 alchemy: 중세와 근세 초 'chemistry'의 의미로 쓰였는데 '만능용
   매'(universal solvent)와 '만병통치약'을 찾는 일과 함께 천한 금속
   으로 금을 만드는 것이 주요 목표였다.
41 versed: 정통한, 조예가 깊은
42 kindly: 친절한, 관대한, 온화한, ~에 알맞은, 자연의, 천연의, 타
   고난
43 simple: 〈명사〉 바보, 속기 쉬운 사람, 약초(로 만든 약)
44 here: 자, 여기 있어
45 administer: 약을 투여하다
46 draught: 물약
47 repell: 물리치다
48 apprehension: 우려, 불안

"Foolish woman!" responded the physician, half coldly, half soothingly. "What should ail[49] me to harm this misbegotten[50] and miserable babe? The medicine is potent for good[51]; and were it my child, — yea, mine own, as well as thine! — I could do no better for it."

{As she still hesitated, being, in fact, in no reasonable state of mind}, he took the infant in his arms, and himself administered the draught. It soon proved its efficacy[52], and redeemed the leech's pledge[53]. The moans of the little patient subsided[54]; its convulsive tossings[55] gradually ceased; and in a few moments, {as is the custom of young children after relief from pain}, it sank into a profound[56] and dewy slumber[57]. The physician, {as he had a fair right to be termed}, next

---

49 ail: 괴롭히다, 아프게 하다.

50 misbegotten: 불운한 태생의, 서출의, 사생아의

51 potent for good: 효능이 좋은. *potent: (사람의 심신에 미치는 영향이) 강한[강력한]

52 efficacy: (약이나 치료의) 효험

53 redeemed the leech's pledge: 의사의 (효험이 있을 것이라는) 장담이 증명되었다. *redeem a pledge: 서약, 약속을 지키다; leech 에는 '거머리'와 '의사'의 뜻이 있는데 서로 어원이 다름. '의사' 의 경우 어원상 one who speaks magic words, healer, one who counsels 등의 의미

54 subside: 가라앉다, 진정되다

55 toss: 뒤척이다

56 profound: 깊은

57 slumber: 잠, 수면

bestowed his attention on the mother. With calm and intent scrutiny, he felt her pulse, looked into her eyes, — a gaze {that made her heart shrink and shudder, because so familiar, and yet so strange and cold} — and, finally, [satisfied with his investigation], proceeded to[58] mingle another draught.

"I know not Lethe[59] nor Nepenthe[60]," remarked he; "but I have learned many new secrets in the wilderness, and here is one of them, — a recipe {that an Indian taught me, [in requital of[61] some lessons of my own, that were as old as Paracelsus[62]]}. Drink it! It may be less soothing than a sinless conscience. [That] I cannot give thee. But it will calm the swell and heaving of thy passion, like oil thrown on the waves of a tempestuous[63] sea."

He presented the cup to Hester, {who received it with a slow, earnest[64] look into his face; [not precisely a look of fear, yet full of doubt and questioning, as to what his purposes might be]}. She looked also at her slumbering child.

---

58 proceeded to: 시작하다, 향하다, 나아가다, ~에 이르다

59 Lethe: 망각의 강, 레테

60 Nepenthe: 시름을 잊게 하는 약, 망각의 약

61 in requital of : 보답으로, 보상으로

62 Paracelsus: 파라셀수스. *스위스의 의학자이자 연금술사

63 tempestuous: 폭풍이 치는. *요동치는 바다에 떨어진 기름은 밑으로 가라앉거나 물과 섞이지 않고 그대로 표면 위에 떠서 요동친다. 그렇듯이, 감정이 요동치는 상태를 묘사한다.

64 earnest: 진심 어린

"I have thought of death," said she, — "have wished for it, — would even have prayed for it, {were it fit that such as I should pray for any thing}. Yet, {if death be in this cup}, I bid thee think again, {ere thou beholdest[65] me quaff[66] it}. See! It is even now at my lips."

"Drink, then," replied he, still with the same cold composure. "Dost thou know me so little, Hester Prynne? Are my purposes wont to be so shallow[67]? {Even if I imagine a scheme of vengeance[68]}, what could I do better for my object than to let thee live, — than to give thee medicines against all harm and peril of life, — so that this burning shame may still blaze upon thy bosom?" — {As he spoke}, he laid his long forefinger[69] on the scarlet letter, {which forthwith[70] seemed to scorch[71] into Hester's breast, as if it had been red-hot[72]}. He noticed her involuntary[73] gesture, and smiled. — "Live, therefore, and bear[74] about thy doom with thee, in the eyes of men

---

65 beholdest: 〈고어〉 behold의 2인칭 단수 현재 시제
66 quaff: 벌컥벌컥 마시다
67 shallow: (생각)이 얕팍한, 얕은
68 vengeance: 복수
69 forefinger: 집게손가락, 검지
70 forthwith: 곧, 당장
71 scorch: 태우다, 그슬리다
72 red-hot: 새빨갛게 단
73 involuntary: 자기도 모르게 하는, 무심결에
74 bear: 견디다, 짐을 지다, 지고 다니다

and women,—in the eyes of him {whom thou didst call thy husband},—in the eyes of yonder[75] child! And, that thou mayest live, take off[76] this draught."

Without further expostulation[77] or delay, Hester Prynne drained[78] the cup, and, at the motion of the man of skill[79], seated herself on the bed {where the child was sleeping}; while he drew the only chair {which the room afforded}, and took his own seat beside her. She could not but[80] tremble at these preparations[81]; for she felt that—[having now done all {that humanity, or principle, or, if so it were, a refined[82] cruelty[83], impelled him to do, for the relief of physical suffering}]—he was next to treat with her as the man {whom she had most deeply and irreparably[84] injured}.

MP3 ★
4장 [2]
시작
"Hester," said he, "I ask not {wherefore, nor how, thou hast

---

75 yonder: 저기 있는

76 take off: 삼키다

77 expostulation: 충고, 충언

78 drain: 액체를 서서히 배출하다, 배수설비를 하다. *drain a house: 집에 배수 설비를 하다; be well[badly] drained: 배수 설비가 좋다 [나쁘다], 잔을 비우다

79 a man of skill: 명인

80 could not but ...: ~하지 않을 수 없다

81 preparation: 준비[하는 행위, 과정]

82 refined: 정제된

83 cruelty: 잔인함

84 irreparably: 회복할 수 없게

fallen into the pit, or say rather, thou hast ascended to the pedestal of infamy, [on which I found thee]}. The reason is not far to seek. It was my folly, and thy weakness. I,—[a man of thought,—the book-worm of great libraries,—a man already in decay, having given my best years to feed the hungry dream of knowledge],—what had I to do with youth and beauty like thine own! Misshapen[85] from my birth-hour, how could I delude myself with the idea {that intellectual gifts might veil physical deformity[86] in a young girl's fantasy}! Men call me wise.[87] {If sages were ever wise in their own behoof[88]}, I might have foreseen all this. I might have known {that, [as I came out of the vast and dismal forest, and entered this settlement of Christian men], the very first object [to meet my eyes] would be thyself, Hester Prynne, [standing up, a statue of ignominy, before the people]}. Nay, from the moment {when we came down the old church-steps together, a married pair}, I might have beheld the bale-fire[89] of that scarlet letter [blazing at the end of our path]!"

   "Thou knowest," said Hester,—for, {depressed as she was},

---

85 misshapen: 기형의(=deformed)

86 deformity: 기형

87 Men call me wise: 사람들은 나를 현명하다 하오. ＊세상에서의 평
    판과 달리 자신의 운명에서 한치 앞을 내다보지 못했음을 자조하
    고 있다고 볼 수 있다.

88 behoof: 이익

89 bale-fire: 큰 화톳불, 봉화

she could not endure this last quiet stab[90] at the token of her shame,—"thou knowest {that I was frank with thee}. I felt no love, nor feigned[91] any."

"True!" replied he. "It was my folly! I have said it. But, up to that epoch[92] of my life, I had lived in vain. The world had been so cheerless[93]! My heart was a habitation[94] large enough for many guests[95], but lonely and chill, and without a household fire. I longed to kindle one! It seemed not so wild a dream,—{old as I was, and sombre[96] as I was, and misshapen as I was},—that the simple bliss, {which is scattered far and wide, for all mankind to gather up}, might yet be mine. And so, Hester, I drew thee into my heart, into its innermost[97] chamber, and sought to warm thee by the warmth {which thy presence made there}!"

"I have greatly wronged[98] thee," murmured Hester.

---

90 stab: 찌름, 찌르는 듯한 통증
91 feign: 가장하다, 꾸미다
92 epoch: 시대
93 cheerless: 생기 없는, 칙칙한
94 habitation: 거주, 주거
95 My heart was a habitation large enough for many guests: 내 가슴은 많은 손님을 맞아들일 만큼 넉넉하다
96 sombre: 침울한, 칙칙한
97 innermost: 가장 내밀한, 가장 깊은
98 wrong: 부당하게 취급하다, 모욕을 주다

"We have wronged each other," answered he. "Mine was the first wrong, {when I betrayed thy budding youth into a false and unnatural relation with my decay}. Therefore, as a man {who has not thought and philosophized in vain}, I seek no vengeance, plot[99] no evil against thee. Between thee and me, the scale[100] hangs fairly balanced. But, Hester, the man lives {who has wronged us both}! Who is he?"

"Ask me not!" replied Hester Prynne, looking firmly into his face. "[That] thou shalt never know!"

"Never, sayest thou?" rejoined[101] he, with a smile of dark and self-relying intelligence[102]. "Never know him! Believe me, Hester, there are few things, — {whether in the outward world, or, to a certain depth, in the invisible sphere of thought}, — few things hidden from the man, {who devotes[103] himself earnestly and unreservedly[104] to the solution of a mystery}. Thou mayest cover up thy secret from the prying[105] multitude. Thou mayest conceal it, too, from the ministers and magistrates, {even as

---

99 plot: 음모, 음모를 꾸미다, 계획하다
100 scale: 저울
101 rejoin: 응수하다
102 intelligence: 지력, 예지, 첩보
103 devote: 바치다, 쏟다, 기울이다
104 unreservedly: 조금도 거리낌 없이
105 prying: 비밀을 캐묻는

thou didst this day}, {when they sought to wrench[106] the name out of thy heart, and give thee a partner on thy pedestal}. But, as for me, I come to the inquest[107] with other senses than they possess. I shall seek this man, {as I have sought truth in books}; {as I have sought gold in alchemy[108]}. There is a sympathy {that will make me conscious of him}. I shall see him tremble. I shall feel myself shudder, suddenly and unawares. Sooner or later, he must needs be mine!"

The eyes of the wrinkled scholar glowed[109] so intensely upon her, {that Hester Prynne clasped her hands[110] over her heart, [dreading lest he should read the secret there at once]}.

"Thou wilt not reveal his name? Not the less[111] he is mine," resumed he, with a look of confidence, {as if destiny[112] were at one with him}. "He bears no letter of infamy [wrought into his garment], {as thou dost}; but I shall read it on his heart. Yet fear not for him! Think not {that I shall interfere with[113]

---

106 wrench: 비틀어 떼어 내다, 끄집어내다
107 inquest: 조사, 규명
108 alchemy: 연금술
109 glow: 빛나다, 빨갛게 타오르다
110 clasped her hands = grab, grasp one's hand: 손을 꼭 잡다
111 not the less(=none the less=no less): 그래도 역시, 그럼에도 불구하고
112 destiny: 운명
113 interfere with: 간섭하다, 참견하다

Heaven's own method of retribution[114], or, [to my own loss], betray him to the gripe[115] of human law}. Neither do thou imagine {that I shall contrive[116] aught[117] against his life; no, nor against his fame}, {if, [as I judge], he be a man of fair repute[118]}. Let him live! Let him hide himself in outward[119] honor, if he may! Not the less he shall be mine!"

"Thy acts are like mercy," said Hester, bewildered and appalled[120]. "But thy words interpret thee as a terror!"

"One thing, thou {that wast my wife}, I would enjoin[121] upon thee," continued the scholar. "Thou hast kept the secret of thy paramour[122]. Keep, likewise, mine! There are none in this land {that know me}. Breathe[123] not, to any human soul, {that thou didst ever call me husband}! Here, on this wild outskirt of the earth, I shall pitch[124] my tent; for, [elsewhere

---

114 retribution: 응징, 징벌
115 gripe(=grip): 통제, 지배
116 contrive: 고안하다, 꾸미다
117 aught: 어떤 것
118 repute: 명성, 평판
119 outward: 표면상의, 겉보기의, 외형의
120 appalled: 섬뜩한, 소름끼치는
121 enjoin: 명하다, 이르다
122 paramour: 정부(情夫), 애인
123 breathe: 나직이[속삭이듯] 말하다
124 pitch: (땅에) 처박다, (말뚝을) 두드려 박다, (천막을) 치다, (캠프를) 설치하다. *〈반대어〉 strike

a wanderer, and isolated from human interests], I find here a woman, a man, a child, {amongst whom and myself there exist the closest ligaments[125]}. {No matter whether of love or hate}; {no matter whether of right or wrong}! Thou and thine, Hester Prynne, belong to me. My home is {where thou art}, and {where he is}. But betray[126] me not!"

"Wherefore dost thou desire it?" inquired Hester, [shrinking, she hardly knew why, from this secret bond]. "Why not announce thyself openly, and cast me off[127] at once?"

"It may be," he replied, "because I will not encounter the dishonor {that besmirches[128] the husband of a faithless woman}. It may be for other reasons. Enough, it is my purpose to live and die unknown. Let, therefore, thy husband be to the world as one already dead, and {of whom no tidings shall ever come}. Recognize me not, by word, by sign, by look! Breathe not the secret, above all[129], to the man {thou wottest[130] of}. Shouldst thou fail me in this, beware! His fame, his position, his life, will be in my hands. Beware!"

---

125 ligaments: 유대, 단결력
126 betray: (적에게 정보를) 넘겨주다[팔아먹다], (정보·감정 등을) 무심코 노출시키다[드러내다]
127 cast off: 벗어 던져 버리다
128 besmirch: (평판) 등을 더럽히다
129 above all: 무엇보다, 특히
130 wottest: wit[알다, 알고 있다]의 2인칭 단수 현재형

"I will keep thy secret, as I have his," said Hester.

"Swear it!" rejoined he.

And she took the oath.

"And now, Mistress Prynne," said old Roger Chillingworth, as he was hereafter to be named, "I leave thee alone; alone with thy infant, and the scarlet letter! How is it, Hester? Doth thy sentence bind thee to wear the token in thy sleep? Art thou not afraid of nightmares and hideous dreams?"

"Why dost thou smile so at me?" inquired Hester, troubled at the expression of his eyes. "Art thou like the Black Man[131] {that haunts the forest round about us}? Hast thou enticed[132] me into a bond {that will prove the ruin of my soul}?"

"Not thy soul," he answered, with another smile. "No, not thine!"

---

131 Black Man: 악마
132 entice: 유인하다

The Scarlet Letter **5장**

Hester at Her Needle[1]

Hester Prynne's term of confinement[2] was now at an end. Her prison-door was thrown open, and she came forth into the sunshine, which, falling on all alike, seemed, to her sick and morbid heart, as if meant for no other purpose than to reveal the scarlet letter on her breast. Perhaps there was a more real torture[3] in her first unattended[4] footsteps from the threshold of the prison, than even in the procession and spectacle that have been described, where she was made the common infamy[5], at which all mankind was summoned[6] to point its finger. Then, she was supported by an unnatural tension of the nerves, and by all the combative[7] energy of her character, {which enabled her to convert the scene into a kind of lurid[8] triumph}. It was, moreover, a separate and insulated[9] event, to occur but once in her lifetime, and to meet which, therefore, reckless of economy[10], she might call up the vital strength {that

---

1 at her needle: 바느질 중에 있는. *at: ~중에 있는; at war: 전쟁 중; at lunch: 점심식사 중

2 term of confinement: 감금 기간

3 torture: 고문, 심한 고통

4 unattended: 지켜보는 사람이 없는, 돌보는 사람이 없는. *unattended patients: 방치된 환자; unattended office[station]: 무인국

5 common infamy: 공통의 치욕

6 was summoned: 소집된, 호출된

7 combative: 전투적인, 투쟁적인

8 lurid: 충격적인, 끔찍한, (색깔이) 야한[야단스러운]

9 separate and insulated: 분리되고 격리된

10 reckless of economy: (그녀가 지닌 에너지의 효과적인 분배의 관점에서) 경제[절약]에 신중을 기울이지 못하고

would have sufficed for many quiet years}[11]. The very law {that condemned[12] her}—a giant of stern features, but with vigor to support, as well as to annihilate[13], in his iron arm—had held her up, through the terrible ordeal of her ignominy. But now, with this unattended walk from her prison-door, began the daily custom, and she must either sustain and carry it forward by the ordinary resources of her nature, or sink beneath it. She could no longer borrow from the future, to help her through the present grief. To-morrow would bring its own trial with it; so would the next day, and so would the next; each its own trial, and yet the very same {that was now so unutterably grievous[14] to be borne}[15]. The days of the far-off[16] future would toil[17] onward, still with the same burden for her to take up, and bear along[18] with her, but never to fling down[19]; for the accumulating[20] days, and added years, would pile up their

---

11 she might call up ... years: 그 사건에 대처하기 위해서, 많은 세월 조용히 보내기에 충분했을 생명력을 불러냈는지 몰랐다

12 condemned: 유죄 선고를 한

13 annihilate: 완파하다, 전멸시키다

14 grievous: 통탄할[극심한](흔히 고통·통증을 야기하는)

15 unutterably grievous to be borne: 견뎌 내기에는 말로 표현할 수 없을 정도로 고통스러운. *unutterably: 말로 표현할 수 없는; grievous: 몹시 고통스러운; borne: bear(참다, 견디다)의 과거분사

16 far-off: 먼, 멀리 떨어진

17 toil: (힘겹게) 느릿느릿 움직이다

18 along: 앞으로

19 fling down: 내팽개치다

20 accumulating: 쌓이는

misery upon the heap of shame. Throughout them all, giving up her individuality, she would become the general symbol {at which the preacher and moralist might point}, and {in which they might vivify and embody[21] their images of woman's frailty[22] and sinful passion}. Thus the young and pure would be taught to look at her, with the scarlet letter flaming[23] on her breast,—at her, the child of honorable parents,—at her, the mother of a babe, that would hereafter be a woman,—at her, who had once been innocent,—as the figure, the body, the reality of sin. And over her grave, the infamy {that she must carry thither[24]} would be her only monument[25].

It may seem marvellous, that, with the world before her,— kept by no restrictive clause[26] of her condemnation within the limits of the Puritan settlement, so remote and so obscure,— free to return to her birthplace, or to any other European land, and there hide her character and identity under a new exterior[27], as completely as if emerging into another state of being,—and having also the passes of the dark, inscrutable forest open to her, where the wildness of her nature might

---

21 vivify and embody: 선명하고 구체화하다
22 frailty: 허약함, 나약함
23 flaming: 활활 타오르고 있는
24 carry thither: 그쪽까지 지고 가야 하는
25 monument: 기념비
26 restrictive clause: 제한 조항
27 exterior: 외양, 겉모습

assimilate[28] itself with a people {whose customs and life were alien from the law that had condemned her}, — it may seem marvellous, that this woman should still call that place her home, {where, and where only, she must needs be the type of shame}. But there is a fatality[29], a feeling {so irresistible and inevitable that it has the force of doom, which almost invariably compels[30] human beings to linger[31] around and haunt[32], ghost-like, the spot where some great and marked event has given the color to[33] their lifetime}; and still the more irresistibly, the darker the tinge[34] that saddens[35] it.[36] Her sin, her ignominy, were the roots {which she had struck into the soil}. It was as if a new birth, with stronger assimilations than the first, had converted the forest-land[37], [still so uncongenial[38] to every other pilgrim and wanderer], into Hester Prynne's

---

28 assimilate: 동화되다

29 fatality: 사망자, 치사율, 운명을 피할 수 없다는 생각, 숙명론

30 compel: 강요하다, ~하게 하다

31 linger: 오래 머물다

32 haunt: 귀신처럼 떠나지 못하고 떠돌다

33 give the color to: 채색하다

34 tinge: (느낌)을 더하다, 가미하다

35 sadden: 슬프게 하다

36 still the more ... the darker ...: the+비교급, the+비교급 구문으로 이 부분의 내용을 풀이하면 그 운명이 훨씬 더 불가항력적으로 (irresistibly) 그 장소에 머물게 할수록, 그 삶(it)을 슬프게 하는 색깔은 더 어두워진다는 의미이다.

37 forest-land: 삼림지

38 uncongenial: 마음에 들지 않는

wild and dreary, but life-long home. All other scenes of earth — even that village of rural England, {where happy infancy and stainless[39] maidenhood seemed yet to be in her mother's keeping, like garments put off long ago} — were foreign to her, in comparison. The chain {that bound her here} was of iron links, and galling[40] to her inmost soul, but never could be broken.

It might be, too, — doubtless it was so, although she hid the secret from herself, and grew pale whenever it struggled out of her heart, like a serpent from its hole, — it might be that another feeling kept her within the scene and pathway that had been so fatal. There dwelt, there trode the feet of one with whom she deemed herself connected in a union, that, unrecognized on earth, would bring them together before the bar of final judgment, and make that[41] their marriage-altar[42], for a joint futurity of endless retribution[43]. Over and over again, the tempter of souls had thrust this idea upon Hester's contemplation[44], and laughed at the passionate and desperate joy {with which she seized, and then strove to cast it[45] from

---

39 stainless: 흠 없는, 순결한
40 galling: 짜증 나는, 화나는
41 that: = the bar of final judgment
42 marriage-altar: 결혼의 제단
43 retribution: 징벌
44 contemplation: 사색, 명상
45 it: 여기의 it은 문장구조상 앞의 seized의 목적어도 겸한다. 의미상

her}. She barely looked the idea in the face, and hastened to bar it in its dungeon. What she compelled herself to believe,— what, finally, she reasoned upon, as her motive for continuing a resident of New England,—was half a truth, and half a self-delusion[46]. Here, she said to herself, had been the scene of her guilt, and here should be the scene of her earthly punishment; and so, perchance, the torture of her daily shame would at length purge[47] her soul, and work out another purity than that which she had lost; more saint-like, because the result of martyrdom[48].

Hester Prynne, therefore, did not flee. On the outskirts of the town, within the verge of the peninsula[49], but not in close vicinity to any other habitation, there was a small thatched cottage. It had been built by an earlier settler, and abandoned[50],

---

으로는 앞서 언급한 '유혹자가 던져 넣은 생각', 즉 이 세상에서는 인정받지 못하나 저 세상의 최후의 심판대에서 함께 서게 할 결합을 이루고 그 심판대를 결혼의 제단으로 삼아 그 후 영원무궁토록 인과응보를 함께 갚아 나가리라는 생각을 가리킨다. {with which … } 부분의 뒷부분은 다소 어색하다, 왜냐하면 문장구조상으로는 {with which … } 안으로 들어가지만 이 생각을 던져 버릴 때의 그녀의 태도가 '열정적이고 필사적인 기쁨'이라고 하는 것은 말이 잘 안 되기 때문이다.

46 self-delusion: 자기기만
47 purge: 정화하다, 제거하다
48 martyrdom: 순교자적인 고통
49 peninsula: 반도
50 abandoned: 버려진

because the soil about it was too sterile[51] for cultivation, while its comparative remoteness put it out of the sphere of that social activity which already marked the habits of the emigrants. It stood on the shore, looking across a basin of the sea at the forest-covered hills, towards the west[52]. A clump[53] of scrubby trees[54], such as alone grew on the peninsula, did not so much conceal the cottage from view, as seem to denote[55] that here was some object which would fain[56] have been, or at least ought to be, concealed. In this little, lonesome dwelling, with some slender[57] means[58] {that she possessed}, and by the license of the magistrates, {who still kept an inquisitorial[59] watch over her}, Hester established herself, with her infant child. A mystic shadow of suspicion immediately attached itself to the spot. Children, too young to comprehend wherefore this woman should be shut out from the sphere of human charities[60], would creep nigh enough to behold her plying her needle at

---

51 sterile: 불모의, 척박한
52 looking … the west: 저기 서쪽으로는, 분지 같은 바다를 가로질러 숲으로 뒤덮인 언덕들을 바라보고 있다
53 clump: (나무) 무리, 무더기
54 scrubby trees: 작은 나무들
55 denote: 나타내다, 의미하다
56 fain: 〈고어〉 (would와 함께 부사로) 기꺼이(흔쾌히) ～하고 싶다
57 slender: 빈약한, 얼마 안 되는
58 means: 돈, 재력, 수입
59 inquisitorial: 조사하는 듯한, 심문의
60 charities: 관용, 자비

the cottage-window, or standing in the door-way, or laboring in her little garden, or coming forth along the pathway that led townward; and, discerning the scarlet letter on her breast, would scamper off[61], with a strange, contagious[62] fear.

Lonely as was Hester's situation, and without a friend on earth who dared to show himself, she, however, incurred[63] no risk of want. She possessed an art {that sufficed, [even in a land that afforded comparatively little scope for its exercise], to supply food for her thriving infant and herself}. It was the art—then, as now, almost the only one within a woman's grasp[64]—of needle-work. She bore on her breast, in the curiously embroidered letter, a specimen[65] of her delicate and imaginative skill, {of which the dames of a court might gladly have availed themselves[66], to add the richer and more spiritual adornment of human ingenuity[67] to their fabrics of silk and gold}. Here, indeed, in the sable[68] simplicity {that generally characterized the Puritanic modes of dress}, there might be an infrequent call for the finer productions of her handiwork.

---

61 scamper off: (특히 아동이나 작은 동물이) 날쌔게 달아나다
62 contagious: 전염되는, 전염성의
63 incur: 초래하다, 처하다
64 grasp: 꽉 쥐기, 통제, 이해, (무엇을 달성할 수 있는) 능력
65 specimen: 본보기, 견본
66 avail oneself of: ~을 이용하다
67 ingenuity: 기발한 재주, 재간, 독창성
68 sable: 흑담비, 어두운, 음침한

Yet the taste of the age, [demanding whatever was elaborate in compositions of this kind], did not fail to extend[69] its influence over our stern progenitors[70], {who had cast[71] behind them so many fashions [which it might seem harder to dispense with]}. Public ceremonies, [such as ordinations[72], the installation[73] of magistrates, and all that could give majesty to the forms {in which a new government manifested itself to the people}], were, as a matter of policy[74], marked by a stately[75] and well-conducted[76] ceremonial[77], and a sombre[78], but yet a studied[79] magnificence[80]. Deep ruffs[81], painfully[82] wrought bands, and

---

69 extend: (영향력을) 확대하다, 늘리다

70 progenitor: 조상

71 cast: 옷을 벗어 던지다. *casting vote: (찬반 수가 같을 때 행하는 의장의 결정투표); cast a role to an actor: 배역하다; be cast away: 배가 표류하다

72 ordinations: 사제 서품식, 성직안수

73 installation: (장비, 가구의) 설치, (특수 장비를 보관 사용하는) 시설, (흔히 공식적인 의식을 통한) 취임[임명]

74 a matter of policy: 정책상의 문제

75 stately: 위풍당당한, 위엄 있는

76 well-conducted: 예의가 바른, 품행이 방정한, 관리가 잘된. *conduct: 지휘하다, 안내하다

77 ceremonial: 의식절차

78 sombre: 칙칙한

79 studied: 세심하게 계획된, 꼼꼼한

80 magnificence: 장려(壯麗), 웅장, 장엄, 호화, 장엄한 분위기, (문장·예술품 등의) 기품

81 ruff: 주름깃

82 painfully: 고통스러울 정도로, 아주 힘들게, 많은 노력을 기울여

gorgeously[83] embroidered gloves, were all deemed necessary to the official state of men [assuming the reins of power[84]]; and were readily allowed to individuals dignified by rank or wealth, {even while sumptuary laws[85] forbade these and similar extravagances to the plebeian[86] order}. In the array of funerals, too,—whether for the apparel of the dead body, or to typify, by manifold emblematic[87] devices of sable cloth and snowy lawn, the sorrow of the survivors,—there was a frequent and characteristic demand for such labor as Hester Prynne could supply. Baby-linen—for babies then[88] wore robes[89] of state[90]—afforded still another possibility of toil and emolument[91].

By degrees, nor very slowly, her handiwork[92] became what would now be termed the fashion. Whether from commiseration[93] for a woman of so miserable a destiny; or

★MP3
5장 (2)
시작

---

83 gorgeously: 화려한

84 reins of power: 권력의 고삐

85 sumptuary laws: 사치 단속법

86 plebeian: 평민의, 서민의

87 emblematic: 상징적인

88 babies then: 공식적인 의식들, 혹은 장례식 등 대사들의 경우에 아이들도

89 robe: (신분의 상징으로 또는 특별한 의식 때 입는) 예복[가운]

90 state: 지위, 신분, 위엄, 위풍

91 emolument: 보수, 수입

92 handiwork: (특히 예술적 솜씨를 발휘한) 일[작품]. *수예(手藝) 혹은 수예(繡藝) 모두의 의미로 통한다.

93 commiseration: 동정, 측은히 여김

from the morbid[94] curiosity {that gives a fictitious[95] value even to common or worthless things}; or by whatever other intangible[96] circumstance was then, as now, sufficient to bestow, on some persons, what others might seek in vain; or because Hester really filled a gap {which must otherwise have remained vacant}; it is certain that she had ready[97] and fairly requited[98] employment for as many hours as she saw fit to occupy with her needle[99].

Vanity, it may be, chose to mortify[100] itself, by putting on, for ceremonials of pomp and state, the garments {that had

---

94 morbid: 병적인

95 fictitious: 허구적인, 지어낸

96 intangible: 뭐라고 (꼬집어) 말할 수 없는

97 ready: 구문을 어떻게 보느냐에 따라 1. 손쉬운[employment를 꾸며 주는 형용사] 2. readily[requited를 꾸며 주는 부사]와 같은 뜻으로 볼 수 있다.

98 requite: 보답하다, (애정에 대해) 반응을 보이다

99 she had [ready and fairly requited employment] for as many hours {as she saw fit to occupy with her needle}: 이 구문의 구조는 다소 모호하다. ㉠ [ready and fairly requited employment]로 묶어서 이를 had의 목적어로 보면, '바느질하는 데 들여야 할 시간으로 적당하다고 생각하는 시간만큼 늘 준비된 듯한, 그리고 정당한 대가를 받을 만한 일이 있었다'는 의미가 된다. ㉡ requited를 employment를 꾸미는 형용사가 아니라 had requited의 동사로 보면, '자신이 일한 시간만큼의 고용 요구 사항에 기꺼이 잘 보답했다'는 의미가 된다. 즉, 앞의 구문 분석에 따라 해석이 달라진다.

100 mortify: 굴욕감을 주다, 몹시 당황하게 하다. *mortify oneself: 고행하다

been wrought by her sinful hands}. Her needle-work was seen on the ruff of the Governor; military men wore it on their scarfs, and the minister on his band; it decked the baby's little cap; it was shut up, to be mildewed[101] and moulder[102] away, in the coffins[103] of the dead. But it is not recorded that, in a single instance, her skill was called in aid to embroider the white veil {which was to cover the pure blushes of a bride}. The exception indicated the ever relentless[104] vigor[105] {with which society frowned upon her sin}.

Hester sought not to acquire any thing beyond a subsistence[106], of the plainest and most ascetic[107] description[108], for herself, and a simple abundance[109] for her child. Her own dress was of the coarsest materials and the most sombre hue; with only that one ornament,—the scarlet letter,—which it was her doom to wear. The child's attire, on the other hand, was distinguished by a fanciful, or, we may rather say, a fantastic[110]

---

101   mildewed: 흰 곰팡이가 핀

102   moulder: 서서히 썩다

103   coffin: 관

104   relentless: 수그러들지 않는, 끈질긴

105   vigor: 정력, 활력, 박력

106   subsistence: 최저생활, 호구. *subsist: 근근이 살아가다

107   ascetic: 금욕적인

108   a subsistence, of the plainest and most ascetic description: 가장 평범하고도 가장 금욕적인 종류의 최저생활. *description: 종류

109   simple abundance: 소박한 풍족함

110   fantastic: 이 단어와 연관된 fancy, fantasy는 둘 다 현실과는 거리

ingenuity[111], {which served, indeed, to heighten the airy[112] charm that early began to develop itself in the little girl}, but {which appeared to have also a deeper meaning}. We may speak further of it hereafter. Except for that small expenditure[113] in the decoration of her infant, Hester bestowed all her superfluous[114] means in charity, on wretches less miserable than herself, and who not unfrequently insulted the hand {that fed them}. Much of the time, {which she might readily have applied to the better efforts of her art}, she employed[115] in making coarse garments for the poor. It is probable {that there was an idea of penance in this mode of occupation}, and {that she offered up[116] a real sacrifice of enjoyment, in devoting so many hours to such rude handiwork. She had [in her nature] a rich, voluptuous[117], Oriental characteristic,—a taste for the gorgeously beautiful,

를 둔, 상상에 의한 작용 및 속성이면서 마음속에 그려 본 이미지를 의미한다. fanciful이 '기발한, 상상의' 정도의 의미라면, fantastic은 '기상천외의'와 같이 좀 더 강력한 의미를 띤다. 어원적으로 볼 때, 15세기 중반 fantasy의 축약형으로 시작된 fancy는 '변덕, 욕망' 등의 의미를 띠면서 현실의 요소들을 결합하든 아니면 완전히 지어낸 것이든 상상력에 의한 것으로 다소 사소한 것에 적용되는 반면, 라틴어 fantasia에서 온 fantasy는 상상력에 의한 산물이되 문학, 예술상에서 좀 더 확장된 형태로 여겨지는 면이 있다.

111 ingenuity: 독창성
112 airy: 환상적인, (공기와 같이) 가벼운, 우아한
113 expenditure: 지출
114 superfluous: 여분의, 남는
115 employ: (기술·방법 등을) 쓰다[이용하다]
116 offer up: [기도]를 드리다, [제물]을 바치다
117 voluptuous: 관능적인, 육감적인

{which, save in the exquisite productions of her needle, found nothing else, in all the possibilities of her life, to exercise itself upon}. Women derive a pleasure, [incomprehensible to the other sex], from the delicate toil of the needle. To Hester Prynne it might have been a mode of <u>expressing</u>, <u>and</u> therefore <u>soothing</u>, <u>the passion of her life</u>. Like all other joys, she rejected it as sin. [This morbid meddling[118] of conscience with an immaterial[119] matter] betokened, {it is to be feared[120]}, no genuine and steadfast penitence[121], but something doubtful, something that might be deeply wrong beneath.

In this manner, Hester Prynne came to have a part to perform in the world. With[122] her native energy of character, and rare capacity, it[123] could not entirely cast her off, although it had set a mark upon her, more intolerable to a woman's heart than that[124] which branded the brow of Cain. In all her intercourse[125] with society, however, there was nothing {that

---

118 meddling: 간섭, 참견
119 immaterial: 중요하지 않은
120 fear: (~일까 봐) 우려[염려]하다, (유감스럽지만) ~인 것 같다.
　　＊It is feared that he may not have read *The Scarlet Letter*. 그가
　　『주홍글자』를 읽지 못했을지 모른다는 우려가 있다.
121 penitence: 참회
122 with: 때문에
123 it: =the world
124 that: =the mark
125 intercourse: 교류

made her feel as if she belonged to it}. Every gesture, every word, and even the silence of those {with whom she came in contact}, implied, and often expressed, {that she was banished, and as much alone as if she inhabited another sphere, or communicated with the common nature by other organs and senses than the rest of human kind}. She stood apart from mortal[126] interests, yet close beside them, like a ghost {that revisits the familiar fireside, and can no longer make itself seen or felt; no more smile with the household joy, nor mourn with the kindred[127] sorrow; or, [should it succeed in manifesting[128] its forbidden sympathy], awakening only terror and horrible repugnance[129]. These emotions, in fact, and its bitterest scorn besides[130], seemed to be the sole portion that she retained[131] in the universal[132] heart. It was not an age of delicacy; and her position, {although she understood it well, and was in little danger of forgetting it}, was often brought before her vivid self-perception, like a new anguish, by the rudest touch upon the

---

126 mortal: 죽을 운명의, 죽음을 면할 수 없는, 인간의, 이 세상의.
      *this mortal life: 인생, 이승의 삶

127 kindred: 일가친척, 〈형용사〉 비슷한, 동류의, 관련된, 가정
      (household)과 관련된. *food and kindred products: 식품 및
      그와 관련된 상품들

128 manifesting: 드러냄

129 repugnance: 반감, 혐오

130 besides: 게다가, 또

131 retain: 유지, 보유하다

132 universal: 만인의

tenderest spot[133]. The poor, {as we have already said}, whom she sought out to be the objects of her bounty, often reviled[134] the hand {that was stretched forth to succor[135] them}. Dames of elevated rank, likewise, {whose doors she entered in the way of her occupation}, were accustomed to distil[136] drops of bitterness into her heart; sometimes through that alchemy of quiet malice, {by which women can concoct[137] a subtile poison from ordinary trifles}; and sometimes, also, by a coarser expression[138], {that fell upon the sufferer's defenceless breast like a rough blow upon an ulcerated[139] wound[140]}. Hester had schooled[141] herself long and well; she never responded to these attacks, save by a flush of crimson {that rose irrepressibly over her pale cheek, and again subsided into the depths of her bosom}. She was patient, — a martyr, indeed, — but she forebore to pray for enemies; {lest, [in spite of her forgiving aspirations], the words of the blessing should stubbornly twist themselves into a curse}.

133　tenderest spot: 가장 약한 곳. *tender spot: 약점, 아픈 곳, 급소; His small height is his only tender spot. 그의 작은 키가 그의 유일한 약점이다.

134　revile: 매도하다

135　succor: 구조, 원조

136　distil: 증류하여 만들다

137　concoct: 만들다, 지어내다

138　coarser expression: 야비한 말

139　ulcerate: 궤양이 생기다, 뭉크러지다, 짓무르다

140　ulcerated wound: 짓무른 상처

141　school: 훈련, 단련시키다, 교육하다

Continually, and in a thousand other ways, did she feel the innumerable throbs of anguish {that had been so cunningly contrived for her by the undying, the ever-active sentence of the Puritan tribunal[142]}. Clergymen paused in the street to address words of exhortation, {that brought a crowd, with its mingled grin and frown, around the poor, sinful woman}. If she entered a church, trusting to share the Sabbath smile of the Universal Father[143], it was often her mishap to find herself the text of the discourse. She grew to have a dread of children; for they had imbibed[144] [from their parents] a vague idea of something horrible in this dreary woman, gliding silently through the town, with never any companion but one only child. Therefore, first allowing her to pass, they pursued her at a distance with shrill cries, and the utterance of a word {that had no distinct purport to their own minds, but was none the less terrible to her, as proceeding from lips that babbled[145] it unconsciously}. It[146] seemed to argue so wide a diffusion[147] of her shame, that all nature knew of it; it could have caused her no deeper pang, {had the leaves of the trees whispered the dark story among themselves,—had the summer breeze murmured

---

142 tribunal: 법정
143 Universal Father: 하느님
144 imbibe: (정보, 사상)을 흡수하다
145 babble: (알아듣기 어렵게) 지껄이다
146 it: 여기의 it은 뜻도 모르고 아이들이 지껄이는 비난과 저주의 소리를 가리킨다고 볼 수 있다.
147 diffusion: 전파, 보급

about it,—had the wintry blast[148] shrieked it aloud!} Another peculiar torture was felt in the gaze of a new eye. When strangers looked curiously at the scarlet letter,—and none ever failed to do so,—they branded[149] it afresh into Hester's soul; so that, oftentimes, she could scarcely refrain, yet always did refrain, from[150] covering the symbol with her hand. But then, again, an accustomed eye had likewise its own anguish to inflict. Its cool stare of familiarity was intolerable. From first to last, in short, Hester Prynne had always this dreadful agony in feeling a human eye upon the token; the spot never grew callous[151]; it seemed, on the contrary, to grow more sensitive with daily torture.

But sometimes, once in many days, or perchance in many months, she felt an eye—a human eye—upon the igno-minious brand, that seemed to give a momentary relief, as if half of her agony were shared. The next instant, back it all rushed again, with still a deeper throb of pain; for, in that brief interval, she had sinned anew. Had Hester sinned alone?

Her imagination was somewhat affected, and, {had she been of a softer moral and intellectual fibre}, would have been

---

148 blast: 폭발, 강한 바람
149 brand: 낙인을 찍다
150 refrain from: 참다, ~을 하지 않다
151 callous: 냉담한

still more so, by the strange and solitary anguish of her life. Walking to and fro, with those lonely footsteps, in the little world {with which she was outwardly connected}, it now and then appeared to Hester, — {if altogether fancy, it was nevertheless too potent to be resisted,} — she felt or fancied, then, that the scarlet letter had endowed her with a new sense. She shuddered to believe, yet could not help believing, that it gave her a sympathetic knowledge[152] of the hidden sin in other hearts. She was terror-stricken[153] by the revelations[154] {that were thus made}. What were they? Could they be other than[155] the insidious[156] whispers of the bad angel, {who would fain have persuaded the struggling woman, as yet[157] only half his victim, [that the outward guise of purity was but a lie], and [that, if truth were everywhere to be shown, a scarlet letter would blaze forth on many a bosom besides Hester Prynne's]}? Or, must she receive those intimations[158] — so obscure, yet so distinct — as truth? In all her miserable experience, there was nothing else so awful and so loathsome[159] as this sense.

---

152 sympathetic knowledge: 교감하는 힘
153 terror-stricken: 공포에 질린
154 revelations: 뜻밖의 사실이 드러남
155 Could they be other than: ~ 외에 다른 것일 수 있었을까?, ~가 아니고 무엇일 수 있었겠는가?
156 insidious: 교활한, 음흉한
157 as yet: 아직
158 intimation: 시사, 암시
159 loathsome: 혐오스러운

It perplexed, as well as shocked her, by the irreverent[160] inopportuneness[161] of the occasions {that brought it into vivid action}. Sometimes, the red infamy upon her breast would give a sympathetic throb, as she passed near a venerable minister or magistrate, the model of piety and justice, {to whom that age of antique reverence looked up, [as to a mortal man in fellowship with angels]}. "What evil thing is at hand?" would Hester say to herself. Lifting her reluctant eyes, there would be nothing human within the scope of view, save the form of this earthly saint! Again, a mystic sisterhood would contumaciously[162] assert itself, as she met the sanctified frown of some matron, who, according to the rumor of all tongues[163], had kept cold snow within her bosom throughout life. That unsunned snow in the matron's bosom, and the burning shame on Hester Prynne's,—what had the two in common? Or, once more[164], the electric thrill would give her warning,—"Behold, Hester, here is a companion!"—and, looking up, she would detect the eyes of a young maiden glancing at the scarlet letter, shyly and aside, and quickly averted, with a faint, chill crimson in her cheeks; as if her purity were somewhat sullied[165] by that

---

160 irreverent: 불손한, 불경한
161 inopportuneness: 시기를 놓침, 계제가 나쁨, 나쁜 시기.
     ＊opportuneness: 시의 적절함
162 contumaciously: 반항적으로
163 all tongues: 〈성서〉 (제 나라 말을 갖는) 모든 국민, 각국의 국민
164 once more: 거듭, 한 번 더
165 sully: 훼손하다, 더럽히다

momentary glance. O Fiend, {whose talisman was that fatal symbol}, wouldst thou leave nothing, whether in youth or age, for this poor sinner to revere? — Such loss of faith is ever one of the saddest results of sin. Be it accepted[166] as a proof that all was not corrupt in this poor victim of her own frailty, and man's hard law, {that Hester Prynne yet struggled to believe that no fellow-mortal was guilty like herself}.

The vulgar, {who, in those dreary old times, were always contributing a grotesque horror to what interested their imaginations}, had a story about the scarlet letter {which we might readily work up into a terrific legend}. They averred, that the symbol was not mere scarlet cloth, tinged in an earthly dye-pot[167], but was red-hot with infernal fire, and could be seen glowing all alight[168], whenever Hester Prynne walked abroad[169] in the night-time. And we must needs say, it seared Hester's bosom so deeply, that perhaps there was more truth in the rumor than our modern incredulity[170] may be inclined to admit.

---

166 Be it accepted as ... that ...: ~이 ~로 받아들여지기를
167 dye-pot: 염료 단지
168 alight: 불타는
169 abroad: 집 밖에
170 incredulity: 불신

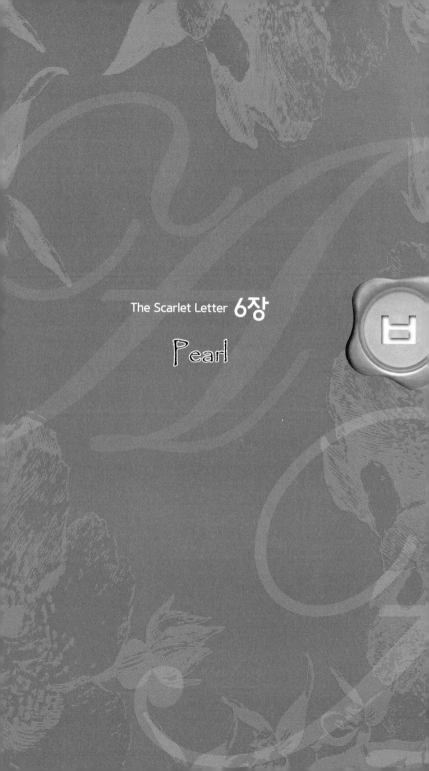

The Scarlet Letter 6장

Pearl

We have as yet hardly spoken of the infant; that little creature, whose innocent life had sprung[1], by the inscrutable[2] decree of Providence[3], a lovely and immortal flower, out of the rank[4] luxuriance[5] of a guilty passion. How strange it seemed to the sad woman, as she watched the growth, and the beauty {that became every day more brilliant}, and the intelligence {that threw its quivering[6] sunshine over the tiny features of this child}! Her Pearl!—For so had Hester called her; not as a name expressive of her aspect, {which had nothing of the calm, white, unimpassioned lustre [that would be indicated by the comparison[7]]}. But she named the infant "Pearl," as[8] being of great price,—purchased with all she had,—her mother's only treasure! How strange, indeed! Man had marked this woman's sin by a scarlet letter, {which had such potent and disastrous efficacy[9] that no human sympathy could reach her, save it were sinful like herself}. God, [as a direct consequence of the sin {which man thus punished}], had given her a lovely child,

---

1 spring: 솟아오르게 하다
2 inscrutable: 헤아리기 어려운, 불가해한
3 Providence: (신의) 섭리
4 rank: 지나치게 무성한, 잔뜩 우거진
5 luxuriance: 풍부, 무성함
6 quivering: 떨리는, 진동하는
7 that would be indicated by the comparison: 그 비교에 의해 표현될, 그 비교가 가리킬
8 as: ~이므로, ~로서
9 efficacy: 효험

{whose place was on that same dishonored bosom}, to connect her parent for ever with the race and descent of mortals, and to be finally a blessed soul in heaven![10] Yet these thoughts affected Hester Prynne less with hope than apprehension. She knew that her deed had been evil; she could have no <u>faith</u>, therefore, <u>that</u> its result would be for good. Day after day, she looked fearfully into the child's expanding nature; ever dreading to detect some dark and wild peculiarity[11], {that should correspond with the guiltiness to which she owed her being}.

Certainly, there was no physical defect. By its perfect shape, its vigor, and its natural dexterity[12] in the use of all its untried[13] limbs, the infant was worthy to have been brought forth[14] in

---

10 God ... in heaven!: 이 문장은 두 가지로 해석될 수 있다. {whose place was on that same dishonored bosom}을 삽입으로 처리하여, God had given her a lovely child ... to connect her parent with ...로 보거나, whose 이하의 부분을 모두 whose로 시작하는 관계절에 속한 것으로 보는 것이다. to connect의 의미상의 주어가 God 혹은 Pearl로 달라지나 God이 Pearl을 통해 뜻을 실현하는 것이므로 결국에는 동일한 의미가 된다. 다소 문제가 되는 부분은 to be finally a blessed soul in heaven이라는 부분이다. 종국적으로 누가 a blessed soul in heaven이 되는가의 문제인데, 문맥상으로 보면 헤스터에 해당되는 것으로 볼 수 있으나 문장구조상 to connect 부분과 병렬배치된 이 부분의 to 부정사의 의미상의 주어를 헤스터로 삼기는 어렵다.

11 peculiarity: 기이한 특징, 특이한 점
12 dexterity: 재주
13 untried: 경험이 없는, 시도해 보지 않은
14 bring forth: 낳다, 생산하다

Eden; worthy to have been left there, to be the plaything[15] of the angels, after the world's first parents were driven out. The child had a native grace {which does not invariably coexist[16] with faultless beauty}; its attire, however simple, always impressed the beholder {as if it[17] were the very garb that precisely became it[18] best}. But little Pearl was not clad in rustic weeds[19]. Her mother, [with a morbid purpose that may be better understood hereafter], had bought the richest tissues {that could be procured}, and allowed her imaginative faculty its full play in the arrangement[20] and decoration of the dresses {which the child wore, before the public eye}. So magnificent[21] was the small figure, {when thus arrayed}, and such was the splendor[22] of Pearl's own proper beauty, shining through the gorgeous robes {which might have extinguished a paler loveliness}, that there was an absolute circle of radiance[23] around her, on the darksome cottage-floor. And yet a russet[24]

---

15 plaything: 노리개

16 coexist: 동시에 있다, 공존하다. *not invariably coexist: 늘 같이 존재하지는 않는다

17 it: =its attire

18 it: =the child

19 clad in rustic weeds: 시골풍의 의복을 입고

20 arrangement: 정리, 배열, 준비, 타협, 계획, 편곡, 장식, 꾸미기. *flower arrangement: 꽃꽂이

21 magnificent: 참으로 아름다운

22 splendor: 화려함, 빛남, 광휘

23 radiance: 빛, 광채

24 russet: 적갈색, 황갈색, 그런 색의 거친 수직(手織) 천, 그 천으로

gown, torn and soiled with the child's rude play, made a picture of her just as perfect. Pearl's aspect was imbued with[25] a spell[26] of infinite variety; [in this one child] there were many children, comprehending[27] the full scope [between the wild-flower prettiness of a peasant-baby, and the pomp[28], in little[29], of an infant princess]. Throughout all, however, there was a trait of passion, a certain depth of hue, which she never lost; and {if, in any of her changes, she had grown fainter or paler}, she would have ceased to be herself;—it would have been no longer Pearl!

This outward mutability[30] indicated, and did not more than fairly express, the various properties of her inner life. Her nature appeared to possess depth, too, as well as variety; but— or else Hester's fears deceived her—it lacked reference[31] and

---

만든 옛 옷

25 be imbued with: (관습 · 습관 등에) 젖어 있다, 어려 있다

26 spell: 주문, 마법

27 comprehend: 이해하다, 파악하다, 포함하다, 포괄하다. *com (completely)+prehendere(catch hold of, seize)

28 pomp: 화려함, 장관

29 in little: 소규모로, 축소하여. *a reproduction in little of: ~의 축소판; the world's knowledge in little: 세계지식의 축도

30 mutability: 변화성

31 reference: 참조. *a book of reference: 참고서; reference to sources: 출전 참조. *(언급, 조회, 신원보증인) who are your references? 당신의 신원보증인은 누군가요? *(관계, 관련) It had no reference to him. 그것은 그와는 관련이 없었다. *(준거) a

adaptation[32] to the world {into which she was born}. The child could not be made amenable[33] to rules. In giving her existence, a great law had been broken; and the result was a being, {whose elements were perhaps beautiful and brilliant, but all in disorder; or with an order peculiar to themselves, amidst which the point of variety and arrangement was difficult or impossible to be discovered}. Hester could only account for the child's character—and even then, most vaguely and imperfectly—by recalling {what she herself had been, during that momentous period while Pearl was imbibing her soul from the spiritual world, and her bodily frame from its material of earth}. The mother's impassioned[34] state had been the medium {through which were transmitted to the unborn infant the rays of its moral life}; and, {however white and clear originally}, they had taken the deep stains of crimson and gold, the fiery[35] lustre, the black shadow, and the untempered[36] light, of the intervening[37] substance[38]. Above all, the warfare[39]

---

point of reference: 평가[판단]의 기준

32 adaptation: 적응

33 amenable: 말을 잘 듣는

34 impassioned: 열정적인, 간절한

35 fiery: 불타는 듯한, 불의

36 untempered: [강철이] 단련되지 않은, 조절되지 않은

37 intervening: 사이에 있는

38 the intervening substance: = the medium = Hester's impassioned state

39 warfare: 전쟁, 전투

of Hester's spirit, at that epoch, was perpetuated[40] in Pearl. She could recognize her wild, desperate, defiant[41] mood, the flightiness[42] of her temper, and even some of the very cloud-shapes of gloom and despondency[43] {that had brooded in her heart}. They were now illuminated[44] by the morning radiance of a young child's disposition[45], but, later in the day of earthly existence, might be prolific[46] of the storm and whirlwind[47].

The discipline of the family, in those days, was of a far more rigid kind than now. The frown, the harsh rebuke, the frequent application of the rod, [enjoined[48] by Scriptural authority[49]], were used, not merely in the way of punishment for actual offences, but as a wholesome regimen[50] for the growth and

---

40 perpetuate: 영구화하다
41 defiant: 반항하는, 저항하는
42 flighty: 변덕이 심한
43 despondency: 낙담, 의기소침
44 illuminate: 밝히다, 비추다
45 disposition: 기질, 성격
46 prolific: 다산의. * a prolific tree: 열매를 많이 맺는 나무; a prolific writer: 다작의 작가. *(많이 산출하는) a period prolific in great students: 위대한 학생들이 많이 배출된 시기. *(원인이 되는) prolific of misunderstanding: 오해의 원인이 되는
47 whirlwind: 회오리바람, 돌개바람
48 enjoin: 의무로서 부과하다
49 Scriptural authority: 여기서 '성서의 권위'는 잠언 13:24로서 '매를 아끼는 이는 아들을 미워하는 이이며, 사랑하는 이는 늦기 전에 [매질로] 훈계한다'는 내용이다.
50 regimen: 섭생, 자양분, 통치, 관리

promotion of all childish virtues. Hester Prynne, nevertheless, the lonely mother of this one child, ran little risk of erring on the side of undue severity[51]. [Mindful, however, of her own errors and misfortunes], she early sought to impose a tender, but strict, control over the infant immortality[52] {that was committed to her charge}. But the task was beyond her skill. [After testing both smiles and frowns, and proving that neither mode of treatment possessed any calculable[53] influence], Hester was ultimately compelled to stand aside, and permit the child to be swayed by her own impulses. Physical compulsion or restraint was effectual, of course, while it lasted. [As to any other kind of discipline, whether addressed to her mind or heart], little Pearl might or might not be within its[54] reach[55], in accordance with the caprice[56] {that ruled the moment}. Her mother, {while Pearl was yet an infant}, grew acquainted with[57] a certain peculiar look, {that warned her when it would be labor thrown away to insist, persuade, or plead}. It was a look [so intelligent[58], yet inexplicable[59], so perverse, sometimes

---

51 severity: 엄격, 엄정
52 immortality: 불멸, 영원한 생명, 정신적인 특성
53 calculable: 계산 가능한, 믿을 만한
54 its: =discipline's
55 reach: [세력, 영향력 등의] 범위
56 caprice: 변덕, 갑작스런 변화
57 acquainted with: ~을 알고 있는, ~와 알게 되는
58 intelligent: 총명한
59 inexplicable: 설명할 수 없는, 불가해한

so malicious[60], but generally accompanied by a wild flow of spirits[61]], that Hester could not help questioning, at such moments, whether Pearl was a human child. She seemed rather an airy sprite[62], {which, after playing its fantastic sports for a little while upon the cottage-floor, would flit away with a mocking smile}. {Whenever that look appeared in her wild, bright, deeply black eyes}, it invested her with a strange remoteness and intangibility[63]; it was as if she were hovering in the air and might vanish, like a glimmering[64] light {that comes we know not whence, and goes we know not whither}. Beholding it, Hester was constrained[65] to rush towards the child,—to pursue the little elf in the flight {which she invariably began},—to snatch her to her bosom, with a close pressure and earnest kisses,—not so much from overflowing love, as to assure herself that Pearl was flesh and blood, and not utterly delusive[66]. But Pearl's laugh, {when she was caught}, [though full of merriment and music[67]], made her mother more doubtful than before.

---

60 malicious: 악의적인

61 wild flow of spirits: 기분의 거친 흐름

62 airy sprite: 비현실적인 요정, 꼬마요정

63 intangibility: 손으로 만질 수 없음, 만져서 알 수 없는 것

64 glimmering: 어렴풋이 나타나는, 기색이 있는

65 constrain: 억지로 ~하다, 부득이 ~하다

66 delusive: 현혹하는, 망상적인

67 music: 음악, 듣기 좋은 소리

Heart-smitten at this bewildering and baffling spell, {that so often came between herself and her sole treasure, [whom she had bought so dear], and [who was all her world]}, Hester sometimes burst into passionate tears. Then, perhaps, — {for there was no foreseeing[68] how it might affect her}, — Pearl would frown, and clench[69] her little fist, and harden her small features into a stern, unsympathizing look of discontent. Not seldom, she would laugh anew, and louder than before, like a thing incapable and unintelligent of human sorrow. Or — but this more rarely happened — she would be convulsed with a rage of grief[70], and sob out[71] her love for her mother, in broken words, and seem intent on proving {that she had a heart, by breaking it}. Yet Hester was hardly safe in confiding herself to that gusty[72] tenderness; it passed, {as suddenly as it came}. [Brooding over all these matters], the mother felt like one {who has evoked a spirit, but, [by some irregularity in the process of conjuration[73]], has failed to win the master-word[74] [that should control this new and incomprehensible intelligence]}. Her only real comfort was {when the child lay in the placidity[75]

---

68 foreseeing: 선견지명이 있는
69 clench: 꽉 쥐다
70 a rage of grief: 맹렬한 슬픔
71 sob out: 흐느끼며 말하다
72 gusty: 거센
73 conjuration: 주문, 주술
74 master-word: 가장 중요한 단어, 으뜸말
75 placidity: 조용함, 평온

of sleep}. Then she was sure of her, and tasted hours of quiet, sad, delicious happiness; {until—perhaps with that perverse expression glimmering[76] from beneath her opening lids—little Pearl awoke}!

How soon—with what strange rapidity, indeed!—did ★ MP3 6장 (2) 시작 Pearl arrive at an age {that was capable of social intercourse, beyond the mother's ever-ready smile and nonsense-words}! And then what a happiness would it have been, {could Hester Prynne have heard her clear, bird-like voice mingling with the uproar of other childish voices, and have distinguished and unravelled[77] her own darling's tones, amid all the entangled outcry of a group of sportive[78] children}! But this could never be. Pearl was a born outcast of the infantile[79] world. An imp of evil, emblem and product of sin, she had no right among christened infants. Nothing was more remarkable than the instinct, {as it seemed}, {with which the child comprehended her loneliness}; the destiny {that had drawn an inviolable[80] circle round about her}; the whole peculiarity, in short, of her position in respect to other children. Never, since her release

---

76 glimmering: 어렴풋이 나타나는, 기색이 있는
77 distinguished and unravelled: (목소리들 속에서) 구별해 내고 풀어내다
78 sportive: 놀기 좋아하는, 장난 잘하는
79 infantile: 어린애 같은, 유아의
80 inviolable: 침범할 수 없는, 불가침의

from prison, had Hester met the public gaze without her. In all her walks about the town, Pearl, too, was there; first as the babe in arms, and afterwards as the little girl, small companion of her mother, holding a forefinger with her whole grasp, and tripping[81] along at the rate of three or four footsteps to one of Hester's. She saw the children of the settlement, on the grassy margin of the street, or at the domestic thresholds, disporting themselves[82] in such grim fashion {as the Puritanic nurture would permit}; playing at going to church, perchance; or at scourging Quakers; or taking scalps[83] in a sham-fight[84] with the Indians; or scaring one another with freaks of imitative witchcraft. Pearl saw, and gazed intently[85], but never sought to make acquaintance. If spoken to, she would not speak again. If the children gathered about her, {as they sometimes did}, Pearl would grow positively[86] terrible[87] in her puny[88] wrath, snatching up stones to fling at them, with shrill, incoherent exclamations {that made her mother tremble, because they had so much the sound of a witch's anathemas[89] in some unknown

---

81 trip: 경쾌한 발걸음, 경쾌하게 움직이다
82 disport oneself: 즐기다, 장난치다
83 taking scalps: 머리 가죽을 벗기는
84 sham-fight: 모의 싸움
85 intently: 열심히
86 positively: 단호히, 분명히
87 terrible: 끔찍한, 소름끼치는
88 puny: 연약한, 조그마한
89 anathemas: 저주

tongue}.

The truth was, that the little Puritans, [being of the most intolerant[90] brood that ever lived], had got a vague idea of something outlandish[91], unearthly[92], or at variance with ordinary fashions, in the mother and child; and therefore scorned them in their hearts, and not unfrequently reviled[93] them with their tongues. Pearl felt the sentiment, and requited[94] it with the bitterest hatred {that can be supposed to rankle[95] in a childish bosom}. These outbreaks[96] of a fierce temper had a kind of value, and even comfort, for her mother; because there was at least an intelligible earnestness in the mood, instead of the fitful caprice {that so often thwarted[97] her in the child's manifestations[98]}. It appalled her, nevertheless, to discern here, again, a shadowy reflection of the evil {that had existed in herself}. All this enmity[99] and passion had Pearl inherited, by inalienable[100] right, out of Hester's heart.

---

90 intolerant: 편협한
91 outlandish: 이상한, 기이한, 이국풍의, 색다른
92 unearthly: 이 세상의 것이 아닌, 초자연적인
93 revile: 매도하다
94 requite: 보답하다, 응대하다
95 rankle: 마음을 괴롭히다, 마음속에서 사무치다
96 outbreak: 발생, 발발
97 thwart: 좌절시키다
98 manifestations: 징후, 표명, (감정, 신념, 진실 따위를) 명시하는 것
99 enmity: 적의, 원한
100 inalienable: 양도할 수 없는

Mother and daughter stood together in the same circle of seclusion from human society; and in the nature of the child seemed to be perpetuated those unquiet[101] elements {that had distracted[102] Hester Prynne before Pearl's birth, but had since begun to be soothed away by the softening influences of maternity[103]}.

At home, within and around her mother's cottage, Pearl wanted not a wide and various circle of acquaintance. The spell of life went forth from her ever creative spirit, and communicated itself to a thousand objects, as a torch kindles a flame {wherever it may be applied}. The unlikeliest materials, a stick, a bunch of rags, a flower, were the puppets[104] of Pearl's witchcraft, and, [without undergoing any outward change], became spiritually adapted to {whatever drama occupied the stage of her inner world}. Her one baby-voice served a multitude of imaginary personages, old and young, to talk withal[105]. The pine-trees, [aged, black, and solemn, and flinging groans and other melancholy utterances on the breeze], needed little transformation to figure as Puritan elders; the ugliest weeds of the garden were their children, {whom Pearl smote

---

101　unquiet: 동요하는, 불온한
102　distract: 어지럽히다, 혼란시키다
103　maternity: 모성, 어머니
104　puppets: 꼭두각시
105　withal: ~을 가지고

down and uprooted[106], most unmercifully}. It was wonderful, the vast variety of forms {into which she threw her intellect, with no continuity[107], indeed, but darting up[108] and dancing, always in a state of preternatural activity,—soon sinking down, as if exhausted by so rapid and feverish[109] a tide of life,—and succeeded by other shapes of a similar wild energy}. It was like nothing so much as the phantasmagoric[110] play of the northern lights[111]. [In the mere exercise of the fancy, however, and the sportiveness[112] of a growing mind], there might be little more than was observable in other children of bright[113] faculties; except as Pearl, [in the dearth[114] of human playmates], was thrown[115] more upon the visionary throng[116] {which she created}. The singularity lay in the hostile feelings {with which the child regarded all these offsprings of her own heart and mind}. She never created a friend, but seemed

---

106 uprooted: 뿌리째 뽑았다

107 continuity: (논리적으로) 밀접한 연관성, (영화, 방송) 대본, 막간물

108 dart up: 화살처럼 날아다니다, 돌진하다

109 feverish: 열광적인, 열이 있는

110 phantasmagoric: 환영 같은, 주마등같이 변하는

111 It was like … northern lights: 북극광의 환상적인 작용과 같은 것은 아무것도 없는 것 같았다

112 sportiveness: 명랑

113 bright: 밝은, 총명한

114 dearth: 부족, 결핍

115 throw: ~로 향하게 하다

116 throng: 군중, 인파

always to be sowing broadcast[117] the dragon's teeth, {whence sprung a harvest of armed enemies, [against whom she rushed to battle]}[118]. It was inexpressibly sad — then what depth of sorrow to a mother, {who felt [in her own heart] the cause}! — to observe, [in one so young], this constant recognition of an adverse[119] world, and so fierce a training of the energies {that were to make good her cause, in the contest [that must ensue]}.

Gazing at Pearl, Hester Prynne often dropped her work upon her knees, and cried out, with an agony {which she would fain have hidden}, but {which made utterance for itself, betwixt speech and a groan, — "O Father in Heaven, — if Thou art still my Father, — what is this being [which I have brought into the world]!"} And Pearl, [overhearing the ejaculation[120], or aware, {through some more subtile channel}, of those throbs of anguish], would turn her vivid and beautiful little face upon her mother, smile with sprite-like intelligence, and resume

---

117 broadcast: 〈자동사, 타동사, 명사, 형용사, 부사〉 방송하다, 방송된, 널리, 광범위하게

118 그리스 신화의 캐드머스(Cadmus)는 페니키아의 왕자로 테베(Thebes)를 창건하고 알파벳을 그리스에 전한 인물로 알려져 있다. 캐드머스의 부계 쪽 할아버지가 포세이돈(Poseidon)이고 손자가 디오니서스(Dionysus)이다. 캐드머스가 죽인 용의 이빨들이 뿌려진 자리에서 군사들이 솟아나 서로 싸운 끝에 5명만 남았는데, 이들이 캐드머스를 도와 테베를 건국하고 귀족가문의 시조를 이루었다고 한다.

119 adverse: 부정적인, 불리한

120 ejaculation: 외침, 고함

her play.

One peculiarity of the child's deportment remains yet to be told. The very first thing {which she had noticed, in her life}, was—what?—not the mother's smile, responding to it, {as other babies do}, by that faint, embryo[121] smile of the little mouth, remembered so doubtfully afterwards, and with such fond discussion whether it were indeed a smile. By no means! But that first object {of which Pearl seemed to become aware} was—shall we say it?—the scarlet letter on Hester's bosom! One day, {as her mother stooped over the cradle}, the infant's eyes had been caught by the glimmering of the gold embroidery about the letter; and, [putting up her little hand], she grasped at it, smiling, not doubtfully, but with a decided gleam {that gave her face the look of a much older child}. Then, gasping for breath, did Hester Prynne clutch the fatal token, instinctively endeavouring[122] to tear it away; so infinite was the torture inflicted by the intelligent touch of Pearl's baby-hand. Again, {as if her mother's agonized gesture were meant only to make sport for her}, did little Pearl look into her eyes, and smile! From that epoch, except {when the child was asleep}, Hester had never felt a moment's safety; not a moment's calm enjoyment of her. Weeks, {it is true}, would sometimes elapse,

---

121 embryo: 배아, 앳된
122 endeavouring: 분투하다

{during which Pearl's gaze might never once be fixed upon the scarlet letter}; but then, again, it would come at unawares, like the stroke of sudden death, and always with that peculiar smile, and odd expression of the eyes.

Once, this freakish[123], elfish[124] cast[125] came into the child's eyes, {while Hester was looking at her own image in them, as mothers are fond of doing}; and, suddenly,—{for women in solitude, and with troubled hearts, are pestered with unaccountable delusions},—she fancied {that she beheld, not her own miniature[126] portrait, but another face in the small black mirror of Pearl's eye}. It was a face, fiend-like, full of smiling malice, yet bearing the semblance of features {that she had known full well, though seldom with a smile, and never with malice, in them}. It was as if an evil spirit possessed the child, and had just then peeped forth in mockery. Many a time

---

123 freakish: 별난, 기이한

124 elfish(=elvish): 장난 잘 치는, 꼬마 요정 같은. *이 작품에서는
elvish가 세 차례, elfish가 네 차례 나온다. 오하이오대학에서 나
온 센테너리(Centenary) 판『주홍글자』의 텍스트 해설에 따르면
elfish가 '요정의 특성을 지닌, 요정과 같은'의 의미이며, elvish는
'요정이나 떠도는 정령과 관련된'의 의미이다. 그런데 이 작품에
서는 모두 elfish의 의미를 담고 있어서 elfish로 통일하는 것이 적
절하다고 한다. 이 주해본에서는 여기 외에 12장에도 elvish가 두
차례 더 나오는데 그 대목에서 elfish와 같다고만 각주 설명을 붙
였다.

125 cast: 색조, 기미, 경향

126 miniature: 축소의, 소형의

afterwards had Hester been tortured, {though less vividly}, by the same illusion.

In the afternoon of a certain summer's day, {after Pearl grew big enough to run about}, she amused herself with gathering handfuls of wild-flowers, and flinging them, one by one, at her mother's bosom; {dancing up and down, like a little elf, whenever she hit the scarlet letter}. Hester's first motion had been to cover her bosom with her clasped hands. But, [whether from pride or resignation, or a feeling {that her penance might best be wrought out by this unutterable[127] pain}], she resisted the impulse, and sat erect, [pale as death], [looking sadly into little Pearl's wild eyes]. Still came the battery of flowers, almost invariably hitting the mark, and covering the mother's breast with hurts {for which she could find no balm[128] in this world, nor knew how to seek it in another}. At last, [her shot being all expended], the child stood still and gazed at Hester, [with that little, laughing image of a fiend peeping out — or, {whether it peeped or no, her mother so imagined it} — from the unsearchable abyss of her black eyes].

"Child, what art thou?" cried the mother.

---

127 unutterable: 말로 표현할 수 없는
128 balm: 향유, 달래 주는 것

"O, I am your little Pearl!" answered the child.

But, while she said it, Pearl laughed and began to dance up and down, with the humorsome gesticulation[129] of a little imp, {whose next freak might be to fly up the chimney}.

"Art thou my child, in very truth?" asked Hester.

Nor did she put the question altogether idly, but, for the moment, with a portion of genuine earnestness; {for, such was Pearl's wonderful intelligence, that her mother half doubted [whether she were not acquainted with the secret spell of her existence, and might not now reveal herself]}.

"Yes; I am little Pearl!" repeated the child, continuing her antics[130].

"Thou art not my child! Thou art no Pearl of mine!" said the mother, half playfully; {for it was often the case that a sportive[131] impulse came over her, in the midst of her deepest suffering}. "Tell me, then, what thou art, and who sent thee hither?"

---

129 gesticulation: 요란스러운 몸짓, 손짓
130 antics: 익살맞은 동작
131 sportive: 장난하고 싶은

"Tell me, mother!" said the child, seriously, coming up to Hester, and pressing herself close to her knees. "Do thou tell me!"

"Thy Heavenly Father sent thee!" answered Hester Prynne.

But she said it with a hesitation {that did not escape the acuteness of the child}. {Whether moved only by her ordinary freakishness[132], or because an evil spirit prompted her}, she put up her small forefinger, and touched the scarlet letter.

"He did not send me!" cried she, positively. "I have no Heavenly Father!"

"Hush, Pearl, hush! Thou must not talk so!" answered the mother, suppressing[133] a groan. "He sent us all into the world. He sent even me, thy mother. Then, much more, thee! Or, if not, thou strange and elfish child, whence didst thou come?"

"Tell me! Tell me!" repeated Pearl, no longer seriously, but laughing, and capering[134] about the floor. "It is thou that must tell me!"

---

132 freakishness: 변덕
133 suppress: 억누르다, 참다
134 caper: 뛰어다니다, 깡충거리다

But Hester could not resolve the query, [being herself in a dismal labyrinth of doubt]. She remembered — betwixt a smile and a shudder — the talk of the neighbouring townspeople; {who, [seeking vainly elsewhere for the child's paternity[135], and observing some of her odd attributes], had given out [that poor little Pearl was a demon offspring; such {as, ever since old Catholic times, had occasionally been seen on earth, through the agency of their mothers' sin, and to promote some foul and wicked purpose}]}. Luther, [according to the scandal of his monkish[136] enemies], was a brat[137] of that hellish breed; nor was Pearl the only child {to whom this inauspicious[138] origin was assigned}, among the New England Puritans.

---

135 paternity: 부성, 아버지
136 monkish: 수도승의
137 brat: 애새끼, 버릇없는 자식
138 inauspicious: 불길한, 상서롭지 못한

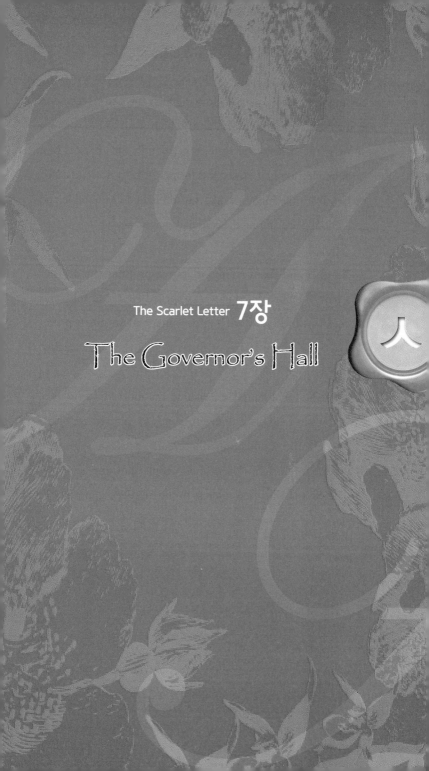

The Scarlet Letter 7장

The Governor's Hall

Hester Prynne went, one day, to the mansion of Governor Bellingham, with a pair of gloves {which she had fringed and embroidered[1] to his order}, and {which were to be worn on some great occasion of state; for, [though the chances of a popular election had caused this former ruler to descend a step or two from the highest rank], he still held an honorable and influential place among the colonial[2] magistracy[3]}.

Another and far more important reason [than the delivery of a pair of embroidered gloves] impelled Hester, at this time, to seek[4] an interview with [a personage of so much power and activity in the affairs of the settlement]. It had reached her ears, {that there was a design [on the part of some of the leading inhabitants[5], cherishing the more rigid order of principles in religion and government], to deprive her of her child}. On the supposition {that Pearl, [as already hinted], was of demon origin}, these good people [not unreasonably] argued {that a Christian interest in the mother's soul required

---

1 fringe and embroider: 술을 붙이고 수를 놓다

2 colonial: 식민지의, 식민지 시대의

3 magistracy: 통치 기간[임기], 치안판사의 직, 치안판사들. ＊리처드 벨링햄은 1641년 총독에 선출되어 1642년에 임기를 마쳤다. 그는 1654년까지는 다시 총독에 선출되지 않았으나 치안판사나 부총독의 지위로 봉사했다. 현재의 에피소드는 1645년 펄(Pearl)이 세 살 때 이다.

4 impelled Hester, to seek ...: 헤스터는 부득이 ~을 찾아야만 했다. ＊impel 주어 (to sth): ~해야만 하게 만들다

5 inhabitant: 주민

them to remove such a stumbling-block[6] from her path}. {If the child, on the other hand, were really capable of moral and religious growth, and possessed the elements of ultimate salvation[7]}, then, surely, it would enjoy all the fairer prospect of these advantages [by being transferred to wiser and better guardianship[8] than Hester Prynne's]. Among those {who promoted the design}, Governor Bellingham was said to be one of the most busy. It may appear singular, and, indeed, not a little ludicrous[9], {that an affair of this kind, [which, in later days, would have been referred[10] to no higher jurisdiction[11] than that of the selectmen of the town], should then have been a question publicly discussed}, and {on which statesmen of eminence[12] took sides}[13]. At that epoch of pristine[14] simplicity, however, matters [of even slighter public interest, and of far

---

6 stumbling-block: 장애물, 걸림돌

7 salvation: 구원, 구조

8 guardianship: 보호자의 임무, 보호, 감독

9 ludicrous: 터무니없는

10 refer: 위탁하다, 맡기다

11 jurisdiction: 관할권, 사법권

12 statesmen of eminence: 명망 있는 정치가

13 It may appear singular ... took sides: 이 문장의 구조에서는 우선 가주어 'it', 진주어 'that ...' 부분을 주목할 수 있는데, 진주어 'that ...' 안에는 다시 주어 'an affair of this kind'를 설명해 주는 'which ... of the town'이라는 긴 관계절이 위치한다. 'on which ...' 부분은 'states of eminence took sides on the affair'로 바꾸어 진주어 'that ...' 절의 두 번째 [주어 + 술어] 부분으로 삼는 것이 문장구조상 자연스럽다.

14 pristine: 원시의, 자연 그대로의, 초기의

less intrinsic weight than the welfare of Hester and her child],
were strangely mixed up with the deliberations of legislators
and acts of state[15]. The period was hardly, [if at all], earlier than
that of our story, {when[16] a dispute [concerning the right of
property in a pig], not only caused a fierce and bitter contest in
the legislative body of the colony, but resulted in an important
modification of the framework itself of the legislature}.

   Full of concern, therefore,—but so conscious of her own
right, {that it seemed scarcely an unequal[17] match between
[the public, on the one side], and [a lonely woman, backed by
the sympathies of nature, on the other]},—Hester Prynne set
forth from her solitary cottage. Little Pearl, of course, was her
companion. She was now of an age [to run lightly along by
her mother's side], and, [constantly in motion from morn till
sunset], could have accomplished a much longer journey [than
that before her[18]]. Often, nevertheless, [more from caprice
than necessity], she demanded to be taken up in arms, but
was soon as imperious[19] to be set down again, and frisked[20]
onward[21] before Hester on the grassy pathway, with many a

---

15 state: 정부
16 when: 관계절로 주어 the period를 꾸며 주는 것으로 볼 수 있다.
17 unequal: 같지 않은, 어울리지 않는
18 that before her: 자기 앞에 가고 있는 여정(벨링햄 집까지 가는 길)
19 imperious: 오만한, 도도한, 긴급한
20 frisk: 뛰어다니다, 뛰놀다, 경쾌하게 뛰어 돌아다니다
21 onward: 앞으로

harmless trip[22] and tumble[23]. We have spoken of Pearl's rich and luxuriant[24] beauty; a beauty {that shone with deep and vivid tints}; a bright complexion, eyes possessing intensity both of depth and glow, and hair already of a deep, glossy brown, and {which, in after years, would be nearly akin to black}. There was fire in her and throughout[25] her; she seemed the unpremeditated[26] offshoot[27] of a passionate moment. Her mother, [in contriving[28] the child's garb], had allowed the gorgeous tendencies of her imagination their full play; arraying[29] her in a crimson velvet tunic[30], [of a peculiar cut], [abundantly embroidered with fantasies and flourishes[31] of gold thread]. So much strength of coloring, {which must have given a wan and pallid[32] aspect to cheeks of a fainter bloom}, was admirably adapted to Pearl's beauty, and made her the very brightest little jet[33] of flame {that ever danced upon the earth}.

---

22 trip: 실족, 헛디딤
23 tumble: 구르기, 넘어짐
24 luxuriant: 무성한, 풍부한. *luxuriant vegetation: 울창하게 우거진 초목; luxuriant soil: 기름진 땅; luxuriant imagination: 풍부한 상상력
25 throughout: 도처에, 전체에 걸쳐, 구석구석
26 unpremeditated: 미리 생각해 두지 않은, 즉석의
27 offshoot: 분지, 곁가지, 산물, 자손
28 contrive: 고안하다, 궁리하다
29 array: 정돈하다, 성장(盛裝)시키다, 차려입히다
30 tunic: 허리 아래까지 내려오는 여성용 웃옷
31 flourish: 화려하게 꾸밈, 장식적 디자인으로 꾸밈
32 wan and pallid: 파리하고 창백한, 핼쑥한, 흐릿한

But it was a remarkable attribute of this garb, and, indeed, of the child's whole appearance, {that it irresistibly and inevitably reminded the beholder of the token [which Hester Prynne was doomed to wear upon her bosom]}. It was the scarlet letter in another form; the scarlet letter [endowed with life]! The mother herself—{as if the red ignominy[34] were so deeply scorched into her brain, that all her conceptions assumed its form}—had carefully wrought[35] out the similitude; lavishing[36] many hours of morbid ingenuity, to create [an analogy between the object of her affection, and the emblem of her guilt and torture]. But, in truth, Pearl was the one, as well as the other; and [only in consequence of that identity[37]] had Hester contrived[38] so perfectly to represent the scarlet letter in her[39] appearance.

{As the two wayfarers[40] came within the precincts[41] of

---

33 jet: 분출, 분사

34 ignominy: 불명예, 수치

35 wrought: work의 과거형을 나타내는 고어. *work out: ~을 성취하다, 만들어 내다

36 lavish: 〈동사〉 아낌없이 쓰다, 〈형용사〉 아낌없는(be lavish of), 풍부한

37 only in consequence of that identity: 그런 정체성의 결과, 즉 펄이 애정의 대상이자 죄와 고통의 대상이라는 정체성을 띤 탓에

38 contrive: 궁리하다, 고안하다

39 her: = Pearl

40 wayfarers: 도보 여행자

41 precinct: 구역, 경계(선), 주변, 근교

the town}, the children of the Puritans looked up from their play,—or {what passed for play with those sombre little urchins},—and spake gravely one to another:—

"Behold, verily, there is the woman of the scarlet letter; and, of a truth, moreover, there is the likeness of the scarlet letter [running along by her side]! Come, therefore, and let us fling mud at them!"

But Pearl, {who was a dauntless[42] child}, [after frowning, stamping her foot, and shaking her little hand with a variety of threatening gestures], suddenly made a rush at the knot[43] of her enemies, and put them all to flight. She resembled, [in her fierce pursuit of them], an infant pestilence[44],—the scarlet fever[45], or some such half-fledged[46] angel of judgment,— {whose mission was to punish the sins of the rising generation}. She screamed and shouted, too, with a terrific volume of sound, {which doubtless caused the hearts of the fugitives to quake within them}. [The victory accomplished], Pearl returned quietly to her mother, and looked up smiling into her

---

42 dauntless: 겁 없는, 불굴의, 용감한
43 knot: 매듭, 마디, 소집단, 떼
44 pestilence: 역병, 악성 전염병
45 scarlet fever: 성홍열
46 fledge: 〈타동사〉날 수 있을 때까지 기르다, 제몫을 하게 하다, 깃 (털)을 달다, 〈자동사〉깃털이 고루 나다. *full-fledged: 깃털이 다 난, 충분히 발달한, 제몫을 하게 된

face.

Without further adventure[47], they reached the dwelling of Governor Bellingham. This was a large wooden house, built in a fashion {of which there are specimens[48] still extant[49] in the streets of our elder[50] towns; now moss-grown, crumbling to decay, and melancholy at heart with the many sorrowful or joyful occurrences [remembered or forgotten], [that have happened, and passed away, within their dusky chambers]}. Then, however, there was the freshness of the passing year on its exterior, and the cheerfulness, [gleaming forth from the sunny windows], of a human habitation {into which death had never entered}. It had indeed a very cheery[51] aspect; the walls being overspread with a kind of stucco[52], {in which fragments of broken glass were plentifully[53] intermixed; so that, [when the sunshine fell aslant[54]-wise[55] over the front of the edifice], it glittered and sparkled [as if diamonds had been flung against it by the double handful]}. The brilliancy might have

---

47 adventure: 모험, 이상한 사건, 돌발적인 일[사건]

48 specimen: 견본, 표본

49 extant: 현존[잔존]하는

50 elder: 손위의, 연상의, 옛날의, 초기의. *in elder times: 옛날에

51 cheery: 기분 좋은, 명랑한, 유쾌한

52 stucco: 치장 벽토

53 plentifully: 풍부하게,

54 aslant: 〈형용사〉 비스듬한, 〈부사〉 비스듬히

55 -wise: 방식, 위치, 방향의 뜻을 지닌 부사를 만든다. *clockwise: 시계 방향으로; sidewise(=sideways): 옆의, 옆으로

befitted Aladdin's palace, rather than the mansion of a grave old Puritan ruler. It was further decorated with strange and seemingly cabalistic[56] figures and diagrams[57], [suitable to the quaint taste of the age], {which had been drawn in the stucco [when newly laid on], and had now grown hard and durable, for the admiration of after times}.

Pearl, [looking at this bright wonder[58] of a house], began to caper[59] and dance[60], and imperatively[61] required {that the whole breadth of sunshine should be stripped off its front, and given her to play with}.

★ MP3
7장 (2)
시작

"No, my little Pearl!" said her mother. "Thou must gather thine own sunshine. I have none to give thee!"

They approached the door; which was of an arched form, and flanked[62] on each side by a narrow tower or projection of the edifice, {in both of which were lattice-windows, with wooden shutters to close over them at need}. Lifting the iron hammer {that hung at the portal}, Hester Prynne gave

---

56 cabalistic: 비밀스러운 신조[교리]의
57 diagram: 도표, 도해
58 wonder: 놀랄 만한 것, 기이한 것
59 caper: 뛰어다니다, 깡충거리다
60 dance: 춤을 추듯 움직이다
61 imperatively: 명령적으로, 단호하게
62 flank: 옆에 있다, 측면에 배치되다

a summons, which was answered by one of the Governor's bond-servants[63]; a free-born Englishman, but now a seven years' slave. During that term he was to be the property of his master, and as much a commodity of bargain and sale as[64] an ox, or a joint-stool[65]. The serf[66] wore the blue coat, {which was the customary[67] garb of serving-men at that period, and long before, in the old hereditary halls of England}.

"Is the worshipful[68] Governor Bellingham within?" inquired Hester.

"Yea, forsooth[69]," replied the bond-servant, staring with wide-open eyes at the scarlet letter, {which, [being a new-comer in the country], he had never before seen}. "Yea, his honorable worship is within. But he hath a godly minister or two with him, and likewise a leech[70]. Ye may not see his worship now."

---

63 bond-servant: 종, 노예, 급료 없는 고용인. cf.) indentured servant
64 as much ... as: ~와 다름없는, (선행하는 수사와 호응하여) 꼭 그
    만큼, (선행하는 글의 내용을 받아서) 그것처럼
65 joint-stool: 조립식 의자
66 serf: 농노
67 customary: 습관적인, 통상적인, 관례적인
68 worshipful: (경칭으로) 존경하는 ~님
69 forsooth: 참으로
70 leech: 의사

"Nevertheless, I will enter," answered Hester Prynne; and the bond-servant, perhaps judging [from the decision of her air and the glittering symbol in her bosom], {that she was a great lady in the land}, offered no opposition.

So the mother and little Pearl were admitted into the hall of entrance. [With many variations, suggested by the nature of his building-materials, diversity of climate, and a different mode of social life], Governor Bellingham had planned his new habitation after the residences of gentlemen of fair estate[71] in his native land. Here, then, was a wide and reasonably[72] lofty hall, [extending through the whole depth of the house, and forming a medium of general communication[73], more or less directly, with all the other apartments]. At one extremity[74], this spacious room was lighted by the windows of the two towers[75], {which formed a small recess[76] on either side of the portal}. At the other end, [though partly muffled[77] by a curtain], it was more powerfully illuminated by one of those embowed[78] hall-windows {which we read of in old books}, and {which

---

71 fair estate: 상당한 재산(토지)
72 reasonably: 당연히, 알맞게
73 general communication: 전체적인 소통
74 at one extremity: 한쪽 끝에
75 tower: 정문 옆에 밖으로 돌출되어 배치된 탑 같은 공간
76 recess: 들어간 곳
77 muffled: 덮여진, 감싸진, 가려진
78 embowed: 활처럼 휜, 활 모양으로 된

was provided with a deep and cushioned seat}. Here, [on the cushion], lay a folio tome[79], probably of the Chronicles of England, or other such substantial[80] literature; even as, in our own days, we scatter gilded volumes on the centre-table, to be turned over by the casual[81] guest. The furniture of the hall consisted of some ponderous[82] chairs, {the backs of which were elaborately carved with wreaths of oaken flowers}; and likewise a table in the same taste; the whole being of the Elizabethan age, or perhaps earlier, and heirlooms[83], [transferred hither from the Governor's paternal home]. On the table — in token that the sentiment of old English hospitality[84] had not been left behind — stood a large pewter tankard[85], {at the bottom of which, [had Hester or Pearl peeped into it], they might have seen the frothy[86] remnant[87] of a recent draught of ale[88]}.

[On the wall] hung a row of portraits, [representing the forefathers[89] of the Bellingham lineage, some with armour on their breasts, and others with stately ruffs and robes of peace].

---

79 folio tome: 이절판(21×33cm)의 두꺼운 책
80 substantial: 실질적인, 묵직한
81 casual: 뜻밖의, 우연한, 이따금의
82 ponderous: 묵직한, 크고 무거운
83 heirloom: 가보
84 hospitality: 친절히 접대함, 환대, 후한 대접
85 pewter tankard: 백랍으로 된 큰 맥주잔
86 frothy: 거품이 떠 있는
87 remnant: 남은 부분
88 ale: 맥주
89 forefathers: 조상, 선조

All were characterized by the sternness and severity[90] {which old portraits so invariably put on}; as if they were the ghosts, rather than the pictures, of departed worthies, and were gazing with harsh and intolerant criticism at the pursuits and enjoyments of living men.

At about the centre of the oaken panels, {that lined the hall}, was suspended a suit of mail[91], [not, like the pictures, an ancestral relic, but of the most modern date]; for it had been manufactured by a skilful armorer[92] in London, the same year {in which Governor Bellingham came over to New England}. There was a steel head-piece, a cuirass[93], a gorget[94], and greaves[95], with a pair of gauntlets[96] and a sword hanging beneath; all, and especially the helmet and breastplate, [so highly burnished as to glow with white radiance, and scatter an illumination everywhere about upon the floor]. This bright panoply[97] was not meant for mere idle show, but had been worn by the Governor on many a solemn muster and training field[98], and had glittered, moreover, at the head of a

---

90 sternness and severity: 근엄하고 엄정함
91 mail: 쇠사슬 갑옷
92 armorer: 무기 제조자
93 cuirass: 가슴 부위에 입는 갑옷, 흉갑
94 gorget: 목에 두르는 갑옷
95 greave: 정강이받이
96 a pair of gauntlets: 갑옷용 장갑 한 켤레
97 panoply: (많은 수의 인상적인) 모음

regiment in the Pequod war[99]. For, [though bred a lawyer, and accustomed to speak of Bacon, Coke, Noye, and Finch, as his professional associates], the exigencies[100] of this new country had transformed Governor Bellingham into a soldier, as well as a statesman and ruler.

Little Pearl — who was as greatly pleased with the gleaming armour {as she had been with the glittering frontispiece[101] of the house} — spent some time looking into the polished mirror of the breastplate[102].

98 muster and training field: 검열장과 연병장

99 Pequod war: Pequot war(1637~1638)를 가리킨다. 피쿼트전쟁 은 신대륙 동부지역을 거점으로 삼았던 피쿼트 인디언(Pequot) 들과 매사추세츠 베이, 플리머스 등의 식민지인 및 그들의 원주 민 동맹[내러갠섯족(Narragansett)과 모히간족(Mohegan)]들 사 이에 토지소유권을 놓고 벌어진 전투이다. 여기에서 패배한 피 쿼트족은 수백 명이 죽고 수백 명이 서인도 제도로 노예로 팔려 가는 등, 최종적으로 대략 700명가량의 피쿼트족이 죽거나 포로 가 되었으며 생존자들은 뿔뿔이 흩어졌다. 이를 계기로 청교도 들은 더욱 노골적으로 정착지 확장에 나서게 된다. 윌리엄 브래 드포드(William Bradford)의 『플리머스 농장기』(Of Plymouth Plantation, 1637)에 피쿼트족과 관련된 분쟁이 기록되어 있으 며, 이 전쟁에 대한 기록으로는 영국군 장교였던 존 메이슨(John Mason)이 남긴 『피쿼트전쟁 약사(略史)』(Brief History of Pequot War, 1736)가 가장 유명하다.

100 exigency: 긴급사태

101 frontispiece: 정면

102 breastplate: 가슴을 가리는 갑옷

"Mother," cried she, "I see you here. Look! Look!"

Hester looked, by way of humoring[103] the child; and she saw that, [owing to the peculiar effect of this convex mirror[104]], the scarlet letter was represented in exaggerated and gigantic proportions, so as to be greatly the most prominent feature of her appearance. In truth, she seemed absolutely hidden behind it. Pearl pointed upward, also, at a similar picture in the head-piece; smiling at her mother, with the elfish intelligence {that was so familiar an expression on her small physiognomy[105]}. That look of naughty merriment[106] was likewise reflected in the mirror, [with so much breadth and intensity of effect, that it made Hester Prynne feel {as if it could not be the image of her own child, but of an imp [who was seeking to mould itself into Pearl's shape]}].

"Come along, Pearl!" said she, drawing her away, "Come and look into this fair garden. It may be, we shall see flowers there; more beautiful ones {than we find in the woods}."

Pearl, accordingly[107], ran to the bow-window, at the farther

---

103 humor: 어르다, 맞장구치다, 비위를 맞추다
104 convex mirror: 볼록 거울
105 physiognomy: 얼굴, 골상
106 naughty merriment: 버릇없는 명랑함
107 accordingly: 그래서, 그 말을 듣고

end of the hall, and looked along the vista[108] of a garden-walk[109], [carpeted with closely shaven grass, and bordered with some rude and immature attempt at shrubbery]. But the proprietor appeared already to have relinquished[110], [as hopeless], the effort to perpetuate[111] [on this side of the Atlantic], [in a hard soil and amid the close struggle for subsistence[112]], the native English taste for ornamental gardening. Cabbages grew in plain sight[113]; and a pumpkin vine, [rooted at some distance], had run across the intervening space, and deposited one of its gigantic products directly beneath the hall-windows, [as if to warn the Governor {that this great lump of vegetable gold was as rich an ornament as New England earth would offer him}]. There were a few rose-bushes[114], however, and a number of apple-trees, probably the descendants of those [planted by the Reverend Mr. Blackstone[115], the first settler of the peninsula; that half mythological personage {who rides through our early annals,

---

108 vista: 경치, 풍경

109 garden-walk: 정원 산책로

110 relinquish: 포기하다

111 perpetuate: 영속시키다, 지속시키다. *perpetuate의 목적어는 the native English taste 부분이다.

112 the close struggle for subsistence: 생존을 위한 각박한 투쟁

113 in plain sight: 앞이 (가리는 것이) 없이 잘 보이는

114 rose-bushes: 장미 덤불

115 Mr. Blackstone: 블랙스톤은 청교도들을 싫어해서 그들이 보스턴 식민지에 도착하자 인디언들과 함께 살기 위해 떠났다고 전해지는 인물이다.

seated on the back of a bull}].

Pearl, [seeing the rose-bushes], began to cry for a red rose, and would not be pacified[116].

"Hush, child, hush!" said her mother earnestly. "Do not cry, dear little Pearl! I hear voices in the garden. The Governor is coming, and gentlemen along with him!"

In fact, [adown the vista of the garden-avenue], a number of persons were seen approaching towards the house. Pearl, [in utter scorn of her mother's attempt to quiet her], gave an eldritch[117] scream, and then became silent; not from any notion of obedience, but because the quick and mobile curiosity of her disposition was excited by the appearance of those new personages.

---

116 be pacified: 진정되다, 달래지다
117 eldritch: 섬뜩한, 으스스한

The Scarlet Letter 8장

The Elf-child and the Minister

Governor Bellingham, [in a loose gown and easy cap, — such as elderly gentlemen loved to indue[1] themselves with, in their domestic privacy], — walked foremost, and appeared to be showing off his estate, and expatiating on[2] his projected improvements[3]. [The wide circumference[4] of an elaborate ruff[5], beneath his gray beard, in the antiquated fashion of King James's reign], caused his head to look not a little like that of John the Baptist in a charger[6]. The impression [made by his aspect, so rigid and severe, and frost-bitten[7] with more than autumnal age], was hardly in keeping with[8] the appliances[9] of worldly enjoyment {wherewith he had evidently done his utmost to surround himself}. But it is an error to suppose that our great forefathers — {though accustomed to speak and think of human existence as a state merely of trial and warfare, and though unfeignedly[10] prepared to sacrifice goods and life at the behest of duty[11]} — made it a matter of conscience to

---

1 indue=endue: 부여하다, (옷을) 입다

2 expatiate on: ~에 대해 상세히 설명하다

3 projected improvements: 계획된 개량작업

4 circumference: 주위, 둘레. ＊the circumference of one's chest: 가슴둘레; This lake is about 2 miles in circumference. 이 호수의 둘레는 약 2마일이다.

5 ruff: 주름깃

6 charger: 크고 납작한 접시(platter)

7 frost-bitten: 서리 맞은

8 hardly in keeping with: 거의 어울리지 않았다

9 appliance: 장치, 설비

10 unfeignedly: 꾸밈없이, 거짓 없이, 있는 그대로

reject such means of comfort, or even luxury, {as lay fairly[12] within their grasp}. This creed[13] was never taught, for instance, by the venerable pastor[14], John Wilson, {whose beard, [white as a snow-drift[15]], was seen over Governor Bellingham's shoulders}; while its wearer[16] suggested that pears and peaches might yet be naturalized[17] in the New England climate, and that purple grapes might possibly be compelled to flourish, against the sunny garden-wall. The old clergyman, [nurtured at the rich bosom of the English Church], had a long established and legitimate taste for all good and comfortable things; and {however stern he might show himself in the pulpit, or in his public reproof[18] of such transgressions[19] as that of Hester Prynne}, still, the genial benevolence[20] of his private life had won him warmer affection {than was accorded to any of his professional contemporaries}.

[Behind the Governor and Mr. Wilson] came two other

---

11 at the behest of duty: 의무의 명령에 따라. *behest: 명령, 요청
12 fairly: 공정하게, 정직하게
13 creed: 주의, 신조
14 venerable pastor: 목사님. *venerable: 존경할 만한, 덕망 있는, ~님
15 snow-drift: 바람에 날려 쌓인 눈. *drift: 이동, 추이
16 its wearer: 수염을 기른 이. 존 윌슨(John Wilson)을 가리킨다. *it은 수염을 가리킴.
17 naturalize: 귀화시키다, 이식하다, 순응시키다
18 reproof: 책망
19 transgression: 죄
20 genial benevolence: 다정한 자비심

guests; one, the Reverend Arthur Dimmesdale, {whom the reader may remember, as having taken a brief and reluctant part in the scene of Hester Prynne's disgrace}; and, [in close companionship with him], old Roger Chillingworth, a person of great skill in physic[21], {who, for two or three years past, had been settled in the town}. It was understood that this learned man was the physician as well as friend of the young minister, {whose health had severely suffered, of late, by his too unreserved self-sacrifice to the labors and duties of the pastoral relation[22]}.

The Governor, [in advance of his visitors], ascended one or two steps, and, [throwing open the leaves[23] of the great hall-window], found himself close to little Pearl. The shadow of the curtain fell on Hester Prynne, and partially concealed her.

"What have we here?[24]" said Governor Bellingham, [looking with surprise at the scarlet little figure before him]. "I profess, I have never seen the like, since my days of vanity, in old King James's time, {when I was wont to esteem it a high favor to be admitted to a court mask!} There used to be a swarm[25] of

---

21 physic: 약, 약제, 의술
22 the labors and duties of the pastoral relation: 목회자의 일과 관계된 수고와 직분
23 leaf: 접이문, 덧문 등의 문짝
24 What have we here?: 이게 뭐야?

these small apparitions[26], in holiday-time; and we called them children of the Lord of Misrule[27]. But how gat[28] such a guest into my hall?"

"Ay, indeed!" cried good old Mr. Wilson. "What little bird of scarlet plumage[29] may this be? Methinks I have seen just such figures, {when the sun has been shining through a richly[30] painted window, and tracing out[31] the golden and crimson images across the floor}. But that was in the old land. Prithee[32], young one, who art thou, and what has ailed[33] thy mother to bedizen[34] thee in this strange fashion? Art thou a Christian child,—ha? Dost know thy catechism[35]? Or art thou one of

---

25 swarm: 무리, 군중
26 apparition: 유령, 허깨비, 기묘한 현상
27 Lord of Misrule: 무질서의 제왕, 무질서 경(卿), (특히 15~16세기에 잉글랜드의 궁정·영주 저택 등에서 베풀어진) 크리스마스 연회 따위를 위해 선출된 사회자. 이 사회자는 농부나 기타 낮은 계급 사람 중에서 임명되어 바보제(Feast of Fools)를 주관한다. 즉, 예컨대 젊은이들이 자기들 중에서 가짜 교황, 대주교, 주교 등을 뽑아 교회의 의식을 풍자하며 대관식 등의 예식을 치르는데, '비이성(非理性) 수도원장', '멍청이들의 대주교', '바보들의 교황' 등의 명칭을 부여하며 유쾌하게 논다. *misrule: 실정, 혼란, 소동, 무질서
28 gat: 〈고어〉 get의 과거
29 plumage: 깃, 깃털
30 richly: 호화롭게, 화려하게, 진하게
31 trace out: 그리다, 찾아내다
32 prithee: 바라건대, 제발
33 ail: 괴롭히다, 번거롭게 하다
34 bedizen: 야하게 치장하다, 장식하다
35 catechism: 교리문답서

those naughty[36] elfs or fairies[37], {whom we thought to have left behind us, with other relics of Papistry[38], in merry old England[39]}?"

"I am mother's child," answered the scarlet vision[40], "and my name is Pearl!"

"Pearl? — Ruby[41], rather! — or Coral[42]! — or Red Rose, at the very least, judging from thy hue!" responded the old minister,

---

36 naughty: 버릇없는, 말을 안 듣는

37 elf, fairy: fairy는 켈트계(대개는 영국, 아일랜드, 스코틀랜드 등) 전통에 등장하는, 작고 추하게 생긴 마귀(goblin, 도깨비), 레프리콘(leprechaun, 아일랜드 민화에 나오는 남자 모습의 작은 요정) 등 대부분의 마법적인 존재를 묘사하는 광범위한 용어. 할리우드 디즈니의 영향으로 fairy는 날개가 달려 있고, 숲에 살며, 소원을 들어 주는 마법적 존재라는 생각이 퍼져 있으나 원래는 인간세상에서 말썽과 혼란을 일으키는 존재였다. elf는 게르만계 특유의 이야기에 등장하는 fairy보다 더 사악한 존재로 아이들을 유괴하거나 여행자들을 숲 속에서 길을 잃게 하는 등의 짓을 저지르는 것으로 묘사된다.

38 other relics of Papistry: 가톨릭의 다른 유물들

39 merry old England: merrie라고 쓰기도 한다. 영국인들이 중세와 산업혁명 시작 전의 시기를 염두에 두고 자신들의 사회와 문화를 전원적 · 목가적인 삶의 방식에 기반을 둔 유토피아적인 것이라고 생각하며 스스로를 부르는 명칭이다.

40 vision: 시력, 예지력, 환영. *have good/perfect/poor/blurred/ normal vision: 시력이 좋다/완벽하다/나쁘다/흐릿하다/정상이다; Cats have good night vision. 고양이는 밤눈이 밝다.

41 Ruby: 홍옥

42 Coral: 산호

[putting forth his hand in a vain attempt[43] to pat little Pearl on the cheek]. "But where is this mother of thine? Ah! I see," he added; and, [turning to Governor Bellingham], whispered, — " This is the selfsame child[44] {of whom we have held speech together}; and behold here the unhappy woman, Hester Prynne, her mother!"

"Sayest thou so?" cried the Governor. "Nay, we might have judged {that such a child's mother must needs be a scarlet woman, and a worthy type of her of Babylon[45]}! But she comes at a good time[46]; and we will look into this matter forthwith[47]."

Governor Bellingham stepped through the window into the hall, [followed by his three guests].

"Hester Prynne," said he, [fixing his naturally stern regard[48] on the wearer of the scarlet letter], "there hath been much question concerning thee, of late. The point hath been

---

43 vain attempt: 헛수고
44 selfsame child: 바로 그 아이
45 worthy type of her of Babylon: 바빌론에 어울릴 법한 유형의 [주홍색] 여인. *worthy of: ~에 어울릴 법한, ~가 할 법한
46 at a good[proper] time: 제때에
47 forthwith: 당장, 곧
48 regard: 관계, 관련, 주의, 고려. *with special regard for your safety: 당신의 안전을 특별히 고려하여. *(주목, 응시, 존경) a high regard for learning: 학식에 대한 높은 존경

weightily[49] discussed, whether we, [that are of authority and influence], do well discharge[50] our consciences by trusting an immortal soul, {such as there is in yonder child}, to the guidance of one {who hath stumbled[51] and fallen, amid the pitfalls[52] of this world}. Speak thou, the child's own mother! Were it not, thinkest thou, for thy little one's temporal[53] and eternal welfare, [that she be taken out of thy charge, and clad soberly[54], and disciplined strictly, and instructed in the truths of heaven and earth]? What canst thou do for the child, in this kind?"

"I can teach my little Pearl {what I have learned from this}!" answered Hester Prynne, laying her finger on the red token.

"Woman, it is thy badge of shame!" replied the stern magistrate. "It is [because of the stain {which that letter indicates}], {that we would transfer thy child to other hands}."

"Nevertheless," said the mother calmly, though growing more pale, "this badge hath taught me,—it daily teaches

---

49 weightily(=weightly): 무게 있게, 중요하게
50 discharge: (어떤 장소나 직무에서) 떠나는 것을 허락하다, (임무 등을) 이행하다
51 stumbled: 발을 헛딛은
52 pitfalls: 위험, 함정
53 temporal: 현세적인, 속세의, 시간의 제약을 받는
54 soberly: 수수하게

me, — it is teaching me at this moment, — lessons {whereof my child may be the wiser and better, albeit[55] they can profit nothing to myself}."

"We will judge warily[56]," said Bellingham, "and look[57] well what we are about to do. Good Master Wilson, I pray you, examine this Pearl, — since that is her name, — and see whether she hath had such Christian nurture {as befits[58] a child of her age}."

The old minister seated himself in an arm-chair, and made an effort to draw Pearl betwixt his knees. But the child, [unaccustomed to the touch or familiarity of any but her mother], escaped through the open window and stood on the upper step, [looking like a wild, tropical[59] bird, of rich plumage, ready to take flight into the upper air[60]]. Mr. Wilson, [not a little astonished at this outbreak[61], — for he was a grandfatherly sort of personage, and usually a vast favorite with children], —

---

55 albeit: 비록 ~일지라도
56 warily: 조심하여, 방심하지 않고. ＊wary: 경계하는, 조심하는
57 look: ~을 주시하다, ~을 눈여겨보다, ~을 조사하다
58 hath had such Christian nurture as befits: ~에 걸맞은 그런 기독
    교적인 양육과정을 거쳐 왔는지. ＊nurture: 양육, 육성
59 tropical: 열대의, 열대 지방의
60 into the upper air: 상공으로, 하늘 높이
61 outbreak: 발생, 발발

essayed[62], however, to proceed with the examination.

"Pearl," said he, with great solemnity, "thou must take heed to instruction, {that so, in due season, thou mayest wear [in thy bosom] the pearl of great price}. Canst thou tell me, my child, who made thee?"

MP3 ★
8장 (2)
시작 Now Pearl knew well enough who made her; for Hester Prynne, the daughter of a pious home, [very soon after her talk with the child about her Heavenly Father], had begun to inform her of those truths {which the human spirit, [at whatever stage of immaturity], imbibes[63] with such eager interest}. Pearl, therefore, {so large were the attainments of her three years' lifetime}, could have borne a fair[64] examination in the New England Primer[65], or the first column of the Westminster Catechism, {although unacquainted with[66] the outward form of either of those celebrated works}. But that perversity[67], {which all children have more or less of}, and {of which little Pearl had a tenfold[68] portion, now, at the most

---

62 essay: 시도(시험)하다
63 imbibe: 흡수하다
64 fair: 정정당당한
65 primer: 입문서, 초급독본
66 unacquainted with: ~에 익숙하지 않은, 경험이 없는
67 perversity: 심술궂음
68 tenfold: 열 배의

inopportune moment[69]}, took thorough possession of her, and closed her lips, or impelled her to speak words amiss. [After putting her finger in her mouth, with many ungracious[70] refusals to answer good Mr. Wilson's question], the child finally announced {that she had not been made at all, but had been plucked by her mother off the bush of wild roses, [that grew by the prison-door]}.

This fantasy was probably suggested by the near proximity of the Governor's red roses, {as Pearl stood outside of the window}; together with her recollection of the prison rose-bush, {which she had passed in coming hither}.

Old Roger Chillingworth, [with a smile on his face], whispered something in the young clergyman's ear. Hester Prynne looked at the man of skill, and even then, [with her fate hanging in the balance[71]], was startled to perceive {what a change had come over his features,—how much uglier they were,—how his dark complexion seemed to have grown duskier, and his figure more misshapen,—since the days when she had familiarly known him}. She met his eyes for an instant,

---

69 at the most inopportune moment: 가장 안 좋은 시기. *inopportune: 계제가 나쁜, 공교롭게 때가 좋지 않은

70 ungracious: 불손한

71 hang in the balance: 극히 불안정한 상태에 있다, 위기에 처해 있다. *balance: 저울, 추, 천칭

but was immediately constrained[72] to give all her attention to the scene [now going forward].

"This is awful!" cried the Governor, slowly recovering from the astonishment {into which Pearl's response had thrown him}. "Here is a child of three years old, and she cannot tell {who made her}! Without question, she is equally in the dark [as to her soul, its present depravity[73], and future destiny]! Methinks, gentlemen, we need inquire no further."

Hester caught hold of Pearl, and drew her forcibly into her arms, [confronting the old Puritan magistrate with almost a fierce expression]. [Alone in the world, cast off by it, and with this sole treasure to keep her heart alive], she felt that she possessed indefeasible[74] rights against the world, and was ready to defend them to the death.

"God gave me the child!" cried she. "He gave her, [in requital[75] of all things else, {which ye had taken from me}]. She is my happiness! — she is my torture, none the less! Pearl keeps me here in life! Pearl punishes me, too! See ye not, she is the scarlet letter, [only capable of being loved, and so endowed

72 constrain: ~하게 만들다, 강요하다, ~하지 않을 수 없다
73 depravity: 타락, 부패
74 indefeasible: 파기할 수 없는, 무효로 할 수 없는
75 requital: 보답, 보상

266

with a million-fold the power of retribution[76] for my sin]? Ye shall not take her! I will die first!"

"My poor woman," said the not unkind old minister, "the child shall be well cared for! — far better than thou canst do it."

"God gave her into my keeping," repeated Hester Prynne, [raising her voice almost to a shriek]. "I will not give her up!" — And here by a sudden impulse, she turned to the young clergyman, Mr. Dimmesdale, {at whom, up to this moment, she had seemed hardly so much as once to direct her eyes}. — "Speak thou for me!" cried she. "Thou wast my pastor, and hadst charge of my soul, and knowest me better than these men can. I will not lose the child! Speak for me! Thou knowest, — for thou hast sympathies {which these men lack}! — thou knowest {what is in my heart}, and {what are a mother's rights}, and {how much the stronger they are, when that mother has but her child and the scarlet letter}! Look thou to it! I will not lose the child! Look to it!"

At this wild and singular appeal, {which indicated that Hester Prynne's situation had provoked her to little less than madness}, the young minister at once came forward, pale, and holding his hand over his heart, {as was his custom whenever

---

76 retribution: 응징, 징벌

his peculiarly nervous temperament was thrown into agitation}. He looked now more careworn and emaciated[77] than {as we described him at the scene of Hester's public ignominy[78]}; and {whether it were his failing health}, or {whatever the cause might be}, his large dark eyes had a world of[79] pain in their troubled and melancholy[80] depth.

"There is truth in {what she says}," began the minister, with a voice sweet, tremulous, but powerful, {insomuch that the hall reechoed, and the hollow armor rang with it}—"truth in {what Hester says}, and in the feeling {which inspires her}! God gave her the child, and gave her, too, an instinctive[81] knowledge of its nature and requirements,—both seemingly so peculiar,—{which no other mortal being can possess}. And, moreover, is there not a quality of awful sacredness[82] in the relation between this mother and this child?"

"Ay!—how is that, good Master Dimmesdale?" interrupted the Governor. "Make that plain, I pray you!"

---

77 emaciated: 쇠약한, 수척한
78 ignominy: 불명예, 수치
79 a world of: 다수의, 다량의
80 melancholy: 구슬픈
81 instinctive: 본능적인
82 sacredness: 신성함

"It must be even so," resumed the minister. "For, {if we deem it otherwise}, do we not thereby say {that the Heavenly Father, the Creator of all flesh, hath lightly recognized a deed of sin, and made [of no account] the distinction between unhallowed[83] lust and holy love}? This child of its father's guilt and its mother's shame has come from the hand of God, [to work in many ways upon her heart, {who pleads so earnestly, and with such bitterness of spirit, the right to keep her}]. It was meant for a blessing; for the one blessing of her life! It was meant, doubtless, {as the mother herself hath told us}, for a retribution too; a torture, to be felt [at many an unthought of moment]; a pang, a sting, an ever-recurring agony, [in the midst of a troubled joy]! Hath she not expressed this thought in the garb of the poor child, so forcibly reminding us of that red symbol {which sears her bosom}?"

"Well said, again!" cried good Mr. Wilson. "I feared {the woman had no better thought than to make a mountebank[84] of her child}!"

"O, not so!—not so!" continued Mr. Dimmesdale. "She recognizes, believe me, the solemn miracle {which God hath wrought, in the existence of that child}. And may she

---

83 unhallowed: 신성하지 않은, 부정한. *hallow: 신성하게 하다
84 mountebank: 사기꾼, 협잡꾼, 광대, 엉터리 약장수

feel, too, — {what, methinks, is the very truth}, — {that this boon[85] was meant, above all things else, to keep the mother's soul alive, and to preserve her from blacker depths of sin [into which Satan might else have sought to plunge her]}! Therefore it is good for this poor, sinful woman {that she hath an infant immortality, [a being capable of eternal joy or sorrow], confided to her care[86], — to be trained up by her to righteousness, — to remind her, at every moment, of her fall, — but yet to teach her, [as it were by the Creator's sacred pledge], [that, {if she bring the child to heaven}, the child also will bring its parent thither]}! Herein is the sinful mother happier than the sinful father. For Hester Prynne's sake, then, and no less for the poor child's sake, let us leave them {as Providence hath seen fit to place them}!"

"You speak, my friend, with a strange earnestness," said old Roger Chillingworth, smiling at him.

"And there is weighty import in {what my young brother hath spoken}," added the Reverend Mr. Wilson. "What say you, worshipful Master Bellingham? Hath he not pleaded well for the poor woman?"

---

85 boon: 혜택, 은혜

86 hath an infant immortality confided to her care: '아이의 불멸성 [=영혼]'이 그녀 자신의 보살핌에 맡겨지게 하다. ＊이다음 부분에서는 여러 개의 to 부정사 부분이 '목적'의 의미를 띠고 있다.

"Indeed hath he," answered the magistrate, "and hath adduced such arguments, {that we will even leave the matter [as it now stands]; so long, at least, as there shall be no further scandal in the woman}. Care must be had, nevertheless, to put the child to due and stated examination in the catechism[87] at thy hands or Master Dimmesdale's. Moreover, at a proper season, the tithing-men[88] must take heed {that she go both to school and to meeting}."

The young minister, on ceasing to speak, had withdrawn a few steps from the group, and stood [with his face partially concealed in the heavy folds[89] of the window-curtain]; while the shadow of his figure, {which the sunlight cast upon the floor}, was tremulous with the vehemence[90] of his appeal. Pearl, [that wild and flighty[91] little elf], stole softly towards him, and, [taking his hand in the grasp of both her own], laid her cheek against it; a caress so tender, and withal so unobtrusive[92], that her mother, {who was looking on}, asked herself, — "Is that my Pearl?" Yet she knew that there was love in the child's heart, {although it mostly revealed itself in passion, and hardly twice

---

87 catechism: 교리문답서
88 tithing-man: 질서유지를 책임지고 있는 교구 관리. ＊tithe: 십일조; tithing: 〈고전법률〉 10인조(열 집을 한 조로 한 행정단위)
89 fold: 주름, 접은 부분
90 vehemence: 격렬함, 열정
91 flighty: 변덕스러운
92 unobtrusive: 불필요하게 관심을 끌지 않는, 삼가는

in her lifetime had been softened by such gentleness as now}. The minister,—for, [save the long-sought regards of woman], nothing is sweeter than these marks of childish preference, [accorded spontaneously by a spiritual instinct, and therefore seeming to imply in us something truly worthy to be loved],— the minister looked round, laid his hand on the child's head, hesitated an instant, and then kissed her brow. Little Pearl's unwonted[93] mood of sentiment lasted no longer; she laughed, and went capering down[94] the hall, so airily[95], that old Mr. Wilson raised a question {whether even her tiptoes touched the floor}.

"The little baggage[96] hath witchcraft in her, I profess," said he to Mr. Dimmesdale. "She needs no old woman's broomstick[97] to fly withal!"

"A strange child!" remarked old Roger Chillingworth. "It is easy to see the mother's part in her. Would it be beyond a philosopher's research, think ye, gentlemen, to analyze that child's nature, and, from its make[98] and mould[99], to give a

---

93 unwonted: 특이한, 뜻밖의
94 went capering down: 깡충깡충 뛰어다니다
95 airily: 대수롭지 않다는 듯
96 baggage: (경멸적) 말괄량이 아가씨
97 broomstick: 대가 긴 빗자루
98 make: ~제(製), 기질
99 mould: 틀에 의해 만들어진 형체, 모양

shrewd[100] guess at the father?"

"Nay; it would be sinful, in such a question, to follow the clew[101] of profane philosophy," said Mr. Wilson. "Better to fast and pray upon it; and still better, it may be, to leave the mystery {as we find it}, {unless Providence reveal it of its own accord}. Thereby, every good Christian man hath a title to show a father's kindness towards the poor, deserted babe."

[The affair being so satisfactorily concluded], Hester Prynne, with Pearl, departed from the house. {As they descended the steps}, it is averred that the lattice of a chamber-window was thrown open, and forth into the sunny day was thrust the face of Mistress Hibbins, Governor Bellingham's bitter-tempered[102] sister, and the same {who, a few years later, was executed[103] as a witch}.

"Hist[104], hist!" said she, while her ill-omened physiognomy seemed to cast a shadow over the cheerful newness of the house. "Wilt thou go with us to-night? There will be a merry

---

100 shrewd: 빈틈없는, 약빠른
101 clew(=clue): 실마리
102 bitter-tempered: 신랄한, 성미 고약한
103 execute: 처형하다, 사형하다
104 hist(=hush): 쉿, 조용히

company in the forest; and I wellnigh[105] promised the Black Man {that comely[106] Hester Prynne should make one}."

"Make my excuse to him, so please you[107]!" answered Hester, with a triumphant smile. "I must tarry at home, and keep watch over my little Pearl. {Had they taken her from me}, I would willingly have gone with thee into the forest, and signed my name in the Black Man's book too, and that with mine own blood!"

"We shall have thee there anon!" said the witch-lady, frowning, {as she drew back her head}.

But here — if we suppose this interview betwixt Mistress Hibbins and Hester Prynne to be authentic, and not a parable — was already an illustration of the young minister's argument against sundering the relation of a fallen mother to the offspring of her frailty. Even thus early had the child saved her from Satan's snare.

---

105 wellnigh: 거의

106 comely: 용모가 아름다운, 어여쁜

107 so please you: 부디, 죄송하지만. *if you please의 의미와 동일하다.

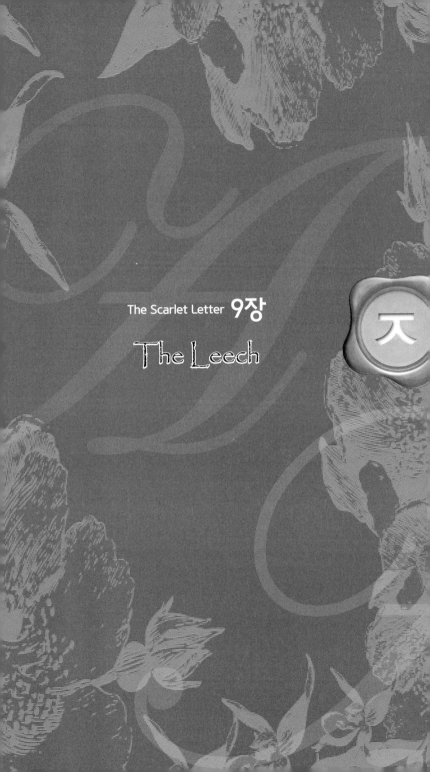

The Scarlet Letter **9장**

The Leech

天

[Under the appellation[1] of Roger Chillingworth], the reader will remember, was hidden another name, {which [its former wearer had resolved] should never more be spoken}. It has been related, {how, [in the crowd {that witnessed Hester Prynne's ignominious[2] exposure[3]}], stood a man, elderly, travel-worn, [who, just emerging from the perilous[4] wilderness, beheld the woman, {in whom he hoped to find embodied the warmth and cheerfulness of home}, set up as a type of sin before the people]}[5]. Her matronly[6] fame was trodden under all men's feet. Infamy[7] was babbling[8] around her in the public market-place. For her kindred, {should the tidings ever reach them}, and for the companions of her unspotted[9] life, there remained nothing but the contagion[10] of her dishonor;

---

1 appellation: 이름

2 ignominious: 수치스러운

3 exposure: 노출, 폭로, 드러냄

4 perilous: 아주 위험한

5 It … the people: 이 문장은 가주어, 진주어(how …)로 구성되어 있다. 진주어 부분의 기본구조는 how a man stood(한 사람이 어떻게 서 있었는지)인데 부사구 in the crowd 부분이 앞으로 나왔고, 주어 a man을 뒤에서 꾸며 주는 부분이 길어서 도치되었다. who … 관계절의 구조는 beheld the woman(목적어) set up(목적보어 과거분사)이며 목적어 the woman을 꾸며 주는 in whom … 이 사이에 위치함으로써 목적어와 목적보어 set up …이 떨어져 있게 되었다.

6 matronly: 가정부인 같은

7 infamy: 악평, 치욕

8 babble: 와글와글, 왁자지껄하다

9 unspotted: 오점 없는, 흠 없는

{which would not fail to be distributed in strict accordance and proportion with the intimacy and sacredness[11] of their previous relationship}. Then why—{since the choice was with himself}—should the individual, {whose connection with the fallen woman had been the most intimate and sacred of them all}, come forward to vindicate[12] his claim to an inheritance[13] [so little desirable]? He resolved not to be pilloried[14] beside her on her pedestal of shame. [Unknown to all but Hester Prynne], and [possessing the lock and key of her silence], he chose to withdraw his name from the roll[15] of mankind, and, {as regarded his former ties and interest}, to vanish out of life as completely as if he indeed lay at the bottom of the ocean, {whither rumor had long ago consigned him[16]}. [This purpose once effected[17]], new interests would immediately spring up, and likewise a new purpose; dark, it is true, if not guilty, but of force [enough to engage the full strength of his faculties].

---

10 contagion: 전염

11 sacredness: 신성함

12 vindicate: 요구하다

13 inheritance: 유산 상속

14 be pilloried: 비판을 받다, 남들이 보는 데서 죄인에게 칼을 씌우다, 웃음거리로 만들다

15 roll: 두루마리, 기록부, 명부

16 whither rumor had long ago consigned him: 직역하면, '그곳으로 소문이 오래전에 그를 보냈다'는 뜻으로 '소문에 따르면 이미 오래전에 그는 그곳[바다 밑]에 잠들어 있다'는 의미이다. *consign: ~에게 ~을 보내다

17 This purpose once effected: 이 목적이 일단 이루어지자

In pursuance[18] of this resolve[19], he took up his residence in the Puritan town, as Roger Chillingworth, without other introduction than the learning and intelligence {of which he possessed more than a common measure}. {As his studies, at a previous period of his life, had made him extensively acquainted with[20] the medical science of the day}, it was as a physician {that he presented himself}, and [as such[21]] was cordially[22] received. Skilful men, [of the medical and chirurgical[23] profession], were of rare occurrence[24] in the colony. They seldom, {it would appear}, partook of the religious zeal {that brought other emigrants across the Atlantic}. [In their researches into the human frame], it may be {that the higher and more subtile faculties of such men were materialized}, and {that they lost the spiritual view of existence amid the intricacies[25] of that wondrous mechanism, [which seemed to involve art enough to comprise all of life within itself]}[26]. At all events, the health of the good town

---

18 pursuance: 추구, 이행

19 resolve: 결심

20 extensively acquainted with: 방대하게 많이 알고 있는

21 as such(=as a physician): 문장 뒤의 received 다음에 놓고 해석

22 cordially: 극진히, 진심으로

23 chirurgical: 〈고어체〉 외과의. *surgical의 의미이다.

24 occurrence: 발생, 사건

25 intricacies: 복잡한 사항

26 작가는 인간의 신체구조를 연구하는 과정에서 신체구조의 기계적·물질적 정교함에 빠져 인간 존재가 지닌 정신적인 측면을 잃어버리는 현상에 대해 언급하고 있다. 의미상으로는 2개의 that 절을

of Boston, {so far as medicine had aught to do with it}, had hitherto lain in the guardianship of an aged deacon[27] and apothecary[28], {whose piety and godly deportment[29] were stronger testimonials in his favor, than any [that he could have produced in the shape of a diploma]}. The only surgeon was one {who combined the occasional exercise of that noble art with the daily and habitual flourish of a razor}. [To such a professional body] Roger Chillingworth was a brilliant acquisition[30]. He soon manifested his familiarity with the ponderous and imposing machinery of antique[31] physic; {in which every remedy contained a multitude of far-fetched and heterogeneous[32] ingredients, as elaborately compounded as if the proposed result had been the Elixir of Life[33]}. In his Indian captivity[34], moreover, he had gained much knowledge of the properties of native herbs and roots; nor did he conceal from

---

연관하여 이들의 더 고차원적이고 섬세한 능력이 물질화함에 따라 점점 더 인간의 기계적인 측면의 정교함에 빠져들면서 인간 존재에 대한 정신적인 측면을 망각한다는 내용으로 이해할 수도 있다.

27 deacon: 교회의 집사

28 apothecary: 약제상

29 deportment: 몸가짐

30 brilliant acquisition: 눈부신 횡재. *acquisition: 취득, 횡재; a valued acquisition: 귀중한 발굴물

31 antique: 옛날의

32 heterogeneous: 여러 다른 종류로 이루어진

33 Elixir of Life: 불로장생약, 만병통치약. *philosopher's stone: 철학자의 돌

34 captivity: 감금, 억류

his patients, {that these simple medicines, [Nature's boon[35] to the untutored[36] savage], had quite as large a share of his own confidence as the European pharmacopoeia[37], [which so many learned doctors had spent centuries in elaborating]}.

This learned stranger was exemplary, {as regarded at least the outward forms of a religious life}, and, [early after his arrival], had chosen for his spiritual guide the Reverend Mr. Dimmesdale. The young divine, {whose scholar-like renown still lived in Oxford}, was considered by his more fervent[38] admirers as little less than a heaven-ordained[39] apostle[40], [destined, {should he live and labor for the ordinary term of life}, to do as great deeds for the now feeble New England Church, {as the early Fathers had achieved for the infancy of the Christian faith}]. About this period, however, the health of Mr. Dimmesdale had evidently begun to fail. By those [best acquainted with his habits], the paleness of the young minister's cheek was accounted for by his too earnest devotion to study, his scrupulous fulfilment of parochial duty[41], and,

---

35 boon: 혜택

36 untutored: 교육을 받지 않은

37 pharmacopoeia: 약전(藥典), 약제의 처방 기준이 담긴 약에 대한 백과사전

38 fervent: 열렬한

39 heaven-ordained: 2판본에는 heavenly ordained로 되어 있다.

40 apostle: 사도

41 his scrupulous fulfilment of parochial duty: 교구를 돌보는 직무

more than all, <u>by</u> the fasts and vigils[42] {of which he made a frequent practice, in order to keep the grossness[43] of this earthly state from clogging and obscuring[44] his spiritual lamp}. Some declared, {that, [if Mr. Dimmesdale were really going to die], it was cause enough, that the world was not worthy to be any longer trodden by his feet}. He himself, on the other hand, with characteristic humility[45], avowed his belief {that [if Providence should see fit to remove him], it would be because of his own unworthiness to perform its humblest mission here on earth}. [With all this difference of opinion as to the cause of his decline], there could be no question of the fact. His form grew emaciated[46]; his voice, {though still rich and sweet}, had a certain melancholy prophecy of decay in it; he was often observed, [on any slight alarm or other sudden accident], to put his hand over his heart, with first a flush and then a paleness, [indicative of[47] pain].

Such was the young clergyman's condition, and so ★MP3 imminent[48] the prospect {that his dawning light would be

9장 (2)
시작

를 세심하게 이행함

42 fasts and vigils: 단식과 철야기도
43 grossness: 거침, 상스러움, 천박함
44 clogging and obscuring: 가로막고 어둡게 함
45 humility: 겸손
46 emaciated: 쇠약한
47 indicative of: ~을 나타내는[보여 주는/시사하는]
48 imminent: 임박한

extinguished[49], all untimely}, {when Roger Chillingworth made his advent[50] to the town}. His first entry on the scene, {few people could tell whence, [dropping down, as it were, out of the sky], or [starting from the nether earth]}, had an aspect of mystery, {which was easily heightened to the miraculous}. He was now known to be a man of skill; it was observed that he gathered herbs, and the blossoms of wild-flowers, and dug up roots and plucked off twigs from the forest-trees, like one [acquainted with hidden virtues {in what was valueless to common eyes}]. He was heard to speak of Sir Kenelm Digby[51], and other famous men,—{whose scientific attainments[52] were esteemed hardly less than supernatural},—as having been his correspondents or associates. Why, [with such rank in the learned world], had he come hither? What could he, {whose sphere was in great cities}, be seeking in the wilderness? In answer to this query, a rumor gained ground,—and, [however absurd], was entertained by some very sensible people,—{that Heaven had wrought an absolute miracle, by transporting an eminent Doctor of Physic, from a German university bodily

---

49 extinguish: 끄다

50 advent: 출현

51 Sir Kenelm Digby(1603~1665). 기상천외한 모험가이자 허풍쟁이 작가로 알려진 한편, 해군 사령관, 외교관, 정부 관리 등과 같이 진중한 지위에 있기도 하였다. 신비주의적인 과학에 큰 흥미를 갖기도 했으며 산소가 식물의 생명에 필수적이라는 사실을 발견하기도 하였다.

52 attainment: 성과, 성취

through the air, and setting him down at the door of Mr. Dimmesdale's study}! Individuals of wiser faith, indeed, {who knew that Heaven promotes its purposes without aiming at the stage-effect[53] of what is called miraculous interposition[54]}, were inclined to see a providential hand in Roger Chillingworth's so opportune[55] arrival.

This idea was countenanced[56] by the strong interest {which the physician ever manifested in the young clergyman}; he attached himself to him as a parishioner[57], and sought to win a friendly regard and confidence from his naturally reserved sensibility[58]. He expressed great alarm at his pastor's[59] state of health, but was anxious to attempt the cure, and, [if early undertaken], seemed not despondent[60] of a favorable result. The elders, the deacons, the motherly dames, and the young and fair maidens, of Mr. Dimmesdale's flock, were alike importunate[61] {that he should make trial of the physician's

---

53 stage-effect: 무대효과
54 interposition: 간섭, 중재
55 opportune: 시의적절한
56 countenance: 지지하다
57 parishioner: 교구 주민
58 from his naturally reserved sensibility: 원래 말을 삼가며 과묵한 감수성을 지닌 목사로부터도
59 pastor: 목사
60 despondent: 낙담한, 실의에 빠진
61 importunate: 성가시게 조르는

frankly offered skill}. Mr. Dimmesdale gently repelled[62] their entreaties[63].

"I need no medicine," said he.

But how could the young minister say so, {when, with every successive[64] Sabbath, his cheek was paler and thinner, and his voice more tremulous[65] than before}, — {when it had now become a constant habit, rather than a casual gesture, to press his hand over his heart}? Was he weary of his labors? Did he wish to die? These questions were solemnly[66] propounded[67] to Mr. Dimmesdale by the elder ministers of Boston and the deacons of his church, {who, [to use their own phrase], "dealt with him," on the sin of rejecting the aid [which Providence so manifestly held out]}. He listened in silence, and finally promised to confer with the physician[68].

"{Were it God's will}," said the Reverend Mr. Dimmesdale, {when, [in fulfilment of this pledge[69]], he requested old Roger

---

62 repel: 거절하다
63 entreaty: 간청
64 successive: 연속적인, 연이은
65 tremulous: 약간 떨리는
66 solemnly: 엄숙하게, 진지하게
67 propound: (사상, 설명)을 제기하다
68 confer with the physician: 의사와 상담하다, 의사의 진찰을 받다
69 in fulfilment of this pledge: [의사의 치료를 받겠다는] 약속을 이

Chillingworth's professional advice}, "I could be well content, that my labors, and my sorrows, and my sins, and my pains, should shortly end with me, and {what is earthly of them[70]} be buried in my grave, and the spiritual go with me to my eternal state, rather than that you should put your skill to the proof[71] in my behalf."

"Ah," replied Roger Chillingworth, with that quietness {which, [whether imposed or natural], marked all his deportment[72]}, "it is thus that a young clergyman is apt to speak. Youthful men, [not having taken a deep root], give up their hold of life so easily! And saintly men, {who walk with God on earth}, would fain be away, to walk with him on the golden pavements of the New Jerusalem."

"Nay," rejoined the young minister, putting his hand to his heart, with a flush of pain flitting over his brow[73], "{were I worthier to walk there}, I could be better content to toil here."

"Good men ever interpret themselves too meanly," said the physician.

행할 때, 즉 의사의 진찰을 받는 자리에서

70 what is earthly of them: 그것들 중에서 지상의 속성을 지닌 것

71 put ... to the proof: 시험해 보다

72 deportment: 몸가짐, 태도

73 with a flush of pain flitting over his brow: 그의 이마 위에 고통의 홍조를 띠면서

In this manner, the mysterious old Roger Chillingworth became the medical adviser of the Reverend Mr. Dimmesdale. {As not only the disease interested the physician, but he was strongly moved to look into the character and qualities of the patient}, these two men, [so different in age], came gradually to spend much time together. [For the sake of the minister's health], and [to enable the leech to gather plants with healing balm in them], they took long walks on the seashore, or in the forest; mingling various talk with the plash and murmur of the waves[74], and the solemn wind-anthem[75] among the tree-tops[76]. Often, likewise, one was the guest of the other, in his place of study and retirement[77]. There was a fascination[78] for the minister in the company of the man of science, {in whom he recognized an intellectual cultivation of no moderate depth or scope; together with a range and freedom of ideas, [that he would have vainly looked for among the members of his own profession]}. In truth, he was startled, {if not shocked}, to find this attribute[79] in the physician. Mr. Dimmesdale was a true priest, a true religionist, with the reverential sentiment

---

74 the plash and murmur of the waves: 바닷물이 철썩 부딪쳤다 잦아드는 소리

75 wind-anthem: 바람의 송가, 노래

76 tree-tops: 나무 꼭대기

77 retirement: 은거처

78 fascination: 매력, 매료됨

79 attribute: 자질, 속성

[largely developed[80]], and an order of mind {that impelled itself powerfully along the track of a creed[81], and wore its passage continually deeper with the lapse of time}. [In no state of society] would he have been {what is called a man of liberal views}; it would always be essential to his peace [to feel the pressure of a faith about him, supporting, {while it confined him within its iron framework}]. Not the less, however, {though with a tremulous enjoyment}, did he feel the occasional relief[82] of looking at the universe through the medium of another kind of intellect than those {with which he habitually held converse}. It was as if a window were thrown open, admitting a freer atmosphere into the close and stifled study, {where his life was wasting itself away, amid lamp-light, or obstructed day-beams[83], and the musty fragrance[84], [be it sensual or moral], [that exhales from books[85]]}. But the air was too fresh and chill to be long breathed, with comfort. So the minister, and the physician with him, withdrew again within the limits of {what their church defined as orthodox}.

---

80 with the reverential sentiment largely developed: 충분히 개발된, 신을 숭배하는 정서를 지닌
81 creed: 신조, 교리
82 relief: 안도, 기분전환
83 obstructed day-beams: 차단된 햇살, 간신히 스며드는 햇살. *obstruct: 막다, 방해하다
84 musty fragrance: 퀴퀴한 냄새, 곰팡내
85 that exhales from books: 책으로부터 뿜어져 나오는 [곰팡내]. *that은 관계대명사 주격임

Thus Roger Chillingworth scrutinized[86] his patient carefully, both {as he saw him in his ordinary life, keeping an accustomed pathway[87] in the range of thoughts familiar to him}, and {as he appeared when thrown amidst other moral scenery, [the novelty of which[88] might call out something new to the surface of his character]}. He deemed it essential, {it would seem}, to know the man, [before attempting to do him good]. {Wherever there is a heart and an intellect}, the diseases of the physical frame are tinged with the peculiarities[89] of these[90]. In Arthur Dimmesdale, thought and imagination were so active, and sensibility so intense, that the bodily infirmity[91] would be likely to have its groundwork[92] there. So Roger Chillingworth — the man of skill, the kind and friendly physician — strove to go deep into his patient's bosom, delving[93] among his principles, prying into[94] his recollections, and probing every

---

86 scrutinize: 세심히 살피다
87 accustomed pathway: 익숙한 길
88 which: other moral scenery가 선행사. *다른 도덕적 풍경(상황)의 새로움[신기함]이 새로운 무엇인가를 그의 성격에서 불러내 표면으로 드러나도록 한다는 의미
89 peculiarity: 기이한 특징, 특이한 점
90 these: = a heart and an intellect. *어떤 이의 육체가 병에 걸렸을 때, 그 사람 병의 특색에는 다름 아닌 그 사람의 감성과 지성의 독특한 특징들이 투영되어 있을 것이라는 의미
91 infirmity: 병약, 질환
92 groundwork: 기초, 토대
93 delve: 탐구하다, 깊이 파고들다
94 pry into: ~을 캐다

thing with a cautious[95] touch, like a treasure-seeker in a dark cavern[96]. Few secrets can escape an investigator[97], {who has opportunity and license to undertake such a quest[98], and skill to follow it up}. A man [burdened with a secret] should especially avoid the intimacy of his physician. {If the latter possess native sagacity[99], and a nameless something more, — let us call it intuition}; {if he show no intrusive egotism[100], nor disagreeably prominent characteristics of his own}; {if he have the power, [which must be born with him[101]], to bring his mind into such affinity with his patient's, that this last[102] shall unawares have spoken [what he imagines himself only to have thought]]}; {if such revelations[103] be received without tumult, and acknowledged not so often by an uttered sympathy[104], as by silence, an inarticulate breath[105], and here and there a word,

---

95 cautious: 신중한, 조심성 있는

96 cavern: 동굴

97 investigator: 조사자, 탐색가

98 who has opportunity and license to undertake such a quest: 그러한 탐색(quest)을 착수할 수 있는 기회와 자유를 가진 탐색가.
   *have a license to do ...: ~할 자유가 있다

99 sagacity: 현명함, 총명함

100 intrusive egotism: 주제넘게 참견하는 자부심[자기중심벽]

101 which must be born with him: 지니고 태어났음이 틀림없는, 그와 함께 생겨났음이 틀림없는(필시 그가 태어날 때 같이 생겼을)

102 this last: = his patient

103 revelation: 드러냄, 폭로

104 an uttered sympathy: 말로 나타낸 동감

105 an inarticulate breath: 말하지 못하고 한숨만 내쉼

to indicate [that all is understood]}; {if, [to these qualifications of a confidant[106]] be joined the advantages [afforded by his recognized character as a physician]};—then, at some inevitable moment, will the soul of the sufferer be dissolved[107], and flow forth in a dark, but transparent stream[108], bringing all its mysteries into the daylight[109].

MP3 ★
9장 [3]
시작
Roger Chillingworth possessed all, or most, of the attributes[110] [above enumerated[111]]. Nevertheless, time went on; a kind of intimacy, {as we have said}, grew up between these two cultivated minds, {which had as wide a field as the whole sphere of human thought and study, to meet upon}; they discussed every topic of ethics and religion, of public affairs, and private character; they talked much, on both sides, of matters {that seemed personal to themselves}; and yet no secret, {such as [the physician fancied] must exist there}, ever stole out of the minister's consciousness into his companion's ear. The latter had his suspicions[112], indeed, {that even the nature of Mr. Dimmesdale's bodily disease had never fairly

---

106 qualifications of a confidant: 절친한 친구[상담상대]라는 자격

107 dissolve: 녹다

108 transparent stream: 투명한 물결

109 bringing all its mysteries into the daylight: 모든 비밀을 백일하에 드러내다

110 attributes: 속성, 특성

111 enumerate: 열거하다

112 suspicion: 의심

been revealed to him}. It was a strange reserve![113]

[After a time], [at a hint from Roger Chillingworth], the friends of Mr. Dimmesdale effected an arrangement {by which the two were lodged[114] in the same house; so that every ebb and flow of the minister's life-tide[115] might pass under the eye of his anxious and attached physician}. There was much joy throughout the town, {when this greatly desirable object was attained}. It was held to be the best possible measure for the young clergyman's welfare; {unless, indeed, [as often urged by such as felt authorized to do so], he had selected some one of the many blooming damsels[116], [spiritually devoted to him], to become his devoted wife. This latter step[117], however, there was no present prospect {that Arthur Dimmesdale would be prevailed upon to take}; he rejected all suggestions of the kind, {as if priestly celibacy[118] were one of his articles of church-discipline[119]}. [Doomed by his own choice, therefore, {as Mr. Dimmesdale so evidently was}, to[120] eat his unsavory morsel[121]

---

113 It was a strange reserve!: 목사가 속을 털어놓지 않으니 실로 이상한 노릇이다! ※reserve: 말이 없음, 내성적임

114 lodge: 숙박하다, 머무르다, 묵다

115 every ebb and flow of the minister's life-tide: 목사의 생명이라는 조수의 모든 밀물과 썰물, 모든 움직임

116 many blooming damsels: 많은 한창때의 처녀들

117 this latter step: 뒤의 take의 목적어로 도치됨

118 celibacy: 독신

119 articles of church-discipline: 교회 기율의 조항들

always at another's board, and endure the life-long chill {which must be his lot who seeks[122] to warm himself only at another's fireside}, it truly seemed {that this sagacious[123], experienced, benevolent[124], old physician, [with his concord of paternal and reverential love[125] for the young pastor[126]], was the very man, of all mankind, to be constantly within reach of his voice}.

The new abode[127] of the two friends was with a pious[128] widow, of good social rank, {who dwelt in a house covering pretty nearly the site [on which the venerable[129] structure of King's Chapel has since been built]}. It had the grave-yard, originally Isaac Johnson's home-field, on one side, and so was well adapted to call up serious reflections, [suited to their respective employments[130]], in both minister and man of physic. The motherly care of the good widow assigned [to[131]

---

120 doomed ... to ...: ~할 운명인

121 unsavory morsel: 맛이 고약한 부스러기 음식

122 his lot who seeks: the lot of those who seek(~하려는 이들의 운명)으로 볼 수 있다.

123 sagacious: 현명한

124 benevolent: 자애로운

125 paternal and reverential love: 아버지 같으면서도 존경하는 사랑

126 pastor: 목사

127 abode: 거주지, 집

128 pious: 경건한, 독실한

129 venerable: 유서 깊은, 고색창연하여 숭엄한, 존귀한

130 suited to their respective employments: 각자의 일을 하기에 적합한

Mr. Dimmesdale] a front apartment, [with a sunny exposure, and heavy window-curtains to create a noontide shadow, {when desirable}]. The walls were hung round with tapestry, [said to be from the Gobelin looms[132], and, at all events, representing the Scriptural story of David and Bathsheba, and Nathan the Prophet[133], in colors still unfaded, but {which made the fair woman of the scene almost as grimly picturesque as the woe-denouncing seer[134]}]. Here, the pale clergyman piled up his library, [rich with parchment-bound folios[135] of the Fathers[136], and the lore of Rabbis, and monkish erudition[137], {of which the Protestant divines[138], [even while they vilified and decried[139] that class of writers], were yet constrained[140] often

---

131 assign to ...: ~에 배정하다, ~로 정하다
132 Gobelin looms: 고블랭 직조기[베틀]. 고블랭은 15세기 중반 이후 파리의 비에브르(Bièvre) 강변에서 염색업을 하던 가문으로 이후 양탄자 직조를 함께 하였다. 여러 세대가 지나 가문이 번창하면서 귀족 작위를 취득하여 다양한 공직에 올랐고 앙리 4세로부터는 공작의 작위와 봉토를 하사받았다. 여기에서 고블랭은 양탄자 직조 기술의 진수를 의미한다.
133 Scriptural story of David and Bathsheba, and Nathan the Prophet: 다윗과 밧세바 그리고 예언자 나단에 관한 성경 이야기. 현자 나단이 남의 아내를 취하려는 다윗을 저주하는 그림의 양탄자로 볼 수 있다.
134 woe-denouncing seer: 재난을 예고하는 예언자. (여기서는 나단을 가리킴)
135 parchment-bound folios: 양피지로 장정한 이절판
136 the Fathers: 교부들
137 monkish erudition: 수도사들의 박식함
138 the Protestant divines: 개신교의 목사들

to avail themselves}]. On the other side of the house, old Roger Chillingworth arranged his study and laboratory[141]; not such {as[142] a modern man of science would reckon even tolerably complete}, but provided with a distilling apparatus[143], and the means of compounding drugs and chemicals, {which[144] the practised[145] alchemist knew well how to turn to purpose}. [With such commodiousness[146] of situation], these two learned persons sat themselves down, each in his own domain, yet familiarly passing from one apartment to the other, and bestowing a mutual and not incurious[147] inspection into one another's business.

And the Reverend Arthur Dimmesdale's best discerning friends, {as we have intimated}, very reasonably imagined {that the hand of Providence had done all this, for the purpose— [besought in so many public, and domestic, and secret prayers]—of restoring the young minister to health}. But—

---

139 vilify and decry: 비난하고 매도하다

140 constrain: 하는 수 없이 ~하게 하다

141 laboratory: 실험실

142 as: 유사관계대명사로 이 절 안에서 reckon의 빠진 목적어 자리에 선행사 such를 놓고 의미 파악

143 distilling apparatus: 증류기

144 which의 선행사는 앞의 장치와 수단들이며, 이것들을 which 절 안의 turn의 생략된 목적어 자리에 놓고 의미 파악

145 practised: 숙련된, 경험이 풍부한

146 commodiousness: 넓음, 편리함

147 incurious: 호기심이 없는

{it must now be said}—another portion of the community had latterly[148] begun to take its own view of the relation betwixt Mr. Dimmesdale and the mysterious old physician. {When an uninstructed multitude attempts to see with its eyes}, it is exceedingly[149] apt to be deceived. {When, however, it forms its judgment, [as it usually does], on the intuitions of its great and warm heart}, the conclusions [thus attained] are often so profound and so unerring[150], as to possess the character of truths [supernaturally revealed]. The people, [in the case of which we speak], could justify its prejudice against Roger Chillingworth by no fact or argument [worthy of serious refutation[151]]. There was an aged handicraftsman[152], [it is true], {who had been a citizen of London at the period of Sir Thomas Overbury[153]'s murder, now some thirty years

---

148 latterly: 최근에

149 exceedingly: 대단히, 매우

150 unerring: 틀리지 않는, 정확한

151 refutation: 반박, 논박

152 handicraftsman: 수공업자, 수공예가

153 Sir Thomas Overbury(1581 세례~1613). 영국의 시인, 문필가로 젊은 남성이 결혼 전에 여성에게 요구하는 게 마땅한 미덕들을 묘사한 시 「아내」("A Wife")를 썼는데 이것이 그의 살해를 촉발한 사건에서 중요한 역할을 했다. 간략한 정황을 살펴보면 다음과 같다. 오버베리의 도움으로 그때까지 보잘것없는 지위에 있던 로버트 카(Robert Carr)라는 인물이 왕의 눈에 들게 되었다. 당시 일인자였던 로버트 세실(Robert Cecil)의 사후 정권이 하워드(Howard) 가문으로 넘어가자 로버트 카는 하워드 쪽에 붙었다가 하워드 가문의 딸로 기혼녀인 프랜시스 하워드(Frances Howard)와 정분이 났다. 이에 대해 오

agone[154]}; he testified to having seen the physician, under some other name, {which the narrator of the story had now forgotten}, in company with Doctor Forman, the famous old conjurer[155], {who was implicated in the affair of Overbury}. Two or three individuals hinted, {that the man of skill, [during his Indian captivity[156]], had enlarged his medical attainments by joining in the incantations[157] of the savage priests; {who were universally acknowledged to be powerful enchanters, often performing seemingly miraculous cures by their skill in the black art}. A large number—{and many of these were persons of such sober sense[158] and practical observation, that their opinions would have been valuable, in other matters}—

버베리가 맹렬히 반대하면서 「아내」라는 시를 발표하였다. 이에 맞서 프랜시스 하워드가 획책한 계략은 제임스 1세(James I)로 하여금 오버베리가 거절할 게 분명한 러시아 대사직을 오버베리에게 제안토록 하여 왕의 미움을 사게 하는 것이었다. 결국 이 거절이 오만으로 간주된 오버베리는 런던탑에 투옥되었다가 그 후 독살되었다(1613년 9월 14일). 그 뒤 프랜시스 하워드가 이혼하고 로버트 카와 재혼(1613년 11월)하였으나 오버베리가 독살되었다는 소문이 퍼져 나가기 시작했다. 급기야 국왕마저 이 살인사건에 연루되어 있다는 소문이 거듭 퍼지자 조사를 시작할 수밖에 없었다. 에드워드 코크(Edward Coke)가 이 사건의 구체적인 조사를 맡고, 프랜시스 베이컨(Francis Bacon)이 재판의 진행을 맡았다. 프랜시스 하워드와 로버트 카는 유죄판결을 받아 사형을 선고받았다가 후에 사면되었다.

154 agone: ago의 고어
155 conjurer: 마법사, 요술쟁이
156 captivity: 감금, 억류
157 incantation: 주문, 요술
158 sober sense: 냉철한 분별력

affirmed {that Roger Chillingworth's aspect had undergone a remarkable change [while he had dwelt in town, and especially since his abode with Mr. Dimmesdale]}. At first, his expression had been calm, meditative[159], scholar-like. Now, there was something ugly and evil in his face, {which they had not previously noticed}, and {which grew still the more obvious to sight, [the oftener they looked upon him]}. [According to the vulgar idea], the fire in his laboratory had been brought from the lower regions[160], and was fed with infernal[161] fuel; and so, {as might be expected}, his visage was getting sooty[162] with the smoke.

[To sum up the matter], it grew to be a widely diffused opinion, {that the Reverend Arthur Dimmesdale, [like many other personages of especial sanctity[163], in all ages of the Christian world], was haunted either by Satan himself, or Satan's emissary[164], in the guise[165] of old Roger Chillingworth}. This diabolical[166] agent had the Divine permission, [for a

---

159 meditative: 명상적인
160 lower regions: 지옥
161 infernal: 지옥의
162 sooty: 그을린
163 sanctity: 신성
164 emissary: 사자, 간첩
165 guise: 겉모습, 변장
166 diabolical: 악마 같은, 사악한

season], to burrow[167] into the clergyman's intimacy, and plot against his soul. No sensible man, {it was confessed}, could doubt {on which side the victory would turn}. The people looked, [with an unshaken hope], to see the minister come forth out of the conflict, [transfigured with the glory {which he would unquestionably[168] win}]. Meanwhile, nevertheless, it was sad to think of the perchance mortal agony {through which he must struggle towards his triumph}.

Alas, [to judge from the gloom and terror in the depths of the poor minister's eyes], the battle was a sore one, and the victory any thing but secure!

---

167 burrow: 파고들다
168 unquestionably: 의심한 나위 없이, 분명히

The Scarlet Letter 10장

The Leech and His Patient

Old Roger Chillingworth, throughout life, had been calm in temperament[1], kindly, though not of warm affections, but ever, and in all his relations with the world, a pure and upright[2] man. He had begun an investigation[3], as he imagined, with the severe and equal integrity of a judge, [desirous only of truth], {even as if the question involved no more than the air-drawn lines and figures of a geometrical[4] problem, instead of human passions, and wrongs inflicted on himself}. But, {as he proceeded}, a terrible fascination, a kind of [fierce, though still calm, necessity] seized the old man within its gripe, and never set him free again, {until he had done all its bidding}. He now dug into the poor clergyman's heart, like a miner searching for gold; or, rather, like a sexton[5] delving into a grave, possibly in quest of a jewel {that had been buried on the dead man's bosom, but likely to find nothing save mortality and corruption}. Alas for his[6] own soul, if these were what he sought!

Sometimes, a light glimmered out of the physician's eyes, burning blue and ominous[7], like the reflection of a furnace, or,

---

1 temperament: 성질, 성미
2 upright: 고결한, 올바른
3 investigation: 탐구, 조사
4 geometrical: 기하학의
5 sexton: 교회지기
6 his: =Chillingworth's
7 ominous: 불길한

300

let us say, <u>like</u> one of those gleams of ghastly fire {that darted from Bunyan's[8] awful door-way in the hill-side[9], and quivered[10] on the pilgrim's face}. The soil {where this dark miner was working} had perchance shown indications[11] {that encouraged him}.

"This man," said he, at one such moment, to himself, "{pure as they deem him},—{all spiritual as he seems},—hath inherited a strong animal nature from his father or his mother. Let us dig a little farther in the direction of this vein[12]!"

Then, [after long search into the minister's dim interior], and [turning over many precious materials, in the shape of high aspirations [for the welfare of his race, warm love of souls, pure sentiments, natural piety], [strengthen<u>ed</u> by thought and study, and illumina<u>t</u>ed by revelation],—all of which invaluable[13] gold was perhaps no better than rubbish to the seeker,—he would turn back, discouraged, and begin his quest towards another point. He groped[14] along <u>as</u> stealthily,

---

8 John Bunyan: *Pilgrim's Progress*(『천로역정』)의 저자

9 ghastly fire ... the hill-side: 천상의 도시를 향해 가는 크리스천 (Christian)의 길에 가로놓인 언덕배기에 위치한 지옥문들의 불길을 뜻한다.

10 quiver: 흔들다, 떨다

11 indication: 징조, 조짐

12 vein: 정맥, 잎맥, 광맥, 방식, 태도

13 invaluable: 값을 헤아릴 수 없는, 아주 귀중한

with as cautious a tread, and as wary an outlook, as a thief entering a chamber {where a man lies only half asleep, — or, it may be, broad awake}, — with purpose to steal the very treasure {which this man guards as the apple of his eye[15]. [In spite of his premeditated[16] carefulness], the floor would now and then creak; his garments would rustle; the shadow of his presence, in a forbidden proximity[17], would be thrown across his victim. In other words, Mr. Dimmesdale, {whose sensibility of nerve often produced the effect of spiritual intuition}, would become vaguely aware {that something [inimical[18] to his peace] had thrust[19] itself into relation with him}. But old Roger Chillingworth, too, had perceptions {that were almost intuitive}; and {when the minister threw his startled eyes towards him}, there the physician sat; his kind, watchful, sympathizing, but never intrusive[20] friend.[21]

Yet Mr. Dimmesdale would perhaps have seen this individual's character more perfectly, {if a certain morbidness[22],

---

14 grope: 손으로 더듬어 찾다

15 the apple of his eye: 눈동자, 매우 소중히 여기는 것

16 premeditated: 미리 계획된, 사전 모의된

17 proximity: 접근

18 inimical: 해로운, 적대적인

19 thrust: 밀다, 찌르다, 강요하다. ＊thrust oneself into: 끼어들다

20 intrusive: 주제넘게 참견하는

21 there … friend: 시치미를 뚝 떼고 언제 그랬냐는 듯한 칠링워스의 태도를 설명하고 있다.

[to which sick hearts are liable[23]], had not rendered him suspicious of all mankind}. [Trusting no man as his friend], he could not recognize his enemy {when the latter actually appeared}. He therefore still kept up a familiar intercourse[24] with him, daily receiving the old physician in his study; or visiting the laboratory, and, for recreation[25]'s sake, watching the processes {by which weeds were converted into drugs of potency[26]}.

One day, leaning his forehead on his hand, and his elbow on the sill[27] of the open window, {that looked towards the grave-yard}, he talked with Roger Chillingworth, while the old man was examining a bundle of unsightly[28] plants.

"Where," asked he, with a look askance[29] at them, — for it was the clergyman's peculiarity[30] {that he seldom, now-a-days, looked straightforth at any object, whether human or inanimate}, — "where, my kind doctor, did you gather those

---

22 morbidness: 병적인 상태
23 liable to: ~하기 쉬운, 영향 받기 쉬운
24 intercourse: 교제
25 recreation: 오락, 기분전환, 취미
26 drugs of potency: 효능 있는 약
27 sill: 문틀
28 unsightly: 보기 흉한
29 askance: 의심의 눈으로, 비스듬히, 곁눈으로
30 peculiarity: 특이한 점

herbs, with such a dark, flabby[31] leaf?"

"Even[32] in the grave-yard, here at hand," answered the physician, continuing his employment. "They are new to me. I found them growing on a grave, {which bore no tombstone, no other memorial of the dead man, save these ugly weeds [that have taken upon themselves to keep him in remembrance]}. They grew out of his heart, and typify, it may be, some hideous[33] secret {that was buried with him}, and {which he had done better to confess during his lifetime}."

"Perchance," said Mr. Dimmesdale, "he earnestly desired it, but could not."

"And wherefore?" rejoined the physician. "Wherefore not[34]; since all the powers of nature call so earnestly for the confession of sin, that these black weeds have sprung up out of a buried heart, to make manifest an unspoken[35] crime?"

---

31 flabby: 축 늘어진, 시든, 무기력한, 연약한. *a flabby man: 무기력한 사람; a man of flabby character: 의지가 박약한 사람

32 even: 바로, 꼭

33 hideous: 끔찍한, 무시무시한

34 Wherefore not: 왜 고백할 수 없었던 거죠?

35 unspoken: 말해지지 않은, 고백되지 않은. *이 부분이 'outspoken'으로 되어 있는 텍스트도 있으나 outspoken(솔직한, 거침없는, 노골적으로 말하는)은 정반대의 의미가 되어 해당 맥락에서 어긋난다.

"That, good Sir, is but a fantasy of yours," replied the minister. "There can be, {if I forebode[36] aright}, no power, [short of[37] the Divine mercy], to disclose, [whether by uttered words, or by type or emblem], the secrets {that may be buried with a human heart}. The heart, [making itself guilty of such secrets[38]], must perforce[39] hold them, until the day {when all hidden things shall be revealed}. Nor have I so read or interpreted Holy Writ, as to understand[40] {that the disclosure[41] of human thoughts and deeds, then to be made[42], is intended as a part of the retribution[43]}. That, surely, were a shallow view of it. No; these revelations, {unless I greatly err}, are meant merely to promote the intellectual satisfaction of all intelligent beings, {who will stand waiting, on that day, to see the dark problem of this life made plain[44]}. A knowledge of men's hearts will be needful to the completest solution of that problem. And

---

36 forebode: 예감, 예견하다

37 short of: 부족한, ~외에

38 making itself guilty of such secrets: 그런 비밀의 죄를 지은

39 perforce: 필요해서, 부득이

40 Nor have I ... understand: ~라고 이해하는 식으로 성서를 읽거나 해석한 적이 없다

41 disclosure: 폭로

42 to be made: 이루어질. (이 부분은 the disclosure를 꾸며 준다.) ＊make a disclosure: 폭로하다

43 retribution: 징벌, 형벌. ＊인간의 생각과 행위가 폭로되는 것이 응보의 한 부분으로 의도된 것이다.

44 to see the dark problem of this life made plain: 이 인생의 어두운 문제들이 명백해지는 것을 보기 위해

I conceive, moreover, that the hearts [holding such miserable secrets as you speak of] will yield them[45] up, at that last day, not with reluctance[46], but with a joy unutterable."

"Then why not reveal them here?" asked Roger Chillingworth, glancing quietly aside at the minister. "Why should not the guilty ones sooner avail themselves of this unutterable solace[47]?"

"They mostly do," said the clergyman, griping[48] hard at his breast, {as if afflicted with[49] an importunate[50] throb of pain}. "Many, many a poor soul hath given its confidence[51] to me, not only on the death-bed, but {while strong in life, and fair[52] in reputation}. And ever, after such an outpouring[53], O, what a relief have I witnessed in those sinful brethren! even as in one {who at last draws free air, after long stifling with his own polluted breath[54]}. How can it be otherwise? Why should a

---

45 them: = such miserable secrets

46 with reluctance: 마지못해, 기꺼이

47 solace: 위안, 위로

48 grip: 꽉 붙잡음, 움켜쥠, 꽉 잡다, 움켜잡다

49 afflicted with: ~로 괴로워하는

50 importunate: 성가시게 조르는

51 confidence: 신뢰, 자신(감), (누가 비밀을 지켜 줄 것이라는) 신뢰, (누구에게 털어놓는) 비밀. *confide: 비밀을 털어놓다

52 fair: 상당한, 꽤 괜찮은

53 outpouring: 발로, 분출. *여기서는 '고백'이라는 뜻

54 after long stifling with his own polluted breath: [밀폐된 공간에서]

wretched man, [guilty, we will say, of murder], prefer to keep the dead corpse buried in his own heart, rather than fling it forth at once, and let the universe take care of it!"

"Yet some men bury their secrets thus," observed the calm physician.

"True; there are such men," answered Mr. Dimmesdale. "But, not to suggest more obvious reasons[55], it may be that they are kept silent by the very constitution of their nature. Or, — can we not suppose it? — {guilty as they may be}, {retaining, nevertheless, a zeal for God's glory and man's welfare}, they shrink from displaying themselves black and filthy[56] in the view of men; because, thenceforward[57], no good can be achieved by them; no evil of the past be redeemed by better service. So, [to their own unutterable[58] torment], they go about among their fellow-creatures, looking pure as new-fallen snow; {while their hearts are all speckled[59] and spotted with iniquity[60]

오랫동안 자신의 오염된 입김에 숨이 막힐 듯하다가. ＊stifling: 숨 막힐 듯한

55 not to suggest more obvious reasons: 더 분명한 이유가 있을 터 이나 그것들을 제시하지 않고 말한다면

56 filthy: 불결한, 추악한

57 thenceforward: 그때 이래

58 unutterable: 이루 말할 수 없는, 형언할 수 없는

59 speckled: 얼룩덜룩한

60 iniquity: 죄, 부정

[of which they cannot rid themselves]}."

"These men deceive themselves," said Roger Chillingworth, [with somewhat more emphasis than usual], and [making a slight gesture with his forefinger]. "They fear to take up the shame {that rightfully belongs to them}. Their love for man, their zeal for God's service, — these holy impulses may or may not coexist [in their hearts] with the evil inmates {to which their guilt has unbarred[61] the door}, and {which must needs propagate[62] a hellish breed within them}. But, {if they seek to glorify God}, let them not lift heavenward their unclean hands! {If they would serve their fellow-men}, let them do it [by making manifest the power and reality of conscience], [in constraining them to penitential self-abasement[63]]! Wouldst thou have me to believe, O wise and pious friend, {that a false show[64] can be better — can be more for God's glory, or man's welfare — than God's own truth}? Trust me, such men deceive themselves!"

"It may be so," said the young clergyman indifferently, as waiving[65] a discussion {that he considered irrelevant or unseasonable[66]}. He had a ready faculty, indeed, of escaping

---

61 unbar: 빗장을 벗기다, 열다
62 propagate: 증식시키다, 늘리다
63 self-abasement: 겸손, 자기비하
64 show: 허세, 가식
65 waive: 포기하다
66 unseasonable: 시기에 맞지 않는

from any topic {that agitated his too sensitive and nervous temperament}. — "But, now, I would ask [of my well-skilled physician], {whether, in good sooth[67], he deems me to have profited by[68] his kindly care of this weak frame of mine}?"

{Before Roger Chillingworth could answer}, they heard ★ MP3 10장 (2) 시작 the clear, wild laughter of a young child's voice, proceeding from the adjacent[69] burial-ground. [Looking instinctively[70] from the open window, — for it was summer-time,] — the minister beheld Hester Prynne and little Pearl passing along the footpath {that traversed the inclosure[71]}. Pearl looked as beautiful as the day, but was in one of those moods of perverse merriment[72] {which, [whenever they occurred], seemed to remove her entirely out of the sphere of sympathy or human contact}. She now skipped irreverently[73] from one grave to another; until, [coming to the broad, flat, armorial[74] tombstone of a departed worthy[75], — perhaps of Isaac Johnson himself], —

---

67 in good sooth: 정말, 참으로
68 whether, in good sooth, he deems me to have profited by: ∼에 의해 내가 나아졌다고 그가 생각하는지 어떤지
69 adjacent: 인접한
70 instinctively: 본능적으로
71 along footpath that traversed the inclosure: 울타리가 쳐진 땅을 가로지르는 좁은 길을 따라. *footpath: 좁은 길
72 perverse merriment: 심술궂은 명랑함
73 irreverently: 불경하게, 불손하게
74 armorial: 문장(紋章)의

she began to dance upon it. In reply to her mother's command and entreaty {that she would behave more decorously[76]}, little Pearl paused to gather the prickly burrs[77] from a tall burdock[78], {which grew beside the tomb}. [Taking a handful of these], she arranged them along the lines of the scarlet letter {that decorated the maternal bosom}, {to which the burrs, [as their nature was], tenaciously[79] adhered}. Hester did not pluck them off.

Roger Chillingworth had by this time approached the window, and smiled grimly[80] down.

"There is no law, nor reverence for authority, no regard for human ordinances[81] or opinions, right or wrong, mixed up with that child's composition[82]," remarked he, as much to himself as to his companion. "I saw her, the other day, bespatter[83] the Governor himself with water, at the cattle-trough[84] in Spring Lane. What, in Heaven's name, is she? Is

---

75 departed worthy: 작고한 훌륭한 인물
76 decorously: 예의 바르게
77 prickly burrs: 가시 돋친 껍질
78 burdock: 우엉
79 tenaciously: 완고하게, 집요하게
80 grimly: 엄하게, 무섭게
81 ordinance: 명령, 법령, 조례
82 composition: 기질, 성질
83 bespatter: 물을 튀기다

the imp altogether evil? Hath she affections? Hath she any discoverable principle of being?"

"None, — save the freedom of a broken law," answered Mr. Dimmesdale, in a quiet way, {as if he had been discussing the point within himself}. "{Whether capable of good}, I know not."

The child probably overheard[85] their voices; for, [looking up to the window, with a bright, but naughty[86] smile of mirth and intelligence], she threw one of the prickly burrs at the Reverend Mr. Dimmesdale. The sensitive clergyman shrank, [with nervous dread], from the light missile[87]. [Detecting his emotion], Pearl clapped her little hands in the most extravagant ecstasy[88]. Hester Prynne, likewise, had involuntarily looked up; and all these four persons, old and young, regarded one another in silence, {till the child laughed aloud, and shouted, — "Come away, mother! Come away, or yonder old Black Man will catch you! He hath got hold of the minister already. Come away, mother, or he will catch you! But he cannot catch little Pearl!"}

So she drew her mother away, skipping, dancing, and

---

84 cattle-trough: 소 여물통
85 overhear: 엿듣다
86 naughty: 버릇없는
87 missile: 던지는[쏘아 보내는] 무기
88 in the most extravagant ecstasy: 지나치게 황홀경에 빠져서

frisking[89] fantastically[90] among the hillocks[91] of the dead people, like a creature {that had nothing in common with a bygone and buried generation, nor owned herself akin to it}. It was as if she had been made afresh, out of new elements, and must perforce be permitted to live her own life, and be a law unto herself, [without her eccentricities[92] being reckoned to her for a crime].

"There goes a woman," resumed Roger Chillingworth, after a pause, "who, {be her demerits[93] what they may}, hath none of that mystery of hidden sinfulness {which you deem so grievous[94] to be borne}. Is Hester Prynne the less miserable, think you, for that scarlet letter on her breast?"

"I do verily believe it," answered the clergyman. "Nevertheless, I cannot answer for her. There was a look of pain in her face, {which I would gladly have been spared the sight of[95]}. But still, methinks, it must needs be better for the sufferer to be free to show his pain, {as this poor woman Hester is}, than to

---

89 frisk: 경쾌하게 뛰어다니다
90 fantastically: 기상천외하게, 변덕스럽게
91 hillock: 흙무덤, 작은 언덕
92 eccentricity: 기행, 괴벽
93 demerit: 잘못, 과실
94 grievous: 고통을 주는, 쓰라린
95 which ... the sight of: 그 고통의 표정을 안 봐도 되었더라면 좋았
    겠지요. *spare: (불쾌한 일을) 모면하게[겪지 않아도 되게] 하다

cover it all up in his heart."

There was another pause; and the physician began anew to examine and arrange the plants {which he had gathered}.

"You inquired of me, a little time agone," said he, at length, "my judgment as touching your health."

"I did," answered the clergyman, "and would gladly learn it. Speak frankly, I pray you, be it for life or death."

"Freely, then, and plainly," said the physician, still busy with his plants, but keeping a wary eye on Mr. Dimmesdale, "the disorder is a strange one; not so much in itself, nor as outwardly manifested, — in so far, at least, as the symptoms have been laid open to my observation[96]. Looking daily at you, my good Sir, and watching the tokens of your aspect, now for months [gone by], I should deem you a man [sore[97] sick], it may be, yet not so sick but that[98] an instructed[99] and watchful physician might well hope to cure you. But — I know not what

---

96 the disorder ... to my observation: 병이 이상하기는 하지만, 그 자체로 이상한 것은 아니며 또 밖으로 드러난 것으로 봐도, 적어도 내 관찰에 드러난 증상으로 보자면 이상하지 않아요

97 sore: 아픈, 슬픈, 〈부사〉 몹시, 심하게

98 yet not so sick but that: 그러나 ~하지 않을 만큼 그렇게 아프지는 않은

99 instructed: 교육을 받은

to say — the disease is {what I seem to know, yet know it not}."

"You speak in riddles, learned Sir," said the pale minister, glancing aside out of the window.

"Then, to speak more plainly," continued the physician, "and I crave pardon, Sir, — should it seem to require pardon, — for this needful plainness of my speech. Let me ask, — as your friend, — as one [having charge, under Providence, of your life and physical well-being], — hath all the operations of this disorder been fairly laid open[100] and recounted[101] to me?"

"How can you question it?" asked the minister. "Surely, it were child's play to call in a physician, and then hide the sore!"

"You would tell me, then, that I know all?" said Roger Chillingworth, deliberately[102], and fixing an eye, bright with intense and concentrated intelligence, on the minister's face. "Be it so! But, again! He {to whom only the outward and physical evil is laid open} knoweth, oftentimes, but half the evil {which he is called upon to cure}. A bodily disease, {which we look upon as whole and entire within itself}, may,

---

100 lay open: 드러내다, 폭로하다
101 recount: 이야기하다
102 deliberately: 신중하게, 찬찬히

after all, be but a symptom of some ailment[103] in the spiritual part. Your pardon, once again, good Sir, if my speech give the shadow of offence. You, Sir, of all men {whom I have known}, are he {whose body is the closest conjoined, and imbued, and identified, so to speak, with the spirit [whereof it is the instrument]}."[104]

"Then I need ask no further," said the clergyman, somewhat hastily rising from his chair. "You deal not, I take it[105], in medicine for the soul!"

"Thus, a sickness," continued Roger Chillingworth, going on, in an unaltered[106] tone, without heeding the interruption, — but standing up, and confronting the emaciated[107] and white-cheeked minister [with his low, dark, and misshapen[108] figure], — "a sickness, a sore place, {if we may so call it}, in your spirit, hath immediately its appropriate

---

103 ailment: 병, 질환
104 You, sir, ... whereof it is the instrument: 그대야말로 내가 알고 있는 어느 사람보다도 정신과 육체가 긴밀히 연결되어 있어서 정신의 도구로서 육체가 그 정신을 흡수하여 정신과 육체가 혼연일체가 되는 사람입니다. ＊conjoin: 결합하다; imbue: 흡수하다; identify: 일체감을 가지다
105 I take it: 내가 생각하기에
106 unaltered: 바뀌지 않은
107 emaciated: 여윈, 수척한
108 misshapen: 기형의, 보기 흉한

manifestation in your bodily frame. Would you, therefore, that your physician heal the bodily evil? How may this be, {unless you first lay open to him the wound or trouble in your soul}?"

"No! — not to thee! — not to an earthly physician!" cried Mr. Dimmesdale, passionately, and turning his eyes, full and bright, and with a kind of fierceness, on old Roger Chillingworth. "Not to thee! But, if it be the soul's disease, then do I commit myself to the one Physician of the soul! He, {if it stand with his good pleasure}, can cure; or he can kill! Let him do with me {as, [in his justice and wisdom], he shall see good}. But who art thou, {that meddlest[109] in this matter}? — {that dares thrust himself between the sufferer and his God}?"

With a frantic[110] gesture, he rushed out of the room.

"It is as well to have made this step," said Roger Chilling-worth to himself, looking after the minister with a grave smile. "There is nothing lost. We shall be friends again anon. But see, now, {how passion takes hold upon this man, and hurrieth him out of himself}! As with one passion, so with another![111] He hath done a wild thing ere now, this pious Master Dimmesdale,

---

109 meddlest: 간섭하다. *고어체로 meddle의 2인칭 단수 표현
110 frantic: 광란의, 미친 사람 같은
111 As with ... with another!: 하나의 열정의 경우에 그렇다면, 다른 열정의 경우에도 그렇겠지!

in the hot passion of his heart!"

It proved not difficult to reestablish the intimacy of the two companions, on the same footing and in the same degree as heretofore[112]. The young clergyman, [after a few hours of privacy], was sensible that the disorder of his nerves had hurried him into an unseemly outbreak[113] of temper, {which there had been nothing in the physician's words to excuse or palliate[114]}. He marvelled, indeed, at the violence {with which he had thrust back the kind old man, when merely proffering the advice [which it was his duty to bestow], and [which the minister himself had expressly[115] sought]. [With these remorseful[116] feelings], he lost no time in making the amplest[117] apologies, and besought his friend still to continue the care, {which, [if[118] not successful in restoring him to health], had, [in all probability], been the means of prolonging his feeble existence to that hour}. Roger Chillingworth readily assented, and went on with his medical supervision[119] of the minister; doing his best for him, in all good faith, but always quitting the

---

112 heretofore: 이전의
113 outbreak: 폭발
114 palliate: 변명하다, 완화시키다
115 expressly: 분명히, 특별히
116 remorseful: 후회의
117 ample: 충분한
118 if: = even if
119 supervision: 관리

patient's apartment, [at the close of the professional interview], with a mysterious and puzzled[120] smile upon his lips. This expression was invisible in Mr. Dimmesdale's presence, but grew strongly evident as the physician crossed the threshold.

"A rare case!" he muttered. "I must needs look deeper into it. A strange sympathy betwixt soul and body! {Were it only for the art's sake[121]}, I must search this matter to the bottom!"

It came to pass, [not long after the scene above recorded], that the Reverend Mr. Dimmesdale, [at noonday[122], and entirely unawares], fell into a deep, deep slumber, sitting in his chair, [with a large black-letter[123] volume open before him on the table]. It must have been a work of vast ability in the somniferous[124] school of literature. The profound[125] depth of the minister's repose[126] was the more remarkable; inasmuch as he was one of those persons {whose sleep, ordinarily, is as light, as fitful, and as easily scared away, [as a small bird hopping on a twig]}. To such an unwonted remoteness, however, had his

---

120 puzzled: 어리둥절해하는, 얼떨떨한
121 Were it ... the art's sake: [다른 게 아니라] 오로지 의술을 위해서라도
122 noonday: 정오
123 black-letter: 고대 영어의, 고딕체의
124 somniferous: 최면의, 졸리게 하는
125 profound: 깊은
126 repose: 휴식

spirit now withdrawn into itself, that he stirred not in his chair, {when old Roger Chillingworth, without any extraordinary precaution[127], came into the room}. The physician advanced directly in front of his patient, laid his hand upon his bosom, and thrust aside the vestment[128], {that, hitherto, had always covered it even from the professional eye}.

Then, indeed, Mr. Dimmesdale shuddered, and slightly stirred.

After a brief pause, the physician turned away.

But with what a wild look of wonder, joy, and horror! With what a ghastly[129] rapture[130], as it were, [too mighty to be expressed only by the eye and features], and [therefore bursting forth through the whole ugliness of his figure, and making itself even riotously[131] manifest by the extravagant gestures {with which he threw up his arms towards the ceiling, and stamped his foot upon the floor}! {Had a man seen old Roger Chillingworth, at that moment of his ecstasy}, he would have had no need to ask {how Satan comports[132] himself, [when

---

127 precaution: 조심
128 vestment: 예복
129 ghastly: 무시무시한, 섬뜩한
130 rapture: 황홀
131 riotously: 떠들썩하게, 요란스럽게

a precious human soul is lost to heaven, and won into his[133] kingdom}.[134]

But what distinguished the physician's ecstasy from Satan's was the trait[135] of wonder in it!

---

132 comports: 처신하다, 태도를 취하다
133 his: = Satan's
134 이 문장에서는 이때 칠링워스의 태도가 악마의 태도와 다르지 않다는 의미를 전달한다.
135 trait: 특성, 특질